What we
Leave
Behind

BOOKS BY ANNA MANSELL

How to Mend a Broken Heart
The Lost Wife
I Wanted to Tell You
Her Best Friend's Secret
The Man I Loved Before

What We Leave Behind

anna mansell

Bookouture

Published by Bookouture in 2020

An imprint of Storyfire Ltd.
Carmelite House
50 Victoria Embankment
London EC4Y 0DZ

www.bookouture.com

ISBN: 978-1-80019-001-6
eBook ISBN: 978-1-80019-000-9

For Lou.

Prologue

'Lisa… I need to say something,' says Paul.

Holly, his sister, who is also my best friend, has just legged it back home after a night in round mine, watching telly and drinking; the new normal for the three of us, since Grandma got too ill to babysit Poppy.

'Right…' he says, looking all serious. This is not his normal face. We've been mates for the better part of thirty years… albeit by proxy for the first twenty. He's a few years older than me and Holly, we probably got on his nerves more than anything back then. The last ten though, we've definitely been mates. Even so, he's rarely shown me this serious face and it's made me feel a bit wobbly.

'Go on then, talk whilst you give me a hand with these.' I eye him carefully as I hand over two dead wine bottles, juggling three glasses and a bowl of crisp crumbs. He follows but doesn't carry on with whatever's given him his serious face, so I default to filling an awkward silence. 'When do you fly?'

'Tomorrow. Two o'clock.'

'God, I'm so jealous!' He follows me into the kitchen. 'What I wouldn't give for a holiday right now,' I groan. 'Maybe after Grandma has… God, that's an awful thing to think… argh, you know.'

'I know.'

'Sorry, sorry. Mood kill.' His face is still serious. 'Sorry, what did you want to say?' I dump the glasses and bowl, taking the bottles from him. 'Are you okay? You look... stressed.'

'Lisa. I...' He looks to his feet, then around the kitchen. The sound of glass clinking into the recycling interrupts him. My chest knots with nerves. The energy has shifted quite substantially, and I don't think it's because of the Chardonnay. When I've stopped faffing, he touches my hand briefly, a request for me to stop. 'I don't know how to say this, Lisa. Christ, I've thought about how to say it so many times.' He turns away. 'The conversations you and I have had in my head.' He offers a shy, embarrassed smile and my heart lurches. 'The thing is, I don't want to make things awkward or difficult for you. I really don't, but...' He clears his throat. 'I have fallen totally, and completely, in love with you.'

Oh God.

'I tried to stop it. We're friends, I know that. I didn't want to complicate things. And then I thought maybe I could ignore it, because I didn't want to not have you in my life, so friends had to be better than nothing at all, if you see what I mean... sorry, that's a bit clumsy, but—'

'Paul—'

'No, please, sorry, I don't want to cut you off, but I need to just get this off my chest now, then I can go. I thought that if I told you now, before I go away, you'll have space from me. Time to think. Making you feel awkward or weird is the very last thing I'd want to do, so I hope you understand why I've chosen now.'

I shuffle my feet.

'The thing is, I suppose, I don't expect you to feel the same way. I don't expect anything, really, I just...' He lets out a heavy sigh. 'I've needed to say it so that I know once and for all. Not now, I don't need you to say anything now. Think about it. But... then... if you don't feel the same way, I would totally understand, and I can just work on getting over it.' He looks at me, dark hair newly cut for his holiday. 'I can work on getting over you.'

'Right.'

'Lisa, you make me want to be the best version of myself. And if you felt remotely the same way, even just a little bit, I would do everything in my power to make you happy. To love you and Poppy the way you deserve. I'm not into all that princess shit, you don't need anyone putting you on a pedestal as such, but... I think you're amazing. Like... the most amazing woman I've ever met. You are generous and kind, you're so smart, you're funny, you're sexy as hell... sorry... that probably sounds weird coming from me but... well, you are. I just think you're the most incredible person and I want to spend all my time proving that to you.'

I swallow. It might be the single most romantic thing anybody's ever said to me. And certainly not what I expected to hear from one of my best mates. We hover in the kitchen, I guess he doesn't know what to say or do next and I've got no idea. For someone who hates people feeling awkward, and always finds a way to fix that for them, I'm dumbstruck.

'Well...' he puffs out. 'I said it. I feel better... maybe. I don't know. Look, I'll let myself out.' He makes to leave, then stops. 'Please don't worry if you don't feel the same. It's fine. I'll be fine.' He looks about the room again. 'I just needed to say it in case there was a chance... So, yeah, I guess I'll see you when I get back.'

He grabs his keys from the side, heading through to the hall. I follow too close behind, which means when he spins round, hand moving to his forehead, he nearly knocks me over with his elbow. 'Sorry... shit, sorry!' He grabs my hand to check I'm okay and my palm tingles.

'Look, I really hope this hasn't just been the most awful thing to do or say.' He stuffs his hand in his pocket. 'I'm not very good at this kind of thing… a little out of practice, I guess. Turns out I've had feelings for you for much longer than even I realised.'

'It's… it's fine… I…'

'Don't rush. I know it's probably out of the blue. You need time to think. I know it's not just you. I know something like this could ultimately affect Poppy too.' He looks through to the lounge. 'And maybe to some it would be stifling, small town, everybody knows us. I don't imagine you dreamed of falling for someone you've essentially grown up around… but just because we live in a small world doesn't mean we can't have big dreams, right?' I swallow, then nod. 'Look, thanks for a lovely night.'

'Oh, it's fine. I mean, thanks for coming round.'

He catches my eye for a second, holding it longer than he ever has before. It makes me notice him. He's tall, almost bearlike, in that he's strong, the kind of man you can curl up into the arms of and know everything's going to be okay. Something in my belly shifts, tilts, then flutters.

'See you when I get back.'

With that, he's gone. And I'm left, behind my closed front door, hot, stunned, and wondering how I hadn't seen that coming.

Chapter One

Three weeks later

I check through my bag, reaching to blindly open the front door as I shout up the stairs. 'Come on, Pops, we need to go!' A rush of cool September air tickles the back of my neck.

Poppy slides down on her bum, each step bumping her pigtails, which bounce like glorious red, coiled springs. She doesn't get her hair colour or the curls from me, they are definitely from her dad.

We stand side by side in front of the hall mirror. Facebook was awash with first day of school photos this morning, but I haven't posted the one I took of her in her bedroom. Though, to most, she looked like an excited, proud and eager five-year-old, ready for her first ever day at school, I hate that I recognised a painted brave face, and faux giddiness. It's not to say she won't be fine, she will be, as soon as we get there and she meets up with Charlie, but right now, she's definitely faking it. I catch my own face and realise where she gets it from; I've had this face on quite a bit over the last couple of weeks. What a bloody roller coaster. 'Well, you look ready to get learning,' I chirp.

She crouches down to fuss Frank, Grandma's old dog who came back with me after the funeral last week. 'So do you, Mum.'

'It's going to be funny, us being in the same building but not really seeing each other all day, isn't it?'

'You'll see me. And I'll see you.' She stands, threading her hand in mine. 'Don't worry, Mum.'

I wonder if I could ever stop her feeling the need to make everything alright for everyone else, or if nature and nurture have this one pretty much sewn up? 'Of course I will. Silly me. Now, come on, grab your coat and let's get going.'

Her rucksack is almost as big as her, yet she casually throws it over her shoulder like a child much older than her years. I squeeze her tight, kissing her pigtailed head, wishing time would slow down as we head out into the September sunshine, almost tripping over a parcel on the top step. 'Woah, careful.' I instinctively put my arm out to stop her falling, checking up and down the road for the postie, she doesn't normally come this early.

'Is it for me?' Poppy fumbles to pick the package up, peering at the name written neatly across the front.

'Erm, no, I think it's for me.' The handwriting is unfamiliar, there's no sender's address.

'Ohhh.' She speaks disappointment but hasn't actually stopped trying to paw at it. 'Who's it from? What is it?' Her tiny hands pull at mine as she tries to get a closer look. 'Open it, open it!'

I'm looking for a clue via the postmark, but there isn't one, it's been hand delivered. My phone dings to say it's half past eight. 'We're going to have to wait until later.' I drop it on the side, shooing Frank and his cocked leg away from the buddleia and back into the house. 'Come on, in the car. We have to get to school, it wouldn't do to be late on our first day, would it? See you later, Frank, I've left the radio on. Do you think he'll like Radio 2, Poppy?'

But she's gone, skipping round to the car, her feet crunching the pebbles on our drive. A breeze whips up scent from the climber that Grandma helped me plant a few years back. I'm really going to miss pottering around the garden with her.

We pass by Dad's house. There's no sign of life, though I've no doubt he'll have been up for hours, probably down in the kitchen, reading today's *Telegraph* or some such. Poppy watches the house as we go past. 'Grandad was sad last week, wasn't he?'

'He was. It was his mummy that died, my grandma.'

'I bet he probably cried. I'd cry if you died.'

I make noises of agreement but don't really want to get in to this. Whether he cried or not doesn't change the fact that he controlled the funeral in the same way he controlled her life in the last few years, mine presumably no longer available to him in quite the same way.

The guest list was small, he didn't invite any of her church group. He refused to play Elvis, which I know she'd expressly asked him to do because she asked me too. Grandma's best friend Iris was allowed to go, but I don't know that she felt all that welcome. As far as funerals go, it was as staged as everything else he's ever done, a show of love because to really feel it might hurt too much. Sometimes I wonder why he lives that way, and how I managed to avoid inheriting his approach to life. I guess I probably have my grandma to thank, or Grandma Elsie as Poppy always called her. Nurture over nature on that one. She was the closest thing I had to a mother, my own having died when I was a baby. And it wasn't always easy with her. I lived with Dad; Grandma lived two streets away. We saw her often, so long as the two of them were speaking. I suppose she was as complicated as Dad, but ultimately, she taught me love and compassion and what it was to be a woman, and… I indicate into the school car park… what it is to be the best mother I can be.

Chapter Two

'Here we are.' I pull up by the staff gate, waiting for it to lift. It feels weird being able to park in this end of the car park. We didn't even dare walk through this bit when I was a kid, it was strictly teachers only. That I'm allowed to park here, the newest member of the team and not even a teacher, feels weird. Like I might get told off. Not that it feels as exclusive as it did back then. There are kids and parents cutting through from their car park all over.

'Come on then. Let's get you round to class, then I'll head over to the office, okay?'

Poppy nods, her voice suddenly lost as she watches a sea of parents, in various states of polish, usher the fruits of their loins towards classrooms.

'Look, there's Charlie!' I say, relieved, hoping her best friend might give her the boost she needs. Me too, for that matter. Charlie's mum is Holly, my own best friend; Paul's sister.

Poppy knocks on our car window, waving. But they both disappear around the corner of the building. Her shoulders sag.

'Come on, let's go catch them up.'

Rules about walking through the car park may have relaxed, but not much else has changed. The same plants grow in the garden, if a little bigger and wilder now. The same smells emanate from the kitchen; that school kitchen smell that is exactly the same regardless of what is actually on the menu. Unless it's curry day, in which case it's that smell, plus spice. Poppy grasps my hand in the way she only ever does when she's nervous or shy. 'It'll be alright, Mum. You'll be fine today, won't you?'

'I will,' I say, squeezing her hand. 'I will be just fine. I'm going to love every second and we can talk about it all on the way home at the end of the day.'

'That's right, Mum,' she says, placated.

'Morning, you, how you doing? Was last week okay? I'm so sorry I wasn't here for you. You're really gonna miss her, eh?' Holly pulls me in for one of her famous, all-encompassing hugs. She's been in Playa Del Inglés for the last three weeks; Grandma died just after she'd gone and she wasn't back 'til late last night so missed the funeral too. It was weird not having her here for such a significant moment in my life and she feels it too, if her extra tight hug squeeze is anything to go by.

'It was… okay, I guess. A bit strange. Dad was in a particularly odd mood, and he wouldn't play the Elvis track she wanted at the funeral.'

'But she told you both that's what she wanted.'

'I know, right.' I picture Dad's face when he was absolute in the fact it wasn't happening. 'I suppose she's not alive to see it, so maybe it doesn't matter? I mean, maybe if she'd chosen something a bit more in keeping with the mood? 'Hound Dog' isn't exactly mournful.'

'Even more reason to have played it, if you ask me. Other than that, was it all okay with your dad?'

Poppy and Charlie are hopscotching by their classroom door.

'I guess. He tried chatting, I did my best to chat back, under the circumstances. I just feel so… confused… actually, not confused, it shouldn't have come as a surprise that he did things that way. It just felt wrong, somehow. And he's definitely acting weirder than normal. Something's brewing, I can feel it. He still hates that I took this job.'

'I can't get over him trying to get you sacked before you'd even started.'

'He didn't try to get me sacked.'

'Well, no, okay. But he did try to persuade them not to employ you.'

'Mmm.' One of his mates is the brother-in-law of the head teacher here. Thankfully she paid no attention, but it was a stark reminder of how controlling Dad can be. He'd laid off for a while, maybe had even started to let me live my life. 'Perhaps losing Grandma has hit him hard. Without her to look after and control, who's he got?'

'I suppose.'

'Says he wants me to focus on getting some kind of degree.'

'Online, presumably?'

'Of course.' Holly remembers when Dad tore up my university offer without my knowing until it was too late to accept. By which time, Billy and I had got back together and I wasn't in such a rush to leave Lincolnshire. Not sure I'd have ever made much of a nurse anyway, I can't stand the sight of blood. 'I've told him I just want to work. I've always been happier when I'm working. I need this, for me and for Poppy. I just wish he'd stop judging every move I make.'

Holly takes a sharp intake of breath. 'Well, he's not the only one judging you.'

'What? Are you judging me? What for?'

'Because you're not wearing the good luck present I gave you!' She fixes me with a look.

'Oh! Was the box from you? Sorry, I didn't get a chance to open it.'

'Box?'

'Yes! On the doorstep, this morning? Though you could have knocked. Or just brought it to school even.'

'What box? I meant the envelope with the ironic friendship necklace I got you from Gran Canaria. I asked Paul to pop it through your letterbox on his way back from dropping me off.'

My heart flips. I've barely had a chance to think about the implication of seeing Paul again. Who, I realised pretty soon after he said how he felt, I've had a crush on for years, probably long ignored because I hadn't for a second thought it would ever be reciprocated. He's known me since I had bruised legs and a fringe my dad cut. How could that ever be considered sexy?

'I can't believe he forgot!' She pulls out a necklace from beneath her T-shirt, hanging it off her index finger. A cracked half of a friendship heart hangs loosely, the word 'Best' on hers.

'I assume "Friend" is on mine then?'

'Gorgeous, right? Word to the wise, mind, don't wear it in the shower. I put mine on so I wouldn't forget it this morning and I think my neck has gone green.' She rubs at a mark where the chain has been and grins. 'Mind you, what can you expect from a five-euro gift?'

'It's the thought that counts.'

'Correct! Which is why I want you to put it on as soon as he's dropped it off. We can show it to all the other mums tomorrow.' She pauses. 'Ha! Who am I kidding? As if I want to talk to any of the rest of them.'

Holly has always pretended she's not interested in making new friends, mainly because she handles rejection badly. She's spiky sometimes, can be difficult to get along with. Some people find her directness off-putting, but I've always admired the fact that she speaks her truth and I know, without doubt, she has my back, no matter what.

I look around at the collection of cliques in the playground. 'Oh God, this is us now, isn't it? For years to come. Mornings and afternoons of having to make small talk with people we have barely anything in common with.'

'That's right. Years of it. Years of avoiding requests to join the PTA, years of wondering which child is repeatedly giving yours nits – and no, lavender and tea tree spray doesn't work. Years of wondering how you can say no to the party invite for the kid whose parents smell, argue, drink, or all of the above.'

'Do you think we're the only ones that feel that way?'

'God knows. If we aren't, they hide it better than us.' She grins at me as the school bell goes and Poppy pulls up short, mid-hop.

I jog over to her. 'Come on, you, give us a kiss. I can't wait to hear all about your day. You're going to have so much fun.' She looks at me meekly. 'Butterflies?' I ask and she nods. 'Me too.'

'You'll be fine, Mummy,' she says, giving me a hug and I bite my bottom lip.

'We both will be. Picky tea tonight?' I know this will be just the motivation she needs to get on with her day because who doesn't like a picky tea? 'I reckon we've still got cake left from Grandma Elsie's fuddle too. She'd be thrilled to know we'd be scoffing it after our first day at school.' She'd been the one to encourage me to go for the job in the first place. She'd always been the one to encourage me to do everything in life. Where Dad locked doors, she snuck a key out and unlocked them.

'Can we have a picnic in the lounge? With teddies?' Poppy's eyes are Disney-wide.

'Of course!'

She gives me a hug just as Charlie runs past her, shouting encouragement to join him. I watch as she disappears into class, her teacher patting her on the head as she moves through the door. I dig deep for some of the same strength of character.

'You're gonna be fine,' says Holly, her hand on my back. 'I'm going to call Paul and kick off about your necklace now.'

The sound of his name, twice this morning, makes me flustered, so I give her a hug and leg it before she notices.

Chapter Three

'And then we had to sit on the carpet whilst Mrs Butterworth read us a story and I got to sit at the front beside her, which was great except that Jacob Lees sat next to me and kept picking at the sole on my shoe.' Poppy yawns.

'Tell him to stop.'

'I did. But he wouldn't.' I twitch at how early 'boys ignoring girls' feelings' begins, but now is not the time for my five-year-old to hear a feminist rant. 'I made a new friend on the friendship bench.'

'Oh yes? Did you sit on it, or did she?'

'She did. I saw her on her own so said hello. She's in the other class actually, she's called Evie. I think she's my new best friend. As well as Charlie.'

'Yeah?' I switch the engine off, sitting for a second as I stifle my own yawn. First day in a new job and whilst I can hardly say nine 'til three is a long day, it's more than I've done for these last few years whilst Poppy was a baby. Dad was insistent, after bringing me back from Edinburgh, a week after Billy left me with just-days-old Poppy, that I stay at home and look after her. 'You walked away from that job you had, they're not going to take you back,' he'd said about my part-time job at the local library. I'd loved that job. If Billy hadn't been so keen to move to Scotland, and me so keen to try and make things work between us, maybe I'd still be there. Maybe, had I not been so crippled with anxiety, hormones and the breakdown of my relationship, I'd have asked to go back. And I should be grateful that Dad put money in my account every month, preferring me to be at home with Poppy anyway. I suppose I should be grateful for all the time I've had to learn to be her mum, courtesy of Dad pretty much paying for everything, and Grandma Elsie showing me the ropes, but now that I'm out the other side, I feel like I've lost a little bit of me in the process.

'Evie likes teddies and the colour blue, not pink like the rest of the girls, so that's probably why we are friends. Did you make a friend today, Mummy?'

I can't admit to how intimidated I felt, sitting in a staffroom full of teachers and TAs who appeared to be full of confidence and clarity on who they are and what they do. Perhaps that's just how they have to present. Maybe if I faked it, I'd make it?

'I don't know about making friends yet, I was pretty busy, to be honest.' Which was true, and the bit I loved the most about today. No time to think about anything other than managing phone calls, letters to type up, forms to get out to classes, dinner monies to look after, the school website and Facebook page to learn how to update. I'm really grateful they gave me a shot at the job because it's probably a bit of a risk for them to take on someone who's been out of the game for so long. 'I think I'm going to love my new job!'

She heads inside first. 'Oooh! Your present, Mum!' She slings her coat off, leaving it on the floor as she leaps on the parcel I'd forgotten about until now. Frank sleepily fusses around our ankles, tail wagging. He's getting too old to do all the jumping he used to when we'd visit Grandma. I tickle the top of his head and he leans into it.

'What could it be?' she says, shaking the box to her ear.

'I'll have that, thank you. You go hang your coat up, please.'

She picks it up and jumps just a little so she can hook her hood over the bannister, which isn't quite hanging it up, but it'll do.

'Can I open it? Please, Mummy, can I?'

'It's for me!'

'Yes but, I can help, can't I?'

Her excitement makes me grin. 'Come on then.'

Together, we unwrap the brown paper to find more paper, white tissue paper this time. Poppy rips against my gentle unfolding. 'Hang on, careful.' I take it from her, unwrapping the last layer to reveal the most exquisite notebook. Handmade with thick brown paper, a stitched cover with an abstract pattern interwoven with gold thread. I run my finger down the front of it, the different kinds of fabric and textures make my hands tingle. 'Wow!'

Poppy leans on me, reaching her hand across to copy me as I stroke the front page. The weight of her feels nice, reassuring. I open the book up and flick through the pages to find tiny headings on alternate pages.

'What does it say, Mummy? What's it for?'

I pause on one of the front inside pages where, handwritten, it says, *Tell me your dreams…*

Chapter Four

'What does that mean?' asks Poppy, frowning as she peers.

'Well, I don't know, I guess it's asking what we want in life?'

'I'd like Evie to come round for tea. And maybe Charlie too. I think they're going to really like each other.'

She climbs on my lap, so I pull her in for a cuddle. 'Are they your dreams?'

'Yes. And also, I'd like a cat.' She looks up at me sweetly, just like she always does when this subject comes up. 'A cat like Scamp.' Scamp being my dad's old cat who she can't possibly remember because Scamp died two and half years ago and I think she's romanticised the grumpy old, scratchy, hissy bugger. Though, in his defence, I'd be scratchy and hissy if a two-year-old was terrorising me like she did him.

'I wonder what Frank would think about a cat in our house? Go on, get changed. Lay your school clothes out on your bed so we can hang them up for tomorrow. I'll start tea.'

Poppy climbs the stairs on her hands and knees and I stand, shaking my head. A card falls out of the gift. *Lisa, here is a place for your hopes and dreams. Writing them down is the first step to making them happen. Good luck in your new job. X*

I study the handwriting, my heart quickens. I don't recognise it. It's definitely not Holly's; hers is unmistakable, sort of fat and loopy, full of flourish and generosity. Is it wrong to say hers is very definitely the handwriting of a woman? This though, it's tight, clean, neither male nor female, just tidy. And whoever it is, knows about my job. I run through the people that know: Holly, already discounted; Paul… I mean, I suppose… it's not really his style though, is it? Dad… I can't remember the last time I saw his writing, though I guess his probably could be described as tight. He's not been one to nurture dreams though, more wrap them up and pack them away in case they take me anywhere but within walking distance of him. I haven't specifically told anyone else, but in our village, everybody knows everything.

I flick through the pages again, finding another where the words: *Who nurtures you?* are handwritten. And another, *How do you feel right now?* and more, *Who do you want to be? What is important?* It's got to be someone who knows me, the questions are so personal, so probing. Paul and I have talked about some of this stuff, when we've all gone out together, usually when Holly is at the bar or chatting some bloke up and we've been left alone. Considering they're siblings, he's definitely a deeper thinker than she is. I guess he always has been, from back when Holly and I were silly teenagers and he was heading to college, his head always in a book of one sort or another. I could see how it might be from him, especially after what he said before they went on holiday. He wouldn't want to admit to it straight away, I guess. He's probably still giving me space. I take my phone out. Should I just message him a thank you? My phone dings in my hand making me jump.

I hope Poppy's first day went well. X

Dad. I read his message a few times, wondering how best to respond. Frustrated that he hasn't mentioned it was mine too. I suppose a first day at school is more significant than a new job. And I should be grateful that he remembered at all, really. He's just lost his mum. He's no doubt grieving. Maybe that was what was behind him interfering at the school? He just wasn't thinking straight? The text is probably his way of saying sorry. Sometimes though, I just wish he'd actually say that. Or not interfere in the first place.

I go to type something back to him, but everything seems not quite right somehow. I'm frustrated with him. He's always tried to control me, my life, my choices. It needs to stop. I thought things were getting better, but with the job stuff, it's like he's reverted. Am I going to be his new focus for control now that Grandma is gone? I don't want it. I need to stand on my own two feet. If Grandma's not there to buffer his mood, I don't know if I can cope with it on my own.

Poppy slides down the stairs on her bum again, a gaggle of teddies clutched tight into her chest. 'I thought we could put the picnic mat out and I'll set them all up. Bear-Bear wanted to come but he's overcomely with sadness, so he's got to stay upstairs.'

'Overcomely with sadness? How do you mean?'

'He's like the little boy in the story we're reading at school. Mrs Butterworth said he's overcomely with sadness.'

'Right.'

'It's really a very shame.'

Her attempts at grown-up chat make me smile, as they always have. 'Do you think Bear-Bear being on his own is the best thing? When I'm sad, I always like to have people around me.'

'No, you don't,' she says, innocently. I look up, sharply. 'You always just pretend you're not sad.' Stunned, I'm not sure what to say, but for her, it seems the moment has passed as quickly as it arrived. 'Right, Mummy, me and my teddies are starving.'

She trots off into the lounge with her teddies, chattering to them about her day and tea and, oddly, Grandma Elsie's funeral. The songs, the glazed windows in the church, the plane that flew over the church-yard as we stood about waiting for the service to begin. Dazed, I take the gifted notebook into the kitchen and start pulling tea together.

Chapter Five

'What? So, you've no idea who it's from?' Holly's feet are tucked up into the cushions on the side of the sofa normally inhabited by Poppy, who fell asleep there not long after dinner, wiped out by her first day at school. Didn't even wake up when I carried her up the stairs. Holly studies the notebook. 'No idea at all?'

'None.' I've since decided it has to be from Paul. It's the kind of thoughtful thing he'd do. But I can't let on. I've not dared mention anything to her about Paul saying he liked me, on the basis that I can't know if he's talked to her or not. I know she's my best friend, but surely blood is thicker than water? They're close, but I'm just not sure he'd have told her. Unless he did and she's playing it uncharacteristically cool? Is she waiting for me to open up and tell her how I feel so that she can relay it back to him? We're not kids anymore, I can't see that would be his style, but then, I also didn't see it coming when he said he had feelings for me in the first place. I've gone round in circles, thinking about it all; caught between a man that I've definitely liked for years, and my best friend. I don't want to mess things up!

'No idea at all?'

'None. It's a mystery.'

She frowns like maybe she does know.

'I thought about asking Iris. Not much gets past her and whenever I've been out for a parcel delivery, they've dropped it off at hers. And, bless her, she does love a good curtain twitch.'

'True.' Holly flicks through the pages, pausing to read the various questions. 'When I lived over the road, she loved a snoop at my expense,' she says, not looking up.

'That's because you were "pashing" in the back of a Ford Fiesta. Even I was intrigued to see how that was going to unfold.'

She gives me a wicked look because we both know how it unfolded. '"*Who Nurtures you?*" What kind of question is that?' She side-eyes the book. 'You'd better put *me* down as an answer.'

'If I fill it out.'

'It was an Escort actually. Ford Escort. And I was not pashing in it, I was merely showing my gratitude for a lovely evening out.'

'With Darren?'

'Yes, with Darren, thank you very much. We did have some of those, before we broke up. In fact, until I got pregnant, he was very generous with his money and time.'

'And sperm, apparently.'

'Well, yes. But that definitely did not happen in the Ford Escort, and certainly not in view of you or Iris.'

'She doesn't mean any harm. She's probably lonely. More so now my grandma's not around. They were best friends since I was a kid.'

'I'm lonely but you don't catch me with night goggles.'

'Iris has not got night goggles!'

'How do you know though?' I laugh at Holly's raised eyebrows and crossed arms. 'Anyway, surely there are other ways to find out who it's from?'

'Like what?' Maybe she doesn't know?

'Facebook!'

I grimace.

'What? If people can find their long-lost brother, thrice-removed, you can find the giver of this secret gift.'

Maybe Paul hasn't said anything. I suppose we both know how insufferable Holly can be when she gets an idea into her head. She'd either hate the idea of us together and make us pay for it. Or love the idea and buy every hat known to man in preparation for a wedding. Before our first official date.

God, do I want to go on a date with him?

I mean… I think I do…

'Look, I am not going back on Facebook just for that,' I say, trying to dampen the flutter of butterflies.

'What do you mean, "going back on"?'

'I came off it months ago. I was losing hours of my life watching everyone else have a really great time. I swear to God my mental health has improved tenfold in its absence. Instagram, now that's where it's at.'

She passes me the notebook back, and I let it sit in my palms, its possibility itching at my heart.

'Instagram?' she says.

'Yes! You should try it.' I realise I sound like it's some kind of new-fangled technology wonder but opt to ignore that fact.

She reaches for her glass of wine. 'As if I need to see Kim Kardashian's perfect pout pose to make me feel good about myself.'

'I don't follow her. I follow people whose lives I relate to.'

'Alright, whatevs. It's still a no from me. But if that's what's floating your boat right now, put a photo of it on there. See who likes it.' She thinks for a second. 'Whoever likes it, they're the sender, right?'

'You've not got the concept of Instagram, have you?'

'Pah! It's all nonsense if you ask me.'

I top up my own wine, enjoying the warmth in my belly as I begin to relax. 'Where's Charlie anyway?'

'At home. Darren's mum came over. Told her I was going to Ballet Barre.'

I cough choke on my wine. 'Ballet Barre?'

'I know. Can't believe she fell for it. I've as much grace as one of those Disney hippos in *Fantasia*. And the stamina of a donkey.'

'I thought donkeys had stamina.'

'Do they? Okay, the stamina of a…' She pauses, searching for something appropriately lacking in stamina.

'A sloth?' I suggest.

'I love a sloth.'

'Me too.' I check my watch. 'So what time do you have to be back?'

'I said it'd be nine thirtyish. I was going to pick up a Chinese on the way back.'

'On the way back? That's really going to fill Darren's mum with confidence that you're committed to health and wellbeing.'

'True. You eaten?'

'I had wake leftovers with Poppy earlier. Not a single item of green on the plate. But a lot of hummus sandwiches. I'm not sure who I thought I was catering for.'

'You are my parenting inspiration.'

'I know, right?'

'So you could go for a bit of fried rice and MSG if I ordered it here instead?'

'I'd prefer pizza.'

'Oooh, good shout. I'll order, while you think about who else nurtures you. Papa Pizza?'

'Yes! Garlic mushroom, please. That'll nurture me.'

'Paul would nurture you if you let him.' She says it out of the blue and once again, I choke on my wine. 'Hashtag just saying!'

'Holly!' I blush at the mention of his name. He must have said something. He could have warned me.

'Maybe he sent it.' She jumps up, dialling the takeaway. 'He does do a good line in gifts, always very thoughtful.' I roll my eyes at her as she backs out of the lounge. 'They're the kind of questions he'd ask, too. Insufferable in his need to encourage.'

She dives out into the kitchen where the phone signal is better. I look down at the book. Is Paul that invested that he'd send me something like this? And if so, why wouldn't he just say it was from him?

Chapter Six

Half an hour later, we're tucking into pizza which was helpfully delivered by a guy Holly's had her eye on for ages. She was on the doorstep far longer than strictly necessary when taking receipt of our food. There was much laughing, and with that, I don't doubt, there will have been hair tossing and coy looks, batting her eyelashes through her fringe. She's always been better at flirting than me. Sometimes, when I've considered the fact that I'm lonely, I've remembered that I'd have to turn on flirting and sexiness in order to be appealing and the idea has fast disappeared. I guess some of that wouldn't be required with Paul.

'So why wouldn't you fill it out?' asks Holly, mid-mouthful, battling with stringy cheese.

'Pardon?'

'The notebook. You said you didn't know if you'd fill it out. Why wouldn't you?'

'I don't know. It's weird, isn't it? A gift like that.'

'What's weird about it? I think it's lovely. Thoughtful, in fact. Someone wants you to be the best version of you and this is how they think they can help.' She's changed her tune. They do say blood is thicker than water.

'What's wrong with the version of me I am now?'

'Literally nothing. You are the epitome of all that is good and kind and hot. I would… if I were that way inclined.'

'Gee. Thanks.'

'I can deffo see what our Paul sees in you.'

I blush, ineffectually hiding my face in my last slice of pizza. 'Has he said something?'

'He doesn't need to. I've seen how he looks at you. His timing is pretty bloody awful though.'

'What do you mean?'

'Look, I wasn't sure if I should tell you this but… Billy's back.'

I look up sharply, garlic butter dripping on to my chin. 'What?'

'Yep. Saw the back of his head down the Co-op. Did a double-take 'cos I couldn't believe it was him, but it definitely was.'

'Did he see you?'

'Don't think so.'

'Why didn't you say something to me? Before now, I mean.'

'I'm telling you now. Why do you think I came round? I love you but it wasn't just for pizza… look, I know that sometimes you—'

'What?'

'Well, for Poppy's sake, I know you wish you had some kind of relationship.'

'Exactly. For Poppy's sake.'

Holly remembers all the times I cried on her shoulder when I wanted to sort things for more than just Poppy's sake, before I really got my head around what a shitty thing he'd done to us both and got the kind of closure I needed. At least, I think I got closure. The weak knees at the sound of his name make me wonder though.

'Maybe he wants to sort things out?'

'Sort things out? There's a bit more required than sorting things out,' I say, ramming pizza in my face to buy me a bit of time to establish how I feel. Angry is one of the things I feel; I am definitely still angry with him. 'He left me with a three-day-old baby telling me I should be more ambitious, that I should want more out of my life! How can you want more when you're a walking milk machine? You've literally nothing else to give at that point.'

'Well, maybe he's grown up. Maybe the notebook is from him and he's going about encouraging you in a more constructive fashion?' I raise my eyebrows. 'You didn't mind being encouraged when you thought it might be Paul.'

'Pfft.'

'Do you think he's changed? Do you think he's capable of it? Was he ever really thoughtful?'

'Not especially. Romantic occasionally, but usually only to get his end away. He said I'd ruined his life by getting pregnant. That he wasn't someone to be tamed and kept under the lock and key of a traditional relationship.'

'Lock and key? Have you got some kind of secret S&M side?'

'Nope. Definitely not.'

'So, and I'm playing devil's advocate here as I was there when you got back remember, I know how you felt about him, but maybe he realises what he lost?'

'Look, whilst I'd always be open to him being in our lives for Poppy's sake, it would be based on a consistent relationship and very much not having sex with me. I can't imagine for a second that he'd have changed enough to send me the notebook for the right reasons, even if it was him.'

'But that's not a good reason not to answer some of the questions it poses. They are pretty valid, I think. Might give them some thought myself.'

'Whose side are you on? You just said I was great.'

'I did. You are. But I also think things like that are good for getting us to think about who we are and what we want out of life.'

'Since when did you get so deep?'

'Oh, I don't know. Charlie starting school has made me think all sorts. Time passes so quickly, doesn't it? Maybe it's time I worked out what I want in life, who I am, you know? We can do it together.'

'I know who I am. I know what I want,' I lie.

Frank wanders in from the hallway where he was guarding the door, his claws clacking on the wooden floor. He jumps up beside me and lets out a deep sigh.

'Shit, is that the time?' Holly jumps up, putting her leftover pizza on the footstool. 'I'd better go.' She bends down to kiss me then breathes into my face. 'Do I smell like cheese and dough?'

'Meat feast?' I say, through a cough.

'Bugger.' She rummages around in her bag for a pack of Polo Mints, dropping three in one go. 'I'll see you in the morning,' she says, mouth full.

The front door slams shut and Frank briefly looks up before shoving his head into a cushion. 'Some guard dog you are!'

I screw the top back on the wine, saving the rest for tomorrow. Reaching for the notebook, I flick through the pages again, pondering answers to the questions with limited success. I think I've spent so much time looking to live in the now that considering the future, my dreams and ambitions seems counter-intuitive. Except that, if I'm honest with myself, the 'living in the now' bit probably comes more out of fear of the future than some inner relationship to my spiritual self.

If Billy is back, is it for me, or Poppy? The handwriting doesn't look especially like his, but then I've not seen him for pretty much five years, so who knows. I pause, trying to hear my feelings. The swell in my stomach, nerves and uncertainty. The memories of how devastated I was when he left. I can't ignore the fact that I loved him, but things have changed. I've changed. And then there's Paul. God, how will Paul feel about him being back? Especially after finally admitting he has feelings for me?

I pick through the notebook, pausing on a question then moving on when my brain wants to explode at the potential answers. Then I find one question that I can manage to answer without too much thought at all: *What nice thing can you do for someone else?* I grab a pen, and start writing: *Chocolate croissant for Holly on the school run, slow walk for Frank, pay for a stranger's coffee.* I pause because I'm aware of the most obvious thing I should do, the thing that I shouldn't even think twice about and yet I'm stuck on it. I take a deep breath and write: *Text Dad back…*then pick up my phone, stop overthinking it and tap out a message back.

She had a great day. Loved it. Is now flat out. Thanks for checking in. x

I consider mentioning something about my day, but he didn't ask and there's no need to antagonise. I know how he feels, I don't have to rub it in his face, so I click send, look down at the list I've written, and draw a line through the text Dad back. If this notebook is from Billy, I can't say I want him back in my life for romance, but maybe we're at a place where we can be friends? And maybe this can help me get a little focus. As for Paul… Grandma died within a few days of him and Hol going away. My sadness drowned out much thought about Paul and my feelings, to be honest. Now though, when it comes down to it, I think I have to admit that I like him.

Chapter Seven

'Here you go.' I hand Holly the paper bag I stuffed a chocolate croissant in when I filled up at the petrol station this morning.

'Pastry? Good God, what did I do to deserve you?' She takes a huge bite before offering me some.

'Just thought it was a nice thing to do for you.'

'You're not wrong. I ended up buying a bottle of wine after I left yours, got a taste for it and, after Darren's mum left, I sank the lot whilst watching *The Crown* on Netflix.'

'Nice.'

'Yeah. Is it weird that I fancy Matt Smith's Prince Philip?'

'Little bit.'

'God, I needed this, you're a bloody angel you are.' She stuffs the other half of the croissant in her face and groans in pleasure.

Poppy drags a little girl up to me. 'Mummy, this is Evie. Can she come for tea?'

'Oh, well, yes, I'm sure she can at some point. No problem.'

Poppy fist punches the air and Evie looks suitably pleased. They run off together conspiring about important things five-year-olds conspire about, before finding Charlie crouched over a slug or snail or something in the corner of the playground.

'I don't wish to gender stereotype here, but why on earth are boys interested in slimy things?' asks Holly, brushing crumbs from her chest.

'I don't think it's just boys.' I point over to Charlie and the girls who have each picked up whatever they've found and are showing it to other kids in the playground, to varying degrees of joy or dismay.

'So, any closer to finding out who the book's from?'

'Nah. Not going to stress about it. It'll come out eventually.' I've decided that I don't want her to know that I'm hoping it's from Paul.

'I'd want to know!'

'Would you want to know for you? Or would you want to know because you're fundamentally nosy and the idea of not knowing who sent it to me is driving you insane?'

'What can I say? My life is very dull, I have to grab moments of vicarious living at any opportunity I can get. Oh, hang on.' She pulls her phone out of her coat pocket and grins before tapping out a response.

'Dull?'

'Pardon?'

'You. And your dull life. Except, I've seen that look before.'

'What look?'

'That look. You. You're sexting.'

'How very dare you. I'm stood in the playground at my son's school. Do you really think sexting in a school playground is appropriate behaviour? You couldn't be further from the truth.'

'Really?'

'Ha! No, I'm totally sexting. Turns out Pizza Delivery Dave is into me.'

'And is that how you've got him saved in your phone?' It will be, it's the only way she can keep track.

'Might be.'

'Before or after Green Dragon Gaz?'

'After, obviously! Come on now, the alphabet!'

I stifle a laugh as the bell goes and Poppy appears out of nowhere, snail in hand.

'Mum, can you look after George?'

'George?' I ask, knowing the answer but hoping I'm wrong.

'George. The snail. I think he should come back and live with us.'

'Right. I mean, you do know I have to go to work now and he probably won't like being in the school office all day.'

'Hmmm…'

'Perhaps you could pop him over there and we'll get him when we leave, later?'

Poppy, thankfully, thinks this is a great idea and pops the snail down by some leaves before coming back with a stern look on her face. 'We must not forget him, okay?'

'Right. Okay.'

She throws her arms around me, giving me a second to kiss the top of her head before disappearing into the classroom with Charlie, waving to Evie as they go in opposite directions.

Holly waves off Charlie before burying her head in her phone. 'How do I look?' she asks.

'Gorgeous as always.'

'Great. I've an impromptu brunch date. Turns out that whilst not currently working is doing all the bad things to my bank account and self-respect, and is without doubt unsustainable, it also has short-term advantages.' She winks and wanders off with more skip in her step than I'm used to seeing at this time of a morning. I briefly envy her.

In the office, I set out my desk: tea to the left of me, computer up in front, phone on the right. I reach into my bag, pulling out the notebook, turning to the page of nice things to do for people and strike a line through croissant for Holly. God, I hope this isn't from Billy.

Teatime. Poppy runs off up ahead, today's school day apparently not wearing her out this time. I yawn, mine having knocked me for six, I'm just not used to being out of the house and having to think all day. But it feels good, I feel… useful. 'Hang on.' I wait for Frank to catch us up in the park. He waddles, sniffing things, cocking his leg for nothing more than a dribble.

'Mum! Can I go on the swings?' Poppy shouts, standing hopefully at the little yellow gate that lets her into the nirvana that is our local park play area.

'Go on then, two minutes.'

I wander over to a bench nearby, letting Frank potter about without pressure to keep up. The grass hasn't long been cut and still smells fresh. The sky is blue, streaked with the occasional wisp of a cloud. Poppy swings her legs forward and back, gaining great height now that she's learned how to do it. 'Be careful!'

'Hey, Lisa. God, she's had a growth spurt!' says a voice and I know exactly who it is.

Chapter Eight

'Paul, hi!' I shift to see better, his head now obscuring the sun behind him. He's got a bit of colour from his holiday. My heart rate quickens, and my mouth feels a bit wonky.

'Three weeks and she's positively shot up. You been putting her in a grow bag?' He half grins, but there's a frisson of nerves too. 'I bet she towers over Charlie, doesn't she?'

'Erm, yeah, ha! She does a bit, all of a sudden. Don't know how it happened.' We both look at her, no doubt searching for what to say. It might be too early to revisit our conversation from before he went away, so I opt for, 'Good holiday?'

'Erm, yeah. Thanks.' He ruffles his hair. 'It was nice. Holly only got hammered and irritating on one occasion. Which I can't blame her for seeing as I'd encouraged her to let her hair down if I looked after Charlie. She went out to some club with a couple of girls she met by the pool and it took her two days to fully recover.'

'Ha! She didn't mention that.'

'No. She can probably barely remember it. Back to reality now though, looking after... Oh God, where's he gone?' Paul looks around, searching for something. 'Jeffrey!' A fox-red Labrador does a downward dog at Frank, bum up in the air, tail wagging furiously. 'He's an absolute idiot, that dog.' Paul shakes his head. 'I don't think he wants to be your friend, you buffoon!'

'That's Grandma's old dog, he can barely walk these days, never mind play. Is he yours?'

'Nah. Toby's. I'm looking after him for a few days whilst he's away. He's a proper dog-botherer though!'

'Yeah, old Frank's not interested in playing any more.'

'Holly said about your grandma. I was really sorry to hear. Are you okay?'

'I'm okay. I mean... it's hard. And God, I'm gonna miss her, but she was in pain, so... She was ready, you know?'

'Doesn't mean you were ready.'

'No. I guess not.'

He shuffles his feet, turning his attention back to Jeffrey.

I should just ask him if he sent the notebook but an odd shyness has come over me. I wonder if that's why he's gone weird, too. Does he want to say something more but doesn't know how? Or is it just the whole Grandma death thing? People are always awkward around death. 'You look like you caught the sun.'

He looks down at his bare arms. 'Yeah, it was pretty hot.'

'Can't remember the last time I went abroad.'

'It's probably my last time for a while, to be fair. I need to knuckle down, try to get the business off the ground.'

'Is it all set up now?'

'Yep. PM Architects is registered with Companies House and I've bought the domain name.'

'That's brilliant. It's going to be so good. I just know it.'

'Thanks. I appreciate it. I've spent the last few weeks panicking that the whole thing's just a pipe dream. It's like I said to you before

I went away…' He stops, presumably because he's realised that's also when he told me he liked me. 'Well…' Cough. 'I've had an enquiry for a garage extension, but it's not quite what I was after.'

'Slowly, slowly. Dreams take time.' I choose my words carefully.

'I guess.' He doesn't flinch. 'Never imagined I'd be longing for a loft conversion.'

'No. Well… all good things come to those who wait and all that.'

He turns to face me, holding my gaze. 'I hope so.' Jeffrey trots over to us, fussing over me, which is a good excuse to break eye contact. 'There's word on the street about some developer buying the land behind Venable's farm. And the old buildings around it. They're wanting to flatten it all and put executive homes on it. Maybe I can find a way to get in there.'

'That'd be great, wouldn't it. You just need a bit of a break, someone to give you a leg up, eh?'

We fall into silence again. I'm sure, before he went away, it would have been comfortable silence, but this time it's very definitely not, so I search for something to say because I've never really been that keen on silences anyway and doing that little sing-song get-out-of-silence hum isn't really appropriate in this instance. 'So!' we both say.

'Sorry, you first.' Which I basically say because I wasn't sure where I was going after 'So' in any case.

'Oh, no, I was just… well, I was going to… ask about Billy,' he says, in the kind of way that makes me think that's not what he was going to say. 'Holly mentioned he was back, I wondered if you'd seen him?'

'Oh! Did she? Right. No, I haven't heard from him.'

'Really? I thought he might have…' He signals towards Poppy who's stopped swinging.

'No. No, not yet.'

'Right. Erm… look… about what I said. I'm sorry if I put you in an awkward position…'

'No, no you didn't.'

'I mean, if Billy's about, you probably need to focus on sorting things out with him, for Poppy.'

'Oh, I don't know about that.'

'It must be easier with two parents, right?'

'We manage. We do just fine. We don't need Billy, or anyone for that matter.' I hear my tone, which is probably a little more irritated than he deserves.

'No, I know, sorry, I wasn't saying you weren't coping or anything. I suppose I also appreciate that what with your grandma, and then Billy back, you've got a lot on your plate, that's all. Emotionally. And I don't want to ruin our friendship, I'm here for you if you need anything. I shouldn't have—'

'Mummy! We forgot George!' Poppy's timing has never been ideal.

'George?' Paul asks, grasping at a chance to change the subject before I've had time to say my bit… not that I know exactly what I want to say, except that I don't think it has to ruin our friendship. Quite the opposite, even. 'Who's George?'

'My pet snail.'

'Wow! You have a pet snail? How cool!' He's bent down to her level, like he always does. She puffs up at being taken seriously, at not being patronised, like she always does.

'We left him at school because snails don't like being indoors and now we've forgotten him he's going to be all sad and alone.'

'Oh no!' Paul looks about. 'What did he look like?'

Poppy jabbers on giving a very detailed description of the snail and I fizz at him taking in her every word, smiling and nodding as if what she's saying is very important. My ovaries ache a little bit.

'So now, I'm just going to have to hope he's still there tomorrow.'

He studies the ground. 'Small, brown and a little bit slimy, you say?'

'That's right.'

He looks around for a moment then, double-takes. 'Wait… that's not… is it?' He points to something beneath the bench. 'Is that George?'

Poppy spins round, pauses, takes a closer look before a sharp intake of breath.

'Wow! George!' she says, gleefully.

Paul winks at me and I try and hide my face in my scarf as it heats up. Poppy lifts the snail by its house, displaying it proudly on her hand.

'He must have known you were coming here and found his way,' Paul says.

'Brilliant, thank you, Paul. You've saved the day,' I say.

He ruffles the back of his hair again, a smile playing on his lips. I want to tell him that I don't think he's ruined our friendship. And I want to ask him about the notebook, but not here, not with Poppy around.

'Right, come on then, Pops.' I round Frank up. 'We'd better get home for tea.'

'Yes, I'd better get off before Jeffrey starts bothering any more disinterested dogs.' As he says it, we both see Jeffrey sniffing a Beagle's backside. 'Oh God.' He jogs off. 'See you soon, we should… catch up. Oh! The present from Holly. I should have dropped it off.'

'Maybe we could do drinks.' We've always caught up. Me, Paul, Holly, it's never been a big deal. Now though, now maybe it is. 'The three of us?' I add as Poppy tugs on my hand.

'You know, Mummy,' she says, thankfully waiting until he's out of earshot, 'this isn't George.'

'No?' I ask, innocently.

'No. I just didn't like to tell him because he seemed so happy to see this snail.'

She pops the not-George snail under a bush and scampers off ahead, chatting to herself as we leave the park, me feeling a mixture of pride in my five-year-old's empathy, and sadness that she even thinks about things like that at her age. Oh, and also excitement. In my belly. I wonder when Paul and I might catch up?

Chapter Nine

With Poppy snuggled down in bed and Frank asleep outside her door, I take a cuppa into the lounge and flick on the telly. Scrolling through the channels nothing really appeals, but I end up leaving it on some house-renovation programme with that Geordie bloke with the grin and dimples. George! Like the snail. That's him. George Clarke. That's when I realise Paul has more than a passing resemblance to him. Maybe it's the eyes, sort of piercing but mischievous. I drift off for a second before realising what I'm thinking about and pull myself together. Not-the-snail George is stood in a fairly beat-up house with the owner, a single woman who's bought it as an investment project. He drapes his arm over her shoulders as they look up and around at what seems to me more like a demolition site than a dream home, vision not being my forte.

'So, Jenny, what do you dream it will look like?' he asks. I cast my eyes down onto the table where the notebook lies, pushing myself off the sofa to reach it before tucking myself up in a throw again, book on my lap.

On my TV, George and Jenny wander around the house and she chats easily about how she wants it to look, the features she'd like to keep and the windows she'd like to open up into bi-fold doors because who doesn't love a bi-fold door? I open the notebook, landing straight on the page that says *Tell me your dreams...*

Paul and I have talked about what our futures might look like, or holidays we'd like to take. Well, he's talked about his future and his holidays and I've been happy to listen. I've never really dreamed much outside of my own life. Which I suppose is a bit sad, really. We've reminisced over school days, mine and Holly's, and Paul's being a bit older than us. We've imagined how things might be for Poppy and Charlie. We've talked about Billy too. He and Paul were inseparable for years; they grew more distant when Billy and I got together that last time. I don't know how much Paul tried to keep in touch after Billy left. I don't know if he bothered trying. Billy was pretty much a no-go zone and sometimes I've wondered if they were basically only mates because of a lack of options in our small town, rather than because they had a huge amount in common.

Billy.

The thought of seeing him again after all this time. If he really wants to reach out for Poppy and me, why hasn't he picked up the phone? Or rocked up at the door? Why hasn't he messaged to let me know he's around? I'll bump into him in the village at some point, bound too.

I think back to when he left, the night I shouted as he took his bag down the stairs of our tenement building. I had Poppy in my arms, stood on the landing outside our flat in Edinburgh. We'd been renting it for less than three of the twelve-month lease we'd signed up to, even though he was shifty the day we signed it. I should have realised, seen it coming. I remember he hovered over the bit where he had to put his signature, as if having second thoughts. I'd nudged him because the estate agent was watching. His hands shook as he handed back the paperwork.

I guess I'd hoped my instincts were wrong, but I knew, the day it happened. I could sense it coming. The whole day dragged, there was an atmosphere until early evening when he finally decided he was going. As I begged him to stay, and Poppy let out a murmur from my arms, he paused on the top step. I told him that if he kept on walking, if he took himself off down the stairs and out of the building, he was never to contact us again. I was exhausted, my boobs hurt because Poppy didn't feed well. I hadn't stopped crying pretty much since the minute she was born. I felt so alone, even with him there... I think it was the first time I realised that I missed having a mother. I wanted to know how she'd handled having me, how her body felt, how *she* felt. Did she feel sad, or overwhelmed? Even beforehand, when I fell pregnant, I tried talking to Grandma, but it didn't feel the same, somehow. It was as if the generation removed put too big a gap between our experiences. She was buttoned up about it all, brushed off the pain, the hormones, the emotions. I could talk to Holly, but she was three months behind me with the pregnancy, so some of it she'd not been through yet. I didn't want to frighten her. And besides, when I was up in Scotland, talking to them on the phone made them feel even further away. All I wanted, was to reach out to someone, to ask advice, be nurtured. A mother would have done that, wouldn't she?

I shiver, remembering how Billy stared at me that night: cold, unloving. How he turned on his heel and left. I waited until I heard the downstairs door of the building slam shut. I waited until a next-door neighbour opened his own door, presumably because he could hear me crying on my doorstep. I went back inside and shut the door behind me, sliding down to the ground, Poppy still in my arms, hoping more than anything that Billy would realise he should come back. But he didn't. We never heard from him again. Dad brought me home to Lincolnshire the following week.

I loved Billy though. I really thought we were happy, even with his uncertainty. I thought that was a phase. I wasn't naive enough to think having a baby would fix us, but I did think it seemed to change how he felt. It took a long time for me to accept that us moving to Scotland was a distraction, a way to delay the inevitable. But when we were good, we were very good. He made me laugh. When he was happy and felt free, he made me feel good about myself and I obliged, I gave him that freedom. I was happy if he was happy because Billy was honestly the first person I ever truly loved. Much to Dad's dissatisfaction. He probably wished we'd never got back together after the first break-up, when he'd split us up on purpose.

Chapter Ten

I pick up my phone and open Facebook. Whilst I have, technically, come off it, I couldn't cancel my account because there were far too many memories and photos on there.

I scroll down the folders until I find what I'm looking for, my head filled with a complicated mixture of nostalgia, love and loathing to see us, fresh-faced. Just after Holly and I finished our GCSEs. Billy was working in McDonald's nearby. He had a car, picked me up from my last exam. English, I think.

Dad hated us being together, said we were too young to be serious, said it would only ever lead to trouble, and I promised him it wouldn't. Which was true, back then. We dated for a couple of years in the end, him still at McDonald's and me at college doing English, Sociology and Business at A-level, even though I didn't know what on earth I wanted to do with them. For years after we broke up that first time, I thought things had fizzled out, as they do when you're a teenager. It's only when we got back together that Billy told me my dad had been the one to pull some strings, got him a job with a travelling food company that went off to festivals all over the world. Dad had masterminded the whole thing, then got me a job clerking down at the bank because I could never answer what I wanted to do with my life and he had decided I was wasting my time.

Then there are the photos from years later when Billy and I got back together, on my thirtieth birthday. I was working at the library by then. The romance of him turning up in the pub and surprising me, telling me that he never stopped loving me. He'd just got back from New Zealand. He was tanned and rugged, his hair kissed by sun, his skin dark and intoxicating. Then after, the days out in Skegness, brown waters and pebble beaches. He'd tell me how much better the beaches in New Zealand were and I felt jealous, until he told me that one day, he'd take me. I liked the idea of it, even though I think I always knew travel wasn't really for me. I like home. I like security. I like to know where I am and who I'll see. I always argued it wasn't small, when he said I should think bigger. I always argued the case that maybe I was content and he was running away… I'm not sure I've ever been certain which was which.

Dad was furious we'd got back together. He never said as much, that wasn't his style, but he didn't approve. The weight of judgement and quiet rage was apparent. Like it always had been when I did something of which he didn't approve, and this time, maybe for the first time, I went against what he wanted, putting love ahead of trying to please Dad.

I pause on a photo of Billy and me stood by a Belgian beer stall at Lincoln Christmas Market. I don't know who took it, but we're looking at each other like we were really in love. And we were. We really were. Despite our differences. Which is why I wasn't worried when I got pregnant. I thought he'd come around to the idea, I thought he'd get there eventually if I gave him space and time. Him saying he wasn't happy was just a symptom of readjusting after years away, travelling. He'd got a job with some computer firm. I was content, I believed he could be too. But instead, he told me that I was holding him back. Keeping him in a small town where everyone knew each other's business and he didn't want that for his life or his child. I think it was an excuse. It's why I suggested we move up to Scotland. Get us out of Lincolnshire. Start anew, prove to Billy that I could think big too, though perhaps Scotland wasn't big enough. Dad said I couldn't go. I don't think I've ever seen him that angry before. Grandma Elsie had apparently smoothed things out in the end. Well, as smooth as they'd ever be. I was thirty-two at the time. No age to be told I could or couldn't do something I really wanted to do. When everyone else's parents were being happy for their children's lives evolving and growing, people getting married and having babies, Dad was clamping down, getting tighter with his expectation. Checking up on me. It felt… controlling. He said I was selfish to go. Threw Grandma Elsie back at me, 'after all she'd done for us' when I was growing up and he'd had to raise me on his own. But I knew she was okay because we would stay connected. And she knew I'd visit, bring the baby to see her. She was never a replacement mother, she and I always knew that, even if he'd tried to convince me otherwise. He'd never done it before, when I was growing up: he was always clear that she was there to support him and I, but that was it. It was such an about turn when I wanted to leave, as if suddenly, he felt I owed Grandma my life. Like I should stay, for her if not for him. But I didn't, I couldn't. And Grandma understood, even if Dad hadn't.

But then Billy left me.

Dad couldn't have been happier the day he arrived on my doorstep to save the day. Poppy was a week old. 'Come on, I'm taking you home,' he'd said, offering me a suitcase. He couldn't understand why I cried all the way back home. Five hours it took us. Edinburgh to Lincolnshire, the village I grew up in, just on the outskirts of Sleaford. Five hours with a restless baby, a suitcase of belongings, and what felt like all my hope left back in that tenement flat.

I reach into the magazine rack beside the sofa and dig out a pen. Billy or Paul, maybe the sender is unimportant. I smooth the page down with my hand. *Tell me your dreams…*

1. *To settle in and enjoy my new job*
2. *To get some financial independence and some savings behind us*
3. *To work things out with Dad… maybe on my terms this time*
4. *To watch Poppy grow into a confident young girl*
5. *To inspire her, to let her see you can achieve your dreams*
6. *To work out what my dreams really are… what do I want in life? What can I strive for? Who do I want to be?*

I pause, writing the number 7 down over and over on itself, circling it, drawing a line beneath it before eventually writing:

7. *Fall in love?*

When I get up to go to bed, there's a small envelope on the doormat. My heart skips as I pick it up, open it, and find the other half of Holly's necklace, nestled within. Paul must have dropped by without my noticing. And he didn't knock to say hi, like he might have done, once upon a time.

Chapter Eleven

Scanning the playground, I'm discombobulated not to see Holly. Especially seeing as I put the necklace on for her. Poppy has run off with Evie and I'm stood alone. I pick out my phone to scroll through Instagram because I'd rather look busy in case any of the mums decide they want to talk to me. I already pissed one of them off yesterday when I told her that her darling vomitous daughter couldn't come into school for forty-eight hours to save her spreading any bugs around. Apparently, I was a 'Bug Nazi' and 'What did a bit of sickness and diarrhoea matter? They all had to develop robust constitutions.' I notice both mother and daughter are here.

'Hi!' says a self-assured voice and nerves spring up out of nowhere. I am basically rubbish in new social situations. 'You're the new school secretary.' Her hair bounces as she talks. She gives off an aura of extreme confidence but not the kind you put on like a cloak when you wake up, more the kind you wake up with, because it's in your DNA. 'Poppy's mum, right?'

On the one hand, I'd like to be known as something other than a mother and school secretary, but on the other, knowing what I know about this woman, or rather her husband and his penchant for my mate, maybe the label is just fine. Where the hell is Holly at times like this? Nobody approaches me when she's around. 'Yes. That's me.'

'I'm glad I've caught you, I'm Felicity. Well, everyone calls me Flick.' She grins bright white teeth and crystal-clear eyes that probably slept beneath a silk mask all night. 'Sorry, what's your name?'

Bugger. 'Lisa.'

'Right. It's Ludovic's birthday at the end of the month and he does so want to invite most of his little friends in class.' I've literally never heard of Ludovic. 'He and Poppy knew each other a bit from before, at nursery. He's always talking about her.' Awkward. 'It's going to be at ARK. You know the exotic animal sanctuary? Such a good cause, we really do love animals. Is Saturday September 26th okay?'

'Erm.' I search for a reason why it might not be, on the basis that I am firmly Team Holly. 'Well…'

'Great!' I didn't say yes. I didn't say yes! 'I'll get the invites out by the end of the week, I just didn't want to waste any on people who can't come because I'm getting them handmade, you see. Keeping it local. Isn't that important? Does Poppy have any dietary requirements? We're strictly dairy-free as Ludo is allergic, so I'm always very aware of people's needs.'

'Well, no, we don't—'

'That's lovely. Brilliant. I'll count you both in then. We're all going to be there, me, Janey, Tash, and Debs is hoping to make it with both Farrell and Bibi, so it's going to be a real hoot for the kids.' She points over to a group of women and their respective children as we talk. They all look immaculate, like they've been up for hours blow-drying their hair and painting on their faces with Charlotte Tilbury and a mere kiss of Touche Éclat, such is their flawless skin tone. In fact, they probably only use Touche Éclat because it's from Yves Saint Laurent, not because they actually need it. I'd need a veritable vat. Not that I could afford it, mind. There are very definitely two camps to this village, and they are in the 'big house, husbands with senior jobs in the army, money isn't really a problem' camp.

'Might even pop a few bubbles for the mums, you know? We do love our bubbles, right?' I hate bubbles. They give me reflux. Maybe that's because I've only ever drunk the kind Holly buys from Aldi? I offer up a polite wave, the mums smile sweetly and wave back. Lady Vomitous is part of the group. I notice she doesn't wave. Felicity leans in conspiratorially. 'Jenna's there too. She mentioned she'd had a run-in with you yesterday about little Jessamy? Don't worry about her, her bark's worse than her bite. She is very stressed out with two kids and a husband that works away – though we're all fairly convinced he plays away too – so you know, a little extra sympathy is sometimes needed.'

She pulls back, standing up straight with a perfect smile across her face, presumably oblivious to the fact her husband isn't so squeaky clean, particularly when it comes to birthday parties. 'You never can tell what's going on behind closed doors, eh?' Her teeth actually sparkle. How is that even possible? 'We could all be fighting a fight that none of us even know about, yes?'

'Yes.'

'Live, Laugh, Love. That's what I say. Ooh, there's the bell. I'll get the invite to you ASAP, okay, Liza?'

'Lisa!'

She waves over her shoulder at me, no doubt not remotely interested in how my name is pronounced. It's not like it's difficult.

*

'Hello, Oakwood Primary, how may I help you?'

'Lisa. It's me.'

'Holly?'

'Charlie's been up all night, I can't bring him in today.'

'Oh no, poor love. There's a bug doing the rounds.'

'They've only been back a few days, I'm raging.'

'I know.' I glance out of the window and catch sight of Lady Jenna of Vomit and scowl through the vertical blinds at her. 'When it starts though, it doesn't take long to get about. I hope he gets better soon!' I make a note so I can update the class register when it comes back.

'Me too. Pizza Delivery Dave was due to pop round today.'

'Meat Feast?'

'If I'd been lucky.'

'You're insatiable.'

'Yup. Typical, eh. Look, Charlie will be back in on Friday, fingers crossed.'

'Alright, love. Oh, and, thanks for the necklace.'

'Great, he dropped it off then?'

'Yes.'

'Did you ask him about the present?'

'No. He just posted it through the letter box.'

The headmistress comes into the office, waiting when she notices I'm on the phone and I immediately feel guilty that our conversation took a non-work direction. 'Thanks for letting me know about Charlie. I hope he gets better soon.'

Chapter Twelve

It's not been the obligatory two days since Charlie was last sick but apparently Holly couldn't have been more keen to get him back to school, not least for the chance to gossip. I point out that it's mums like her that stopped her Pizza Delivery Dave date, but she wafts the suggestion away. I'm judging her as I judged Jenna's mum.

'I can't believe you got invited to a Felicity Perfect party!' She pushes her arm through mine as we walk down the path.

'Well, *I* didn't get the invite, Poppy did. And Felicity's surname is not "Perfect", is it?'

'No. It's Smith. Which serves her right.'

'Holly!' She's mean about her, but I know why. And this invite will have touched a nerve.

'Whether *you* got the invite or Poppy is just semantics, either way you got invited to a Felicity Perfect party! You'd better be careful.'

'Of course I will.' I dig around in my bag for my phone to look at the list of jobs I need to do today. Fridays are my day off and after my first four, full days at work since before Poppy was born, there's a fair bit to catch up on, including taking Iris out to do her food shop. 'Do you know, all I want to do today is flake out in front of daytime telly.' I sigh.

'Don't change the subject.'

I roll my eyes at her. 'Look, Flick said she was inviting everyone from class, so Charlie will get an invite too, won't he?'

'I doubt it.' Holly offers me gum.

'Did she really never believe you?'

'Nope. As far as she was concerned, in fact, all of them, I got pissed on Prosecco and came on to her husband.'

'At a kids' party?' Flick and her gaggle of mums jog past us. Ordinarily I'd be admiring in a This Girl Can kind of way, but they're all so tight-arse spandexed, and I'm feeling particularly unfit at the moment, so I'm rather more irritated than inspired. 'Why would she think you'd do that? Did she not notice the special attention her husband gave you? I'd have bloody told her.'

'Oh, totally. Million per cent. Every time he topped me up, I saw her clock me and scowl. I gave up trying to reject it in the end, mainly because I was irritated by her assuming I'd be remotely interested, or a threat to her. I was gutted when you said Poppy was poorly, I had a bad feeling about going anyway. You know when you get that sixth sense that something's gonna happen? But I went anyway, so really, it's probably my fault.'

'It is not your fault. He made a pass at you.'

'Yeah, well. I probably didn't help things when I started dirty dancing by the breakfast bar. I knocked off the dairy-free cheese rolls in the process, and that, apparently, *is* a crime.'

'I remember you saying. Dairy-free cheese rolls, though? I don't even understand how that's a thing.'

'What can I say? She played Timberlake, I'm a glutton for Timberlake.'

I give her a look because I know she's trying to shake it off, but I also remember how she shook and cried that night she told me what had happened with Felicity's husband in their utility room loo. At least, what he wanted to happen until she managed to knee him in the nuts and make a run for it. No matter how many times I tried to get her to report him, she wouldn't. She never has.

'Anyway, dairy-free cheese really sticks to your teeth. I did them a favour,' she says, sadly. 'Just make sure you have Paul's number to get him to pick you up. God knows what I'd have done had I not been able to call him.'

'Did you ever tell him?'

'Course not. He'd have royally kicked off in a way I absolutely did not need. He just thinks I got hammered and embarrassed myself. Right.' She pulls out her house keys, shaking off the mood that threatens to dampen her fire. We rarely talk about that party. 'I've now got to Veet downstairs before Pizza Delivery Dave makes his reappointed swing by.'

'I think I wish you hadn't said that.'

'Why?'

'Well, now I know what you're going to be doing until school pick-up.'

'It's not that hairy!'

'I meant after he's arrived.'

'Yeah, fair enough. If I'm lucky… or should I say, if he's lucky, right?'

'You can gob off all you like, but I can see that look in your eye. You like him.'

'Hush now, let's not have anyone believe I have a heart!' She waves over her shoulder as she heads off inside her house.

I briefly envy her freedom to do with her body and life whatever she pleases. Even with someone attempting to assault her, she's never let it stop her living her life, seeing people if she wanted to. It's good, I think, that she refuses to let Felicity's husband take any more of her energy. I've never been that free, never had casual sex, and I definitely can't be arsed to Veet down there. Though, I'm not sure I'd bother even if sex was on the cards.

'Oh, hi, Paul!' I pull up short at the corner, just moments away from walking straight into him, colouring at the idea he might know what I was thinking about. I bend down to give Jeffrey the dog an ear scratch. 'Sorry, I was miles away.'

'Don't worry. You okay?'

'Yeah, fine, just wishing I was a bit more like your sister, that's all.'

'Oh God, no. The world can only handle one Holly March.' I grin, he's probably right. 'She okay?'

'Yeah, she—' I stop myself because I'm sure he doesn't need to hear about her sex-capades, though now I feel the need to follow up with something else. 'She was just laughing at my misfortune, Poppy's been invited to a school birthday party. Same mum whose house Holly was thrown out of at the kids' party last year.'

'Oh, the one when she got absolutely shit-faced? She was in a right tangle after that.'

'Yeah, that's the one… though I don't blame her getting pissed. Kids' parties and nursery school mums, I can't think of anything worse. I'm now wondering how to get out of it.'

'Ahhh, poor Poppy.'

I scratch at my arms, the idea of the party growing more and more uncomfortable in my chest. I've never been good in big groups. 'Kids have no idea what it's like, navigating other children's parents.'

'No, but they bloody love a party, don't they?'

'I guess so.'

'Write a list.'

'Pardon?'

'A list. Of all the reasons she would love it. Pros and cons. Then you'll read it, feel bad at even suggesting you didn't go, and it'll become all the more manageable.' I should just ask him. I should ask him now. 'Alright, if not more manageable, the guilt will consume you and you'll just get on with it anyway.' Jeffrey starts pulling at the lead. 'I'd better go, this one is desperate for a run and I've actually got a meeting about a job this lunchtime, so I need to prep.'

'Oh, that's good news. Fingers crossed for you.'

'Cheers, erm…' He pauses. I want to say something. Apparently neither of us can. 'See you later.'

I walk a few paces then turn around. 'Paul!' I shout, but he turns to me with phone to ear, apologetically signalling that he can't talk.

Chapter Thirteen

When I get home, I see the notebook on the side and think about Paul's suggestion to make a list of pros and cons about the children's party. Was that his way of subtly suggesting the notebook was from him? God, I should have just bloody well asked. We're as bad as each other, clearly. He's not said a word about declaring his feelings and I'm not asking about the notebook. Does that make us both as useless, or a match made in heaven?

I smile at the thought of him. Would it be weird? To date someone I've known for so long? Would Holly be okay with it? We've hung out together for years, I suppose most of it wouldn't really change. Except that I'd have someone who cared about me. Who thought about me and wanted what was best. Someone who made me laugh and was kind. Thoughtful. Someone I definitely fancy.

I open the notebook and find a blank page towards the back. I don't know why I'm so anxious about it really. I didn't do many parties as a kid. Dad kept us to ourselves, maybe because he found the idea of spending time with other mums – as it largely would have been back when I was a kid – too much. I can't say I don't get it. I hated feeling so removed from friends though. I remember all the things people went to that I missed out on. The parties, the gatherings. I went to some, but not nearly as many as my peers. I always felt so left out…

Party pros:
1. *It'll help Poppy make friends*
2. *It'll be good for her confidence*
3. *Kids love parties*
4. *Party rings!*

Party cons:
1. *Other mums*
2. *No Holly*
3. *…*

I snap the book shut, irritated that I've even thought of letting my own neurosis get in the way of Poppy's life. Paul's right. She'd love it. I can't do to her what Dad did to me, just because he didn't want to take me places. I remember Grandma tried to encourage him to take me to stuff, a few times. A kids' club that had been set up in the village hall. She walked round from hers to collect me and Dad, said she wanted to come too. But he'd organised something else to clash so that we couldn't go. I think maybe she tried a few times after that, I remember hushed conversations between them. I'd strain to listen but could never make out what they were actually saying. It makes me wonder what was going through his mind all the while; was it just discomfort at being the only Dad flying solo with his child? Embarrassed to be there with his mum instead of his wife? I suppose people ask questions and maybe that was too much for him to bear. It can't have been easy explaining that my mother was dead. And yet I relied on him to be the grown-up, to be strong for us both, to raise me the way Mum would no doubt have wanted. My world was so small growing up, and mine and Poppy's world is pretty small now, but I want different things for her childhood. I can't do to Poppy what Dad did to me.

I just need to overcome the crippling anxiety and get on with it. What would Grandma say?

'Well, I imagine your grandma would be supportive and gentle and try and encourage you to do what was right, knowing you'd come round eventually,' says Iris, rooting round in her bag for the key to her house, which is next door to mine. We've enjoyed fish and chips in the car, overlooking the park. We chatted about Grandma. Iris, I know, on this occasion, bit her tongue about Dad, frustrated with him about Grandma's funeral too. But biting her tongue isn't really on brand. 'I, on the other hand, would say: get your arse to the party and stop being so self-involved!' She looks up with a grin and I can't help but laugh because whilst Grandma was never one to force her views on anyone – perhaps a product of her time in which women weren't particularly forthright – Iris was clearly cut from a different cloth. A bright, vivacious, unapologetic Pucci cloth with chandelier earrings and lavender perfume. 'Now give us a hand with these bags, will you? I put me back out lifting some King Edwards yesterday.'

'Oh no! You should have called me, I'd have come round and sorted it for you.'

'If I can't try and shift a kilo of potatoes round me pantry, there's no hope for me. You're not next door to act as my housemaid. I'm supposed to be looking out for you!'

'Says who?'

'Never mind, look, that's what the Radox is for. A nice bath with Muscle Unwind and I'll be right as rain. Thanks for this, love, I really appreciate it.'

'No problem.'

I carry her bags in, popping them on the worktop in her kitchen. 'Oh, I keep meaning to ask—'

'Yes?' Iris starts steadily unpacking shopping, pottering between pantry and cupboards, flicking the kettle on as her hand passes the switch.

'Was the notebook from you?' I haven't really kept meaning to ask but as we went round the shops it occurred to me that I'd basically narrowed it down to two people and, realistically, it could be from anyone.

'The what?'

'The notebook. It was on my doorstep on Monday morning. A good luck in your new job present.'

'Oh, no... no, I don't know what you're talking about. A notebook, you say?'

'Yes.'

'Right. No.' She huffs a packet of rice onto the top shelf before turning to smile at me. 'How lovely.'

'It is, I just wish I knew who sent it. You didn't see anyone come by, either?'

'Me? No.' She says it as if she's never at the window, which makes me smile as she thinks for a moment. 'A secret admirer I shouldn't wonder. Very romantic. And couldn't we all do with a bit more romance in our lives? Ever since my Bernie died, it's been a bit lacking on the romance front round here. There was the nice chap I met down the butchers who sent me a pound of pork mince...'

'Pork mince!'

'I know. I don't really like pork and a pound of mince could never replace a nice bunch of daffs.'

'No.'

'Right you are, thank you, love. I'll let you get off.' She ushers me out of the door. 'Erm… do let me know if you find out who it's from.'

Chapter Fourteen

The front door grazes over the post as I push it open, my own shopping bags scuffing against the wall. Frank totters through to me, no doubt desperate for a wee because I was definitely out longer than I expected, but it was nice for me and Iris to remember Grandma as she'd have wanted, albeit in my car with my phone streaming Elvis.

Frank's scraggy tail wags as he briefly fusses me then trots out to cock his leg against the climbing rose. 'Go on! Do it in the garden, you mucky bugger!' I shoo him away, round the back of the house.

Absentmindedly picking through the post, I wander down to the kitchen. I file the bills – bills I'm determined to cover on my own from now on. There's a card from the daughter of an old friend of Grandma's. She apparently heard about Grandma and wanted me to know she was thinking of me. I remember the bits that need to go in the freezer and quickly sort those before I forget again and defrost the Nobbly Bobbly ice cream that Poppy asked me to buy. Getting a glass of water, letting it run a second to cool before sloshing it into a pint glass, I watch Frank sniff his way around the garden before pausing in a shaft of sunlight, sniffing up at the shrubbery. I need to cut the grass.

Frank's claws on the parquet let me know he's back in, so I go to shut the front door before coming back to open the last of the mail, pausing on a menu for the new Indian that's opened because wouldn't a korma be good for tea?

And that's when I open an envelope that contains nothing but a photo. Of me. As a kid.

I drop it on the kitchen side, then peer to make sure it's definitely me. Weirdly, the hairs on the back of my neck stick up and I look over my shoulder and out into the garden as if someone might be watching me.

I reach for the photo again, taking a closer look. What I think might be five-year-old me stares back: eyes and grin wide, a carrier bag in my hands with, I remember, swimming costume and towel contained. It's a photo I've not seen for years. Lost in the annals of time. I'm sat on a wall beside four other girls. Michelle, her knees red raw and bruised, as they always were. Elaine, her head protected from the sunlight in a flowery bonnet that ties beneath her chin. Rachel, her giant NHS glasses dominating her face, and Holly, whose birthday party it was. It must have been a Saturday afternoon. Sometime in June. Late 1980s. We tiptoed through the manky bit of water that was between the changing rooms and pool, the one that always had plasters floating around in it. We screamed and laughed amongst the inflatables. Afterwards, we sat in wet pants eating chips soaked in vinegar because none of us could dry ourselves properly and we were too hungry to care. Holly's Mum and Dad had a Polaroid camera and we'd take photos of each other, then marvel at the magic of them appearing before our eyes. I loved Holly's birthday parties, they were always such fun, so vibrant somehow. Swimming one year, Skegness another, film nights in their separate kids' lounge – well, converted garage – when we got older, sleepovers. Hers was the only place Dad freely let me go to as a kid, her dad and mine good mates since school themselves.

I turn the photo over, my hands shaking as I search for the scribble of our names that I wrote when organising photos years later. And there it is, crude letters written in Bic biro. Now a faded sort of brown colour rather than the black it would have been originally. When did I lose this? I've not seen it in years. It had been in my room, Blu-Tacked to a mirror. I suspect I lost it years before I noticed it had gone. I suppose I didn't have many people round, but I do remember Holly went through a bit of a light-fingered stage. She swore down for years she hadn't nicked Crystal Barbie's wrap, but she definitely did. I get it, her Barbies were all knock-offs from the market, and it *was* a pretty covetable kind of fabric.

Then I think logically. I was talking to Paul about the party this morning. He knows I was stressing about it. He's got most of their parents' stuff, he's probably dug it out and sent it as a reminder of something I'd love Poppy to experience. I bet you Holly did lift it. It ended up in their house and, when he inherited all the photo albums, he'd got hold of it. I suppose it's sweet really. A subtle nudge rather than barging in and telling me I should let Poppy go to her friend's party. I put the photo in the back of the notebook, sticking it down with tape before studying it whilst drinking a mug of tea. Memories like this are so precious, and so few for me. Too few. I want more for Poppy. Not more stuff, but more life, more experience. I want to build memories and teach her joy. She's growing up in a world so wrapped up in stuff, in things, in material wealth, but she needs to learn richness from moments of happiness that come from having good people in your life.

With Paul and Holly, I have good people in my life. And who knows if Ludovic Perfect will turn out to be one of the good ones? But it's not for me to choose, is it? Dad chose for me, for so long.

Then I remember.

That party was the first time Billy and I met each other.

He was at Holly's house afterwards with Paul. I remember him playing on Paul's computer, barely saying anything to me. Neither of them did, me and Holly weren't cool. What would he have been, seven? Maybe eight? Dad was late picking me up, work I think, and so I sat with Holly, Paul and Billy in Paul's room, just watching them play computer games, even though we weren't really invited. Weird green people lurched awkwardly on a black screen, games like Sonic and Mario Kart a mere glimmer into the future.

Is it Billy thinking back to those first moments? Did I still have it when we moved up to Edinburgh? I did have photos, from all through the years. Did he take it as a reminder for some reason? What might come next, if so? The photo he always said he loved best of us? The one we took in a passport booth, the two of us looking direct to camera, him with his arm awkwardly around my shoulder, me with a silly grin? I've not seen that one for years either. Did he lift them both when he left, in a moment of uncharacteristic sentimentality?

Chapter Fifteen

'I swear to God, it's been years since I've had an orgasm like that,' says Holly, dreamily, as we wander from our cars to the park, the kids already enjoying the see-saw after badgering us into taking them straight from school.

'Mmhmm.' I don't really want her to expand because I can't actually remember the last time I had one and I want to ask her about the photo.

'Also, I know I started out thinking it was a bit of fun, but you're right, I think I do like him. We laugh, like I've never laughed before. Proper belly laughs and silliness, he makes me feel young again.' I give her a look because it's unusual to hear her talk from the heart. 'What? There's also the fact that I get discounted pizza, though I'd pay full price if he's going to do that to me.'

'Does that make him sound a little bit like a male sex worker?'

'He'd make a fucking fortune! More than delivery driving, I can tell you.'

'You're hiding your real feelings with jokes. Lovely.'

'*Lovely?*' Holly leans up against the park railings as the kids chase each other round, whooping with delight. 'What's up with you? Oh wait, has Billy been in touch?'

'Nope. Not heard a peep. Keep wondering if I should reach out to him, actually.' I drop rubbish in the bin, checking where Frank is.

'You will not!'

'We should talk about Poppy!'

'Yes. But knowing him, he'll see it as you making a move and he'd bloody love it if you did.'

'What if he's already made it?'

'The notebook?'

'Yes. And today, a photo.'

'What?'

'A photo. Through my letterbox.'

'A photo of what?'

'Us at your birthday party, your fifth, I think, maybe even sixth, I can't remember. We were all—'

'Sat on that wall! Yes! Elaine had that sun hat on that she hated but her mum made her wear. You were in an electric pink towelling jumpsuit!'

'Yes!'

'God, I wanted that jumpsuit so badly.' She chews on the inside of her mouth before pouting, then saying, 'If this is all from Billy, he's playing a weird game and I do not remember him being a particularly patient, long-game playing kind of guy. And like you say, actually, you just need to talk about Poppy.' I shrug, maybe she's right. 'Paul, on the other hand...'

'Holly!' I walk on.

'What? I'm just saying...'

'Alright, if he did send it, then that means you had to have nicked it.' She catches me up. 'Hang on! Why would I have stolen the photo?'

'You stole Crystal Barbie's wrap.'

'I did. It was incredible.' I pull up because that's the first time she's ever 'fessed up. 'I also took that strawberry rubber you wouldn't stop sniffing!'

'I knew that was you! I never did find one that smelled as good as the original.'

'But I swear down, I didn't steal the photo. I don't know how our Paul would have got it, but it wasn't from me. Can you get copies of Polaroids?'

'No idea. But it had my writing on the back, so it was definitely the original. He got all your mum and dad's photos, right?'

Two paws land on my waist and I look down to see Jeffrey, Paul's mate's dog, wagging his tail enthusiastically, a ball grasped between his teeth.

'Get down!' Paul appears, a little out of breath after chasing the dog. He pushes him off me. 'Sorry, he's bloody filthy!' He tries to wipe at my coat to get rid of the mud prints left behind, before realising he's brushing quite high up my thigh. 'Oh God, sorry. He's an absolute fool, that dog!'

My cheeks prickle.

Holly rolls her eyes. 'Fancy seeing you here, at school chucking-out time, when we might be coming for a walk in the park too.'

Paul shifts from one foot to the other and I avoid his eyes.

'Come on then, when does the dog go back home?' she asks with a sigh that suggests she's not going to be the one to call us out yet, but her patience is wearing thin.

'A week on Tuesday.' He watches, dismayed, as Jeffrey runs over to Frank, trying once again to get him to play. 'And not a day too soon, he's so far eaten my vintage Golas, and a steak I was going to cook but got distracted from with a text message. Plus, he seems to have taken a shine to one of the pillows and won't stop humping it. I'll be burning that when he's gone. You two alright?'

'Yeah, good thanks, you?' Holly gives her brother a hug.

'Very good actually, thanks. Despite canine distractions I've managed to land myself an eco-home build on the edge of Cranwell Village. RAF Officer who's retiring next year wants a new home to lord it up in after he gives his digs back.'

'That's amazing! Well done!' I say and he beams at me. 'I'm so chuffed, you're making it happen. I knew you could.'

'I hoped. In fact, I've been doing a lot of crossing my fingers and praying.'

'Which god?' asks Holly.

'All of them.' Paul grins. 'Just to be on the safe side. What you been up to?'

'Well! I've had quite the day,' says Holly.

'By the look on your face, I'd say I don't want to know?'

'Probably not.' She leans nonchalantly against the railings watching the kids chase each other into a slide tunnel. 'Paul,' she drawls, and I panic. She may have changed conversational tone but she's still capable of going rogue. 'Guess what Lisa got in the post today?'

Oh God.

'What?'

'A photo from when we were kids, sat on a wall outside the swimming baths for my party.'

Part of me wants to die and part of me wants to watch his every move and see if he gives himself away.

'Oh man, I so wanted to go to that party and Mum wouldn't let me. Told me I had to stay at home with Dad and Billy, who took over my computer and, until you two got back, he wouldn't let me have a go. I hated him that day.'

'Anyway, she has no idea who sent it.'

'What?'

'The photo. Or this lovely little book with all these life exploring questions in. All nicely handwritten.'

'Oh, right?' He reaches down to fuss at Frank who's seeking solace from Jeffrey at our feet. I can't see his face. 'Nice.'

I twist my fingers into the lining of my coat pocket. 'Yes… they are. Really lovely.'

'Actually, she'd really like to know who they're from though.' Sometimes I hate her. 'In fact, so would I!'

She peers at Paul for just a little too long, he bends down to fuss Frank fully, scratching at his belly until his leg does a little repetitive motorbike kick.

'Right! Come on, Charlie, let's get back.' She claps her hands as if that's the end of that. He had his moment to confess and didn't. 'Your dad's picking you up in time for tea.' She turns back to me and Paul. 'I've got a kid-free weekend. You wanna go to the pub tonight and celebrate this job then, Paul?'

'Can do, I've nothing else on.'

'You coming, Lis?'

'I can't, can I? Poppy's only ever had Grandma looking after her if I've gone out. I don't really want to ask Dad, and I've no idea who else to ask. You could always come back round to mine,' I say, avoiding Paul's eye.

'I bet if you asked Iris she'd pop round for an hour or so. Go on, come for one. I love being at yours but… you know, the pub's nice too.'

'Oh… I don't know.'

She grabs hold of my arms, eyeballing me in a way that says, *Do as you're told, or I'll make this moment even more painful for you.* 'Live a little. That's what that book has been encouraging you to do, hasn't it?' She's grinning at me, eyes devilish.

'It *has* been ages,' says Paul. But we look at each other because *ages* is really only a few weeks, and the last time was when he told me he liked me.

Holly drops my arms. 'We'll see you around eight, okay?' She jogs over to fetch Charlie, Paul rolls his eyes at her then wanders off after Jeffrey, and I stand in the park, my heart racing.

Chapter Sixteen

'Pint?' asks Paul as I get to the bar.

'Go on then.' My hands are stuffed into my pocket because the closer I've got to the pub, the more nervous I am. And I wonder if he can tell that I had put bright pink lipstick on before realising I've never worn bright pink lipstick to go to the pub with Paul and Holly and why would I suddenly start doing that now. I wiped it off but there's still a stain. 'Guinness, please.'

'Two pints of Guinness, mate, and are you still serving food?'

'Yes, 'til eight, mate,' says Jed, the pub landlord. He hands Paul a menu whilst pouring the drinks.

'You eaten?'

'Yup. And I can't stop too long anyway, Iris is with Poppy, but she looks tired and I don't like to take advantage.'

'Fair enough. Can I have the curry please, Jed?'

'Sure thing.'

We make our way over to the seat in the corner by the window where we've pretty much always sat. Birthdays, a few Christmas Eves, my eighteenth, Paul's twenty-first a few weeks after. In fact, we came here for farewell drinks before heading up to Scotland. I remember Billy slagging everyone off by the end of it. He was hammered and kept telling people, Paul included, that they had no ambition. Being stone cold sober and six months pregnant, I was mortified.

Paul takes out his phone, reading it. 'Typical!'

'What?'

'Holly's bailed. Apparently, she's got pizza and nachos coming and she can't leave the house.'

I wonder how much time I'd get for murder? And how I didn't see her bailing out coming. I should totally have seen it coming.

'Never mind, eh? So, you're deffo letting Poppy go to the party then?'

'I think I probably always was,' I say, studying him.

'You just seemed a bit resistant to the idea.'

'Yeah, I think I was mostly resistant to an afternoon with a load of mums I don't really know.'

'Oh! It's the mums not the kids you live in fear of. Yeah, from what little I've seen, I get that. They seem kind of—'

'High maintenance? Judgmental? Perfect and polished? I think they're practically all vegan and regular Pilates goers.'

'I didn't realise either of those things were bad? I mean, they say veganism is better for the environment—'

'Chicken curry?' says Danny, steaming plate in hand.

'Oh. Erm. Yeah.' Paul looks sheepishly at his food. 'Chicken's not that bad, is it?' He prods at his dinner as if suddenly a bit guilty before seemingly deciding that his environmental concern is not something that's going to stand in the way of his dinner. 'And isn't Pilates supposed to be good for your mental health? Centring, breathing, using your body.'

'I don't know. Probably. They're not that bad really, I'm sure some of them are perfectly lovely. We're probably all stood in the playground feeling awkward. I just feel guilty that I don't move, or eat healthily, or have a body like theirs.'

'You have a lovely body.' I look up sharply as he scoops curry with a poppadom. 'Oh, shit, sorry, I didn't mean… I was just trying to…'

'Don't worry. And thanks, I guess?'

I sip at my Guinness feeling my cheeks flush. Paul concentrates on a particularly interesting piece of chicken for a second. 'Oh God, Lisa, I'm sorry. I'm so rubbish at this… I should probably apologise.'

'What for?'

'Before I went away. Saying what I said. I mean, not because I don't mean it, I do. I really like you, I just didn't want to put you in an awkward position and maybe I shouldn't have said anything.'

'Paul, I think I'm—'

'I know you probably don't feel the same way, I mean, who really fancies their mate's older brother, but—'

'Paul, I've been thinking too, and—'

'Oh God!'

'What?' I follow Paul's gaze. 'Jesus… Billy?'

Billy has his back to us, he's enthusiastically hugging a bloke he's just bumped into, chatting to a group of people that I recognise from around and about. He's casual, relaxed, seemingly happy to see everyone. The ex-boyfriend I haven't seen in five years has literally just rocked up into our tiny world as if he never left. Just as Paul and I were about to talk.

I shuffle my chair wondering if I can hide behind Paul a bit. 'Shit.'

'You okay?' He checks over his shoulder at Billy before turning back to me. 'Do you want to leave?'

'No. Yes. I don't know.'

'We can, if you prefer.'

'But why should I?' I grab hold of my pint as if it can help, heart racing at the sight of Billy, and awkward at the start of a conversation with Paul that needs to happen but probably can't right now. Billy is at the bar, ordering a drink, still with his back to us, still talking to the group that greeted him so fondly. Of all the times he could pitch up. I sip at my drink and Paul goes to take another bite of his dinner before pushing his half-eaten plate away from him.

I fake okay, shaking off my mood, though opt for a change of subject. 'So?' I chirrup. 'What else have you been up to today?' The beer mat I'm picking at is starting to disintegrate. It'll make a mess on the table, Jed hates beer mat mess.

'Oh, well…' Paul looks confused by my tone shift but goes with it. 'After I saw you, I went back home and did some work. Prepped some drawings for that job I landed. I erm…' He sips at his drink as if buying time. 'I went for a walk at lunchtime.'

'Mmhmm.'

'Had the meeting for that job, walked Jeff again, that's when I bumped into you two, then back home and worked a bit more until we came out. Boring day really.'

He keeps trying to return my gaze but breaks off every now and then. I notice him shift his chair so that he can see in the mirror behind me, occasionally watching Billy through the reflection. I'm still fairly well hidden, I think.

'Must be nice to get lost in your work?' I've drained my glass.

'Do you want another?'

Technically it's my round but I can't go to the bar yet and if he goes, I can't hide behind him. I check my watch, we've only been here twenty minutes, leaving seems defeatist. And besides, if it is Billy sending the stuff, maybe he'll see me and say something. Paul would surely have 'fessed up by now if it was him? Or was that what he was about to do? And Billy *is* Poppy's father, I can't just run away. 'Maybe in a minute.'

'Right.'

'You always did like drawing and art and stuff.'

'Pardon.'

'Your job. I remember you were always drawing when we were kids. It must be nice to do it as a job now.'

I can see he's weirded out by the direction of my conversation. We've sat at this table and discussed life and the universe before now, we've made each other laugh reciting funny film lines, we've played cards and joined forces when Holly was cheating. It's always been so straightforward, so easy, and yet here I am now, small-talking about his job and his day like we barely know one another.

'It's a bit more than colouring in these days. A seven-year degree and I'm pretty adept at actually designing buildings now.' He smiles. 'Yeah, I love it.'

He's talking and I've drifted off, watching Billy's every move. He's as confident as always, holding court for the group he's now sitting with, to listen and laugh. I don't think any of them have noticed I'm here. That pretty much sums things up with him though, I was always invisible around him; people are drawn to him, he has them eating out of the palm of his hand within seconds, even the most cynical of people can be turned around by Billy. Well, everyone except Dad.

'You okay?' asks Paul, who appears to have realised that I've not actually been listening.

'Sorry. Yes. I'm okay. It's just…'

'A shock. I understand. You've not seen him in years. It must be strange.'

'I'd send photos of Poppy to begin with. I stopped when he didn't respond. It hurt too much, you know?'

'I remember.'

'Rejecting me was one thing, but Poppy too? His mum and dad didn't seem to want to know either. When they moved away, they just never bothered keeping in touch, no matter how much I tried.'

'I never understood that. How could they not want something to do with Poppy? If that was my mum or dad, or Holly for that matter, they'd have hunted me down. After buying her all of the stuff and doting on her.'

And that's when Billy turns around and sees me staring.

Chapter Seventeen

Our eyes meet. Anger burns in my belly, but my heart flips too. He's not changed a bit, well, maybe he has a little bit. He's more tanned now, his hair is a little longer, wilder. His eyes crease and his smile widens. He stands, shaking his head, his arms open wide as he strides across the pub. Paul watches me out of the corner of his eye. I'm standing, Billy's arms are around me. He smells the same, he feels the same, same wooden beads around his neck, same collection of leather and festival pass wristbands. He holds me tight for just a touch too long, taking in a deep breath as if smelling my hair and I feel weak and weird and frustrated that he thinks this is okay and annoyed at myself that I'm letting him. I pull back, but he's still got hold of me. He's got new tattoos on his forearms. 'Fuck, Lisa. I knew I'd see you but...' Hands on my shoulders, he holds me out, looking me up and down. I grit my teeth and stand back, out of his grip. 'Wow. You look amazing!'

There is a moment's pause where I don't say anything because I'm stunned and don't know where to begin, and unusually, he doesn't seem to know what to say next either. Paul breaks it eventually. 'Billy.' His voice is flat, not terribly warm or friendly.

'Paul! Oh my God! Hi, mate! I didn't realise that was you.' He opens his arms to hug Paul who doesn't stand. Billy doesn't flinch at the rejection, holding his hand out to shake it instead. Paul does at least do that.

Apparently failing to sense he's not welcome, Billy pulls up a stool in between us. 'Not interrupting, I hope?'

'No, course not.' I know I say it a little too quickly. Paul has gone back to watching me. I've come over quite hot. 'I heard you were back.'

'Yeah. I meant to message you, then time ran away with me. You've not changed a bit! I was looking through old photos earlier today. God, some of them date right back…' He pauses, head to one side, eyes soft and surprisingly sincere. 'How are you?'

'Erm… well…'

'How long has it been?'

He's bright and open, seemingly oblivious to the fact that I can tell him exactly how long it is based on how old our daughter is. This fact instantly brings me back into the room. 'Well, Poppy started school this week, so… yeah, I guess about five years.'

His smile falters a little and it's nice to see the mask slip. The one on the back foot is now him. 'Ah. Yes. I wanted to talk about that, obviously.'

'That?' Paul nearly chokes on his drink, then shakes his head, looking out of the window for a second before focusing back on Billy, jaw tight.

'Well, Poppy. I meant I wanted to talk about Poppy.' Billy adjusts the stool slightly, not so cool and confident now. 'Maybe I could come round and meet her?'

His disregard for the weight of responsibility parenthood brings picks at me, nagging at the bit of my heart that flipped at the sight of him, pinching the bigger bit of my heart that is wholly and solely reserved for Poppy. 'Yeah, I mean, it's probably not that straightforward,' I say.

'What? Meeting her?'

'Yeah. I mean, we don't often talk about you.'

'Right. But… I'm her father?'

Paul lets out a cough that suggests he's holding in things he wants to say. I'm glad that, despite my initial distraction, he recognises I've got this.

'A father doesn't walk out on their child. A father doesn't ignore letters and photos. A father doesn't rock up, five years later, assuming that he can just wander back into his child's life without so much as a conversation first.' My voice falters with nerves but there are some things I'm just not moveable on. Basically, anything relating to Poppy. I fiddle with my fingers, reminding myself that he can't just assume all is okay, I'm right to not just let him walk back into our lives… even if it is Billy. The man I thought was the love of my life. Poppy's dad.

'Paul…' I check the time. 'I think I'll head off in a minute. Are you—'

He jumps up. 'Yep. Sure. I'll walk you home.' I look at him, wondering if he'll sense that I could do with a second on my own with Billy, which apparently he does. 'You okay if I just nip… to the loo?' I nod as he jogs off.

'You two aren't…?' Billy points to me and where Paul had been sat.

'We were just having a drink.' Not that it's any of Billy's business.

'Right. He seems a bit… pissed off?'

'Billy.' I cock my head to one side, fully back in control. 'Why are you here?'

He looks down at his fingers, then fiddles with a couple of bead bracelets he's wearing. 'I ran away. From lots of things before. I've been travelling around, living, experiencing what the world has to offer, settling in a new city, working, but… I guess I've felt as if there's unfinished business.'

'Unfinished business?'

'Well, you know what I mean.'

I grab my coat, my resolve wavering. 'No. I don't know.'

'Please, Lisa. I know you're probably angry with me. And you've every right to be.'

'You think?'

He reaches for my hand, I let him take my fingers, interlinking them with his own. 'I want to reconnect. I want to see if there's any way to fix things.'

'Things?'

He stares at me. His eyes bearing into mine. 'Lisa, you're the only woman I've ever—' I put my hand up and he stops. 'Look, here's my number. I want to see you. I want to meet Poppy. Maybe she doesn't have to know I'm her dad.' Paul now stands by the pub door, arms tightly folded. 'Not yet anyway, if you're worried about that. I mean, I guess I understand, but I have a right to—'

'You gave up your rights when you walked out on us.'

'I know. And I want to make it up to you.' He lets my fingers go. 'Will you call me? Please?'

I look around, the pub is full of familiar faces, some giving us a side eye, perhaps aware of our past. Others apparently not paying any attention, but bets on it'll be all over the village by tomorrow. There are a few parents from school, an infant school dinner lady and her husband, the old couple whose house Billy and I used to walk past when we first got together and went down to catch the bus into Lincoln. Jed, the landlord, who's run this pub for as long as I can remember, his eyes darting over in our direction occasionally. He's the biggest gossip of them all.

'Are they from you?' I ask, piercing his eyes with mine.

'What?'

'The notebook and photo. Did you send them?'

'Erm, well...' He frowns then throws a smile at someone over my shoulder, cocky and self-assured returns to his face as he leans in. 'I mean, if you liked them...'

I study him for a second, take his number, stuffing it in the back pocket of my jeans. Paul pushes open the pub door as I get to him, and I'm relieved for a blast of fresh air as I dip out beneath his arm. Through the window, I see Billy adopt his winning smile as he swaggers back over to the group he'd been chatting to. The gifts were far too thoughtful to have been from him, surely?

Chapter Eighteen

I do that fast walk, jog thing, trying to keep up with Paul. 'Thanks, it was nice to get out for an hour or so.'

'Mhmm.'

'Shame Holly couldn't make it.'

'I guess.'

'Still, I'm sure she'll come out next time, ooh, ouch.' Paul spins round as I nurse my ankle where I've just lost my footing.

'You okay?'

'Yeah, sorry, I just twisted it a bit.' I put some weight on my ankle and it stings a little.

'What did you do?' He looks around at the ground in search of something to blame my trip up on.

'I was... trying to keep up with you.'

'Oh, right. Sorry.'

'Are you okay?' I lean against a garden wall for a second, rubbing my ankle.

'Me? I'm fine! Are *you* okay?'

I try putting weight on it again, the sting subsides. 'I think so, it'll probably walk off.'

'No, I mean with Billy. Just then.'

'Oh, right. Yeah... well, no... I don't know.'

'No. Me neither, to be honest. Can you walk?' He offers me an arm and I take it, his warmth reassuring. It's the closest we've been in weeks. It feels nice. 'It's none of my business, but... God, I dislike him.'

'You were best mates, once upon a time.'

'That was before he became a total dick. I could put up with it when it was an occasional thing.'

'Yeah, me too. I mean, I always knew he had the capacity to behave badly, but I suppose I just accepted it as part of who he was. I'm not perfect.'

'None of us are perfect. But he's used that as an excuse for years, like owning that fact means he doesn't have to think about the consequences of his behaviour. How he left you, after Poppy. I just... I wanted to...' He side eyes me. 'Sorry. Not my fight.'

'How do you mean?'

'Stuff with you and Billy, it's between you two. Nothing to do with me. Sorry. I've no right to be angry.'

We walk on in silence, me still hanging on to his arm. He is tense, I can feel it in his arm.

'How do you feel about him?' Paul asks after a few minutes.

'Oh God, Paul. I don't know. Seeing him just now, it was a shock. I mean, maybe it shouldn't have been because I knew he was in town and it's too small a place to keep missing each other but... I don't know.' We turn the corner into my road. 'I guess he's in the past,' I say, which is the most I can manage after what just happened.

'He's the father of your child, though, Lisa. You loved him.'

'I did. And I so wanted to have him in Poppy's life. For the first few years of her life, I was desperate for him to call or turn up. I'd have flung open that door and just let him waltz in because two parents are better than one, aren't they?'

'I don't know about that.'

We stop outside my house. 'I do. Or at least, I wish I'd had two.'

Paul looks up at my house, then around everywhere but at me. 'You said the notebook had questions for you to complete? Things to fill out?'

'Yeah.'

'Maybe the person sending it thinks it might help. I have a notebook. I use it all the time: make notes, doodles about ideas I've had, things to do, plans.'

'Yeah?'

He nods, tension shifting. 'And this is between me and you, right? I mean, I'd never tell Holly because she'd absolutely rip it out of me, but I also write a list of things I want to achieve each year in mine.'

'Yeah?'

'Yeah. It's the whole law of attraction thing. Asking the universe.'

'Wasn't that Noel Edmonds's bag?'

'I think so. But don't let that put you off. Honestly, even if it doesn't come true, it focuses your mind, helps you work out what you want.'

'Wow. Right.' I let go of his arm, reaching into my pocket for the house key. 'I didn't know you were that deep a thinker.'

'Yeah, well, there's a lot about me that you don't know.' Paul kicks a bit of stone. 'I know that now probably isn't the time… for us, but…' We stand far enough apart not to be touching but close enough that I can feel the shift in energy. 'Maybe we could spend more time together. I mean just as friends. But, together, just you and me. No Holly… no Billy!'

We lock eyes, his are dark, familiar yet unfamiliar in equal measure. For the first time tonight, and maybe for a long time, he's not afraid to look at me. 'It was from you, wasn't it?'

'What?'

'The notebook. The photo too…'

Just as he's about to answer, the front door opens on the chain, Iris peers out between the gap. 'I heard voices and I thought it couldn't possibly be you back already and then I wondered who it'd be. You're home early.'

Chapter Nineteen

I hold out her coat for her as she feeds thin arms into it. 'Thanks so much, Iris, I really appreciate it.'

She buttons up, smiling. 'Oh, it's my absolute pleasure. Important you get time to be a human being as well as a mum. Thanks, Paul.' She adjusts her scarf, so it sticks out of her coat, always so immaculately presented, then weaves her arm through his. 'You could have stayed longer, though?'

I glance at Paul. 'I'm tired, to be honest.'

'Well, I imagine with the funeral last week, the new job this week… not to mention them mystery gift whatnots…' She rummages for a tissue, stuffing it up her sleeve as I flick my eyes anywhere but in Paul's direction. 'It's been a big week, or two, eh, love?'

'I guess so.'

She lets Paul guide her out of the door and down the path to the little gate at the front of our house. It squeaks as he opens it. 'You know I'm happy to do it anytime, especially when I've a suitor as gallant as this to see me home. I know it's only a few paces, but you never know what can happen between here and there.'

'I'll bear it in mind.' I grin at her flirting with Paul and him not really being sure quite what to do about it.

'Thanks for the drink, Paul.'

'No worries.' He pulls the gate to. It squeaks again. 'Hey, I was wondering… well, I'm taking Charlie to ARK next weekend, you know the zoo sanctuary place that Ludo kid's having his party at. What with Charlie not getting an invite, I thought I'd just take him. Turns out he's been pretty down about it. Maybe you and Poppy would like to come, too?'

'Oh! Well, erm… I'm not sure.' I want to say yes. Now that he's said it, moments after whatever we were about to share by my front door, I really want to say yes. But with Billy's arrival tonight, Poppy has to be my priority. I'd love for her to have two parents in her life, and it's not that I want to get back with Billy so much, but I need to sort things out. I don't need the distraction of whatever this might be with Paul and me? We've known each other years, a few more weeks, even months, can't cause any harm, can it? 'I'll see. I don't know what's happening yet.'

Paul's shoulders sag. The first time he's come out and asked me to go somewhere with him and I don't commit. 'Right. Okay. Well, no worries either way, it was just a thought.'

'Thanks. I mean, maybe another time?' I say, feebly trying to rescue the moment. 'I'm a bit strapped, that's all. I don't get my first pay cheque 'til the end of the month…'

'I was going to pay.'

Iris raises her eyebrows at me.

'Oh, no, no, I couldn't ask you to do that. Thanks, I mean it's kind, but… I don't know. I'll see. Okay, lovely to see you, thanks so much, Iris. Thank you. Bye then, bye.'

I shut the door on them both, leaning against it, my heart racing. The door into the lounge is open and Frank is watching me from his spot on the sofa. 'You're not supposed to be up there.' I sit down beside him, cuddling him into me. Grandma always let him on the sofa, I've not had the heart to tell him he can't do it here. There's a definite Frank shape developing in the corner that's positioned by the bookshelf. I reach for the notebook and pen, pausing briefly at the photo.

Billy always did like me to think about stuff. He always wanted me to think differently, or bigger. He wanted me to explore beyond the boundaries I set myself. But he'd never have done it so generously as this, so encouraging of my own free thought. He'd have done stuff that made it clear what he thought I should think or do. He'd have made the lists for me. He'd have seen it his business to lift me out of the hole he thought I was hiding in, regardless of how I felt. Billy said the gifts were from him if I liked them. I know him well enough to know that means it wasn't him. Paul, on the other hand. All that chat about lists and notebooks. They have to be from him. But if Billy wants to connect with Poppy, managing that has to be my priority. Growing up as a single-parent family, there was always a gap. A hole where Mum should have been, and as Poppy gets older, she's going to feel that gap, too.

I take out my phone and bring up a message to Paul. *Thanks for seeing Iris home. And bear with me… I like you, I really do. I just can't rush things, especially not now that Billy is back. x*

I understand. x

Thank you. I pause, then add, *and thanks for the presents. Xxx*

It's fifteen minutes later when I get a message back saying, *They're not from me. X*

Chapter Twenty

Monday morning has come back around all too quickly. I hand Poppy her school bag as the bell goes. 'Make sure you give Ludo that RSVP, won't you!'

She flings her arms around me, squeezing about as tight as a five-year-old possibly can. 'Yes, Mummy. Will do.'

I watch as she runs off to class. It's only their second week yet she seems somehow to have grown. We spent the weekend watching films and baking, a bit of gardening to get fresh air, but basically just hunkering down together because that's all I wanted to do, and she always seems so chilled when it's just us. I thought about talking to her about her dad. But he rarely comes up and when he does, it's usually her asking basic questions. I've always said that he had to go away, that he loved her but sometimes mummies and daddies need to be apart. Somehow, she's never questioned that further, which meant that this weekend at least I could put Billy's number in the notebook and shove it in the drawer. I'm okay with giving myself permission to have space to think. Not about *if* he should meet Poppy, but when, how. What are my terms, for her best interests?

I've also spent a lot of time wondering: if Billy didn't send the presents, and it wasn't Paul either, then who did?

'Nice weekend?' Holly appears beside me as Charlie runs past and up the steps to class.

'Lovely thanks, you?'

'Great!' She beams.

'I missed you on Friday, thought you were coming out too. Can't believe you sacked me off for Pizza Delivery Dave.'

'I think we should probably just call him Dave, you know.'

I grab hold of her elbow as she begins walking. 'Have you amended his name in your phone?'

'Might have.'

'Christ, it's only been a week. This is huge!'

'So's his—'

'Liza,' a voice drawls, interrupting us. Holly looks at me confused. 'Liza, have you got a second?' Felicity adjusts the beret she's wearing at a jaunty angle. Her blonde soft curls cascade from beneath it over her shoulders. Parisian chic.

'Liza?' Holly mutters under her breath.

'Ssshhh! Yes, hi, Felicity.'

'Please. Call me Flick,' she drawls.

'Yeah, Liza! Call her Flick,' says Holly, with a grin.

Flick narrows her eyes in Holly's direction, who smiles sweetly in return. 'I just wanted to check that Poppy can make it to the party? I know I said I'd wait on the RSVPs but seeing as I've seen you.'

It seems like something of a waste with regards to what must have been extortionate handmade, personalised invites, to then just ask in the playground as opposed to waiting for the return of the little self-addressed envelope that came with the invite. 'Yes. She's got her RSVP in her bag.'

'Oh, lovely. I'm so pleased she can make it.' She looks at Holly as if suddenly realising that she has no justification for not inviting Charlie, other than not believing that her husband was a sleaze and Holly is not a bad person, however acerbic she can be. 'That's lovely, great… erm… I'm so sorry about Charlie. We just didn't have the room for everyone. We had to go with the register. Top twenty-five children, you know? Right, anyway, bye then, thanks.' She jogs off all light and bouncy.

Holly scowls the kind of scowl when she's feeling rejected but doesn't want anyone to know she cares. 'She does know that C for Charlie comes before P for Poppy in the register, doesn't she?'

'Isn't it done on surnames?' I give her a hip bump, just a little bit of contact so she knows I've seen her hurt.

'Alright.' She smiles, sadly. 'Charlie Betts probably still comes before Poppy Gill, though, eh.'

'Erm. Yeah, I guess so… maybe she thought Charlie had your surname?'

'*March*… I mean, I don't care. It's not about me. I just feel bad for Charlie. That's why Paul's taking him to ARK next weekend. Charlie can get into school afterwards and gloat about the fact that he's already been, and the rest of the class are losers cause they've got to wait until they can go.'

'I'm not sure that's the healthiest approach to dealing with rejection.'

'To be honest, I said the same thing. You'd have been proud of me, I said it felt a bit mean. Suggested it might be better to take him after the party, but Paul was insistent. Something about them being overdue an outing together. To be honest, Dave's invited me out for the day, well, he invited us both but it's a little soon to be introducing Charlie to him just yet. Paul having him works for both of us. So… are you going to go?'

'To the party? I think I have to.'

'No. To the sanctuary. With Paul. He said he'd invited you.'

'Oh, that.' I feel heat prickle up my neck. 'I don't know. Apart from anything else, do I really want to go twice in two weekends? I mean, I've heard it's nice but… I'm not sure.'

'You know, you're probably why he wants to go sooner, rather than later.'

I pull at my coat. 'Well… I'm absolutely broke until payday anyway.'

'I'll lend it you if you need money.'

'Where are *you* going to get it from?' I say it a bit quick and Holly looks bruised. 'Sorry, I didn't mean that to sound so harsh. But neither of us are exactly rolling in surplus cash, are we?'

'I've got a new job actually.'

'Oh?' We've reached the office door and I really do need to get in.

'Yeah. Dave put a word in for me. I'm on the phones down the pizza place. Cash in hand. Thursday, Friday, Saturday nights. Paul's going to babysit whenever Darren can't have Charlie. It'll top me up a bit. I can start saving for Christmas. You never know, I might have a boyfriend for this one.' She shoves her hair behind her ear, kicking at something on the ground before beaming up at me.

'Christmas? You're planning ahead, aren't you! I have literally never seen you like this before. Even Darren felt like he had a sell-by date.'

She breaks into a grin. 'Well, maybe it's time I let someone into my heart and not just my—'

'Please don't.'

'If you insist. Okay, I'll see you at pick up! Maybe we can walk back together, and you can tell me about seeing Billy?' She eyes me, eyebrows raised because I haven't mentioned it to her first. 'Look at you! Billy! Paul! Two men chasing after you!'

'What? Wait, no! It's not like that!'

She winks, blows me a kiss and flounces off, shouting over her shoulder, 'You're basically Bridget Jones!'

Chapter Twenty-One

I'm sat in the staffroom, Tupperware of leftovers resting on my lap as I pretend to scroll through my phone as the others talk. They do try and involve me in their chatter, but I still don't feel like I entirely belong. Probably not helped by the fact that the room hasn't changed since I was at school here and going into the staffroom was always something you did if you were naughty and on your way to the headmaster's office. I only ever went in twice: once for copying maths answers off Marcus Davies, the clever boy I sat next to, and once for leading a revolt against a science teacher who set us a test paper without teaching us any of its contents – both times I was given lines to write, both times Dad was furious at my alleged behaviour and sent me to my room.

I take a mouthful of lunch and scroll through the BBC News app but jump as my phone starts ringing and Dad's number comes up. My heart rate spikes and I wonder if I can cancel it – I'm in a room full of people, it's rude to answer. But they're looking at me now because I'm just staring at it, so it would probably seem weird to ignore it and what if he's had an accident or something awful has happened? Or it's something about Grandma Elsie that he needs help with. I can't keep on keeping my distance, not really, he doesn't have anybody else.

'Dad, hi. Sorry, I didn't hear the phone.' I don't know why I say it, and clearly Poppy's teacher doesn't either because I see her surreptitiously clocking me.

'Hi, I was just ringing to see how you are.' His voice is strained, uncertain. It makes me feel guilty for not having called him since the funeral. Did I say I would? I suppose it doesn't matter.

'Oh, right. Yes, I'm fine thanks. You?'

'Oh good, good. Yes, I'm okay. You know...' He pauses. I don't know what to say. I've never really known how to talk to him but usually I can find something to stop him feeling awkward. Yet today, I'm a bit lost. 'And Poppy?' he asks, eventually. 'Is Poppy okay?'

'Yeah, yeah, she's good. Enjoying school, settling in. It's lovely.'

'That's nice.'

'Erm... is there anything you need? It's just... I'm at work, Dad.'

'Oh! Oh, yes, I remember now. Is it going okay?' Again, his tone is strained but this time I can imagine his face too, a look of disapproval as he asks the question because he thinks he knows better about what I should and shouldn't be doing.

'It's really nice to settle in somewhere, it's not been long but it's nice to feel that I'm finally earning my own money again. Fending for myself, you know? I've missed working.' There's a pause where he doesn't respond and to fill the gap I just say, 'I need some independence, eh? Let's face it, you won't be here forever.' Poppy's teacher looks up, not remotely surreptitiously this time. 'Shit, sorry, Dad... you know what I mean.'

'I suppose so.' I pull at my blouse, feeling really hot and awkward. 'So, the reason for my call is that I was thinking of going away for a few days, this weekend, actually.' I get up with my mug and head for the kettle. 'Normally on a weekend I'd be taking Grandma Elsie shopping or helping out round her house and, well… obviously I don't need to do that any more.' Guilt picks at my chest. 'So… I was wondering if you'd like to come with me. We could go anywhere. Straight from school on Friday, then home Sunday so Poppy doesn't miss school. We all need holidays, don't we?'

He sounds as awkward about the proposition as I feel. 'Oh, well, I don't think—'

'Or if not a whole weekend, we could just go out for the day, this Saturday.' He says it really quickly as if wanting to give me options that might be more palatable but basically don't give me a get-out, and that's the kind of claustrophobia that I don't have to keep accepting. 'The forecast looks good, maybe we could jump in the car and go to Mablethorpe. You used to love Mablethorpe.' I loved Mablethorpe because it's the only place we ever went – day trips only – and I knew no different. 'I think we should spend time together. It will be good for Poppy.'

Not, *I'd like to*, or *wouldn't it be nice if*, but 'I think we should'.

'Life is short, and family is important.'

When some people say that, it's usually just an observation. When he says it, gruff and determined, it's an instruction. The feeling of claustrophobia creeps in. The memory of the times he took me on the day trips, but I was barely allowed any freedom, how tightly he'd hold my hand. How all I wanted to do was run the length and breadth of the beach, picking out stones, paddling on the shoreline, but how we only ever used to look at it all from a distance. Which was my childhood all over, watching from the sidelines whilst everyone else threw themselves into it, full force, neck deep in fun and candyfloss, parties and silliness. I pick at my blouse, wafting it a little to cool me down.

'I'm really sorry, Dad, but we already have plans for Saturday, I'm afraid.' I put my hand up to my mouth as I talk, the guilt shifting from chest to deeply set into my bones.

'Who with?'

'Paul.'

'Who's Paul?'

'Holly's brother, remember?'

'Oh right. Yes. Can't you cancel?'

Like he always did? Anytime I got excited about something. I wouldn't say I was exactly excited about the park trip with Paul. I'd effectively turned him down because I don't need the complication of a Paul and me situation right now. But now it's offered a useful excuse not to see Dad, which is shitty of me on both counts and yet...

'No, sorry, Dad. We've had it planned for ages. We're taking the kids to a rescue zoo and they're super excited, so I'd hate to let them down. It's lovely and it'll be nice to spend that quality time with Poppy out and about, you know?'

I feel churlish, childish even. But I'm also bitter that he can go for so long not really knowing what to say to me, or how to communicate, then expects me to drop everything to spend quality time together, right after effectively judging my life choices. The choice to work and support myself so that Poppy can see her mother as an independent woman who doesn't need to rely on a man to survive, even if that man is her father. It sums up our relationship, the constant push and pull of closeness versus distance. Dad apparently never comfortable with either. But I have to remember not to do to her what Dad did to me. Seeing her grandfather regularly should factor in, shouldn't it? The bell goes for end of dinner break.

'Look, I need to get back to work, Dad, I'll call you next week and maybe we can arrange something else.'

'Right then. I suppose.' He sounds old, older than he did when he was urging me to give up work and rely on him. Not to take this job. To study, if it kept my brain busy. Presumably, that meant study from home. God forbid I should go anywhere, live my life, expand my horizons. 'I'll wait to hear from you then.'

I shove my phone in my pocket, pouring water on a tea bag for a drink I don't want; and not just because it's herbal. I wait until pretty much all the teachers have left the room and take my mug of rooibos, or whatever other crime against tea I appear to have picked out in all the stress. There's an ache in my gut like the one I always get when I talk to him: guilt, responsibility, echoes of a contradictory childhood. Maybe he tried his best – at a time when a single father raising his child was looked upon with surprise and judgement – but it was lonely, suffocating, intimidating at times. Should I be grateful that he didn't just marry someone else to give me a mother, like I imagine was often the way back in the 80s? Or should he have been bolder and allowed himself to move on after Mum passed? I think about Poppy. The last thing I ever wanted was for history to in any way repeat itself. And yet, look where we are.

Chapter Twenty-Two

Poppy swings her legs under the table, waiting for me to place her dinner down. 'Mrs Butterworth was telling us all about a monster today.'

'Was she?' I set a steaming bowl of pasta pesto down in front of her, and she hungrily dives in, shoving a forkful into her mouth.

'Yeah, and she—' She pauses to chew, taking a breath as if to speak again.

'Manners, please.'

She finishes her mouthful. 'Mrs Butterworth says that when she was our age she used to sit by a big lake or something and wait for a monster.'

'Oh, Loch Ness, you mean?'

'Yes! That's it. Apparently, it has a monster.'

'That's what they say.'

'I'd love to see it!'

'Wouldn't you be scared?'

'Miss says it's a nice monster. One that looks after the lake and the fishes and just swims about.'

'Ah, yes, she's probably right. You know, when I lived in Scotland, I wanted to go to Loch Ness but never got there.'

'You lived in Scotland?'

I smile, sadly. 'I did, for a few months anyway, not long. In fact, you did too. For a few days, anyway. You were born in Scotland.'

'Wow, really? I'm Scottish? I never knew that.'

'Well, no, you're not Scottish because me and your dad are from Lincolnshire.' As I say it, I feel like I'm playing with fire a little. Unsure how much to say today. Will Billy stick around long enough to meet her? Will he want anything to do with her after he's met her?

'Where is my daddy?' I look up sharply. 'Everyone in my class has a daddy, most of my friends live with their daddies. Where's mine?'

I push my bowl away, wiping my mouth. He's here. He wants to meet her. I don't know how long he plans to stick around, but still. 'Would you want to meet your daddy?' I ask, forcing a kind of nonchalance that I hope she'll believe.

She looks at me, still eating, eyes wide. 'Yes,' she says, her voice quieter than normal. My heart pings at how brave and strong she is. How smart and thoughtful, often well beyond her five years. 'I'd love to have a proper daddy.'

The doorbell goes and I jump up. 'Oh, who could that be?' She watches me intently, not breaking eye contact, please God, don't let it be him. 'Just a minute.' I jog through to the door, pausing before opening it, collecting myself. Whoever is here has just saved me from that conversation but I'm going to have to have it at some point.

'Hello?' But there's just a small brown package on the doorstep. I step out over it, looking round to the drive and the big gates. Nobody's there. I never heard the squeak of gate or footsteps on the gravel. I pick up the parcel then jog down the path to the small gate, looking up and down the road. Over the way, there's an older lady in a red coat walking a dog, she holds a phone to her ear in deep conversation. Down the way, a man jogs. 'Excuse me?' I shout after him. 'I'm sorry, excuse me!' I try again, out on the pathway now. He jogs to the kerb, looking up and down the road to check for traffic before crossing. I try waving but he's gone. I look down at the parcel, my hand shakes. My heart is in my mouth. When I turn back around, Poppy is at the door.

'Who was it, Mummy?'

'I don't know. There wasn't anybody there.'

'Did you get another present?'

'I think I did.'

'Oooh. What is it? What is it?'

Chapter Twenty-Three

I usher Poppy back inside, giving one final glance around before closing the door behind me. 'Open it!' She tugs at the package. 'Open it, open it!'

I stick my finger beneath a fold of paper, pulling at the sellotape until it unsticks, and the paper easily unwraps. A small cream jumper is inside, a plain white envelope sits on top. When I lift the jumper both Poppy and I can see it's not for me.

'Look, look, that's too small for you, Mummy!'

She tries to pull it from my hands. 'Poppy!' She steps back, scolded. 'Do you mind?'

I snatch the jumper back, not sure what to say. My hands tremble as I look at it, then back in the envelope. There's a printout in it and pulling it out, the hairs on the back of my neck stand up. Two tickets to ARK. Poppy looks hopefully at the jumper again and I quickly wrap it all up and put it on the side.

'Come on now, have you finished your tea? It's getting late and you need a bath yet. Sit down nicely and finish your tea whilst I run the water. Every last mouthful please and finish your drink.'

'But, Mum—'

'No buts, come on, please.' Stung, she goes back to her chair, glancing up at me as if trying to work out what's going on. I go back into the hallway and glance at the package. I open the front door again, checking up and down the road, checking for any clue or hint as to who left the parcel. The light has shifted, it's grey and dusky, the nights beginning to draw in. Iris's curtains are closed so I can't even check if she saw anyone. A car drives past, the driver notices me, and I get a shiver down my spine. I jog back into the house and lock the door behind me. Shoving the parcel into the sideboard I run upstairs and start running Poppy's bath. Perched on the edge of the tub, I catch sight of myself in the mirror opposite. I'm white as a sheet, my eyes small and frightened. This is stupid. It's just a parcel. It must be Paul. He's the only one, other than Holly, that knew about the trip. Oh, and Iris, she was there when Paul mentioned it, but there's no way she could deliver something then leg it so quickly. I've not mentioned it to anyone else, have I?

It has to be Paul. It *has* to be. And if it is, why did he say they're not from him?

I call Holly.

'Hello?' Her voice is reassuring. 'You okay, chuck?'

'Erm, yeah, I'm fine. I just… God, this is ridiculous. I just…'

'What's up?'

Poppy pads through to the bathroom, still looking wounded. She lifts her arms as I take her jumper off, my phone in the crook of my neck. 'Hang on, let me get Pops in the bath.' I put Holly on speaker as I finish helping Poppy undress; I can hear her moving about her own home. We do this sometimes, have each other on speaker whilst we carry on doing whatever we need to do and, in this moment, it's like having a housemate. I wish she still lived over the road. 'In you go, that's it. I won't be long,' I say to Poppy, twisting the taps off and heading onto the landing. I push the door open wide so I can see her clearly from my bedroom, lowering my voice. 'I got another present.'

'Oooh, what this time?'

'A jumper for Poppy. And tickets to ARK.'

'Oh wow! Actually, that's really sweet. Quite romantic. Must be Paul, then, right?'

'But he says the presents aren't from him. Has he said anything to you?'

'Well, no, but who else could it be?'

'I don't know. I thought Billy, but he said no as well. Well, he said they were from him if I liked them. It wasn't terribly convincing.'

'And when did Paul say they weren't from him?'

'The other night, after we saw Billy.'

'Oh, right…'

'What?'

'Well, I don't know but… maybe he didn't want to confuse you by admitting to them when you'd just seen Billy. Maybe he thought he should back off.'

'But then he asked me to go to ARK, after that? And this gift has only just arrived. I was here when it came. Sat having dinner with Pops. Whoever it was rang the doorbell and when I opened the door, there was nobody there. Why the secrecy?'

'Because he's scared? Because he's always been a bit rubbish with telling girls how he feels? Because he's trying to win you over with gestures?'

'Gestures are pointless if you pretend they're not from you!'

'Well, yes. That's true. Do you remember when he liked Jane Mawson? He basically just hung out at the park so that he could see her house. Would sit at home drawing pictures for her. Never actually told her until it was too late, and she got together with that lad from the army base. What was his name?'

'Can't remember.'

'She's down Corsham way now, apparently. Five kids!'

'Blimey.'

I hang some clothes up, Holly still on speaker on my bed. I catch sight of myself in the mirror, all comfy clothes and no makeup. Christ knows why he'd be interested in any case. 'I'm so confused, Hol.'

'About what?'

'Paul, Billy, the presents.'

'Why would you want them to be from Billy?'

'I don't know that I do, necessarily, but if it was, at least it might mean there's a chance we could reconnect for Poppy's sake.'

'Because relationships of parental convenience always work.'

'Oh God, I don't know. I don't think I mean that really.' I drop onto the bed, with a groan. And then I realise. 'Wait, shit! What if it's all from Dad?' I scrunch my eyes shut and as I do, there's a crash, a splash and a scream from the bathroom that makes my blood run cold. 'Holly, I've got to go.'

Chapter Twenty-Four

I burst through to the bathroom to find Poppy cradling her head. 'Poppy, what on earth happened? Are you okay?' She's sobbing uncontrollably, unable to get her words out, occasionally not even able to breathe enough to cry, great moments of silent sobbing where you wonder if they're even going to stop the silent bit long enough to fill their lungs. 'Hey, hey, sssshhh. Calm down. Hey.' I pull her into me, her wet body seeping through my T-shirt, almost as much as the guilt for leaving her in the bath alone seeps into my bones. I could see her, I was watching. I shut my eyes for a split second.

'I wanted my book'– sob – 'so I tried to reach it' – sob, breathe, sob – 'but I slipped and banged my head on the sink.' Sob. I kiss the top of her head, I can feel an egg bump growing beneath my hand.

'I'm sorry, baby, I'm so sorry, I was just...' But I don't bother trying to explain why I wasn't sat in here with her because she doesn't care and I should have been in the room instead of talking about mystery presents and, worse, men! We're good on our own. She's never slipped in the bath before. Emotion rises from deep in my bones as it so often does when I feel like I've let her down or done something stupid and irresponsible. Nobody tells you about the guilt that arrives the second you give birth, the guilt that consumes you every time you get something a little bit wrong. Grandma used to say that 'in every mother, was a Catholic just waiting for confession'. As I hold Poppy in my arms, growing cold until her cries subside and she's just sniffing, I bite down on my lip and refuse to give into how I feel.

'Come on, let's get you out and dry, shall we? Pick out some PJs, let's get cosy.'

'I want the jumper.' Sniff.

'What jumper?'

More sniffs. 'The one that came in the parcel. It looks cosy.' I chew the inside of my mouth. Would Dad have chosen this for her? It would be out of character, totally off brand, and yet, there's a tiny part of me that does wonder. He's never been one for gifts, not really. Grandma bought all the birthday and Christmas presents, I'm sure of it. I don't even think he wrapped them up. In fact, it begs the question, what's he going to do now that she's gone? But maybe they are all from him and that's why he's sending them. Because he knows that I'm all he has and perhaps he's frightened, but too buttoned up to admit it.

'Please can I have it, Mummy?'

I nod and, towel still wrapped around her, little wet footprints in the carpet, she runs down the stairs to fetch it. 'Careful down those stairs!'

I take her a hot water bottle through, finding her curled up on the sofa next to Frank. Her hair is still damp. It's left an imprint on the cushion she rests her head on. 'Charlie says his Uncle Paul is taking him to the zoo. He said we could go. Can we go, please, Mummy? I really want to go. I can wear my new jumper.'

My resistance dissolves, as most things do when it's something I can see Poppy needs. 'Of course we can go.' The envelope with the tickets is on the sideboard, cast aside when Poppy dug out the jumper. 'It'll be lovely, won't it?'

She does a little dance on the sofa before snuggling into me, content, as we watch reruns of old *Horrible Histories*. She belly laughs at *Stupid Deaths*, even though I think half the jokes are lost on her. I laugh with her because I'm so grateful to hear her giggle, and because the jokes aren't lost on me. Eventually, it's time to put her to bed.

Tiptoeing downstairs, leaving her tucked up in her room, I see the parcel on the side in the hall. I suppose I should be touched that Dad heard me talk about the visit. I've so rarely felt heard over the years and maybe he knows it. And it would make more sense for him to have sent me the photo if Holly can't remember stealing it, though I don't know why he'd have sent that or the notebook. The notebook especially goes against his want to keep me in a place that he is happy with, but maybe he's begun to realise he can't do that forever? He's talked about me studying, maybe it's all part of that plan… though that was about stopping me working, which doesn't make any sense. Why would a parent want to restrict his child's life? Don't you want them to grow bigger than you? To see more, do more, be more? Maybe he does and just isn't sure how to show it. Maybe I'm being unfair, maybe he finally can see that I need to spread my wings. For all I know, Grandma Elsie told him he should be encouraging, not stifling me. She tended not to tell him how she really felt about things. But maybe, feeling death draw closer, she made an exception?

I pick up the notebook from the side, flicking through the pages, pausing on *What plans do you have? This week, This month, This year.* Dad never made plans, not so as I knew, anyway. Over the years, Grandma used to ask him about holidays or trips. What we were doing at Christmas in case we wanted to walk round for Christmas dinner. Or whether we wanted to pop over at Easter. I remember how he'd always waffle his way through a response, not really ever answering. Planning wasn't his thing, as it isn't mine. Maybe he's begun to realise that living in the moment is no good if it means you never do anything or go anywhere. Poppy has dreams, ideas of things she'd like to do. Between her and this notebook, maybe it's time I learned from Dad's mistakes? Maybe that's what he wants me to do too and that's why he sent the notebook?

I let my mind wander over possibilities for this week, this month and this year, then start writing:

This week: Make a plan to save up for holidays and trips with Poppy.

This month: Start saving, research experiences we can have, sell things on eBay to raise funds.

This year: go to Scotland and sit by Loch Ness with my girl.

Okay, so maybe it'll be within the next year as opposed to this one, we've only a few months left, but we could get to Scotland by next summer, couldn't we?

Then I flick to the page that says *Tell me your dreams…* and I write:

Find a way to connect with Dad

Because if these gifts are from him, he's making the kind of effort that must be so alien to him, the least I can do is respond.

Chapter Twenty-Five

Flick approaches in the school playground, her face stern. I look behind me at first, assuming she must be marching to speak to someone behind me, but when I turn back she's right in front of me. 'I hear you're going to ARK this weekend?' she spits. Holly ducks down, out of the firing line, pretending she has something important to say to Charlie.

'Oh, erm… well, maybe, yes. How did you know?'

'Oh, you know what kids are like, they gossip more than the mums do.' She raises her eyebrows pointedly, which is unfair given the fact that Holly and I aren't the only gossipers in this playground. 'I think Jenna told me after Jessamy told her.' Point proven. I look over at Lady Vomitous and clench my teeth. 'I have to say, I'm a little disappointed, to be honest.'

'Pardon?'

'I'm disappointed. You have been invited to Ludo's party and you know that's where we're going. Don't you think it's a bit like raining on his parade to go there before his special day?'

Holly jumps up beside me. 'His special day,' she hoots. 'It's just a birthday party and I think you'll find it's a free country where Lisa… sorry, Liza, can go anywhere she likes.'

I try to feel my feet on the ground in the hope it might soften and swallow me whole.

'You don't think that maybe it's like opening a Christmas present before it's actually Christmas?'

Holly huffs. 'No. I think—'

I grab hold of Holly's hand, logic and reason evades her when it comes to Felicity. 'I'm sorry, I didn't think. I didn't realise it would upset you. Or Ludo for that matter. It's just that Holly's brother wanted to take Charlie and he invited Poppy to go along too. And me. She was very excited. I suppose I just didn't have the heart to say no.'

'Oh right! Yes. I see now.' Flick folds her arms. 'This is because Charlie wasn't invited, isn't it? What a cheap shot. Undermine a child's party because yours wasn't invited. I have never heard of anything so tragic in all my life. Is that really what this is?' She has left the shock behind her and is now apparently staggered, if the disdain and shake of her head is anything to go by. She crosses her arms so tightly I worry she might not be able to breathe. 'So, it's a pity trip then, essentially.'

'Oh, no, I don't think—'

'Yes. It probably is,' Holly interjects, squeezing my hand to let me know that she's not lost all control. 'But it's one my brother, Charlie's uncle, has said he'd like to do. For the record, I had suggested it may be better for him to go after the party, but he wanted to do it this weekend and, as he's organising it, paying for it, and taking him, I didn't think it my place to argue too hard.'

Holly mirrors Flick, arms folded, but with eyebrows raised, lips pursed. They're like a pair of judgmental bookends, me the encyclopaedia – or should I say pamphlet, given my lack of contribution to the conversation – caught in the middle.

'This is just how it's worked out. A bit of uncle-nephew bonding. With added best mate. I'm sorry if it upsets you.' She doesn't sound terribly apologetic, but I'm kind of impressed that she's suggested she might be. 'I wouldn't worry about it, Flick. I don't imagine for a second that Charlie or Poppy will ruin anything for your darling little Ludo. Your party will be absolutely perfect, irrespective of the fact Poppy will have already been. Before Ludo.' I wince. 'Assuming you're not about to rescind her invitation?'

Flick pauses and I brace myself because how the hell would I explain that one if she decided to.

'What kind of woman do you take me for?'

'Someone who spent a fortune on party invites and doesn't want to waste an opportunity to show off about how perfect her life is?' Holly's tried to whisper that one to me but as Flick opens and closes her mouth, I'm under no doubt she heard.

Holly raises her eyebrows, cocks her head to one side, then turns away.

I, somewhat guiltily, plead a silent apology with my eyes and really hope that Flick is more aware of subtle body language than she is of how unimportant her argument is. She purses her lips even tighter, about turns, and struts back across the playground. A huddle of mums welcome her back into their coven, rubbing her arm, passing her a tissue, sending us death stares over her shoulder.

'Was I a bit harsh?'

'Well… maybe a little, yeah.'

'Should I apologise?'

'That's up to you, but… probably, yeah. Be the bigger person.'

'Might let her sweat over it a bit first. Charlie was gutted he didn't get invited! Thank God for Poppy, cause he's really feeling this transition from nursery to school, and not in a good way. God, they don't warn you about this bit when it comes to parenting.'

'Nope. They don't. The guilt is real.'

The bell goes and I jog over to Poppy, relieved with the get out of jail card. I pack her off to class, showering her in kisses she doesn't want.

'Right, I'd better get to work.'

'Okay, oh, Lis?' I stop. 'I've been thinking about you and Paul.'

'There is no me and Paul.'

'No, but the more I think about it, the more there definitely should be.'

I look over to the gates that lead to school reception. 'I really need to get to work.'

'Look, I just wanted to say to you that I can really see you and him working.'

'Holly!'

'No! Hear me out. You want someone smart. Someone who understands you, who lets you be you.'

'Do I?'

'Yes! I know you think you're okay on your own, and of course you have been for ages, but I really think you'd make a good team. He's smart, you're smart. He's kind, you need kindness. And don't tell him I ever said this, but he is very funny. I mean, maybe even funnier than me.'

'At the moment, you're not being funny at all.'

'He makes you belly laugh.'

'So did you, once upon a time.'

'Just… think about it.' She winks, slings her bag over her shoulder and before skipping off says, 'Give him a chance.'

Chapter Twenty-Six

Butterflies in my stomach, I sling my bag in the car, jogging back to the door. 'Hurry up, come on, get your shoes on!' Whilst I'm buzzing about like I've had too many coffees, hands shaking, heart racing, Poppy is still half asleep, despite it being ten in the morning. I'd love to go back to bed and hide under my duvet, except that I haven't stopped thinking about what Holly said all night and needed a change of scenery before I sent myself crazy with what ifs.

In the past few days, I've looked at Billy's mobile number several times, remembering the look in his eyes when he asked me to call him. I suppose I should be grateful that he's prepared to give me some space, that he hasn't pestered or badgered me to get in touch. He could very easily find out where I live, maybe he already knows. At any point he could have turned up to see me, to introduce himself to Poppy. I know I need to sort it, for Poppy's sake if not mine, I just don't know where to start. He's asked after me. So, Iris said yesterday when I took her shopping, looking over my shoulder the entire trip for fear of bumping into him again. She'd seen him when she was out getting some fresh air and they chatted. He asked her to put a word in for him. She told him she wouldn't, and that he had to be patient. But she also told me she'd seen him. Was that her way of keeping him in my thoughts? Or was she just trying to be supportive because she knows Poppy would be better off with both of us in her life, together or not? And, on that basis, she's right, I know she is. I pull my phone out to text him. 'Come on, Pops! Paul and Charlie will be waiting for us.'

I tap out a message with one hand, waggling her shoes beneath her nose with the other. I tell Billy I'll be in touch next week, that he and I should meet up first, work out how to handle things. I click send whilst ushering Frank outside before we go. He sniffs about, stands looking through the fencing, then plods and waits, not doing a wee. 'Why is everyone else in this house on a go-slow this morning?'

'Mummy, I wanted to wear my jumper.' Poppy rubs her eyes as she slips her feet in the wrong shoe.

'No. Come on, you're fine as you are.' I grab her shoes, pull her feet out and put them on the right ones.

'But it's a zoo jumper. I want to wear the jumper.'

I'm due on. My hormones are through the roof. I've just agreed to meet up with Billy after five years apart and I'm terrified about the day ahead because I really like Paul and we've never spent so much time together without Holly. And certainly not since he told me how he felt. Or since I realised that I might feel the same way. Four times this morning I've picked my phone up to cancel before remembering something about feeling the fear and doing it anyway. 'Just get in the car, please.'

'But—'

'Poppy!'

Her face falls, her bottom lip wobbles but, characteristically when I raise my voice, she doesn't let herself cry. 'Come on, baby, get in the car. Where's your coat?'

Poppy wanders out to the car as I grab her coat, shooing Frank back inside and slamming the door, shoving the key in to lock it. Then I catch sight of Poppy's face and guilt ramps up, so I open the door back up and run upstairs for her jumper. My phone dings out a text with a response from Billy. *That would be great, let's go somewhere not in the village, somewhere nobody knows us.*

'There you go.' I throw the jumper into the back seat beside her and opt not to bother responding to Billy just yet. I don't know why it matters where we meet, so long as we do, surely? Then I see myself in the rear-view mirror, pause, breathe and readjust. The truth is, if I let myself believe it, I'm looking forward to this, I want to see Paul. I like him, I always have, and, yes... I think maybe we would make a good team.

Taking the back way through Lincolnshire, we pass through small villages with thatched roofs and tiny cottage gardens in early autumn bloom. I spot a couple walking arm in arm, a young child on a balance bike just up ahead of them.

'Mummy, I can't wait to see the pigs. Charlie says he thinks they're really, really small and maybe we'll be allowed to feed them or pet them.'

'That'd be nice, eh.' I smile at the image of her. I glance through the rear-view mirror as she picks through the books she keeps in the car. Saturday mornings are normally filled with slow get-ups and reading, cuddles on the bed and laughter. This is new, it's nice, I don't have to be frightened.

'Are we nearly there?'

'Yes, five minutes or so.'

Poppy gabbles on about the various animals she's going to see. And then something hits us hard from behind, the back window smashes and Poppy screams. I try to reach back to hold her leg, but we're shunted again. I see walls and buildings spin around me, my body pulled left with the force. There's another shunt and through the rear-view mirror, I see Poppy's head smash into the side of the car. I grip the steering wheel, my body rigid, eyes now screwed tightly shut. The airbag explodes in my face and I'm thrown from side to side before suddenly coming to a standstill.

Then silence.

Chapter Twenty-Seven

Voices and footsteps grow closer. I smell burning rubber. My ear, hands, and the side of my face are hot, stinging. I'm still gripped to the steering wheel.

'Hello? Hello?' says a voice.

I try to shift round to check on Poppy, but it hurts to move at first. 'Poppy?' I try to see her in the rear-view mirror, but it's moved. 'Poppy, are you okay?'

'Hello? Can you hear me?' A man appears by the side of us, he glances in the back of the car then quickly back to me, his face drains of colour.

'Poppy, Poppy?'

'Are you okay? Are you okay in there?'

'Oh my God, she just spun into my path, I couldn't stop,' says someone else, someone I can't see.

'Are you okay?' asks the man beside me, his eyes still flitting between me and the back seat.

I croak, 'Yes.' Then, ribs stinging, neck stuck, I manage to turn just enough to see Poppy. Her body lifeless, her eyes closed. 'Oh God, oh God. Poppy!' The book she was reading is caught between her legs and the passenger seat. 'Poppy!' I try to unbuckle myself. Breath leaves my chest, winding me.

'Please, please don't move.' The man reaches into the back-passenger side, broken glass allowing him to unlock the door. 'Someone call an ambulance,' he shouts over his shoulder. 'Don't move,' he repeats, pulling the door open.

'My daughter!' I try and reach for her foot. 'Poppy!' I shake it but she doesn't respond. 'Poppy!'

'Please don't move. Let me try.'

I ignore his instructions, fumbling with the seat belt to free myself as he carefully opens her passenger door, peering at her.

Pain sears through my side. 'Poppy, it's Mummy. Can you hear me?'

A woman appears on the other side of us. I notice her glance around at the debris, drystone wall, glass and car now settled in a garden.

'I couldn't stop. I tried but… you just… you were just there. On my side of the road,' chokes the voice I heard before. He surveys the scene, hands on his head, he paces, and the woman tries to comfort him, but he can't stand still, he just keeps staring then looking away, up to the sky, back to us. 'The car shunted her into my path. I couldn't do anything!'

'An ambulance is coming,' a man shouts, jogging over to us. He's still on the phone, reciting the scene, telling his phone about me, about Poppy. 'Yes, the driver in this car is awake. There's another, the one that went into the back of her, they're not responding at all. This one? Yes, a passenger, in the back, a young girl…' He pauses. 'No, no, she doesn't seem to be.'

'Poppy, open your eyes, Poppy,' I try again, ignoring the red-hot pain that stabs my side as I reach again over to the back seat. Her skin is warm to the touch, it's like she's asleep but I've always been able to wake her from sleep. The smell of rubber and oil makes the back of my throat sore. 'Poppy, Poppy, can you hear me? She can't hear me. Oh my God, she can't hear me. Poppy! Poppy!'

'Hey, hey, please try not to move,' says the man on the phone. 'They say someone will be here very soon, they say you might be hurt.' He manages to open the driver's side passenger door, though it creaks heavily as he pulls it open. 'Yes. I'm just climbing in now. What's her name?'

'Poppy.'

'Poppy, can you hear me? Poppy,' he says. 'Right, okay. Where?' His fingers feel along the side of her neck. 'I don't know, I'm not sure.'

'Sirens!' says someone nearby.

'I think they're on their way,' the man says to his phone before focusing on me. 'Can you tell me your name?'

'I'm… I'm Lisa.'

'Hi, Lisa, I'm Jonathan.' He forces a smile. 'How old is Poppy?'

'She's five.'

'She's five,' he says back into his phone. 'What day is it?' he asks me.

'Saturday.'

'Yes. She knows.' He peers out the front window. 'They're here now.'

Someone manages to open Poppy's side of the car and her arm falls as they do, hanging limply out as her body slumps slightly. The new man, dressed in green, takes her tiny wrist in his hand, placing thumb and forefinger in search of a pulse. He exchanges a glance with the first guy.

'Tell me she's okay! Tell me! Oh my God, Poppy, be okay, Poppy, be okay.' I push one of the men out of the way, pulling Poppy onto my chest holding her tight into me, my heart beating against her cheek. Maybe it can beat enough for us both. Maybe it can help hers. 'Poppy, Poppy, it's Mummy. Wake up. Wake up. Come on, baby, it's all going to be okay. Can you hear me? Can you feel my heart? Come on, baby, you're going to be fine. Somebody help me!' I scream. 'Please! God, somebody, please help me!'

Chapter Twenty-Eight

I am lying in a field, tall grass and poppies surrounding me. The sun shines and I feel warmth on my face and peace in my heart. I feel clear on who I am and what my purpose is in this life. My heart is calm. When I open my eyes to look up at the sky, I see birds soaring, no clouds. I smell the grass around me. A bee buzzes, landing on a poppy, crawling around inside the petals. I hear music, somewhere in the distance, maybe a prayer chant, beautiful sounds, an organ, perhaps a choir. I feel like I want to stay here, never move. I want to sink into the earth and feel it envelop me, nurture me, caress me. I feel like I could live forever just here. I think about my life, beautiful moments wash over my mind: the day I met Holly in the playground when we were kids; the days hanging out in the park as a teenager, sun kissing our shoulders, laughter, hope, everything as it's meant to be, freedom. I remember the day I met Billy, the love I felt, so deep, so right. I remember us walking and talking, holding hands, our connection. I feel love in my heart so intense I can barely breathe, yet I know I am breathing because I don't feel panic or fear. I close my eyes and colours swirl: reds and oranges, yellow and green; clouds, mixing and swishing like a Van Gogh painting in my mind's eye, before eventually they part, leaving bright blue skies in front of me, just like those I can see when I open my eyes.

Up ahead, I hear giggling, playing, the sound of a tiny voice. The voice calls out 'Mummy, Mummy' and I sit up, peering over the poppies and grass, the bee buzzes off and I watch it before the child's voice calls my attention again. I stand, looking around to see where it's coming from and, up ahead, I see flame red hair, curls, bouncing as the child runs this way and that. I watch for a moment, my heart explodes. I walk towards her, this little girl, dressed in white, her face bright as she swirls and twirls, dancing in the sunshine. As I get closer, she notices me and breaks out into the biggest smile. Pausing for a second before she runs towards me, 'Mummy! Mum!' she says, her arms open wide. Red curls flow out behind her. The bee settles on another flower, going about its work, and as the little girls gets closer, she leaps at me. I catch her, no question, standing strong as she wraps her arms and legs around me. 'Mummy, you're here,' she says. 'You're here.' And I hold her tight.

'Where else would I be?'

And then I hear my name. Called gently by someone else. I put the little girl down, she stands by my feet, pressing her tiny hand in mine. When I turn around to hear the voice better, the sun goes, and a darkness appears and the voice gets louder and the feeling of warmth and peace leaves me and it's cold and bright and sterile and when I wake up, I'm in a hospital room, eyes fixed on the ceiling, body too stiff to move. I can't feel, hear or smell Poppy near me.

Chapter Twenty-Nine

'Lisa? Hey, Lisa. Are you okay? She's awake, she's awake!'

The male voice is familiar, but my eyes blur, focus, then blur at the ceiling, my body locked into the bed for a second before something shifts and I can move. I try to sit up, but somebody places a hand on my shoulder, gently keeping me where I am.

'Lisa?'

And that's when I see Billy, for only the second time in five years, here by my bedside. I blink, confused. 'What? Why are you…?' I look around, for anybody else. Holly, Dad even… Paul?

'God, Lisa, I've been so frightened. I can't believe you're okay.' He leans in, scooping my head into his arms, kissing me. 'God, sorry, sorry,' he says, letting go. He pats my arm as if that's a more appropriate show of affection after all this time. 'Sorry. I saw Paul, he was dropping Charlie back with Holly. He told me what had happened, so I came straight here.' He looks up at the clock, it's quarter to six. Dusk outside.

Billy looks tired, drawn. He moves his hand from my arm to my hand, taking it in his. My heart lurches as confusion sets in. If Paul was dropping Charlie back, why didn't he come?

'What are you doing here?' I frown, then scan the room again. It's almost dark outside. 'Where's Pop…?' The strain of trying to speak is too much though and my voice breaks.

'Hey, hey, ssshhh,' he says.

Coughing doesn't help, and it hurts. Everything hurts. And my belly is ravaged with fear as reality creeps in. 'Where is she?' I manage, my eyes darting between him, the door and the room. 'Where's Poppy?'

I try and push myself to sit up again but Billy holds my hand more tightly, before making way for a woman in smart clothes and a white coat who has appeared at my bedside. She perches on the side of my bed, her hand resting on my arm.

'Where's Poppy?' I demand.

'Lisa, my name is Lydia, Lydia Whiting.' Her voice is calm and gentle. I look to Billy then back to her. 'I'm your consultant.'

'Where's my daughter? I need to see her.'

'You can, soon.' My head drops back onto my pillow. 'We need to talk to you first.'

Billy sits beside me, still holding my hand, staring at the consultant, expectantly. I want him to let go of me.

'Can you remember what happened?' she asks.

I search my mind for clues as to how I got here, shaking my head because I can see moments, flickers of memory, but nothing quite pieces together. 'I was driving, I was in my car with Poppy…' I search for more images, more memory to make itself known to me. 'We were going somewhere.' I scratch at my brains to try and remember 'To meet Paul! We were meeting Paul and Charlie.'

Billy stands, letting go as he folds his arms, moving to the window.

'It was a day trip,' I say to the consultant. 'I was just driving… I don't know what happened. Where's Poppy?' I can feel myself getting increasingly agitated.

Billy moves to come back beside me and I flinch.

The consultant shifts to catch my eye, drawing my attention back to her as she passes a file to one of the nurses stood behind her. Does she notice my response to him? Should I again ask why he's here? 'You were in a road traffic accident, Lisa.' I close my eyes, I feel heat, I smell fuel. 'A car hit you from behind, nudging you into the path of a van. You've fractured some ribs, there's bruising, a little concussion. It'll take time to heal. We're keeping you in for observation, you've been lucky though, there don't appear to be any other injuries.'

'And Poppy?' I plead at the consultant.

'Lisa, you're in shock, after the accident. You'll notice there are also some friction burns to your hands.' She has her hands in mine and when I look down, she shows me red marks, raw and sore. 'That's from the air bag.'

I clench my fists; my knuckles complain. so I close my eyes and feel how my body aches. Then something comes to mind, Poppy's arm falling limply as the car door opened. 'Oh God, she's dead.'

The consultant looks briefly at Billy before back at me. He rushes to my side. 'She's in intensive care.' She waits a second and a swell of relief replaces devastation, but the fear remains. Billy's hand is alien in mine. 'Lisa, Poppy is very poorly.'

'Oh God, oh no.'

'We've explained it to your partner already.' It's Billy's turn to flinch this time, but he says nothing, and I want to scream out that I barely know him anymore, but convention, or maybe fear and exhaustion, swallows my voice.

'It would appear that the first impact shunted you from behind, then the second impact was on Poppy's side as your car spun into the path of a van.'

'Oh God, oh my God. But she's alive?'

'She was unconscious when we got to her. Initial checks suggested she may have experienced some severe swelling to her brain, and we couldn't be certain how much trauma there was.'

My eyes fill, and I don't have the strength to fight the tears. Or let go of Billy's hand. Or ask him why they think he's my partner. Or ask him why he's here. Or ask why Paul isn't.

The consultant gives me a moment. 'When something like this happens, people's bodies often shut down. They operate on a kind of base level to protect them, to keep them alive. Your daughter's body is looking after her.'

'What does that mean? What are you saying?'

'Lisa, Poppy is in a coma.'

I try to sit bolt up but sickness and weakness crashes over me. Billy looks up to the ceiling, biting down on his bottom lip. I want to scream at him, why are you here? How can you care about us now? Is this what it takes to make you realise? Some people knew it all along… and yet, somehow, I can't find the strength to argue what I know he'll find a way to justify. And he's not my priority right now.

'She is being closely monitored. We're running tests and scans to get a picture of the damage.'

'But she'll be okay, right? She has to be okay.'

The consultant clasps her hands in front of her. Her nails are short and clean. She's tight, in control, empathetic yet sort of disconnected.

'Please tell me she'll be okay.'

'It's very difficult to say at this stage.'

I blink, forcing the tears out of my eyes so I can see properly. 'I need to see her!'

'You can. Soon. We're just running a few more tests. I know it's probably impossible, but you have to try to think positively and let us do what we need to do first.'

I open my mouth to speak but nothing comes out. I close my eyes and I can see Poppy, smiling, bright, healthy. I can hear her voice, telling me she wants the jumper.

'She is stable, Lisa. That is a good sign. The next twenty-four hours are critical, but we are doing everything we can to ensure that your daughter has the best chance of recovery.' I give a shallow nod, my throat closing, increasingly unable to breathe. 'You will need to rest, you've had a traumatic experience yourself. It's important you sleep.'

'I want to see Poppy,' I say, but I can feel myself drifting despite fighting it, exhaustion suddenly overwhelmingly in control, despite all the questions, uncertainties and falsehoods in the room.

'As soon as we've finished assessing her and we're happy that you're well enough,' I just about hear her say.

I'm in my head. Nothing is real. 'I *need* to see her,' I hear myself say. Then there are words exchanged, I don't hear exactly what. Some voices I don't recognise, Billy's in amongst them. I feel cold, detached. I think he asks if he can stay. I think they say of course he can and I want to shout out, *Why are you here?* but I can't speak.

I force my eyes open for a second. The tiles on the ceiling are stained, brown marks that creep out from beneath a metal grid. The brightness fades again. Then returns as I fight the need to sleep. A light in the corner of the room is low, darkness kisses the edge of its glow until you get closer to my bed where another light above me seems to leak out and meet the shadows. My eyelids are heavy. My head feels like cotton wool. Flashes of memory are now replaced with something more washed out, neutral watercolours, no images, sound disperses. I feel someone brush my forehead, their touch warm and gentle on my skin. I drift away.

Chapter Thirty

Billy's voice is low, reserved, but I can't quite open my eyes. 'She's okay. At least, she will be.' I manage to force my eyes over to see him stood by the window. 'I don't know.' His movements lurch, his shoulders sit high up around his ears, tension caught up in his body. 'I don't think that's a good idea. If she'd asked for you, then maybe, but, look, she needs time and space, man.' Pause. 'Yeah, I'll tell her.' Pause. 'Yes. Yes. I'll try to call you later.' He hangs up, stuffs the phone in his pocket before turning to see me. 'Sorry, I didn't mean to wake you.' He moves towards me, his face full of worry, though he avoids eye contact. 'They did say you'd drift in and out of sleep. The pain relief they've given you is quite strong.'

I shift slightly, my body stiff but this time, there's no pain. 'Tell me what?'

'Pardon?'

'Then, on the phone. You'd tell me what?'

'Oh, that? No, no, not you. Sorry. I was… it was Dad. About Mum. They've fallen out. Nothing for you to have to think about. Sorry!'

It's now completely dark outside. 'How long have I been asleep? Have they said anything about Poppy?'

He checks his watch. 'Nearly two hours?' He folds his arms. 'And no, not yet. They said it would be soon.' He studies my face, his own etched with concern. 'How are you feeling?'

He turns his back, gazing out of the window. 'Oh, erm… Holly called, by the way. She's worried about you. Said she's been to feed Frank. Apparently, Iris has offered to walk him. I think she wondered if you wanted her to take him back to hers, or ask Iris maybe?'

'Why are you here?'

'I didn't want you to be on your own.'

'But how did you hear?'

'I went for a walk. Bumped into Paul outside Holly's.' I swallow. 'He was dropping Charlie back. He said what had happened. I was so worried, Lisa, I…' He stuffs his hands in his pockets. There's something about him that I've not seen before. I mean, I know he always cared in his own way, but his own way was never enough for me before. This though, it feels different. Maybe. 'The police tried calling your dad. His phone's off and he's not at home.'

I think about all the years Dad took the phone off the hook, locked the door and told me we were going to pretend to be on holiday. We wouldn't answer the door, nor leave the house; we'd live in a make-believe world where the sun shone and we built sandcastles out of cushions, toasted marshmallows on the fire in the lounge. I wonder if he's really gone away, like he said he was going to, or if he's hiding at home like he always did? And if so, I wonder why.

'Shall I try calling him?'

'No,' I croak, my voice scratchy from sleep and stress. 'Thank you, I'll call him when I'm ready. Was Paul okay? When you saw him?'

Billy looks down at his fingers, fiddling with a ring on his right hand. 'Shaken up, I suppose. Worried about you, but more so Charlie, really, I think.' I frown. 'When he told me what had happened, I just… I don't know… I couldn't not come here. I had this vision of you waking alone, frightened, I couldn't do that to you.' I stare. 'They weren't going to let me in at first, I had to tell them I was Poppy's dad.' He holds his hands up as if he can tell how that's just made me feel. 'It's not a lie, is it? I guess, they just assumed we were together then. Maybe I should have been more honest, but… you shouldn't be alone at a time like this, Lisa. I know you, you'd close off. Hide away, focusing just on you and…' He's about to say Poppy, I know it. 'You don't have to do this on your own.'

It would be easy for me to forget how well he knows me considering how long we were together. That he was a bastard in the end doesn't delete our history.

'I'm here for you, Lisa. I'm here for both of you.'

I try to adjust my body, leaning on to my side, away from him. 'Have they said anything about her?'

'Only that they'd try and let us see her soon.'

I'm just about to ask him to leave because none of this feels right, when a nurse appears. She chirrups a hello whilst picking up my paperwork and checking down the forms.

'I need to see Poppy.' Billy moves out of the way as the nurse comes right beside me, taking my pulse, counting as she watches the seconds pass on her fob watch. 'I need to see her now. It's not right that she's somewhere on her own and I'm here. There's a hole in my heart, a gap in me, in who I am. I'm alone here and so is she. She's too small.' The nurse goes to interrupt me. 'I know she's asleep' – I can't bring myself to say coma – 'but, please, you *have* to let me see her.'

'Can you sit up at all?' The nurse stands back and watches as I try and shift myself up, wincing at bruising despite the pain relief. I can't imagine what it might be like without it. 'You're due more meds in an hour.'

'I just need to see my daughter.'

The nurse makes a note on the file that hooks over the end of my bed. 'Let me have a chat with the nurses on ICU and see what I can organise. Can I get you anything else in the meantime? There's a drink on the side there. Are you hungry?'

I shake my head. 'No.'

'We'll try and get you both down as soon as possible.'

'No! Just me.' Billy shifts where he stands, the nurse looks between us both. 'Just me,' I repeat, firmly.

The nurse looks at Billy as if trying to work out what's going on.

'That's fine,' he says. 'Just Lisa. I can wait here. Poppy needs her mum.'

The nurse raises her eyebrows. 'Okay.' She pauses, shifting so that she's between me and Billy. 'Is everything else okay?' she asks, carefully.

I pause. Now is the time I could have him removed. But instead, I just nod, too tired for any scene my rejection might cause. She tops up my cup with water, adjusts the bed sheet slightly, side eyes Billy, then leaves. I see her out in the hallway, talking with a friend, they both look in my room's direction.

'Pass me my bag, please.'

Billy, silently, does as I ask. I reach into it, pulling out the notebook.

'Lisa…'

I open it to a blank page, click the pen. 'You can leave now,' I say, quietly.

'Lisa, please.'

'Leave. I said I'd be in touch and I will.'

'You're allowed to be vulnerable. You're allowed to show weakness.'

I glare at him, put pen to paper and write: *Please let Poppy be okay. Please let Poppy be okay. Please let Poppy be okay.* And I keep writing the same thing, over and over.

A few moments later, Billy leaves.

Chapter Thirty-One

My phone interrupts the mantra I'd got into, my writing sloppy but the sentiment remaining the same. 'Hello?'

'Oh God, Lisa, Lisa, are you okay?' Holly's voice is breathless. 'I've been so worried, I'm so sorry I've not tried calling until now. I wanted to call sooner but Charlie's been in a mess. He and Paul saw the accident. They were a few cars behind you.'

'Were they?'

'Yes, Charlie has been so upset. He's only just gone to bed.'

I check the clock, it's nearly half ten. It feels like days have passed, weeks even. Yet only this morning, everything was fine, life was exactly as I understood it.

'Billy said you'd asked Paul not to call?'

'I never said that.'

'He's beside himself, he tried to get to you, when it happened, but there were people everywhere, someone had sort of taken over, was telling people not to overcrowd the scene. Charlie was screaming, and Paul was so torn.' I scrunch my eyes shut, not able to cope with any trigger back to what happened. 'He tried to get in to see you at the hospital but they wouldn't let him in. They said your partner was with you?'

'That's what Billy told them. To be allowed in.'

'I can't believe him! Jesus!' She's shuffling about, there's rustling down the phone line. 'Billy came past ours, just when Paul got back. He was so distressed, I think it all just blurted out. Fuck! I can't believe Billy would do that to you! How dare he?'

I don't have the energy for her rage, however much I might agree.

'Paul's beside himself, Lisa. He feels it's his fault. That if he hadn't invited you, you'd never have been in the car. I keep telling him that's not true, but he's devastated.'

I think about what it would be like to have him here. His own particular brand of calm. His gentle touch. How much I would prefer it. 'It wasn't his fault,' I say, exhausted.

'I told him you'd say that, but he's in a tangle. You know what he's like at the best of times, and you... you mean a lot to him, Lisa.'

I do know what he's like. Which is to say that he's the kind of bloke who would feel wholly responsible and stay away from me if someone suggested it was in my best interests, even if that someone was Billy. 'I'm just waiting to see Poppy.'

'Where is she?'

'She's...' I struggle to find the words. My best friend on the other end of the phone has unzipped my resolve and all of a sudden, I'm fighting back a tsunami of grief.

'Oh God, Lisa. Do you need me? I can get Paul to stay with Charlie? I'll get a taxi.'

'No, no,' I squeak. 'No, it's okay. I'll be okay.' I massage the frown and fear on my forehead as there's a knock on the door and a nurse comes in. 'Hol, I have to go, someone's here. I'll call you back, okay?'

'Lisa, any time. Day or night, okay? Call me. I'll come in, or Paul can. He can get rid of Billy if you need it.'

'It's okay,' I manage. 'Billy's gone for now. Look, I'll talk to you later. Tell Paul what I said, it's not his fault.' I hang up as the nurse perches on the side of my bed. I shove my phone and the notebook away.

'I'm here to take you to see Poppy, if you're up to it?' she says and something like relief kisses my chest but it's short-lived, her face solemn.

'I'm up to it!'

'And her dad? Is he still here?'

'No,' I say taking a deep, restorative breath and wiping my face. I have to button back up again. Poppy needs me. 'Her dad's gone for now.'

'Right.' The nurse looks around before asking, gently, 'Is everything okay?'

I nod, not prepared to go into the detail. 'So, Poppy.'

It's her turn to take a breath now. 'Okay, Lisa. I need to prepare you for what you will see.' I hold her gaze, jaw tight. 'Your daughter is currently on a ventilator. There are lots of tubes and wires. Some people find that understandably distressing, especially in their children.'

I swallow, my throat feels sore. 'Why a ventilator?'

'As I think your consultant mentioned before, Poppy's body is operating at its lowest state of alertness, it's closed down to give her brain time to recover from the impact. There is swelling that needs to reduce and, until that time, we want to make sure she is safe. The ventilator ensures she is breathing.'

I bite my lip, my eyes sting.

'I know you want to see her, and it might just help her too, we don't know for sure if a coma patient can hear, but we can't be certain that she can't. Your voice might be just what she needs.'

'To wake up?'

'Well, no. Probably not yet. But to help her through, to know she's not alone.' She passes me a tissue and I dab at the tears now coursing down my cheeks. 'Are you ready?'

I wipe my eyes, sit up as tall as I'm able and nod. The nurse brings a wheelchair in, helping me shift across from the bed. I feel stronger than I did when I tried to move earlier, more able to support my own weight, albeit with her help, but in truth, everything hurts, aches; I'm sore.

She wheels me through the darkened corridors, low lights keeping things visible as we move through the hospital. The occasional door to a ward is open but dark, it being well past normal visiting hours. The way is lit by lamps at nurses' stations, low lighting through corridors. We go up in a lift, down another corridor, eventually we reach a lobby; to one side is a ward door painted in bright colours, animals play in trees. On the opposite side, a plain door faces us. The nurse pushes open the plain door and wheels me in. We arrive outside another door. 'Okay?' she asks. 'Are you sure you're ready?'

I nod, take a deep breath and brace myself. Which, as the door opens, I can tell is foolish, optimistic at best. Because nothing can prepare you for the sight of your baby swallowed up by a large bed. The sight of the most important person in your world, tubes coming out of her nose and mouth, wires attached to her fingers, a machine to the side of her squeezing up and down, rhythmically. I close my eyes for a second, the pain in my heart now sharper than anything I felt climbing from bed to wheelchair, more painful than anything I've ever felt before.

The nurse pushes me closer still and all breath leaves me as I reach out to touch Poppy's hand, taking her tiny fingers in mine. They're warm, like they were in the car. I go to speak but a sob escapes before the words. I pause, try to regain the strength she needs from me before managing, 'Hey, baby.' I breathe. 'It's okay, Mummy's here,' I whisper. I take the now disintegrated tissue from my lap and wipe hard at the tears that serve Poppy no purpose. I stroke her hand then wait, eyes fixed on her face, trying to take it all in because I'm so desperate for something in return and I don't want to miss a flicker, a tiny promise that she's still inside this little, sleeping body.

But there's nothing, and I am crushed.

Chapter Thirty-Two

'She was so tiny, Holly,' I say with a sniff, back in my room, the darkness swallowing me whole, as it has for the last few hours since I was told I had to come back. 'I held her hand, I watched her so intently and she didn't move, she didn't flinch, she couldn't hear me.'

'You don't know that, Lisa. She might have been able to hear you.'

'So why didn't she wake up?'

'Because she's not ready? Because she needs time? We all need time sometimes, Lisa.'

It's the middle of the night. Later, three-ish. I've wanted to call Holly since I got back to my room but kept putting it off until it got so bad that I just needed to hear her voice, I need her to reason with me. To hold my hand, if not physically, then metaphorically.

My mind is racing over Billy's arrival, him bringing some supplies, a phone charger, some books to read. I've turned myself inside out with questions about how and when to bring him in to Poppy's life. What if he could help? What if her desire to know more about her dad would give her body and mind the motivation to open her eyes? What if she could hear him? But the questions, and the uncertainty, it all got so bad that I could feel myself trying to climb out of my chest, clutching at the desperation of the situation, and the only person who's ever been able to ground me is Holly. To some, she comes across as brash, outspoken, spiky even. But they don't know her, or they've judged her before taking the time to work out who she is. And she sees it, always. For all the front, she is sensitive. She sees when people judge her, and she retreats. Maybe because we've been mates since we were kids, maybe because she's my opposite in every way, shape and form, or maybe because she's the only person who's ever really known when to bring humour and when to bring peace, I don't know what I'd do without her.

'Lisa, she's in the best place. They will be doing everything they can for her.'

'I know they will. They will. But…' I push my head back into my pillow, pinching at my eyes until they star. 'I just want her to be awake. I want this to be over and for her to be home with me. Tucked up in her bed with Bear-Bear beside her. Me downstairs watching telly and eating a takeaway, wondering what you're doing before reminding myself I don't want to wonder because you'll probably be with Dave and… oh God, I'm so sorry to call you, Holly. It's the middle of the night.'

She covers the phone, I hear the rustle.

'Is he there now? I shouldn't have called.'

'Of course you should have! That's what best mates are for. You can call me at any time. And, yes, he's here. Well, he's just gone downstairs to make us tea, actually. He came over after Charlie had gone to bed. He's being lovely. Has promised to creep out first thing before Charlie wakes up.'

'I don't even know what day it is.'

'It's Saturday night, well, no, Sunday technically.' Her voice is soft and patient. There's no rush to get me off the line, no need to fix me other than to just be present in the moment with me.

'I feel like I've been here for days.'

'You will do.'

'This is the worst twenty-four hours of my life, Holly. I want to go back to before it happened. I want to have stayed at home. What if—'

'Don't!' She cuts me off and I pinch my lips together until they hurt. 'Don't say anything, Lisa. We are not entertaining any idea other than that she is going to be fine, okay?' I nod even though she can't see me. 'Okay?'

'Yes! Yes. Okay.'

'Right. So, put any of those thoughts as far away as you can. Bury them deep. We get what we invite, right? You need to imagine her at home, playing in her room. You need to imagine the sun streaming into your kitchen, the radio's playing and you're singing along. Actually, no, don't sing. We both know that's not your forte.'

I laugh a bit, in spite of my fear. And that's why I needed to call Holly. I can already feel myself climb back inside of me.

'Can you picture it?' she asks, and I close my eyes. The sun is warm on my face, the radio plays something I can't quite imagine but I know it's playing. 'She is upstairs, Charlie's there too. They're making up some game and she is healthy and happy. Can you feel it?'

I breathe for a moment, fear and panic is being replaced with... well, I wouldn't go as far as to say calm, but it's being replaced with not quite as fearful or panicked.

'She is going to come through this, Lisa. She is.'

'What would I do without you, Hol?'

'I don't know. I really am great.'

I let out a small laugh. 'I'm fucking terrified.'

'I know you are. I would be too. But this is not your story, okay? This is a pause, a minor diversion. I know it doesn't feel minor, maybe minor is the wrong choice of word.'

'I know what you mean…' Her phone rustles again and I hear her say thank you. 'You got tea?'

'I have.'

'Nice.'

I look over to the table beside me, reaching for the plastic cup containing oxygenated water. I grimace as I sip, it tastes grey somehow.

'So… Billy then. Did he see her too?'

'No. No, I asked him to leave. And now I'm wondering if I should let him. He's her dad, it might help her.'

'Maybe it's the thing he needed to realise what you and Poppy mean to him?'

'He's had plenty of time to realise that. If I let him in, it's for her, not him.'

'I know… I know. And I'm not saying that you need to have this big reunion or anything, you know my thoughts on that one, I just…' She stops herself, perhaps thinking about what she really means. I imagine her tucked up in her own bed. Leopard-print bedding and dark green walls. 'I suppose it's nice that he was there for you?'

'Maybe.' I'd rather it had been Holly. Or Paul.

'And we can all do stupid things sometimes. We can all own them and make amends. If he has been trying to reconnect, for whatever reason, you need to think about how you feel. And if you want him to see her.'

'What if she's not ready?'

'Lisa, she's…'

Holly stops herself but I know what she's thinking. If Poppy's not ready, it's because she's… asleep. If she's not ready, it's because she doesn't know her dad is in town. But more than any of those things, if Poppy's not ready, it's because I'm not ready. And it's not my right to use that as an excuse to build a barrier.

Later, I pick up my phone to check the battery, plugging it in to the wall. I see a message, from Paul, that I hadn't heard come through.

I can't stop thinking about you, about Poppy. If you need anything, anything at all, please call me. I can come in, or I can stay away, whatever you need. I can have Charlie so Holly can visit, whatever is best. I'm here for you. x

Chapter Thirty-Three

It's Tuesday. My strength is returning and today is the first day I can walk through to Poppy on my own. I smile at the nurse at her desk but she's mid phone call, so waves me through. When I get into Poppy's room, I pause at the door, the sight of her still connected to tubes and wires not yet normal. I guess it couldn't possibly be. They've been checking her daily, pushing pins into her to check auto reflex responses, tissue in her eyes, each test making me wince and recoil and hold my breath in the hope it's the one she responds to.

'Morning, Poppy, it's Mummy.' I drop my handbag on the chair. It hurts to lean over but I do it anyway, kissing her gently on her forehead, then pausing just in case she reacts. My lips just touch, my breath is held, her forehead feels warm, but there's nothing.

I pull the chair closer to her bed. 'They've talked about discharging me today. I won't have to keep leaving you for check-ups or anything, I'll be able to sit here, beside you, for as long as you need me.' I yawn, checking the clock. I've barely slept these last few days and when I do, I get flashbacks, the accident happening all over again in my dreams. Each time the lead-up to it is different, the accident is slightly different too, but each time the outcome is the same for Poppy.

'Knock, knock,' says the nurse, sticking her head around the door. 'You okay?'

I gaze at Poppy. 'I'm okay.'

'The sun is shining, Poppy.' She breezes into the room and opens the blinds a little. A shaft of light hits her bed. 'Some positive news for you this morning, Mummy. Some of this morning's tests have shown us a change in Poppy's auto reflexes.' My heart lifts the most it has for days. 'We're going to start reducing Poppy's sedation this afternoon, see if she responds to breathing on her own, monitor her responses to sound and touch. It's all routine stuff, based on test results and monitoring and it'll give us a sense of how she's doing.'

'What if she doesn't respond?'

'We try again tomorrow.'

I rub my thumb over my hand, fingers clasped in fingers, knuckles white. 'Okay.'

The nurse comes round to my side, there's a parcel beneath her arm. 'I know this is incredibly difficult for you, we are doing everything we can for her, okay?' I nod. 'And look, Poppy, this arrived for you.'

She passes me the parcel. 'When?'

'I'm not sure. It could have been today but sometimes people drop things at reception and it takes a little longer to make its way up to the patients.' I rip it open. 'Oh, how thoughtful.'

I stare at *The Clockwork Dragon*, a book Grandma bought for Poppy years ago, she always loved it. I flick it open to the front page, searching for Grandma's handwriting but there's nothing there. No dedication or year as in her copy at home, and it's too new to be hers anyway. No tell-tale bolognese marks from when she has sat with it at the dinner table.

'Who's it from?' chats the nurse as she routinely checks Poppy's pulse and makes notes on her file.

I shove it back in the wrapping. 'I don't know.'

'Oh, a surprise. Nice.'

'Mmhmm.' I shove it beneath my bag.

The nurse clocks what I've done out of the corner of her eye. 'You could read it to her, you know, if you liked? Sometimes it helps to do that sort of thing. And we never know for certain, but it couldn't harm things for Poppy.'

'I talk to her.'

'Yes, I know. Which is great. I just meant if you were struggling for things to say. I suppose it might be hard after a while, being in here.' I cock my head to one side. 'Finding new things to tell her, when you're here all the time. I imagine it might be hard.'

'Not so far.'

There's a knock on the door and a head pops round. 'Chelle, can you come with me to do obs in bay six, please?'

'Yes of course.' She tidies her side of Poppy's bedding. 'I'll be back in a bit, but shout if you need anything.'

'Okay.'

'They'll be round with tea soon, if you want a cup.'

'Thanks.'

I wait for the door to close, watching Poppy's face. Her eyelashes, long and full. They always have been, since she was a baby. People always commented on her eyelashes and her hair, the rich red curls she got from her dad.

Her dad.

Billy's called several times, somehow managing to resist just turning up again, which I must say I'm grateful for. Paul, on the other hand, hasn't done anything since he messaged. I messaged back, when I had the energy. I told him it wasn't his fault, that he wasn't to feel guilty. I didn't ask him to come in even if, to be honest, I wanted to. But I know I've needed space to try and straighten my thoughts out. Maybe Billy has changed. Maybe this *was* the shock that he needed. I mean, it shouldn't come to this for him to realise what he had, what he walked away from, but if he has, how could I stop Poppy seeing him? How could I even think about pursuing anything with Paul at a time like this? Even though part of me niggles that maybe we're a passing fad. For Billy, that is, not Paul. But how could Billy not be bowled over by the tiny version of us that we created? Is a father's connection less strong than a mother's?

Which leads me to think about Dad. Does he still have no idea what's happened? Or does he know and has just not called? Surely that's not the case. If these gifts are from Dad, surely he hasn't just sent the book instead of actually turning up to see me and Poppy? Maybe he has gone away. But if so, where to? Who with? Why hasn't he tried calling? He doesn't take real holidays, he hides. But if several people have tried to make contact, me included, his house phone just ringing out, his mobile switched off, how could he keep ignoring it? The village is too small for him not to know...

'What do you think, Poppy? Eh? Does Grandad know and he's keeping his distance? How could he keep his distance from you? That's what I'd like to know.'

I glance over at the book. He must know, mustn't he? Or the gifts aren't from him after all?

Chapter Thirty-Four

I'm sat with Poppy, her hand in mine, the picture book to my right on the bed. My head is noisy with confusion. Dad's the only person I've not out-and-out asked about the gifts, but why would he send them? Especially now, if he knew we were in here, why hasn't he just come? He's always been so protective of me, overly so, he'd be here, I'm sure of it. Towering over the nurses to make sure I had all that he thought I needed, irrespective of what the nurses thought.

But as blood family goes, we're all each other have: me, Dad and Poppy. Are we so broken that he can't admit he's the one to be sending the gifts? Are we so broken that I end up in hospital and this is the best he can do? Is it my fault? Have I pushed so hard to distance myself that I've silenced his feelings, and this is the only way he's known how to convey them? If I look back, did he ever talk about how he felt, and I've just forgotten? Or is this new? Since Grandma died? Was that a catalyst for change in him?

'Eeh, Poppy. If only I knew.'

I drop back into my chair, uncertain how I feel about any of it. Once upon a time, when I was small, Dad would have been the first person I ran to if I felt worried or afraid. As a kid if I fell, or fell out with a friend, he was always there, always on hand. Even when I didn't think he'd be nearby, he always suddenly appeared. When I was young, that was reassuring, perhaps more so because of not having a mum around; I never felt alone. Then as I got older, sometimes, I *wanted* to feel alone. I wanted space. I wanted to navigate the murky waters of being thirteen, fourteen, Christ – even fifteen, and fifteen was the murkiest of them all – but I wanted to navigate them alone, or at the very least with friends. It was never about not wanting to talk to him about periods or sex, boyfriends or drinking, not as such, it was just… I needed to be able to say my piece and not feel judged.

And now we're so far apart, that I can't even reach out to him when, perhaps, I've fallen the hardest, need him the most. And if the gifts are from him, we're so far apart, that he can't even be there for me.

Putting him at arm's length didn't happen overnight and I'm not even sure it happened consciously. But it happened, and as I've got older, the lines have forged deeper. When he came to 'rescue' me, when Billy left and I was alone in a strange city with a tiny baby, I wanted him at arm's length. I hadn't really wanted to leave, but I couldn't see how I could make it work to stay. And as we made the five-hour drive back to Lincolnshire, in almost total silence save for BBC Radio 4 and Poppy's occasional grumblings for food or a nappy change, I felt further and further away from him, the closer we got to home.

I remember when he bought Poppy and me the cottage to move into, his own mortgage had been small, paid off with some inheritance from when Grandad died. He told me he could afford it, that it was no different to when he had his own mortgage to pay, that he wanted us to have somewhere of our own, so I didn't have to worry about a landlord. Even when I tried to resist it, he told me it was an investment. Something that might one day give him a return on a collection of bonds and savings he had squirrelled away. People, old friends, peers, people I vaguely knew in the village who felt they were entitled to an opinion, they were so envious, told me how lucky I was, how great Dad was. And I admit, walking through the front door, closing it behind Poppy and me, knowing it was effectively ours for as long as we wanted it, I did feel safe. It has been my sanctuary, but it felt like it always came with a caveat. *You live there, behave as I expect, I'll pay the bills then I know how much electricity you're using, I'll know where you are at all times.* I guess ultimately, something about it felt more manipulative than generous.

Holly was the only one that understood, she couldn't believe he'd never taken me to view it first. That he'd not so much as asked where I might want to live, if he really wanted to buy me somewhere. 'Why does everything have to be on his terms?' she'd said, outraged.

Eventually, it felt like the only thing connecting Dad and me was Grandma. For her sake, I would talk to him when we were both round her house. I would take his calls, in case she was ill. Now she's gone and I don't know where we stand, or how we fit. Then something like this happens and it makes you wonder if the need for independence has done more harm than good. Maybe it's not his fault that he's never been one to talk. He's a product of his time, his own parents weren't big talkers. I loved Grandma, but did I always know how she felt? Definitely not. There were often things left unsaid and perhaps that was for the good, perhaps it was their own family upbringing, a Victorian era, inherited from her own parents, not quite shaken off. It doesn't make Dad a bad person any more, perhaps, than I am for pushing him away. We all do what we need, when we need it. I just can't work out if I feel the need to close my circle because of what's happened or open it up wider. If they are from him, I suppose Dad's trying. And it would make sense. After all, paying for things has usually been his way to fix a problem. 'Things' never quite being what I really needed.

But if it's all he's able to do, it's better than nothing, right? What's Billy done for Poppy? Left her and me to fend for ourselves until now. He never even managed 'things'.

'Men, eh?' I say to Poppy. The machine that breathes for her pushes up and down, the noise eating away at me. My sweeping generalisation about the opposite sex sticks in my throat. I've never been one for gender stereotypes. They're not all the same. Paul isn't like any man I've known before... an ache in my heart creeps in. The strength and focus I've been finding, for Poppy's sake, falters, and the only person I want to reach out to is Paul.

Chapter Thirty-Five

They said the airbag burns would subside, and now it's Friday, they no longer sting. Getting dressed is easier. The bruising is really coming out on my ribs too. Arnica, that's what Grandma would have prescribed. I daren't ask for it in hospital though. Still, they're pretty shades of purples, pinks, greens and blues. I suspect they'll take on a yellow hue soon and that's never really been my colour.

Paul's phone barely rang when I called it, his voice crept into my heart and immediately made me feel like I could do this, I could be okay, for me and for Poppy, if he was beside me. Even for just a few minutes. I could have asked Holly to bring the clothes in, she was fetching them for me, but I felt like he needed to see me to know I'm okay, and if I'm honest, I needed to see him.

'Can I come in?'

I spin around to see him and my legs feel weak, as if I don't need to stand up on my own now that he's here. 'Paul!' He pushes the door open, tentative. 'It's so nice to see you…'

'And you.' He looks me over, his eyes falling to what's left of the marks on my hands. I study them too, self-conscious. 'I'm so sorry, Lisa.'

'Paul, please—'

'I just… I feel so responsible.' He reaches for my hands, running his thumb over the marks. 'If it wasn't for me…'

'Please, don't. You had no idea this would happen.'

'I saw it, I watched it all, it was like a nightmare.' He drops a bag down to the floor. 'Charlie was in the car with me, I'd just pointed your car out to him. He screamed out when he saw what had happened. I tried to get to you, but there were people trying to keep the situation calm, they wouldn't let me close and Charlie was sobbing, just…' He seems to remember the moment, his own experience of it, the sights and sounds. 'I was so torn… it was… well, sorry, I'm not here to tell you how awful it was for me. That's not… that's not it.'

'It's okay.'

'And then Billy, he was walking past Holly's when I got back. I was so distressed, I just told him everything.'

'It's fine, honestly.'

'I never for a second thought he'd force his way in like that. Holly said he'd told them he was Poppy's dad? I'm so sorry!'

'It's okay. Honestly.' I squeeze his hand, and when he finally allows himself to catch my eye, I see how frightened he's been. 'Come here.' I pull him into me and we hold one another, tightly. It's not the first time we've been this close, a hug at the start or end of a night out was standard, but this time it's different. It's not just the tops of our bodies, connected, chest and shoulders to hug, it's our whole bodies, tight as he holds onto me like he needs me to hold him up and I'm holding him the same way. When we finally pull apart, he moves hair from my face, smiles in a kind of resolute way, then steps back.

'Is this everything?' He picks up the bag the nurses gave me for my few bits I need to take away.

'Yeah. Haven't needed much, though I might do now. Can't stay in these clothes forever.' I pick at the jumper I was wearing in the accident.

The coat that I'm sure I bled onto. The jeans that now feel baggy and constricting in equal measure.

'Holly sent you some bits, it's all in here.' He points to the bag he'd dropped on the floor when we hugged. 'God knows what's in it.'

'Probably a lot of leopard print.'

'I think she got it from your house.'

'Phew. I'm not sure I'm quite ready for her style.' He smiles. 'I'll change later, I just want to get to Pops now.'

He jumps as if just remembering the fact. 'Of course, do you need anything else? I can go and get stuff for you?'

'No, no, it's fine.'

'Right. Okay.' He looks at the door. 'I'd better go then…'

'You could walk me up to Poppy?'

He grabs the bag he brought in for me. 'Of course, no problem.'

I pass through the open door as he stands, wedging it with his foot. I wait for him as he closes it. We walk close enough to be touching, but kind of unofficially, our arms lightly brushing. He reaches for the lift button, his eyes focused on the numbers up above us, watching intently as the lift descends to our floor. I want to ask him to stay. The lift doors open, we step aside for a porter pushing a man in a hospital bed. I want to ask Paul to stand beside me for this whole thing, until Poppy wakes up, just beside me, so I know I'm not alone. The doors close. It's my turn to fix my eyes on the numbers lighting up each floor now. I feel him watching me out of the corner of his eye. I feel his body lean, just slightly in my direction. Someone else gets in the lift and we have to shuffle to the back. We share a smile.

When we approach the door to Paediatrics ICU I stop, staring out of the window into a garden below, before turning to face him.

He passes me my bags. 'Anything you need, just call me, okay?'

'Okay.'

'Literally anything. Any time.'

'Okay.'

'And let me know how she is.'

'I will.'

We hover, opposite one another. Clearly, neither of us are certain what to do. It's not the kind of courtship you dream of and yet, maybe, here we are. He steps towards me, plants the gentlest kiss on my cheek, his hand briefly in mine, then he waits for me to go through the ICU Paediatrics door. And somehow, as I allow it to close softly behind me, I don't need to look back to know he'll be watching me walk down the corridor with concern in his eyes. But it's enough to make me feel like I'm not alone. Like I can do this. Like I am everything I need to be for Poppy. And I've always known that, in my heart, I've known I can be everything she needs me to be if I just believe it, but I suppose he's just reminded me, perhaps when I needed it most.

Chapter Thirty-Six

Poppy's condition hasn't changed since I left her last night. I say hello, kiss her, pause in case she senses I'm there and wakes up, then I drop into my chair more quickly than normal, the ache of her lack of response in stark contrast to the love and support I was feeling moments before.

I close my eyes, head back, then reach for the notebook inside my bag. Whoever sent me this blessed notebook, if they want to help, I'll bloody well let them.

I start making a list of the pros and cons of calling Dad again, or trying at least, seeing as he hasn't tried calling me. Surely, he would have, had he known? Even if he didn't pick up to anyone ringing him, he'd have called me? I consider another list for having Billy here for Poppy, the possibility that he might be good for her, the chances of him taking over, bombastic in good intention that railroads my gentler approach.

'What do you think, Poppy?' The list of pros outweighs the list of cons when it comes to Dad. I dig out my phone and press to call him, thinking about what message I'll leave.

'Lisa? Oh, Lisa!' He's breathless. He sounds old. I haven't really thought about it before, he's sixty-six, that's not that old, is it? 'Are you okay? Oh my God, are you okay?'

'Yes, yes, I'm okay.'

'I've been away. I had no idea. Iris just came past. I was about to come over to the hospital. How did it happen? This is why I never wanted you to drive that car! It's a death trap. I always said it.' His energy rushes through the phone and silences me from defending my right to drive, or my right to own the car that I bought with the only savings I had left from when I worked in the library. Bought because I needed the independence. 'How's Poppy? Is she awake yet? What are they doing for her?'

'She's...' I look over to her, the machine in the corner keeping her alive. 'She's stable.' The word the nurses have said each time I've asked.

'I shouldn't have gone away. I should have stayed here!'

'You couldn't have known what might happen,' I say, irritated by how quickly I find myself trying to appease him. And why would he have stuck around, just in case? The only time we've spoken in recent months has been to talk about Grandma. We've not spent any time together.

'What happened?'

'We were hit from behind into the path of another vehicle.'

'Jesus, Lisa.' His voice shakes, there's a tone to it that I've not heard before. 'I was so worried, I didn't know if you... well, you could have...' But he doesn't finish the sentence that I've thought myself a million times: we could have died. He takes a breath, pausing, before saying, 'I'm so glad you're alive.' And I bite my bottom lip because he sounds like he means it and I feel, without question, how much he loves me and even though part of me doesn't know what to do with that, I also know that it is the same as the love I have for Poppy, a love I don't know that I've ever really understood him to feel. Or perhaps I underestimated it? Him? Poppy's monitor breathes in and out and I scrunch my eyes up tight. 'Do you need anything? Can I bring you anything? I can be there in half an hour,' he says.

'No. No. I'm… it's okay.'

'I can come over. I can get whatever you need. Is she in a private room or a ward? I can talk to George Green and get her moved.' Doctor Green was his go-to on anything medical, a GP in the local surgery, his long-time friend. The same doctor he took me to every time I got ill as a kid, the same doctor he made me see when I was feeling low, when I hit eighteen, the same doctor he made me see when I first got pregnant even though I'd booked to see someone else. I had to politely ask Doctor Green if he minded my changing to a female doctor. He'd been reluctant at first, but presumably knew he couldn't ignore my request. Dad hadn't liked it, said it was far better to see someone we knew and trusted. 'He probably knows people at the hospital. I can get him to help if you need it.'

I close my eyes. I can hear him pacing around and wonder where he might be: the lounge, looking out over the back garden by the radiator, or the drive by the bay? The kitchen, pacing around the dining table? His office?

'She's in a room just off the main ward, Dad. It's just her. She has her own nurse to keep an eye and monitor everything. They come in regularly. It's fine.'

'Okay.' He lets out a heavy breath and we fall silent. I hear the squeak of his office chair as he presumably sits in it and now, I can exactly picture him, phone to his ear, spare hand cradling his head, as I've seen him on occasions before, when he didn't know I was watching.

'Could I come over to see you both?' he asks, his voice more uncertain than it was when he was offering to get Doctor Green to fix everything. A side of him I rarely see. 'I feel like I need to see your face, look into your eyes to know you're okay… well, as okay as you can be with Poppy…'

I pinch the bridge of my nose. 'They don't really like visitors on ICU, Dad. And I don't really want to leave her side. They're going to start some tests this afternoon to try and get her to respond.'

'Perhaps you should have a break, before then, then? Get some fresh air even. Have you been out since you arrived? I could take you for coffee, get you something to eat. I could drive you to the Costa nearby. Or maybe I could run you home, you can have a shower, pick up some fresh clothes, then I'll bring you straight back.'

My heart lurches at the idea of leaving Poppy. 'I have clothes. Paul brought me some.' My belly rumbles for the first time in days, probably at the mention of food and coffee. 'She might wake up.'

'You said they were doing tests this afternoon? They mustn't think she's likely to wake up on her own just yet. And you won't be gone for long? If that's all you do, just home and back, I'll bring you takeaway coffee and lunch, we can just drive to yours. You can freshen up then I'll take you straight back.'

I think about Poppy's bedroom full of toys, things that might help. She hasn't been away from Bear-Bear since the day she was born, her tiny, now grotty-pink, slightly limp bear, its ribbon round its neck all crumpled from too much cuddling… if it's even possible to cuddle a bear too much. She loves that bear. Its smell. The feel of its worn feet on her cheek as she watches TV, the touch of its ears on her chin as she falls to sleep. How could I have not thought about him before now? He might help. 'Okay. Okay, if you can come now, maybe I could pop home. Just quickly though, please, I don't want to be away from her for too long.'

'I'm on my way.' I hear the creak of the chair again as he jumps up. I hear the scrape of car keys from his desk and his footsteps on the staircase. 'I'll be twenty minutes. Twenty-five, actually, give me time to get you lunch.'

'I don't need anything.'

'You need to eat, Lisa. It's important. You have to keep your strength up for Poppy, if not for you. That's what parents do…' His words wobble, and I imagine him biting back some emotion he daren't express. Just as he always has. There was something in his tone this whole conversation, yes, there was judgement, but it was different. Yes, there was solutions to problems I wasn't giving him, but they were different too. 'I'll text you when I get to the pick-up point, okay?'

'Okay.'

He sounds like a father I don't recognise, maybe even a father I've long wished for. One that is there for me, one that sees what I need before I've seen it myself. One who can nurture and provide without question, without judgement, taking over when I need guidance, but not squashing my choice. One that helps me to breathe, even when it feels impossible. Has he always been there, and I've been too self-centred to see it? Or has something given rise to a change?

Chapter Thirty-Seven

I climb in the passenger seat of Dad's car. I've not seen him since the funeral, neither of us lean to kiss or hug the other. He's different, but the same somehow.

'Any news on Poppy?'

'Not yet.'

'You look tired,' he says as I buckle up.

'I am.'

'Do they have a bed for you?'

'Well, until this morning, I had my own bed on a different ward. I usually came back to try and sleep but couldn't much. The first two days I could barely move on my own, they kept me in for observation, I think maybe because Poppy was in too. Everything hurts but I'm okay… it's just hard to sleep…'

'Right. Of course.' He stares at me for a moment. It feels awkward. Eventually, he starts the engine, nods, and fixes his eyes on the road up ahead. We're queuing for the lights, the hospital just behind us. I feel sick at leaving Poppy behind and my eyes sting. I shouldn't have left her, I should still be there. Everything about this is wrong. And the car, the car feels too small, I feel vulnerable. Other cars settle beside us and behind, queuing. I lean away, closer into the middle of the car, which is closer to Dad, I press myself into the car seat, hyper aware. My heart races.

'What time do you want to be back for?'

Now! I want to shout. 'If we can be back by two at the latest, please.' I'm watching the hospital disappear from view in the wing mirror, flinching as a cyclist undercuts us.

'She'll be okay, for an hour or so,' Dad says, nodding to the direction of my gaze. 'Remember what your grandma always said, if *you're* not okay, she won't be. And you are not okay.'

I bite down on my bottom lip to try and stop my chin from wobbling, the rise of emotion and fear and guilt suffocates.

'There's a cheese sandwich in the bag there, and some crisps. I didn't know what flavour so bought a few.'

'Thanks.'

'You need to eat, Lisa.'

His tone is back to normal, dictatorial. The tone you don't ignore, and the teenager in me wants to rebel but the mother in me knows he's right. I swallow a sigh, reaching for the bag of food, pulling out the Tupperware box that always contained my school pack-up. Nostalgia overwhelms me for a moment, my emotions raw. Opening the box, I find sandwiches carefully made, cut just so, only a scraping of butter because it's bad for me, a layer of salad because it's good. Home brand crisps that don't really taste of anything, yet nobody here to swap them and my Breakaway bar with in favour of a Monster Munch or Quaver.

'Iris said she'd been feeding Frank for you.'

'Yes. Holly did it the first day, but Iris offered to take over. I think it's given her something to focus on. She goes in and sits with him for a bit, he seems fine. Sleeps most of the day, anyway.'

We pull up onto the drive, noticeably empty with a lack of my car.

'Will they send you a courtesy vehicle?'

'I don't know. I've not really got that far. I just know that my car was a write-off.'

'I'm not surprised. You could have written it off with a can opener.' I stare at him. 'You could do with something newer, safer, Lisa. I always said that when you bought it. I don't know why you didn't just let me buy you a car, like I said I would. Something more robust.'

'I don't need you to buy me a car, Dad.'

'If it means you and Poppy are safe, I don't know why you wouldn't let me.' His eyebrows are raised, as if he perhaps thinks I'm being reckless. 'One of the guys down the tennis club owns the Volkswagen dealership in Lincoln. He'd do me a good deal.'

'I liked my Fiesta.'

'It was fifteen years old.'

'It was ours: mine and Poppy's.'

Dad turns the engine off on his car. He looks out of the windscreen at the red-bricked wall that separates my drive from the field behind my house. I finish my sandwich, not wanting to get out of the car because I don't want to go into the house. I'd been in it alone when she started nursery, before I got the job at the school, so it's not like it's never happened. But that was because she was safe, she was playing, having fun, making friends. Not because she was asleep, being made to breathe by machines, watched over by nurses.

'I need to go back!'

'Lisa, just shower. Get changed. Pick out some new clothes, for you and for Poppy.'

'This was a mistake, I shouldn't have let you bring me here. Holly sent me clothes, I have all I need. Poppy doesn't need clothes!'

'Lisa!' His tone is sharp, authoritative. It makes me feel eleven. 'She's going to be okay.'

'You can't say that! We don't know!'

He turns to face me. 'She needs you to hold it together, she needs you to be strong. Not…'

'Not what?'

'I'm here now. I'm back. Come on, the sooner you're in the house, the sooner I can get you back to the hospital. Okay?' I don't move. 'Okay?'

Resolve drains away as quickly as it arrived, my mood lurching from strong to weak, to needy to needing nobody except myself and my girl. This shift brings sudden exhaustion; at the situation, or at him, I'm not sure. He comes round to open my door and I heave myself out. He faffs with his car whilst I walk round to the front door, digging around in my bag for my keys. And on the doorstep, wrapped around its base in brown paper with a purple bow, is a lavender plant. I'm stock still staring at it. 'Is this from you?'

'What?' asks Dad, locking his car, the alarm bipping on.

I pick the plant up. 'This!' I shove it toward him. 'Is this from *you*?'

'Oh!' He shifts from one foot to another.

'And everything else! It is, isn't it!' I lurch again, anger this time. 'It's from you? The picture book, the notebook, the tickets, even!' I shake my head in disbelief. 'And if you sent all these things, that means you knew! About the accident, about Poppy! You knew and you couldn't bring yourself to call me? I just… I can't even…'

Dad looks stunned by my outburst, my heart is racing, frustration coursing through my veins.

'Why? Why would you send it all to me? Why can't you just talk to me? I've been in hospital, Dad. Desperate for Poppy. Terrified. I had to do it alone, the one time I probably really needed you and you couldn't find a way.'

'I wasn't here, Lisa!'

'So, what? It wasn't all from you...?'

He scratches his head, he looks around to see who might be about, always keen to keep up a pretence of everything's fine, nothing to see. 'Yes.' He sighs, heavily. 'Yes, they're from me.'

I stand back, stunned.

Chapter Thirty-Eight

In seconds, my physical exhaustion has turned to the emotional kind. I'm so tired of his inability to just open up, say what he thinks, own his thoughts and feelings. 'Why, Dad? Why does everything have to be cloak-and-dagger or secrets all the time? Whenever we've been detached in any way, separated for any time, it's always been secrets or manipulation. I should have known all along that these gifts would be your way of getting to me even when I was keeping my distance.'

'Lisa…'

'Was it because I'd closed off? Was it the job? You hated that I'd taken that job. I know you tried to get them to change their minds. The head told me. I couldn't believe it, I was so embarrassed. And what was it you said? I needed to be around for Poppy, as if by me demonstrating being an independent woman, a mother who could care for her by myself, earning my money, on my terms, was not a good enough example to give? What better example could there be? Should she really think I need to be kept by a man? Is that what you want my daughter to learn? That her only place of value is in the home?'

I run out of steam, my outburst as much a surprise to me as it must be to him, judging by the look on his face.

'Let's go inside.' He ushers me into the house, checking over his shoulder again.

'I feel like you've never understood, Dad. You've never known what I needed because you've never listened. You've always just assumed that you knew best.' I sling my bag on the floor, the last fumes of energy ebbing away with the sudden voicing of things I've never said before. 'It's all I've ever wanted. To be heard.' I close my eyes. 'For you to listen to what I'm saying. If you could just realise that all I want is to *breathe*.'

'I understand. But what if that space might bring you harm? I've tried to do my best.'

'Did you? With me? Were you mollycoddled when you were first a parent? That can't work for me, I *need* space, I need to be me. To learn to be a single mum, to learn to be strong for her, to stand on my own two feet.'

An image of her in the bed, all trussed up in wires and tubes flashes into my mind, the plant is suddenly leaden in my arms. My heart races, tears stream. I drop down, steadying myself with the plant. 'She *has* to live. She has to learn to breathe on her own, she has to be okay to run and play and tell me what needs doing round the house. She has to be okay.'

Dad comes closer, standing right beside me, though not crouching down. Not touching me. Grandma would have. She was buttoned up, a tough nut to crack, but when I needed it most, she cracked. She'd have wrapped her arms around me, she'd have held me until I was ready to stand. But Dad? He just waits. Hovering. Close enough to overbear, not close enough for me to feel held up.

Eventually I manage a quiet, but certain, 'Why?'

He swallows. He looks down the hallway. He studies the lavender. A car goes past then the road falls silent again. Through smoky glazing to the side of my door, I see plants in the garden sway gently in the breeze.

Eventually he says, 'I was trying to reach out. I just didn't know how. You talk about feeling claustrophobic, I did too.'

I run my hands through the lavender releasing its scent, breathing it in.

'I've never got it right with you, Lisa. I know that. I've never known what to do but I have tried your whole life to protect you.'

He goes through to the lounge, sitting down by the table for two where Poppy and I eat each day. I remember having left her breakfast pots as we were running late. Somebody has cleaned them away, somebody has cleaned everything. The cushions on the sofa are neatly plumped, the post isn't in a pile on the mat but stacked carefully on the table beside the remote control for the TV and a handbook about the heating. It feels cold in here, un-lived in.

'You've always been so independent, Lisa. Fiercely so. You'd leap on up ahead as a toddler, whenever we went anywhere, you'd run off. Not away from me as such, just off. I'd have to jog to keep up with you. At school, you walked to your own beat. You didn't get drawn in to what everyone else was doing. I was always hugely proud of you for that, you reminded me so much—' He stops himself, as he always has when he's suggested I might be like my mother. 'It's difficult to support someone who's never wanted to be supported.'

His description of me sounds like Poppy too, wildly living her own life on her own terms, yet I don't feel like she does this without me. I just feel as if I have to work harder to be the support she needs. That's parenting, isn't it? Working out how to be the best version of you that they need?

'Your grandfather always said that I should have been stricter with you, been more specific about how you should be, but your grandma always encouraged you. I was conflicted, I never wanted to raise you alone and yet sometimes, raising you with them being so close, they're opinion rarely withheld, it was hard.'

I wonder if he sees how much of this I recognise for myself. His opinion rarely withheld.

'And I felt such guilt,' he says, his voice quieter. 'That your mother and I weren't married, that she was so young…' He rarely mentions this. The age gap, ten years between them. He rarely mentions her at all. 'You are a mystery to me, Lisa. I have never known how to do right by you and though I've always tried my best, I'm aware it's rarely been good enough.'

I lean against the lounge door, his last words picking at my conscience.

'My world has been turned upside down, recently.'

I catch sight of a photo of Grandma on the wall. His loss suddenly brought into focus for me. I've never lost a mother, I never had one to lose, but Dad… Am I the reason it hasn't been easy? Have I always pushed him away or was that only as I got older, teen years, early twenties? Did it then become habit? Something that's become so deep-rooted I can't even see it differently now? Am I too much for him? I think, if I was honest with myself, that's what I always felt. Too much. Too loud. Too many opinions. Noisy, wearing. A reminder of what he lost.

He lets out a sigh. 'I'm sorry… I just… I've not known what to do.'

'Were you at home?' He looks up sharply at my words. 'When people were trying to tell you what happened. When you sent the book, were you at home, or did you really go away? And if so, where to?'

He looks to his feet. 'I just… I had to… I just needed to get away…'

Chapter Thirty-Nine

A key in the front door makes us both jump, Frank skitters in, eventually followed by Iris. 'Frank, oh, Frank, I totally forgot about you. How did I not notice you weren't even here?'

He sniffs around me, trying to jump up in excitement but his doddery old legs don't quite let him. I crouch down and nuzzle into him.

'Ahhh, he's pleased to see you,' says Iris, hanging his lead over the bannister.

'Thank you so much for walking him, Iris.' I stand up, Frank now cumbersome and fussy in my arms.

She gives him a scratch behind the ears. 'Oh, it's no bother at all. How's Poppy?'

'She's… well, she's stable,' I recite.

'Oh, love, I can't imagine how you must feel, it's such a worry.'

'They're going to try and reduce her medication later this afternoon, see if she responds.'

'Such a wee little thing to have to go through this, she is.' I nod, biting down hard on my lip. 'I didn't expect to see you,' she adds.

'No, I just popped back to pick up a few things for Poppy.'

'Right, of course.' She notices the lavender on the bottom step of the staircase. 'Oh, that's pretty.' She runs her hands over it, smelling them afterwards. 'I do love lavender, it's very healing.'

'I bought it for her,' says Dad, appearing into Iris's view.

'Oh! Hello. I didn't realise you were here too.'

'I picked Lisa up from the hospital. I'll drop her back over when she's got what she needs. It's to stimulate Poppy's senses. The lavender. You should talk to them, read even, touch and maybe offer them things to smell.'

'Right. Of course. Very good. Thoughtful.'

There's an awkward pause. Any other time I'd have the energy to fix it. Or Poppy would have. It's not my job right now, though.

'Well, I should probably leave you to it. Oh, before I go,' Iris says, hand on the door handle, 'I can't get the heating to work. I know it's only the end of September, but the temperature took a dip and I just couldn't help thinking Frank might get cold. I did wonder about taking him back to my house, but he doesn't seem too unhappy here and I know it's only next door, but he has had to move recently so I didn't want to upset him.'

'Oh, thank you, Iris. I appreciate that. I'll take a look at it, no problem.'

'Keep me posted on Poppy, won't you? I'll keep on with Frank until you're back. It's done me the world of good getting out the house and it's like I can chat to your grandma whilst I'm with him. I tidied up a bit for you too, I hope that was okay. Just wanted to make myself useful whilst I was here with him.'

'Thank you! Thank you so much. You didn't have to.'

'I'm happy to be able to help.'

'Thank you!'

I drop Frank down, closing the door behind her. He wanders into the lounge, awkwardly jumping up on the sofa to nestle in some cushions with a heavy sigh.

'You get what you need from Poppy's room, I'll take a look at the heating,' says Dad, our previous conversation now apparently closed.

Wherever he was, he wasn't here. He knew… he sent the book… why didn't he come back early? Something doesn't add up and yet I nod, not sure what else to say or do.

At the top of the landing, I pause outside Poppy's bedroom, suddenly overwhelmed. In the bathroom, her towel is stuffed behind the radiator as she would have left it last Saturday. Her toothbrush is beside mine in the cup and the sticker on the mirror that she put up there when she thought I wasn't looking. On the little radiator on the landing there are a couple of her T-shirts. I stare at them, I've so often thought she's turning into my big girl but seeing them there like that, she's still so tiny.

Pushing open her bedroom door, I'm greeted with the smell of her. My little girl. And that's when it really hits me, exactly what's happened. I go from detached from reality to drowning in it, barely able to breathe, lungs tight, no room for air. Tears stream down my face and my heart hurts so hard I want to rip it out of my chest and throw it away from me. I pull at my T-shirt, my legs weak, everything closing in. Falling onto her bed, I pull her duvet up around me, breathing the memory of her in. The sleepy look on her face when I woke her Saturday morning before her eyes widened when she remembered what we were doing. How she threw the covers back and leapt out of bed, wrapping her little arms around me and squeezing me so tightly she nearly knocked me off my feet. I push my face into her pillow, trying to drown out the sound of pain that I feel, curled up in a ball, Bear-Bear pulled close into my chest.

She should be here.

She should be playing, laughing, reading, writing, tickling Frank under the chin, or building a den for her and all of her teddies. She should be running up and down the stairs to get toys she wants to play with, or to fetch a change of clothes because whatever she had on this morning just couldn't possibly do for this afternoon too. She should be brushing her dolls' hair or having races with her superheroes. She should be poring over her books, feet tucked into her cushions as she flicks through the pictures and sounds out the words she knows.

I feel a warm hand on my back. It doesn't move. The heat from it seeps into my back and through to my chest, my heart. It doesn't take away the pain but maybe it dilutes it. As does the weight of the person who sits on the bed beside me, saying nothing, just being. No judgement, no suffocation, just patience. Despite the anger I've just shown him, the despair, he's here. And that's when I wonder if I've misjudged all Dad has done over the years. Perhaps it's not that he hasn't wanted to be affectionate, or hasn't been able to be there for me. Perhaps it's just that his way was too much, it crushed me. Perhaps he tried quiet and steady, and I rejected it. Perhaps he then pushed and pushed to make me hear? But, in fact, all it did was crush me. And perhaps in this instance, he doesn't have to push so hard, because quiet is what I need.

'I can smell the rubber and fuel. The wet earth from the ground around where we came to a standstill. I can hear the voices and when I close my eyes, I can see her. What if she wakes up and she can hear, smell and see it all too?'

'She won't.'

'How do you know? How can any of us know.'

'Memories fade.' He looks to his feet. 'Especially in young people.'

'But—'

'I promise you, she won't remember it,' he says, firmly. 'She won't remember,' he says again, but more gently this time, as if perhaps for the first time, he's caught himself.

'What am I going to do, Dad?' I turn my face just enough to see him.

'You're going to do what you have to do because she is your child.'

'But what? What does that mean?'

I shift and he takes his hand back. 'You are going to be patient and calm. You are going to be there, beside her bed. You are going to talk to her, read to her, write a story that she can hear, let her smell the lavender, let her know you're there so that when she's ready, she will wake up and know you've been there all along. Just waiting until she needs you.'

I shift my legs round, planting my feet on the floor beside him. We're no longer touching.

'Do you need anything other than her bear?' he asks.

I shake my head.

'Come on then, let me get you back to her.'

He stands. He doesn't hold a hand out to me. But he waits until I'm standing too. And then he leads the way, back down the stairs, waiting by the front door.

'I've had a look at the heating. I can't get it to work so I'll call someone for you, get them to come take a look.' I nod, holding Bear-Bear close into me. 'Have you a key I can take, so I can let them in?'

Reluctantly at first, but knowing I need to make some changes, I pull one out of the small cupboard by the door, handing it to him. The first time he's ever had free access to our home.

'And here, I cut off some of the flowers as I didn't think the hospital would want you taking the whole plant in, but maybe this will be enough?' He hands me a few stems of the lavender wrapped in dampened kitchen roll. 'Come on, love. Let's get you back to your little girl.'

Chapter Forty

'Shall I stay?' Dad asks as we pull up to the drop-off zone. 'I can park up. Wait downstairs.'

'No, it's fine. You go home.'

'But... this afternoon... it's important.'

'It is. But I'll be with her. I won't leave her side, especially not whilst they're doing the tests.'

'Right. Of course not.' He looks down, scratching at a mark on his neatly pressed trousers.

'I'll call you, later. Let you know how it goes.'

Unspoken words hang between us. Perhaps it's harder than I imagine, having to watch me go through this when I clearly don't want him too close. If it was Poppy pushing me away, how would I feel?

'Take this with you.' He reaches into the back of the car for another carrier bag. 'It's just a few bits, snacks to keep you going.'

'I can eat in the hospital.'

'Yes, but you might not like what's available. Or you might get hungry when there's nothing about and not want to leave her side. I just thought... I just want to make things as easy as possible for you.'

I grab hold of that and my other bag, tucking Bear-Bear safely under my arm. The concrete hospital building feels ominous, bigger than normal, it looms over me.

'Go on. She needs you,' he says, perhaps picking up on my mood.

I nod, climb out of the car, force a half-smile, and leave him waiting, I guess, until I'm out of sight.

'The consultant will be coming in around three o'clock,' says the duty nurse as I make my way onto the ward.

'Great, thank you.'

'Have they told you what they'll do?' she asks, stepping out from behind her desk.

I check Poppy through the door window, my heart drops to see nothing has changed. 'No. Not really. Just that they were going to run some tests. Reduce her medication?'

'Yes. They'll reduce her medication whilst monitoring her heart rate; this is to see if she can stabilise her own markers without the additional support. They'll do some of those other tests you've seen already.' I shudder at the idea, flinching myself when they press her skin with a needle, or the tissue into her eyes. 'She's been for a scan whilst you were out.'

'What? When? Nobody told me that was happening!'

'It's fine.' The nurse steps towards me, cupping my elbow briefly. 'You couldn't have done anything, they just want to get the latest picture of her brain to see how the swelling looks, get a sense of how quickly it's reducing.'

'Right.'

'Go in, sit with her. Talk to her, you know?'

'I will. I do.'

The nurse smiles then goes back to her desk, immediately focusing back on her paperwork. I steel myself before pushing open Poppy's door. 'Hey, baby, I'm back. Did you miss me?' I kiss her forehead again, this time pushing my hand into hers. It's clammy and unresponsive. It hurts. 'I brought Bear-Bear. Thought you might be missing him.' I rub the side of her face with his paw, her nose with his ears. I hold him beneath her nose for just a second in case she can smell him. When she doesn't respond, I tuck him into the crook of her arm.

'Grandad took me home so I could fetch him for you. I thought it might be nicer for you to sleep with him.' My vision blurs as I stare at her, the reality of what is happening still so overwhelming. 'The nurse says they're going to do some tests later. See if we can't get you to breathe on your own maybe, or open your eyes.'

I reach out to her tiny arm, so fragile in my hands. 'And if you can hear me, I want you to try as hard as you possibly can to do anything the doctor asks of you, okay? You try really, really hard to breathe on your own, or open your eyes maybe. Even for just a second. Anything to let us know that you're still in there, that you can hear me.'

I look around the room, cutting off my line of thought before I break down beside her. Then I remember the lavender stem. 'Hey, here, Grandad bought you a plant. It's a lavender. We both love lavender, don't we? Do you remember the big lavender bush in Grandma Elsie's garden?' I look over my shoulder in the direction of the door, keen to keep it secret until I've had chance to let her smell the plant, not certain if the nurse would approve. 'Here, can you smell it?' I lay it beneath her nose for a second, then run my fingers up the stem, rubbing the flowers between thumb and forefinger before holding those beneath her nose. 'Isn't it beautiful, that smell? Such a gorgeous scent. Can you smell it, Poppy? Can you? Its stem is rich and green, the flowers tight and purple. It's come off a whole bush that Grandad wrapped up and left as a surprise on our doorstep. Wasn't that kind of him? We can plant it in the garden when you're better.'

I wait, watching her eyes, studying her tiny lips. The lack of moisture and the temperature in the room making them dry. I reach for the cup that has water in it, taking out the small sponge and pressing it gently on her mouth. 'There, that's better, isn't it?'

The lack of response to anything I do makes me sag, tired and frightened, dropping back into the seat, screwing my eyes shut just long enough for an image of the crash to burn into my retina. I jump up, heavy breathing. I move to the window, and though it's closed, there's some relief being where it's brighter. And I wonder how long I'll have to see and hear what happened? And I wonder if she will see and hear it, too? If she can see and hear it now? If she dreams. If she relives the moments leading up to the accident, or after, in the moments of silence that followed. Does she remember anything? If she wakes up, will she remember it?

'Lisa?' I spin round toward the voice. 'We're going to start the tests, okay?'

I nod. Adjusting my body, realigning everything so I can stand tall, and strong, planted in the room, ready for whatever follows.

Chapter Forty-One

I've been staring at Poppy's face since the consultant left the room, my eyes dare not flicker away from hers. A *reassuring sign* is what they said when they managed to get her to breathe without the use of apparatus. The sound of her gentle breaths has filled my heart, it's all I can hear, every few seconds, a breath in, then out, barely audible under the noise of nurses chattering, the telephone and various buzzers going off in the corridor outside. But those things can't interrupt what I prefer to listen to. The swelling is subsiding. The doctors are happy with her progress. I've never really cared about progress before, that percentile nonsense, then those required in education – even just at nursery – they were never things I marked her life on, I never cared. She was always doing fine. So long as she breathed and ate and, most importantly, laughed, the rest was unimportant. Now though? Now I care about her progress. Now I want to know every detail about how things are going. I pinch at my shoulders, my muscles rock solid. The machine, before, it was a reminder each time it breathed on her behalf that I almost lost her, and I felt like the noise tightened my muscles with each mechanical breath. That I don't know how much of her I'll get back is still better than being taunted by it, my sleep disturbed, its rhythmic sound monotonous, like a ticking clock or a metronome.

My phone dings. *I'm grabbing a coffee, do you want one?*

My tongue clacks, nothing having passed it since Dad dropped me off. *Please, yes. Americano with hot milk, thank you.*

Ten minutes later Holly arrives, coffee cups steaming, a paper bag of treats sticking out of her handbag. 'Hey,' she whispers, putting the cups and her bag down. She pulls me into an embrace, holding me tight. We stand, her holding me up, as a wash of relief at having her here swells over me. She pushes me back, studying my face with a gentle smile before turning to check on Poppy. 'Hey, little one.' She brushes hair from Poppy's face. 'How are you?' Her eyes flick over Poppy's face before she turns to me. 'Breathing is good.'

I half smile. 'It is.'

She pulls the spare chair up, placing it down carefully beside me. 'It's not dinner, I should probably have brought you dinner, but I brought you pastry. With chocolate. Chocolate pastry.'

'I don't know if I can eat.'

'You need to.'

'I know. Dad fed me at lunchtime.'

'You've seen him then?'

I nod. 'He took me to get Bear-Bear for Pops.'

Holly looks over, noticing the teddy tucked into the bed beside Poppy. 'That's why she's breathing! With you and Bear-Bear, she's got all she needs, right?'

I blow over my coffee.

'Here.' She offers up some of the chocolate pastry, shoving the other half in her mouth. 'I don't mind helping if you can't eat it all but at least try a bit.' Flaky pastry crumbs drop from her fingers to her dress, an emerald green dress with hot pink animal print markings. 'Sorry I've not been able to get in until now. It's been mad at home.'

'It's okay. Is Charlie okay?'

'He is. A bit weepy. Misses his little mate. Not sleeping so well, but he'll be okay.'

I nod, staring at Poppy, nudging away the prick of guilt that wants to blame me for Charlie struggling. How weird that I'd feel that and yet...

Holly stretches her legs out before her.

'Nice dress,' I say, nodding down to it.

'Thanks. It was a gift.'

I raise my eyebrows waiting, because although she's a dialled down version of herself, kind of sixty per cent Holly, I can tell there's more she wants to say. 'Go on. Tell me.'

'Dave bought it for me,' she says, permission to be excited – granted. 'What for?'

''Cause he saw it and thought it'd look nice on me. We're going out for a meal after this.'

'Ahhh, that's really lovely. It's going okay then?'

'It is. He's downstairs now actually. Drinking coffee and studying whilst he waits.'

'Studying?'

'Yeah. He's doing a degree, part-time.'

'In what?'

'I don't know. Something to do with numbers. He's really smart!'

'Wow.'

'And much younger than I realised!'

'Oh?'

'I thought he must be late twenties, maybe even thirty. Turns out, he's only twenty-four.'

My eyes widen. 'Twenty-four? Christ alive, we were fourteen when he was born... Weren't you snogging Richard Middleton when you were fourteen?'

'And the rest, yes, I bloody well was.' She looks off wistfully before coming back to the present day. 'But I really like him, Lisa. He's funny, he's kind, he's—'

'Smart, you've said. So, basically, he's all the things you would have turned your nose up at before.'

'What can I say? I wasn't mature enough to appreciate smart men who treated me with respect. And who knew you could get all that, in someone who's hot too?' She grins at me, but there's a look behind her eyes that tells me she knew, she just hadn't quite figured out she was worthy of them. 'I've got to tell you, it's really nice to feel like you know where you stand.'

'You think?' I smile but I don't know if I've ever really known that. Certainly not with Billy and I've not bothered much since because of Poppy.

'Yeah, I mean, it's early days, of course it is but...' She brushes crumbs off her leg to the floor then brushes them under her chair with her foot. 'I'd really like to introduce him to Charlie.'

'Wow. It's only been a couple of weeks.'

'It'd only be as a friend. I'm just interested to know how Charlie is with him, if he takes to him. And vice versa.'

'Are you sure it's not a little soon?'

'I've talked to Darren about it. He said the same, but like I said to him, this feels different. Dave feels different. We talk, about everything, all sorts. He's clever, he really thinks before he gives his opinion on stuff. He's gentle, kind. He respects me. I mean, I haven't mentioned it to him yet, he might not want to, but I suppose I want to just test the water a little. I've never introduced anyone to Charlie before, it's not like I have them traipsing in, lined up: a new dad every week. This would be the first person since his dad.'

'Did Darren agree to it then?'

'He trusts me. It's funny, somehow, it's helping us too. We've always made it work for Charlie, but something's shifted, it's like we like each other again. Maybe I've changed?'

'Maybe.'

'I almost like me.'

'Wow… that's big.'

'I mean, I know I can be a dick, but I've got a good heart, right?'

'You have. He's so young though.'

'He is, but… he's lived. He's had tough times. His dad died when he was doing his A-levels. Can you imagine? I don't know how he still passed them! I lost my hamster just before geography GCSE and I swear that's why I got a U.' I laugh at her. 'Seriously though, you don't go through that and not grow up, do you?'

'I suppose not.'

I sip at my coffee and she sips at hers, pulling back sharply. 'Shit, that's still hot. Have you got an asbestos mouth?'

'No. I think sometimes it's quite nice to feel something other than total despair and exhaustion.' I nod in Poppy's direction. 'I'm really happy for you, chuck. You look so happy, it's lovely.'

'I just wish you were too.'

'Hey. I will be. She's improving. She's going to wake up.' A pregnant pause follows. 'What?' Holly shakes her head. 'What?' I ask again.

'I just… I wondered if they knew how she'd be? Afterwards? When she wakes up?'

'They don't know. She's responding well. It's only been six days. Best-case scenario, she'll wake up soon and it'll be limited damage. It can happen, in kids especially.'

'Worst case?' she asks, tentatively.

'They don't really say. I guess they don't want to frighten me? They come in and do physio with her, trying to keep her mobile. I suppose I hope that's our worst-case scenario, that she needs physio to help her walk, talk and eat again.'

'Oh man…' She stares at Poppy. I do too, her chest is gently rising and falling. Her eyes, though, they remain static, closed, switched off. We sit in silence for a while, each sipping our coffees, both watching Poppy. The phone rings outside in the corridor. Footsteps. Voices. This time though, I don't feel so alone.

'Was it nice to see Paul?' she asks, after a few minutes.

I smile at her. 'It was.'

'He looked better, when he got back. Managed to find the energy to get on with some work. You mean a lot to him…'

'He means a lot to me.'

'And Billy?'

Chapter Forty-Two

I shift, uncomfortably. 'What about Billy?'

'Have you spoken to him since he left here?'

'No. Not yet.'

'Any thoughts?'

'On what?'

'On what he wants? Why he's back? Why he suddenly leapt to be your saviour!'

'I don't know. I think, he just wants to be there for me and Poppy. He said it made him realise what we mean to him.'

'But he was already back?'

'Yes, but I think the accident just highlighted what he really wants. Well, so he says, I don't know. I'm confused by the whole thing, but I just keep thinking that if she wakes up—'

'When!'

I nod. 'Yes, when, she's got every right to two parents. She deserves to feel loved and cared for. He can be there for her in ways I can't, and I know how it is to only have one parent.'

'So do lots of people, and they manage.'

'She shouldn't have to manage.'

'He didn't need to desert you when she was first born.' I notice her watch Poppy for a minute. She's considering what she wants to say next and it's not often she does that. 'You know he warned Paul off.'

'He did what?'

'When Billy left you, he came back to find Paul. He said that you were the mother of his child, that Poppy might need her father. He said that he loved you both and was going to prove it, starting straight away.'

'Paul never said.'

'Well, he wouldn't, would he? He doesn't want to cause problems or get in the way. I'm surprised he came in at all, to be fair. He told me you didn't need the complication of him around at the moment.'

'I need the support of people I love…'

Holly studies me for a second, no doubt wondering what I mean. What kind of love? I suppose, I wonder myself. 'Paul and I aren't together, there was no need for Billy to warn him off.'

'He saw that you were close, I guess? I don't know.' She runs her finger round the plastic lid on her coffee. 'Paul will want to do what's best for you and Poppy.'

'Can I not decide what's best? What is it with men thinking they have a right to assume what we want or need?' My heart thunders in my chest, frustration, irritation and confusion swamping anything I felt before. 'God, I don't know! I'm not saying I want to get back with Billy but…' Holly follows my gaze, us both landing on Poppy.

'I suppose you were good together for years. You know, playing devil's advocate.'

'We were.'

'You brought out the best in him.'

'Until he left me.'

'And I am in no way defending him. Let's face it, blood is thicker than water… but I suppose it's not out of the question for him to want to change things.'

'No. And that's where I come unstuck. What's best for Poppy? What's best for me? How much do I want Billy in my life? Really? And Paul? Things were just beginning, it was such early days. But I suppose I could see how he and I could work. And if I work, that's good for Poppy. But how would Billy be, if that's the choice I made? Would he back off, hurt? Would he get angry? My choice could push him away from Pops and that's not fair on her. I feel torn.'

'Lisa, Paul will kill me for saying this but, where you're concerned, he hasn't always known what to do for the best. He's always had feelings for you.'

I shift to face her. 'Always?'

'Pretty much.'

'Why have you never said?' My brow furrows, how could I never have known?

'I love you, but like I said, blood is thicker than water. He's my brother. Had we been teenagers, I might have said something, just to piss him off, but I suppose I didn't realise it was the case until I was mature enough not to get involved.'

'Since when are you mature?'

'Shut your face.'

We fall silent for a few minutes.

'How long then?' I eventually ask.

'Well, I think pretty much since we were kids, really. Not in a Ross Geller hopelessly devoted to Rachel Green kind of way, but... I don't know, actually, maybe it *is* a bit like that. I don't think he ever played a Bontempi keyboard to impress you though.'

'Dubious detail around the Ross and Rachel relationship aside, maybe things would have been different if he had.'

Holly pauses, once again really giving thought to what she wants to say. 'I love my big brother and I know that where you're concerned, he's…'

'What?'

'Vulnerable.'

'Right.'

'And, you're…'

'Also vulnerable?'

'Not normally, I wouldn't necessarily say, but maybe, yes, at the moment. And maybe now isn't the time to think about anything with him or Billy, but then… I don't know, maybe it is.'

I groan. 'Poppy is my only focus at the moment. Paul and Billy can both just…' I stop talking because it's not true. I mean, yes, Poppy is my only focus and Billy is treading a fine line, but if these last few days have taught me anything, it's that time is precious, and anger is pointless.

'Maybe having someone to lean on whilst you focus could be a good thing.'

'Whilst you're off jumping Pizza Delivery Dave.'

'His name is Dave!'

'I know, I know.' I force a smile because I don't want to be cross with Holly.

She checks her watch. 'I'd better get going. Our table's booked for eight.'

'Where you going?'

'I don't know. An Italian he knows of in some village, somewhere.'

'Sounds lovely.'

She checks my cup is empty before collecting it in hers, slinging her bag over her shoulder. 'Call me if anything changes, otherwise I'll try and swing by on Monday, okay? When Charlie's back in school.'

'Okay. Thanks, chuck.'

I watch her leave, turning my attention back to Poppy. If Paul and I had got together years ago, instead of Billy and me, Poppy wouldn't exist. And I know without question that if it came down to it, she is all I need.

Chapter Forty-Three

Glancing at the clock I realise it's almost nine. I must have dropped off after Holly left, only waking now because my phone buzzes on the table. I reach to silence it, checking Poppy first before answering, her little face as still and peaceful as it's been since getting here. No change.

'Lisa?' Dad's voice sounds strained. 'Lisa, how is she?'

'Oh, sorry, Dad, I meant to call you, I must have dropped off. She's breathing on her own,' I say, tired but as proud as I was the day she took her first steps in a shop in town, teetering across its filthy brown carpet before landing on her bum and smiling up at me with glee. 'She's still…' I can't bring myself to say it. 'She's not awake, but she's breathing on her own.'

'Oh, Lisa. Oh, Lisa, that's… Oh, I'm so pleased. When I hadn't heard anything, I've been so worried. You should have called… Sorry, sorry, that's unfair.'

I don't say anything. I'm not sure I've ever heard Dad apologise for anything, least of all his expectation of my behaviour.

'Are you okay?' he asks.

'I'm okay. Tired.'

'Can you get some sleep? Can they give you anything to help? Doctor Green could probably prescribe something, if you need it.'

'It's fine. I've been snatching catnaps. I don't want to sleep for too long, I want to be awake if she wakes, you know?'

'Of course you do. Of course. I understand.'

I sit back in the chair, watching her. Dad's breath echoes down the phone. 'Are you sure she won't remember it, Dad?'

'No,' he says, quietly. 'I don't think she'll remember a thing.'

'What if she does though? What if it haunts her like it haunts me? Sometimes, when I close my eyes, it's all I can see. Or suddenly, when sleeping, I'll wake to the sound of metal on metal. Or the smell…'

'She won't remember it, Lisa.'

'She's so young, too young to have to go through something like this.'

'She is.' He sighs. 'Look, I'll leave you to it. Oh, I've got a couple of people coming over to look at your heating. I'll let you know how I get on.'

'Okay. Thanks, Dad… and… I'm sorry.'

'What for?'

'For not letting you know as soon as things changed.'

'Well… when something threatens our children, we sometimes lose sight of things… Lisa, I know things haven't been easy for us.' I shift in my seat, uncomfortable at his uncharacteristic confrontation about the fact. 'Maybe when things improve, we can spend a bit more time together. Try and work out how we fit.'

I scratch and fidget. 'Yes. We should.'

My eyes fall on the intravenous drip attached to Poppy. Where I've watched the ventilator for so many hours, I find this a new distraction to what's going on. The drip from bag to bag to tube. The bubbles moving through. The curl and loop before it reaches her tiny hand, delivering food or medication, I'm not really sure, but whatever it is helps keep her alive. I wonder what it is about Dad that's always been so difficult to navigate, or maybe what it is about me. I wonder how we can fix it and what I need to do to make things easier. I wonder how I'd feel if Poppy felt towards me the way I feel about Dad. Disconnected. Detached.

I can see all that he's done for me has always been in good faith and I should be grateful. He's a diluted version of his dad. Grandad always seemed so unapproachable, so closed off to life, to anything that wasn't written in his Bible. Somehow Dad never had that same commitment to religion. I'm not sure Grandma did, really. It always felt like Grandad's thing, and certainly, she never went to church after he died. Is Dad more like Grandma or Grandad? The control and manipulation would suggest Grandad, but there have been moments, over the years, where I've seen a glimmer of the other, just now a case in point. And he was a single parent, that's something I should relate to. He was a man, raising a daughter, Christ knows that can't have been easy at any time, but back then? What resources did he have? What tools to guide him through it? Grandma helped where she could, Grandad was so in control of everything until he died. How old was I then? Fourteen? Maybe fifteen? Even losing his dad though, he can't have felt totally alone, can he? But there were definite gaps in my dad's relationship with his parents. Moments where you could tell there was an undercurrent of something. A dissatisfaction. Did they feel he'd let them down, having me? Did he feel they let him down, in some way? Did he feel they controlled him, as I have felt? Is it my generation's responsibility to bridge inherited gaps in our relationship? For the sake of Poppy's?

I pull my chair in closer to Poppy and stroke her face. I reach for the lavender and run it beneath her nose again. 'I promise I won't make the same mistakes, Poppy,' I say. 'As soon as you wake up, I can prove it to you. I'm going to do better, be better, just you wait and see.' I study her eyelashes, thick and long. Her nose, like a button. Her hair, a fiery halo on the pillow, around her face. 'Hey, would you like me to read you your book?' I pull it onto her bed, opening on the first page. 'I wonder how many times we've read this, Poppy? And I wonder how many times you've heard it, because if it wasn't me reading it, it was Grandma Elsie. I think you've even had Holly reading it to you and Charlie before now. What is it about the story that you love so much? How fierce the characters are? You do love a dragon.'

I flick through the pages, exquisite illustrations in bright colours on each page. 'Hey, look at this,' I say, lifting the book up to her eyeline. 'This is your favourite page, isn't it?' I press the page open even further for her. When I look back up, I swear I see her eyes flicker open. 'Poppy?' I stand, putting the book down on her bed and reaching for her arm. 'Poppy? Can you hear me? Did you just open your eyes? Poppy?'

Through the window in the door, I see a couple of the nurses in the corridor. I want to shout out to them, but I don't want to startle Poppy if she's waking up and I don't want to leave her in case she opens her eyes and there's nobody there. 'Poppy? Poppy, can you hear me?' Her eyes are fixed closed again, her chest rising and falling gently. I grab the book, showing her the page again. 'Here, look, it's here. Your book, here, can you see, Pops? Can you? It's beautiful, you love this page. Poppy?' Her eyes flicker again and my own fill with tears, my shoulders lifting in relief. 'Poppy, Poppy, I'm here. It's Mummy, can you hear me?' She flickers again and this time I run to the door, flinging it open. 'Nurse, anyone, please, she's opened her eyes. She's opened her eyes!'

Chapter Forty-Four

'This is common, Lisa,' says one of the nurses, checking Poppy's stats as the other shines a light in her eyes.

'I promise you she opened her eyes. I showed her the book, I told her to look and she opened her eyes.'

'We believe you.'

'Poppy, can you do it again? Can you open your eyes?' I grab the book, holding it in front of her face. 'Here, here you go, it's this one, isn't it. You love it. Come on, Poppy, open your eyes for us, open them for Mummy. Come on, baby.' Salty tears stream down my face as desperation replaces relief. 'Just one more time,' I plead. 'Just so we know you're in there, just one more time.'

An arm moves around me. 'This is a good sign, Lisa. Now she's breathing on her own, this is a sign she's improving further. It just might not all happen at once, okay?'

'How long? How long 'til she's awake?'

'We can't say,' says the other nurse opposite me. 'It could be soon, it could be days still. The important thing is to keep doing what you're doing. Keep talking to her, stimulate her senses. Know that it all helps, however much at times you might feel like it's in vain, it helps. Okay?'

'Okay.' I nod, dropping down into the chair beside Poppy, letting my hand rest on hers.

'Now, you look tired. Are you comfortable enough here? You could go home if you wanted? Just for a night.'

'I'm not leaving her. Not on her own.'

'We can sit with her. She won't be on her own.'

'I'm not leaving her.'

'Okay, okay. Try to get some rest though, yes? She needs you to be here and ready for her when she does finally wake, yeah? You can't burn out now.'

I nod, exhaustion kicking in.

'We'll update the consultant. Let us know if you see anything else, okay?'

'I will.'

The nurses leave. The room falls silent again. 'I'm still here, Poppy. Okay? I'm still here.' I stroke her hand, watching for any movement at all, my eyes growing heavy as I stare at hers.

When I wake, it's Saturday morning. A week since the accident. Light leaks in through a gap in the blinds. I rub and pull at my neck, yawning and clicking as I try to stretch out the night's sleep sat upright in the chair beside her bed. My belly is full of nerves and memories, last week we were getting ready to go out. Everything was as it should be. If I'd have only known, just an inkling that something wasn't right, I'd have stayed at home. Wouldn't I?

'Good morning, baby,' I say, kissing her forehead then waiting. 'Did you sleep okay? Did you dream?' I ask, wishing she could answer me with tales of her night-time adventures as she so often has in the past. 'Shall we open the blind, let some light into the room. It looks like a nice day,' I say, watching the green, gold and auburn of the leaves on the tree opposite light up, their colours warming in the autumn sun. A gentle breeze blows the boughs and a few leaves drop to the ground, a smattering of red, orange and brown collects at the tree's base.

'Knock, knock.' I turn to see a head popping round the edge of the door. 'This was left downstairs at reception for you,' says a woman I've not seen before, dressed in civvies.

'Oh, right. Thank you.' I take the parcel from her.

'It's quite heavy, careful.'

'Oh right, yes, thank you.'

She disappears off down the corridor.

'Look, Poppy. We have a present.' It's wrapped in the same brown paper the lavender was in. 'Grandad must have brought it for us. Maybe he couldn't sleep. He's been so worried about you. About us both I should imagine.'

I perch on the end of her bed, watching to see if she responds before I continue. 'Shall we open it? See what's inside? Do you want to look? Come on, baby. Have a look, let's see what we've got.' I rip open the paper to reveal an old tape machine. A black one with silver buttons. I frown. 'What's this? I haven't seen one of these for years. Used to have one when I was a kid. Just like this. I think Grandad must have been keeping it safe for nostalgia's sake.'

I press the button on the top that opens the cassette holder, pulling out the tape inside. In biro is written *Hits from the 90s* and I laugh. 'Good grief, hits? There can't be many of those on here. The nineties brought us 2 Unlimited and Color Me Badd, Poppy? Let's hope they're not on there. Shall we listen? You'll laugh.'

Closing the lid again, I push my finger down hard on the play button. The old whir of tape reel starts before the first song. 'Ace of Base! Christ!' I nod my head along to the music. 'This one's called "The Sign",

Pops.' I sing along, briefly taken back to my teen years. All the angst and drama. The years of trying to look like Gwen Stefani and totally not understanding Nirvana. I grab Poppy's hand and dance with her, swaying it from side to side as I jig about for the entire song, letting my memories wander over school, GCSEs, first kisses, house parties.

'I wonder what's next?' I say, about to drop her hand except that I'm sure I felt her fingers move in mine. I freeze. 'Poppy?' Ace of Base shifts to Alanis Morissette, one of my favourite songs to sing on karaoke: 'Forgiven'. 'Can you hear that, Pops?' I stare at her fingers in my hand as the music plays. I sing along. I perch on the edge of her bed, her hand still in mine. Bjork, 'One Day', comes on next. I remember this song, I borrowed the album from the library and listened to it on repeat for weeks. There was something so evocative about it, other-worldly. It made me feel creative, artistic, like I'd maybe stepped away from commercial pop and embraced music that came from something higher than a drive for money and recognition. Dad hated it. Why would he send it now? Acceptance, perhaps? That this music was part of my childhood? Part of me? Has this situation made him think, too? My eyes sting as I begin to sing to this one, the lyrics feeling potent in the moment. And when I open them again, a deep restorative breath helping push me to stand, I see Poppy has been watching me and I don't know how long for.

Chapter Forty-Five

'Poppy? Poppy, can you hear me?' She sort of stares, eyes glassy but open. I move in a little closer to her. 'Poppy? Poppy, follow my eyes, follow me.' I move gently from side to side, but she doesn't follow. I put my hand back in hers, holding it there so gently that if she moves, I'll be in no doubt, I'll know. I sing along to Bjork, gently, quietly, holding her gaze even though I don't think she's holding mine. By the end of the song, she blinks a few times before eventually, her eyes drift closed.

I switch the tape off and fall into the chair beside her, frustrated, tired, overwhelmed. 'You sleep,' I say to her, defeated. 'Sleep for as long as you need to get you better, okay? To heal. Sleep for as long as it takes for you to come back to me, whole, fully formed, refreshed. Ready to craft on Sundays, bake whenever you get the chance. Ready to play games and watch films. Ready for school. Ready for hugs at bedtime. Sleep for as long as it takes for all of these things to happen so readily, so easily, that this week pales into our memories.' I run out of steam, uncertain I could ever imagine this horror paling into my memory.

Then I reach for my bag, pulling the notebook out. Whilst I've no energy to talk, whilst I can, suddenly, barely stand, I feel like there are things I need to say, things I need to document about how I feel right now. How this has unfolded.

A week is a very long time when you're waiting for the only person in the world who matters to wake up. It's a very long time when your body feels old and broken, when your breath falls short of what you need it to do for your lungs, heart and soul. A week is a very long time when all you want is to stop the clock, push it back, start again and stay at home. Or fast forward until you're awake and we can get back on with our lives, our way, on our terms.

What do you want from your life, Poppy? What do you need to help you realise your dreams? What even are they? Will they still be the same when you're older? When you wake? Will you always want to be a 'vet doctor' during the week and paint pictures on a weekend? Will you go to college? Should I start saving to make sure we can afford it? Where will you go? Who will you be? Will you keep your red curls long or crop them short? What will you wear when your favourite dungarees don't fit any more? Will you always hate baked beans but love broccoli?

I pause.

Then I write: *To Do* and underline it several times.

Redecorate Poppy's room in purples and green, just the way she wants.

Set up the craft area she keeps asking for by taking out the chair in the window.

Open a savings account for her, then move all the money Dad's given me across into it.

Buy seeds to grow our own veg for next year, and sort Poppy's own area in the garden for all the things she wants to grow herself.

'What else, baby?' Her lips move, a small bubble forms then pops as she breathes.

Get a new car when the insurance paperwork resolves.

Then I draw a line through it. Dad never wanted me to have that car. Said it was unnecessary. That he could drive me anywhere I wanted to go. I bought it for £1000. It was all I had. It's failed every MOT since, and I've always had it fixed. If it's too cold, it doesn't always start. If it's too hot, it doesn't always start. I have to carry water in the car because the screen wash has a small hole somewhere that I've never been able to find. Sometimes it leaks oil out onto my driveway and sometimes the petrol gauge doesn't work. And I never cared before because it was ours. When Dad told me it was a death trap, I was even more insistent. It felt like he was using salacious words to get me to stop doing something he didn't approve of. Sensationalising something to frighten me and I was desperate to have something that would let me get out of the village and away from prying eyes when motherhood was overwhelming me in those first few weeks, when I first came home, and it felt like everyone whispered. Then the months when she was still small but growing faster than I could cope with. When everything seemed to be flying past me and I kept missing life because I was so wrapped up in her and when I would look up, life felt small, claustrophobic. I loved her with every ounce of my being but sometimes I needed to breathe, albeit with her. Because of our car, I could travel to garden centres and woodland walks far away from home. Villages in the middle of Lincolnshire's giant flat expanse where nobody knew me, and nobody cared. Where the only acknowledgement I'd get was for my placid girl, playing with her toes in her pram, stretching one out towards me if she wanted me to tickle it before giggling from her boots, toothy grin and eyes crinkled.

And now it was the car that couldn't protect her. The car that crumpled around her instead of holding strong. And the sound of the accident hasn't left me. The smells, the sight of her limp in her seat. I don't know if I'll ever be able to drive again.

Chapter Forty-Six

My phone startles me awake. I fumble to answer whilst checking on Poppy. 'Hello?'

'How is she today?'

'Oh, Dad, hi. She's… she's okay, I think. I don't know, I must have dropped off.' The clock says it's lunchtime. I can hear chatter out in the corridors.

'Sorry. I didn't mean to interrupt you sleeping.'

'It's okay, it's fine.' Every time I think of him, I think about the look on his face when he admitted to sending the gifts. The loss he's just had with Grandma. The shock of finding out what had happened to Poppy and me. We can't carry on like this, we have to be better, for me, for him, for Poppy. I pull at a crick in my neck, feeling guilt in the pit of my belly at the fact that I think I've slept most of the night and certainly didn't stir when they came in to do checks on her this morning. 'Don't think I've slept that well since before the accident,' I say through a yawn.

'Oh, well that's good, isn't it?'

'I guess. Thank you for the music by the way.'

'Pardon?'

'The music, this morning. It was perfect actually. In fact, she opened her eyes and moved her hand a bit to it. Sorry, I should have called you to say thanks but—'

'She opened her eyes?'

'Just for a moment, and she moved her fingers.'

'Well, that's brilliant! Oh, love, that's...' He trails off with a sniff. 'Gosh, you must be feeling relief?'

'I don't know, I mean, maybe? Maybe that's why I dropped off? I don't know. They've said it's still a long way to go. It doesn't mean she's waking up as such, but she can breathe on her own now, that's a good sign and—'

'Sorry to interrupt you, Lisa.' A nurse pops her head around the door. 'I noticed you were awake. Just to say that we're reducing her medication again, after yesterday's breakthroughs and so on. So, I'll be in in a bit to give her the next batch but it's not as high a dosage as before. We can keep an eye on her then, see how she responds. Maybe you could play that music again? It seemed to help.'

'Okay, thank you. Yes.'

'So... what did she say? The music helped?' Dad asks.

'It did, yes. Thank you so much, it was such a surprise, though I can't help wondering if something a bit more modern might have been better for her.'

'How do you mean?'

'Well, all that nineties stuff, I mean, obviously I remembered them all, but she wouldn't have a clue. Sorry, sorry, that sounds really ungrateful, doesn't it?'

'No. No. Not at all, to be honest I didn't... well, I didn't think, just grabbed whatever I could.'

'Maybe it was one of my old mix tapes. I made loads, back in the day. Christ, I don't know where you keep all this stuff. I bet your office is a real treasure trove of childhood memories.'

'Oh, no, not really. Just a few things, you know...'

I yawn again. 'Did Grandad do that? In his office? Keep things from your childhood to bring out at various appropriate times?'

'Of course he did. How else do you think I still have all my school report cards? Look, I was actually calling to let you know that I've had a couple of plumbers round to your place this morning. I was sort of hoping it would be a straightforward fix, but it looks like your boiler needs replacing.'

'Oh God, that's all I need.'

'It's fine. You're not there for now, you don't need it.'

'No, but I will, when I get back. And what about Frank?'

'I've brought him back to stay with me. He looked lonely on his own. I think he liked the peace and quiet to begin with, didn't you, old boy, but he is much happier here on the sofa.'

'I'll bet he is.'

I wonder if it's hard for Dad having his mum's dog at his place. He hadn't been all that keen to have him when I originally offered to take him back with me. Like it was a reminder that his mum had passed. 'Hey, Dad, if you can, send me a video of him, would you? I think maybe Poppy might like it.'

'Of course, anything at all.'

'And thanks again for the tape, it was a lovely thought.'

'Oh, it's fine. Yes. No problem.'

I take the tiny brush I bought from the shop down in the hospital entrance, running it over Poppy's fringe and down the bits of her hair that I can see. Her hair pulls through it, briefly straightening before the curls bounce back in place. I dampen a flannel I also bought, making sure the water is neither too hot nor too cold. 'Here, you go.'

I gently wipe her face, paying attention to the dryness in the corners of her mouth, taking her hands and running the flannel down each palm, holding her fingers afterwards to see if they move. I turn her hand over in mine, looking at her little fingers and tiny fingernails. Nails she loves to paint with every shade of nail polish she can find in my drawer – most of which have been there years and are just gloopy, sticky shades of pink or red from back when I bothered with things like that. I remember the day she pampered me, a facial using toilet roll and soap that got in my eye. A manicure that went up my hands and a foot massage that basically just tickled.

'Well, getting all nostalgic isn't any good, is it?' I sniff up hard. 'Grandad's going to send us a video of Frank so you can see him. They won't let him in the hospital, so this is as good as you'll get until you wake up and we can go home. You know, when you're ready. Oh, that must be him now.'

I throw the flannel on the side and wipe my hands on my jeans. 'Oh wait, hang on, no it's not, it's Paul. He's checking up on you and wondered if he could bring me some food in today.' I read over his message, my heart flipping slightly. My belly grumbles. I am hungry. And I don't know how many dry cheese sandwiches or slices of toast I can manage. I'd like to bet that whatever he brings in won't be dry or toasted. 'He also says Iris wants to visit, if we don't mind. Apparently, she's been worrying about us both and just wants to know that we're okay. Well, maybe not okay, but surviving, eh?' I place my hand on her leg.

Her eyes flicker beneath her lids so I wait a second. 'Maybe he could bring in a roast dinner for us?' I say. 'We both love a good roast dinner, don't we? Eh? Grandma Elsie's cauliflower cheese, apparently she learned how to make that off Iris. Now I miss that, almost as much as I miss

Grandma, don't you?' I move a stray bit of hair that has stuck to her damp cheek. 'Will you remember how you love cauliflower cheese?'

I tap out a response: *Thank you, that'd be good. It'd be lovely to see Iris, bless her. Just so you know, they've started reducing Poppy's medication, so I don't want to leave her side really. But you can come in her room for a short while, if you both like? X*

That's fine. We'll come in around three, let me know if anything changes and that time's no good for you. x

Chapter Forty-Seven

'Knock, Knock.' Paul pushes the door open slightly, noticing the physio is in, carefully manoeuvring Poppy's legs as they have started doing each day for the last few days. 'Oh, sorry, shall we come back?'

'No, no. We're about done here, aren't we, Poppy? You're doing very well; those legs are starting to really move. We'll have you hopscotching in no time.' She gives her leg an affectionate pat before tucking it back in again. 'I'll leave you to it.'

Paul stands back for the physio to leave, then opens the door for Iris who totters in with a helium balloon bouncing off a string attached to her handbag.

'Nice balloon,' I say with a wink.

'Oh, yes. I thought Poppy might like it, they do love a balloon, don't they? Kids.'

'They do.' I pull Iris in for a hug. She's tiny. Much smaller than Grandma ever was. Her perfume washes over me and soothes again.

'Oh bless, look at her. Oh, Poppy love.' She puts her fingers to her lips as if to stop any emotion. 'She's so wee in that bed.'

'She is.'

Iris takes the balloon from her bag and ties it to the bed. 'Here you go, my love. This is for you. Now, if you could make us all feel better and wake up, that'd be very good of you because we do so worry.'

I half expect Poppy to wake up at the instruction.

'Any update?' asks Paul, who hovers by the door.

'Nothing more than I've already said. They seem to be hopeful that she may wake up soon, but they can't say when. Or if they can, they aren't. I suppose they have to manage expectations, don't they?'

'Of course.' He stares at her.

'You can come in you know. Sit down.'

'Oh, I don't want to crowd her. I just wanted to let Iris see her. I can come another time, I mean… if you wanted. I'll leave you this, then head downstairs until you're ready, Iris.' He hands me a plate covered in a beeswax wrap. 'It's only chicken salad, I'm afraid. With some pasta, just a bit of homemade pesto, I hope that's okay. I wasn't really sure what food you could get in here and you need to eat well when you're dealing with all of this.'

'Oh, wow. Thank you. I mean, the food here's not great, this is…' Disappointed he's not staying, I gaze down at the plate, which I can now see is full of colourful salads, pasta, a little bit of potato salad. 'This looks delicious, thank you.'

'I put a few onions but just on the side in case you didn't like them.'

'No, I do. Thank you.'

'Isn't that thoughtful of him? He brought one round for me too.'

'I just had loads left. Pasta. You never get the quantity quite right, eh?'

'I'll look forward to that for my dinner,' says Iris, trying to pull the spare chair closer to the bed.

I go to jump up and help her, distracted by the dinner, overwhelmed by people in our little room. Paul beats me to it though and our bodies brush. 'Sorry, are you okay?' he asks, steadying me first before pulling the chair for Iris.

'I'm fine, yes, thank you.'

'There's cutlery in there, a flask of tea and some juice... I didn't know which you'd prefer.'

'Thank you... thank you so much.' He scratches the back of his head and blushes. 'You can stay... if you like.'

'No, no. It's not good for Poppy, is it. Too much noise with us all rattling on beside her. I think they say only two at a time anyway, don't they? No, I've got a bit of work to do anyway, so I'll just go sit down in the coffee shop and wait.' We lock eyes briefly. 'Call me when you're ready, Iris. I'll come back up for you – and say goodbye.'

'Alright, love. Thank you.'

He ducks out the door leaving us sat beside one another.

'You look exhausted,' she says, taking the bag off me and passing me the cutlery. 'Get that down your neck, it'll do you good. I'll pour you some of this tea and all.'

'Do you know what, Iris, I've drunk that much tea in the last week, I don't think I could stomach a single drop.'

'Oh, no bother. I'll have that then, wouldn't want him to think it'd gone to waste, would we?'

'No. No, not at all.'

'Such a good lad. Not sure I'm taken in by the too-much-pasta chat though.'

'Eh?'

'Too much pasta! I mean, we've all put a bit too much in a pan. But enough to feed two more mouths? And potato salad. And pesto. And all the other lovely things he's put in there. Seeds, I think there's some seeds. That's not a bit of overcooking, that's planned.'

I fork a mouthful of the salad, shoving it greedily in.

'Nice that he cares.' She's looking at me pointedly. I've never been good with being looked at pointedly. 'We all need someone that cares.'

I shovel another mouthful before trying to say, 'Mhmm.'

She pours tea into the little cup on top of the flask as I keep eating. It's been easy to ignore the belly rumbles – I just haven't been that interested in food and I hate leaving Poppy for any length of time – but to have a plate full of good stuff on my lap has just sent my belly into overdrive and I'm ramming it in like someone might take it away.

'Is he single?' she asks, casually, and I nearly cough out my potato salad. 'I just wondered, you know. I suppose you're a bit distracted with Poppy really, but then you never know when love can tap at your door.'

'As you say, I'm a bit preoccupied with more important things.'

She nods, letting the conversation stall for a minute before saying, 'Hearts should always be open. That's what my old mum used to say to me.' I feel myself warm. 'So, what have they said?' She turns her attention to Poppy. 'Will she be…' She pauses, looking over her, all love chat evaporating as if she's just re-seen what I'm dealing with here. 'Will she be okay? When she wakes up?'

I run my tongue over my teeth before answering. 'They don't know. The physio has been working her legs daily, they say things like that may need a bit of work, it depends how long she's in bed for. They can seize up, even in little ones. They can't say about her speech until she wakes. It doesn't look like the swelling to her brain has caused any lasting damage, or so they say, I don't know how they tell this sort of thing but still, it's good to hear that's what they think. I just have to be patient now.'

'Never was your strong point, was it?'

I look up sharply. I've known Iris all my life, via Grandma, but I suppose I'm still surprised at her character observation.

'I remember when your grandma bought you a Doozer for Christmas, do you remember? Those little green things off that kids' programme you were obsessed with.'

'*Fraggle Rock.*'

'You couldn't wait to open it. Didn't you find it in her wardrobe and bring it downstairs a week before Christmas?'

'I was playing hide and seek. I had no idea it was for Christmas. As far as I knew then, Santa brought presents.'

Iris laughs. 'Well, he does, doesn't he,' she says, nodding towards Poppy. 'And I'll bet he'll be bringing you big presents this year, Poppy, rewards for being so brave.'

I smile, sadly.

Chapter Forty-Eight

An hour passes. All the tea from the flask has gone and my plate of food is empty, washed and back in the bag Paul brought it up in. I've pressed play on the tape machine and Whitney Houston is belting out 'I Will Always Love You'.

Iris pats her hand on her knee. 'You know Dolly Parton sang this originally.'

'Did she?'

'Yeah. She wrote it. Me and my Bernie used to love this song. Well, when Dolly sang it.'

'Right.'

'I mean, there's nothing wrong with this version, but it's a bit…' She wrinkles her nose up. 'Didn't think I'd be fussed about marriage 'til things changed with me and Bernie. Was never the settling-down type. Think he wore me down in the end. Doesn't sound romantic, but it was.'

'Yeah?'

'Yeah. I'd known him years.' She gets out her old mobile phone as big as a house brick. 'Paul? It's me. Iris. Are you ready?' I pause the tape player so she can stop putting her finger in her spare ear. 'I think we should leave Lisa and Poppy in peace for a bit.' I can hear his muffled voice on the other end of the phone. 'Alright, love. See you in a minute.'

She hangs up and drops her phone in the bag with a thud. 'By the way, I brought this for you.' She passes me a small blue box. It's leather, but old. A little battered. 'Your grandma gave it to me, years back, but I always thought you should have it. Seeing as she's not here to tell me off now, I wanted to give it to you.'

I open the box and inside is a gold chain with a small gold ball on the end of it.

'To be honest, I'm not sure your grandad shouldn't have given it back at some point, when he stopped being in the Masons.'

'What do you mean?'

'It's a Masonic ball. A gift to the Masons' wives.'

'Oh gosh, wow.' I pop the ball open. It unfolds into a cross of Jesus with a series of markings on each pyramid side that makes up the ball.

'Probably some kind of magic in that, or top-secret sign that nobody outside of the Masons is supposed to know about. I was never sure about them myself, always thought they were dodgy buggers, but they put on a good do and your grandma always loved this.'

'I don't remember it at all.'

'No? Oh... well, she probably wouldn't have worn it every day. Special, isn't it? Stuff like this.'

'Yes. Of course.'

The door opens. Paul and I catch eyes, he half smiles.

'Right, we'd better go.' She goes over to Poppy and with a kiss on her own fingers, transfers it to Poppy's cheek. 'Now, you hurry up and wake up, please, love, you've had quite long enough in that bed.'

'Thanks for coming,' I say to them both.

'Oh, it's no bother, when Paul said he was coming over I just asked if he'd room for a little one. I haven't half been worried about you both and I did want to give you that necklace; maybe it'll bring you a bit of good luck?'

I look over to Paul whose cheeks flush and I wonder if it's because he'd said Iris had asked him if he could bring her over, not the other way around.

'Keep us posted, won't you, love?'

'Of course. No problem. And thanks for the lunch, it was really lovely.'

He takes the bag from me, pleased. 'Oh, good. I'm glad you enjoyed it. Holly said she might pop in Monday, after morning school run. I could send more food in with her if you like?'

'Oh, I wouldn't want you to go to any bother.'

'It's no bother. I'm happy to help.'

'Well, I don't know. Whatever. It's fine. Thank you.'

We stand, awkwardly.

'I think they said there's a new cook starting tomorrow. I imagine the food will be better. Don't you worry about me, I'll sort myself out here. It's fine.'

'Right. Okay. Well. See you, then.'

'Yeah. Bye.'

'Bye, love.' Iris totters out, just as she'd arrived. As they head off down the corridor, she hooks her old lady arm into the crook of his, chatting to him. Paul takes a glance back in my direction and I dip out of view. I wanted to say something to him, I wanted to tell him not to listen to Billy. What was emerging before all this hangs between us, and whilst now isn't the time to think about my love life, it is a time I need the people I love and rely on to be there for me even more. But it's also a time I should be thinking about Poppy. Which means Billy too. I dig my phone out. *Hi. Poppy has shown signs of improving. Maybe you'd like to come in?*

Chapter Forty-Nine

In the last twenty-four hours, Poppy's eyes have flickered open several times. Her hand has, I swear, curled around mine, once even holding on to my finger. I have sung to her, I have danced for her, I have read her favourite book and I have, this morning, wafted toast underneath her nose because who doesn't love the smell of toast in a morning? She loves toast.

She loved toast.

God, I hope she'll still love toast when she wakes up.

I have responded to a text from Dad, asking how I am, and if Poppy is okay. He texted back straight away, despite the fact it was barely six in the morning. There was no undertone to his message, I didn't feel watched or judged.

And now, Billy is here.

'Can I come in?'

I don't know what I expected when I agreed he should come. He called after I sent the message and asked if he could see us both. I know I have to give him a chance. Not for his sake, but for Poppy's. He is still her father...

I nod, motioning to the spare chair in the corner of the room, but he doesn't take it. His eyes, instead, are fixed on Poppy. He steps towards her, taking his cap off and wringing it in his hands. 'She's so small,' he says, his voice fractured.

'She'd be furious to hear you say that out loud. She's a big girl, you know.'

A cry laugh escapes his mouth as he wipes his eyes. I wouldn't say he was all that emotional in the past, it surprises me.

'Hey, Poppy, we have a visitor. This is Billy. He's an old friend of mine.' He looks at me, uncertain. It's my turn to take the lead, something that so rarely happened in our relationship. 'We met at school. I've known him as long as Holly and Paul.'

Billy forces a smile as if she could see him. 'Hi, Poppy,' he says with an awkward wave.

'Have a seat.' I realise my words come out more as an instruction than an invite but where before, around Poppy, I've been worried and nervous, quiet and a bit broken, now, with him here, I feel stronger. She's mine to protect and I will do that, no matter what.

'Any progress today?'

'Nothing new. You're not quite ready, yet, eh, Poppy?'

We sit in silence for longer than I imagined we might when I ran through possible conversations in my mind. I'd thought over the things I've always wanted ask, about what was going through his mind when he left us. I've thought over the questions about where he went and who with. Over how we came to be so broken in our communication, was I always like that? My memory is that we talked, to begin with at least. He knew how I felt about everything, always, or so I thought. Have I romanticised that part of our relationship? Have I forgotten what he was really like? My anger subsided years ago, well, most of it. But the questions never stopped, I just pretended not to hear them after a while. What was the point in asking them if I couldn't offer an answer?

'I think I went a bit mad,' he says, quietly. I look up, feeling heard. Taken aback, but happy to wait for him to expand. 'It sounds like an excuse. I don't want to make excuses but... I think it's true.' I let my eyes rest on Poppy's. 'It was before you got pregnant. I think I'd already started to feel panicked by life. I'd look around at the village and it felt too small, stifling. I'd think about how you felt about your dad, how he clipped your wings, and I felt the same about the village. It was like life was mapped out for us. We'd stay there, get married, have kids, die there.'

'Who says I wanted to marry you?'

'I know, I know. But... you get what I mean, don't you? That idea that this was all there was for us. Confirmed when you fell pregnant. I was so angry with myself for letting it happen.'

'It takes two.'

'But it shouldn't have.'

'She's not a mistake!' I say, my voice low, but strong in case she can hear.

'I didn't mean that.' He takes in a deep breath, reversing interlaced hands to stretch them out in front of him, his fingers grazing the bed. 'She wasn't... isn't... but everything I did and said, was. I wasn't ready for any of it, I wasn't clear on what I wanted. I remember how frustrated I'd get with you, and everyone here, how small I thought their lives were. How they lacked ambition. The truth was, I did too. I just knew I didn't want what I had.'

'Thanks.'

'I mean me, it was all me.'

'Save me the excuses.' I don't mean to say it with venom, but he leans forward, pinching his nose, both elbows on each knee. 'Sorry. That wasn't meant to be antagonistic.'

'The second I walked out of that door, when you were on the landing, I wanted to turn back.' I raise my eyebrows. 'I knew as I walked down

Princes Street that I was making a mistake. That I would regret it every day. And not because you and Poppy were something I wanted.'

'Wow!'

'I'm not here to lie to you, Lisa.' I suppose I should be grateful for that fact. 'We should probably have separated a long time before I left. I wasn't good for you and you…'

'What?'

'You weren't right for me either. Not back then. And not because of anything you did, it was—'

'All you. Yes, you said.'

He spins round, taking my hands in his. 'You will never know how sorry I am, or how much I regret not being in her life, letting you do this alone.'

'So why come back now?'

'Because I've finally found the balls to own my—'

'She's not a mistake!' I hiss.

'No, I know. I wasn't going to say that! To own my choices, to acknowledge where I let you down. Where I… let myself down. And I know that probably sounds self-indulgent, but I did. And I don't want to do that anymore.'

I take my hand back from his.

'I know people think I swagger around, that I hold court and demand all the attention, I can't help who I am.' I raise my eyebrows at him. 'But I can help how I apply that in life, I can help how I manage relationships… friendships. I want to be there for you and for Poppy. I want to be in her life, in any way you see fit.'

'Right.'

'But I'm here to try and fix what I can, work out a new way to be a father.'

'From where? Are you moving back?'

'Well, I mean… that depends…'

'On?'

'On what's here for me. It depends on… Poppy…' He gestures towards her, then looks at me. 'It depends on us.'

Chapter Fifty

I lean against the wall outside the hospital doors, no coat, the hairs on my arms stand on end. I asked Billy to leave and I've sat for the rest of the day, studying Poppy, replaying our conversation, drifting in and out of broken sleep. I need time to think, to process what's already happened, and what happens now. Stars appear the longer I look up in the dusk, and as I try to get rid of the tension in my chest, I watch my breath twist and disappear. He was disappointed, he didn't want to go, but I appreciate that he did. And that he hasn't tried to call or text me since.

Just like with Dad, I needed this: space, air to breathe. Car headlights sweep through the grainy, not light but not yet fully dark night as people arrive for evening visiting hours. An ambulance leaves the hospital, sirens kick in as it hits the main road. Another arrives, silently. As I peer in the direction of A & E, I see the paramedics hop out and greet nurses who leave the building in their direction. I wonder if they met me when I was brought in? I wonder if it's the same people? The same shift? Do they remember Poppy, when she arrived? Or are they so used to seeing people come and go that they lose track, nobody standing out in the sheer numbers. A woman hobbles out in a thick coat with surgery socks and the gowns they give you when you're admitted without your nightwear. She stands beneath a tree, her face briefly lit by the glow of her cigarette lighter. I've never smoked; well, I tried it one night at a mate's house party. Felt really grown up and quite sexy to begin with, until the nicotine hit my veins and I went a bit dizzy, then felt sick for the rest of the night. It's just never really been my thing. Nor has drinking. Probably because I hated being out of control.

'It's a bit fresh for standing beneath the streetlights,' says Paul, appearing out of nowhere. 'You want my coat?'

'Oh! Hi! Erm, no, thank you. I was just getting some air. Kind of like the cold on my arms for a minute.'

'Beautiful evening for it.'

'It is.'

We both stand looking up to the sky.

'Holly said you'd said you wanted casserole?'

I groan a bit. 'Did she now.' He holds another bag up for me. 'Funny that, seeing as I've not had a chance to speak with her today.'

'Oh… erm…'

I shake my head and a resolute smile plays on his lips. We both know what she's like. 'You didn't have to do this.'

'I know I didn't.'

I take it from him, but he holds on for a second, we're connected, albeit via an insulated food bag. 'I need to get back to Poppy. I don't like to leave her too long.'

'Of course not. Go on…'

I turn away, pulling the food bag into me.

'Lisa.'

When I turn back to face him, he looks different to the Paul I've known for years. He's uncertain, vulnerable even. 'There's something I need to say.'

'Paul, I really do need to get back to Poppy.'

'I know, I know, it's just… I think I need to be clear about something…'

'Alright, mate? How are you?' A bloke in ripped, baggy jeans and a thick jumper brushes past us. Hanging on to him is a heavily pregnant woman who's stopped dead in the doorway and is breathing with low groans. 'Sorry, looks like we're about to add to the brood.'

'Bloody hell, Scott. I didn't know, wow, congratulations!'

'Thanks.' The woman's breaths grow more shallow, quieter, less cow-like, and it's as if she climbs back out of herself. 'Okay?' he asks and she nods, her body still doubled. 'Come on then, at least we made it this far, this time.' She nods and breathes, before he slowly walks through into the main entrance with her. 'Head wetting'll be on Friday, I reckon, if you're passing the Lion?'

'Right. Sure thing,' Paul shouts after his mate, grinning until he's out of sight. 'That's their sixth. Think I might buy 'em a telly.'

His comment makes me laugh.

'Sorry, I was—'

'Come up. If you like.'

He looks around at the various people coming and going. 'Are you sure?'

'I'm sure. Come on. She might like to hear your voice.'

We've made small talk all the way back up to Poppy's room. When inside, he stands around awkward. 'Is that a tape player?'

'Yeah. Dad brought it in for me yesterday. It's got a tape full of 90s hits on it.'

'Short tape.'

'You'd be surprised.'

'She's got a better colour,' he says, pressing play on the machine as Ace of Base starts up again. 'Jesus, I hated this song.'

'Rude.'

I perch on the bed, taking Poppy's hand in mine. 'What did you want to say, Paul?'

His back faces me. I notice him take a deep breath before turning round. 'The thing is… well… it's all a bit embarrassing and I'm not really sure how to say this.'

'Do you need to?'

'Well… probably, ideally not like this, but, yes, I feel like I do. I've kept playing it over in my mind. I wanted us to spend the day together last Saturday because I wanted to give us a chance to see one another in a different way. And now, perhaps when you need me the most, I feel like you can't lean on me because things have changed. We've been friends for so long. I wanted to rush to your side when this happened, I wanted to hold you and make it all go away and of course I knew I couldn't and then… I don't know, I suppose I thought it best to pull back. You didn't need complications right now.'

'And Billy told you to.'

'I wouldn't have listened if I didn't think he might have a point.'

'I don't need people to make decisions for me.'

'Of course. But you also don't need anybody needing anything from you now. You don't need to worry that you can't ask a friend for help in case he thinks it means more to you than just that, help, from a friend. I just need you to know that I understand nothing can happen between us, I really do. I understand it's important to try and sort things with Billy, for Poppy's sake.'

'Paul.'

'I…' He pauses, adjusting his body language. 'I love you, Lisa. I do. And that's why I want you to know that I am here for you, but in the way you probably need, right now, as a mate. The food yesterday and today, it's as mates. Yes, I did bring Iris yesterday to give me an excuse to come over but it was because I wanted to try and say this then, but I didn't really think it through and when I saw you, I just wanted to get some space and work out how to deal with things.'

'Iris was here, we couldn't have talked with her here.'

'She'd already guessed what was going off. Said she wanted to pop and visit an old neighbour that she knew was up on a different ward.'

'She never said anything.'

'I think she might have been lying. I don't know. Thing is, I just need you to know that I'm sorry if I've made any of this awkward. I really didn't mean to. If I thought it was appropriate to fight for you, to make you know how serious I am, then I would. But now is not the right time.'

'Is there ever a right time?'

He's about to respond when the door opens and Billy stands there, arms laden with teddies and a giant card. 'I'm sorry, I just wanted to bring her these. I wanted her to have something of me. I know we've got a long way to go, I know you need time to think about my offer but…' Paul shifts into Billy's view. 'Oh… *you're* here.'

And it's in this moment that I feel it, the smallest of movements in my hand. Just a gentle uncurling of her fingers, tiny to begin with, so small I might not have noticed. Except that like the other times, it doesn't flicker on then off. It stays, her fingers stay threaded through mine. And when I turn my head towards her, I see her eyes open, glassy, but open, she looks around the room, at Paul, then finally at me.

'Poppy?' I jump off the bed. 'Poppy?'

She opens her mouth, no sound comes out.

'Poppy? Poppy? It's me, can you hear me, can you see me?' She stares at me for what must only have been a second but feels like too long, before eventually she gives the shallowest nod. 'Oh my God.' Instinctively, I reach out behind me, grabbing someone's hand. 'Call the nurse, quickly, get the nurse!'

Chapter Fifty-One

I look down to see Billy's hand in mine, Paul at the door waiting for the nurses to jog in. When he turns back around, he clocks Billy and me holding hands and I let go, quickly.

'Ahh, Poppy. Hello,' says the first nurse, at the end of her bed, the second one round the other side of my little girl. Poppy goes to open her mouth again and again, nothing comes out. She looks around the room, confused, uncertain, her hand still in mine and this hand I daren't let go.

'Is your throat sore, Poppy?' asks one of the nurses and Poppy nods. At least, I think she nods. I'm struggling to see anything through the tears and the relief. Paul and Billy stand just behind me, one on either side. I feel their presence, their energy radiates. 'You've had something down your throat to help you breathe, that's why it might be sore. But it will get better, okay?' She nods again. 'We'll get some medicine to help it, if you like.'

Poppy nods again, just a shallow one, too aware of the other nurse who is taking her temperature and pulse. Poppy's eyes flit between the two nurses, the balloon that floats above her pillows, Billy and Paul beside me, and then me.

'Gosh, little one, you gave me quite the fright.' I lean over her, repeatedly kissing her forehead and cheek, brushing hair from her eyes and kissing her again. 'Can you speak? Can you say my name?' She opens her mouth but nothing comes out. 'Oh, it's okay. Don't force it. It's fine. You're awake, God.' A heavy breath leaves me. 'You're awake.' I rest my head on her chest, her heart beats against my cheek.

'Where…' Her little voice tries but breaks. I haven't heard that voice for well over a week and it's so tiny and broken but it's there, and she still sounds like her. Croaky, but her.

'Take your time,' I say.

She coughs and swallows, wincing. She didn't show pain before, if she ever felt ill, she was always stoic. She'd cough then carry on. Even now, the wincing, she does it, but she doesn't let the pain sit in her face. She blinks, as if clearing her mind of how she feels.

Paul pulls the chair closer for me, Billy eyes him, then says to me, 'Sit down.'

I drop down beside her, pulling the chair closer to her bed, still not daring to let go of her hand. 'We had an accident.'

'You've been having a lovely long rest,' says one of the nurses with Poppy's folder open, pen poised. 'Your body needed to stay asleep until it was feeling a little better and now, it must be feeling better.'

Poppy nods as if she understands. She notices Bear-Bear in the crook of her arm and pulls him into her.

'Look at the balloon from Iris. And all these cards, Poppy. There's one from Charlie, and Evie, look, too. Class One have sent one, they all want you to get well soon.'

'Yes, look, I brought you a teddy and a card too.' Billy thrusts it out and I scowl at him because if ever there wasn't a right time to ingratiate himself with her, now is it.

I pull her focus back to me. 'And here, look, Grandad sent us some music. I've been playing it to you, and oh look, this book too.' I hold it up for her, but I can already see, as I waffle on, that she's overwhelmed. 'Hey, hey, it's okay. I'm here. None of that matters now anyway, it's all fine.' I reach out to cup her face in my hand, then look over my shoulder to the boys. Billy is right beside me, Paul has stepped back.

'I should go, leave you to it. Unless you need anything?' We hold each other's gaze.

Billy shifts even closer to Poppy's bed. 'I mean, I'd like to stay, though?'

'Billy, I think it might be best for Poppy if it's just her and me.'

'But she needs—'

'Peace and quiet to recover,' Paul says, then clamps his mouth shut straight away, his face etched in apology. I offer a smile because he's right. He said what I was about to.

'She needs space,' I say, pointedly. 'Please, leave us. I'll call you later, Billy.'

One of the nurses steps closer to me. Billy stares at her, then me, then Paul. I can see he wants to give me all the reasons why he should stay but I am relieved he doesn't. Paul opens the door, gives me a smile, then steps out, holding the door open for Billy who pauses.

'I promise I'll call you,' I repeat.

He nods, smiles at Poppy and then puts the teddies and card on the end of her bed. She watches him as he leaves. Paul closes the door behind them both, offering me one final, gentle smile before he does.

'Lovely presents, eh, Pops?' She nods, her eyes quickly drifting from the gifts back to me. 'Just us though for now, eh? Until you're feeling stronger.'

*

An hour later, the nurses have been in and out. Poppy's consultant has been in to see her and softly talk me through the next stages: seeing if there's been any cognitive damage, assessing her mobility, observing her to make a full and informed diagnosis as to the next course of action. It's all words. Words I wish I could follow, but there were too many and I didn't really understand what was going off myself and all I could do anyway was look at Poppy and hold her hand and feel my heart beat again at the sight of her awake.

I wrote notes in my notebook, stuff they said so I could go back and read it, except that I don't want to read it, I just want to sit here and look at her. Watch and wait until she wakes up from what they promise me now is just a sleep, a little rest after the last hour of being checked and prodded and manoeuvred.

It's now that I let myself really lean into the feelings I've been ignoring since I found out about the accident. I've cried, for sure, and I've felt fear and uncertainty. But I think I've also been ignoring the noise of all my emotions because, apart from when I was at home, with Dad, I've just not wanted to feel any of it. And I didn't want to then, it just overwhelmed me. But now, now I sort of want to face it all. Allow myself a moment to acknowledge what this last week has really been like because the only way I can be here and present for Poppy now, as she will need me to be, is if I let go of all that I've been carrying since the minute I woke up in that hospital bed.

Sometimes you have to face how you feel head on, let it do its thing. Respect the hurt and the anger and the confusion. Let it do the damage it wants to do but just for a moment, just long enough for you to know it's been and left footprints in your soul, then you can move forward with new purpose. Refreshed and ready to tackle whatever it is that might face us next. Alive. Together. We've made it this far. She's made it this far. There's a new page to turn.

Chapter Fifty-Two

Monday morning. I responded to one of Billy's four text messages this morning, apologising for not having updated him last night, but letting him know she was okay and that I'd be in touch. He'd pleaded with me to not make him wait too long. I also messaged Dad, just to say that she'd woken last night and that I'd call him later to update him properly when all the tests had finished, so it's something of a surprise when he bursts into the room, searching out eye contact with both myself and Poppy. He pulls up short just before me and for a moment I think he is going to give me a hug. I stay seated, wondering why all the men in my life can't get over themselves.

Poppy is awake again, just like they said she would be. She stops looking at her book, the one thing she's managed to focus on in between tests and visits from various doctors, nurses and specialists this morning. And it's not even ten a.m. She forces a smile for Dad, though she still seems exhausted.

'Poppy, look who it is.'

He hovers.

'You okay, Dad?'

'Yes, yes. I'm fine. Thank you. I'm just so relieved for you. I had to come over, I needed to see you both. Is she okay?' He addresses me, though he's always done that, rather than talk to her direct.

'You're doing well, aren't you, Pops? Your throat's sore, isn't that right?' Dad looks to me. ''Cause of the tube. And your body aches a bit, right?' She nods. 'There's some bruising, but really, she's okay. No other injuries. They're going to see if you can manage to stand and take a few steps later today, aren't they? They just want to check what her muscle tone is like, see how she is, what kind of physio she'll need, that sort of thing. We think she might need some speech therapy, isn't that right, Pops? Just to help her with all her sounds, that's something to do with the brain stem damage, I think. I can't remember, there's been so much said, I'm just grateful she's awake.'

Poppy goes back to reading her book, pausing on each page to study the photos, occasionally drifting off before her focus returns, and slowly, her fingers not yet quite as nimble as they were before, she moves on to the next page.

'Where did you get that?' Dad asks.

'What?'

He stares at me. 'That necklace.' I reach for the chain Iris gave me, having forgotten I'd even put it on. 'Where did you get it?'

'Oh, Iris brought it in for me.' I pull the ball out of my top so he can see it better.

'When?'

'The other day. Paul brought her in to visit us.' He pulls it from my neck and the chain digs into my neck a bit. 'Dad. Careful.'

'Why was she here?'

'She's been worried about Poppy, and me for that matter.'

'But I saw her. I told her how you were.' His tone is no longer concerned and caring; it's darker, it puts me on edge. 'Why did she need to come in?'

'I suppose sometimes it's nicer to see people face to face, isn't it? When you've been worried about them.' He nods, stiffly, his gaze still on my necklace before eventually drawing his eyes up to mine. 'It was nice to see her, Dad. It's been a bit lonely in here on my own, sometimes.'

'I could have come in. If you'd said. If you'd let me.' Claustrophobia claws back into my chest. 'You've only got to ask, Lisa, I'd be right here. I mean, I've tried to do the right thing and give you space, but perhaps that was the wrong thing? I can't know this if you don't say.'

'It's fine. I suppose I didn't realise I would enjoy the visit until she was here. Maybe I didn't realise the loneliness until she'd gone?'

'Right.' He stares back at the necklace with suspicion before pulling a chair up beside me and we sit in silence.

The energy in the room has shifted and unusually I'm not quite sure what to say, relieved when I remember. 'Plumbers.'

'What about them?'

'Did you get in touch with anyone? About the boiler?'

'Oh! Yes. Well, I've had three over to price it up, but then one of them noticed a problem in the kitchen and upon investigation…' He glances back at the necklace, preoccupied. 'Well, it looks like there's some other work needs to happen at your place.'

'What do you mean? What kind of work?'

'I'm not exactly sure. I think it's to do with the extension. Whoever did it, didn't membrane the walls properly, which means there are bits of damp forming. I got a builder out to look at that for us and when they investigated, it looks like there's no insulation.'

'Right. But it's not cold in there.'

'Well, no, maybe not but it's not good for the house, so I've arranged for them to come in and get it all sorted whilst you're not there.'

'But what if they say we can go home? It's not good for Poppy if there's building work going on.'

'No, that's true but you can't leave it as it is, and she might be in for a while longer yet. If not, if they let you come out, you'll have to come to stay with me.'

'Or Grandma's?' I suggest, quickly.

'No, no, I've accepted an offer on hers so that won't suit, I'm afraid. It's fine, I've plenty of room. You can have your old room together, or she can have your old room and you can be across the hallway. It's silly me having all that space and you not staying with me when you need help.'

'Well, how long will the work take?'

'It depends. I mean, they need to basically pull all the kitchen out, take the walls down and start again. It's a big job, I'm afraid. Could take quite a few weeks and the guys I want to give the work to, well, I'm not sure they're available for a while yet. Dennis, from golf, he's having them do an extension for him. That's how I found out about them you see, you need to get recommendations for workmen and so I'd rather wait for them and get the job done right.'

I feel sucker punched. Taken from a blind spot and wrestled to the ground. This is what he's done all of my life, taken over and dictated how things must be because he's got the money and the contacts. 'Maybe it can wait, until next summer.'

'You can't leave a job like that over winter, that's the worst thing you could do. If it gets any worse, it'll be a much bigger job. To be honest, you could do with the whole place repainting too.'

'I don't want it repainting!'

'Well, when did you last do it? You don't have time for that sort of thing now you're working.'

'I have weekends.'

'Which you should be spending with Poppy. Especially now, you don't need that distraction. I'll pack up a few things for you both, make sure she's got some bits to play with, that you both have clothes.'

'Holly brought me stuff, I don't need anything.'

'Well, I'll just get Poppy sorted then. It's no trouble. Let's get it done whilst we can.'

At any other time, for any other person, his logic probably seems sound. It *is* looking tired at my house. I love the walls and the decorations but, yes, there are scuff marks, chips on paint, and I know it gets a bit damp around the windows if I forget to put the dehumidifier on, but I can wipe them off. It's my house. My home. I don't want to go to live with him. But I can hear my inner narrative, I hear how ungrateful it sounds, how rude it would appear to him if I were to reject him getting things organised. And I do have stuff from Holly, she brought plenty in. It is only Poppy's bits that I might need. I guess I could give him a list.

'I won't get them to change anything you like.'

'I like my kitchen!'

'Well, they'll be putting the same one back in. It needs doing, Lisa. Just be pleased that we have the means to do it. Grandma's estate is getting sorted, there's money coming from there and she'd love to know it went on your home.' I grit my teeth together, my jaw tight. 'Oh, and about your car. They're just waiting on conformational paperwork then they'll pay out. I think you should put the money in the bank for now.'

'Dad, I don't know how I feel about driving yet, but… I need a car.'

'I already said, I'll get you one. Something a bit newer and sturdier.'

'I liked my car. I paid for it. It was my car.'

'And I always told you it wasn't as safe as it could be. You've had it too long already. And I understand the freedom you felt it gave you.'

I want to point out it wasn't something I felt, but fact. The car did give me a freedom that, had I listened to him, I'd never have had. When he was so insistent I shouldn't buy one. So insistent, in fact, that where normally he'd have bought it for me, he flat out refused the idea that it would be good for me. I always knew he hated that I bought it without him knowing. 'I need a car, Dad.'

'And like I said the other day, I can get you sorted.'

Whatever energy that had been in the room has now gone. Any whisper of fight I might once have had, has disappeared. The sand has run out of my independence and I've no energy to turn the timer over.

'I'd better go, leave you two to it. I guess it'll be lunchtime soon. I didn't bring anything in for you today, so hopefully you'll be able to get something from the cafe, now that Poppy's awake?' I nod, fighting back the overwhelming urge to cry. 'I'll let you know what the builder says and as soon as I've a car sorted, I'll text you the details so you can sort your insurance out, okay?'

'Okay,' I croak.

'Right, Poppy. Grandad had better get off,' he says to her.

She opens her mouth but nothing comes out again, so she smiles, weakly.

He smiles back and behind the glasses, I think I can see love. Maybe even warmth. Sometimes I just wish it was enough to give him pause for thought about all the things he does for our benefit, and whether we really want them.

Chapter Fifty-Three

Poppy rests again, worn out by lunch. Watching her grow tired just trying to feed herself is soul destroying. My little girl reduced to a tired, frustrated shell of who she used to be. I offered to help but didn't expect her to want me to. When they tried helping her to stand this morning, her legs weak, unable to take her weight, she wouldn't give up until she'd been able to stand alone, for just a second. I wonder where she gets her grit and determination from because I don't really think it's me. When I think back to the conversation with Dad over the house, I kick myself at how quickly I let myself be run over by his solutions. I suppose it's the reason I took myself so far away from him, emotionally and then, with Billy, physically, when we went to Scotland. Dad couldn't railroad so easily if I wasn't available.

But I've no strength for that right now, it's easier to roll over. Let him do what he wants, the way he wants it. Even if that does mean doing things I don't want to. If it's in Poppy's best interests, then I guess I can let it slide. And he's probably right, it's not fair on her to live amongst a building site after all she's already been through. Maybe this comes back to what he said before, how hard I make it for him to care for me. I should be grateful.

I grab my notebook and pen, finding that each time I feel frustrated or confused, writing it down has helped me to unlock certain thoughts, perhaps offload certain feelings. Pen poised, I start writing. I make notes about the house and how much I just want to go home. I write about Dad's and how uncomfortable it makes me feel when I have to stay there, how tight my chest feels, how much I feel the need to choose my words. I write about Holly and how perhaps she's the one to help me if I can make sure to spend time with her. Her light and froth has always lifted me, she's always been the person I call on if I want to have fun, be silly. Not that I find that easy any more.

I write about Billy. About the look on his face when he saw Poppy but how surplus he clearly felt when he noticed Paul was there. And as much as I'd like Poppy to have a relationship with her dad, on the basis that two parents have to be better than one like I had, I realise I don't want the kind of father that I imagine he would be. One where delivering gifts was more important than waiting until I was ready to speak to him about how we go about introducing them, how we make them fit. How the three of us fit. Becoming a parent changed me, a lot for the better, sometimes maybe for the worst, in as much as I'm one-dimensional these days. I don't feel like I'm much more than a mum, like in gaining a new side to me when I had her, when I fell pregnant even, other parts of me faded away. Perhaps that's why I'm so easily knocked off my perch, because there's not enough of me to stand my ground or be confident in who I am and what I think at the moment, unless it's about Poppy. Everything else though, everything, feels fluid, maybe even a little out of reach.

Which makes me think of Paul.

Quietly arriving. Quietly being. Quietly leaving when he could see there was a moment for me to treasure and be present and he was surplus to requirements. Quiet, yet firm, supporting what I needed instinctively. The only messages I've had from him since, are just little ones checking in. 'Are you okay? Do you need anything? Call me if I can help.' It's never about him, always about me, me and Poppy.

'Mummy,' croaks a whispered voice beside me.

I close the notebook and place it on the side. 'Hey, you, how are you feeling?'

She nods, which I know means she's okay.

'Anything hurting?'

She shakes her head.

'Throat?'

'A little,' she croaks.

'We'll get them to top up your medicine soon, okay.'

Another nod.

She shifts on to her side. 'You want me to put the telly on?'

A shake of her head.

'Music?' I point to the tape player. She nods. 'Here you go. You've been listening to this for the last few days.'

'Have I?' she manages.

'Yeah. Whilst you were sleeping. We've sung and danced to it.'

She shrugs as if she doesn't remember.

'No, well, you were sleeping.'

'What happened?' she manages, tracing her finger around my palm like I used to when doing ring-a-ring-o'-roses on hers. Her fingers jerk a little, tiny, fine movement not available to her just yet.

'We had a car accident, baby.'

I watch her for a moment, still tracing her finger across my palm. I wonder if the words go in, if she really understands what any of it means. Maybe Dad was right when he said she wouldn't remember, and I'm glad of that. I don't want to trigger or unlock any memories by saying too much.

'We were going to ARK with Charlie and Paul.'

She nods. I don't know if she remembers or just accepts what I'm saying. I curl my hand around hers. 'I think we might move in with Grandad, just for a little while. Is that okay with you?'

She nods.

'Do you like his house?' I ask, aware how different it is to ours. And how rarely she's been, particularly in recent months. 'He has a slide in the garden, do you remember?'

She nods. She takes her hand back, pulling Bear-Bear back into her, her eyes heavy, the chat easily wearing her out. I stroke her arm, just like I used to when she was a baby and struggling to get back to sleep, until I hear her breath shallow, as she moves into sleep. If it's in Poppy's best interests, I can do anything. Including moving in with Dad.

Chapter Fifty-Four

'Here you go, there, careful, that's it. Go steady, here, let me take these upstairs and you can make yourselves comfortable in the lounge.'

Dad pushes the lounge door open for Poppy and me. It's been just over a week since she woke up. Just over two since the accident. The physiotherapy has been quite intense, the team getting enough strength back in her legs for her to get as far as the bathroom with minimal support. Her cognitive skills are beginning to return, she can concentrate a little longer, her voice is returning, albeit a little on the raspy side. She can hold cutlery in her left hand, though her right is a little trickier. She's managing the iPad, mind you. A fact I smiled at when I noticed. She had been loving the feel of fresh air on her face as Paul carried her from the car to the house, as her little legs still easily tired. In Dad's place though, the fire rages, piled high with red and yellow burning logs, the heat hitting us square in the face as we step in from the hall. Neither of us turn our faces to it, I guess because, with the exception of a few trips down in a wheelchair to a small garden in a courtyard at the hospital, fresh, moving air feels somehow new to us both. It smells both autumnal and clean. Fresh.

'Thanks, Paul, Holly. I can take it from here, I think,' says Dad as he jogs the wide staircase with our bags, leaving Paul and Holly in the hallway.

Holly follows me into the lounge. Frank the dog is stretched out in front of the fire, vaguely noticing my arrival but not doing anything about it. 'Are you sure you're going to be okay? Do you want me to stay?'

'No, and yes, but it's fine. We'll adjust.' She smiles sympathetically at me. 'Go on, it's fine, honestly.'

I flick the telly on for Poppy, Paul having lifted her up on to the sofa. She puts her little arm out, trying to encourage Frank to come over to her and he does, slowly, stretching and groaning before plodding towards her. She fusses him as best she can, whilst I pull a throw over her, though it's not long until she's kicked it back off again and I can't blame her, it's tropical in here. She settles with Frank leant up against the sofa below her as I head over to the window, wrestling with the clasp to try and open it.

'You'll let the warm out,' says Dad, reappearing.

'Right, it's just that—'

'She needs to stay warm, doesn't she? Isn't that what the hospital advised?' He looks between me and Holly.

'I think they just want her to be comfortable, really,' I say.

'Right. Well cold isn't good for your bones, is it? I've made soup. And there's bread in the oven too.' I hadn't smelled the bread because the kitchen is down some stairs and the lounge had overwhelmed all my senses in any case. 'I'll put the kettle on. Are you two staying or is it just me and the girls?' It's not really a question, however he poses it.

Paul and Holly pick up the signals. 'No, no, we need to get off anyway. I need to get over to school to pick Charlie up and...' She points to Paul as if handing over the conversation reins.

'Yeah, I have some work to do.'

'Ah, right. Well that's a shame but thanks for bringing them back. I hope it's not put you out too much? Can I refund your fuel at all?'

'No! No.' Paul backs off towards the door. 'It's no trouble.'

'Right, okay, I'll just pop the kettle on then, see you, you two. Thanks again.'

Dad jogs off down the hallway, his footsteps trotting down the stairs to the kitchen. He's got more energy than I've seen in years and already I'm feeling claustrophobic.

'Take me with you!' I whisper to Holly as she follows Paul to the door.

She pulls it open. 'You're going to be fine, okay? Honestly, I promise. It'll all be okay. A bit of time with your dad might be just what you need to get things back on an even keel and Poppy needs peace and quiet and there definitely won't be any of that at your place currently. Look, chill out. Let your dad look after you, okay?'

I nod, unconvinced.

'And if you need anything, as always, you know where I am, yes?' asks Paul. He's been attentive since arriving with Holly to pick me up, attentive but guarded in some way. As if he's holding back. I wish he wouldn't. I wanted him to hold me. I wanted him to wrap his arms around me whilst relief rushed out of my veins. Leaving hospital with Poppy felt like it might never happen. We caught one another's eye in the rear-view mirror at one point, holding it for just long enough that I could be reminded of his feelings for me, and mine for him.

'You're seeing Billy this evening, right?' asks Holly as she climbs into Paul's car.

I notice Paul pretending to act nonchalant, snatching occasional glimpses at me as he puts the boot down.

'Yes. As long as Pops settles okay, I'll give him an hour. Dad's out at some men's club tonight so I can see him without Dad hovering.'

'Let me know how it goes.'

'Will do.'

She pulls the door shut with a wave.

'Thanks, Paul, I appreciate it.' I move around to his side of the car, threading my arms around his waist as I would have before, when we were just friends. He reciprocates, squeezing me tightly, planting a kiss on the top of my head in a way he probably wouldn't have before. I want to tell him not to worry about Billy, that he and I will talk too… but I also know I can't be clear about anything right now. Poppy has to come first.

Chapter Fifty-Five

Dad is by the hat stand, buttoning his coat up, adjusting his hat.

'I can stay if you want,' he says, stopping me halfway up the stairs, just about to check on Poppy. 'Maybe it'd be better if I didn't go?'

'No! Please!' I stop myself because I can hear my tone and it's a little too desperate. 'Go on, it's fine. We're fine. She'll be asleep and Billy is coming round so we can talk. Honestly, go on. Have a good evening.'

Dad nods. He doesn't approve of Billy. Never has. I think he was going to suggest he shouldn't come round, but, in fact, he seemed to stop himself from commenting and turned his focus to our dinner instead. That's some kind of progress, I think. And maybe that's what this next few weeks of us being under the same roof will offer, progress. I really do want to make things work between us, and I feel as if he does too.

The front door slams shut, Dad's car pulls off the drive and I let out a breath. Poppy is fast asleep having not moved from the position I left her in when I tucked her up in bed, Bear-Bear snuggled into her chest. I watch her for a moment, my heart full of love and relief that even though we're not home, home, we're here. Not in hospital. Not surrounded by illness and fear. No longer reliant on other people to cook for us and clean around us. I wish we were home, I wish she was in her own bed and me tucked up on the sofa. Because, to be honest, Dad hasn't stopped fussing until he went out and I don't know how many weeks I can cope with him trying to do everything for us, but I do appreciate that he's trying.

I pull the door to mine and Poppy's room too, just as the doorbell goes. It's a short, sharp ring of Dad's Victorian bell and I pause to see if it disturbs Poppy, but she doesn't flinch.

Jogging down the stairs, I narrowly avoid Frank, who has apparently taken to resting at the bottom of the staircase, no longer bothered about climbing it but presumably wanting to protect anyone asleep upstairs. I pull open the wide, stained-glass door to the porch of Dad's house. Billy's reflection meets me through the glass. There's a brown envelope with my name on the mat.

'Hi,' I say, grabbing the envelope then standing back for Billy to come in.

'Hi.' He offers up a generous bunch of flowers, autumnal coloured gerbera, roses and carnations. 'I thought you might like these.'

He only ever bought me flowers when he'd done something wrong, and I'd forgotten that fact until he presented these to me just now. I resist asking him what it is. 'Hi, come in, thanks, they're… lovely.'

'How is she?' He takes off his coat and scarf, looking around for somewhere to put them.

'Here, on the bannister,' I say, as I thumb the envelope from the mat open. He looks around for where to go and I head off down the stairs to the kitchen. 'Tea?'

'Great. Thanks.'

Then I pull up short at the bottom of the steps, Billy careers into the back of me. 'Shit, sorry… I…' But I can't find the words because I can't stop looking at the lock of my hair, tied up in a short braid, within the envelope. I know it's my hair because there's a tag attached to a bobble that keeps it together with my name and the month and year on it. I think it's in Grandma's handwriting and there's a vague recollection at the back of my mind about the day I went to a hairdresser to have all my hair cut off short. I'd grown it down to my waist and was so proud, but Dad wanted it cutting short and neither myself or Grandma got a say in it when he'd decided, especially when he was backed up by Grandad.

I remember crying in the hairdresser's chair as she snipped it off. I remember feeling like a boy, which now I know is probably gender stereotype stuff but back then it felt like I'd had all kinds of girly taken from me.

'Are you okay?' Billy has come to stand beside me.

'I don't understand.' I pull the hair out, studying it.

'What?' He peers more closely, then grimaces. 'What the hell is that?'

'My hair.'

'In an envelope on your doorstep? Bit dark.'

'Did you see anyone when you arrived?'

'No.'

'Nobody hanging around? No cars?'

'I saw your dad leave. To be honest, I'd been waiting until he came out before pulling out the side road and coming over. He always terrified me, your dad.'

'So, you saw nobody.'

'No! I told you. Your dad left, I pulled out the side road and came here. Well, not straight here, I went to get these from the garage first, but when I was here before, I didn't see anyone and by the time I pulled onto your drive, there wasn't anyone there. Does it matter?'

I pull absentmindedly at the necklace Iris gave me. 'I don't know. Maybe.'

'Right.' He grows impatient with my distraction and takes it upon himself to put the kettle on.

'Sorry, here, let me.' I take the kettle from him, filling it up as I stare out of the window into the pitch black of our back garden, suddenly wishing Dad had blinds down here.

'So, how's she doing?'

'Yeah, she's good. She's doing really well. There'll be quite a bit of physical therapy and some speech stuff to do, she struggles with some sounds it turns out. She's lost a bit of the fine motor neurone stuff, holding a pen is tricky, but the physio says it'll come back. She's pretty good in herself, though, which is the main thing really. The rest just needs patience.'

'Good, good. That's great.'

I pass him a cup of tea, the envelope of my hair on the kitchen table.

Chapter Fifty-Six

'So. How are you?' he asks, reaching out for my hand. I let him hold it for a second before cupping my hands round the mug.

'I'm okay.'

'Rough few weeks.'

'You could say that.'

'It's been torture waiting to hear from you, I've felt so removed from everything. At a real loss.' I look at him, clearly not hearing himself. 'It's like I came back, wanted to connect with you, do the right thing by Poppy and then I've had to wait.'

'I see.'

'Which has been so hard because I've missed out on so much already, I just wanted to be there for you both.'

I cock my head to one side.

'What?'

'Why now?'

'What do you mean?'

'Why now? Why is now the time you want to be there for us both and not before when I fell pregnant, or when she was born? What's changed?'

He presses his palms together, holding them to his heart. 'I've changed.'

I wonder how true this is. It's been hard to notice, given all that's gone off, but there are still signs of the old Billy there: the swagger in the pub, the turning up with gifts for Poppy, the competition between him and Paul.

'How?'

'I've travelled. I've seen the world and learned about the universe. About myself. I've had time to study me.'

'Your favourite subject.' I've said it before I realised I was going to.

'Ooh. Ouch. You're angry.'

I stand up, pushing my tea away from me. It spills slightly onto the envelope of hair, so I move it to the kitchen side, still freaked but only able to deal with one thing at a time. 'Yes, I probably am. Have you any idea what you put me through?'

'I'm sorry!' He reaches his hands out across the table in my direction. 'Truly. For everything. I know it must have been hard.'

'Hard? Hard! You've no idea how hard.'

'But you had money, you had your dad to keep you covered whilst she was young and you're working now, right?'

I don't know if it's the hair on the doormat or him, but I can feel a bubbling undercurrent in my chest, and I don't know if I have the strength to keep it in check. 'This isn't about money, Billy… though that wouldn't go amiss too. This is about emotional support. It's about taking responsibility for your daughter, for your pregnant girlfriend, then the new mother that I was when you decided to just up and leave.'

He looks over his shoulder as if someone might hear my raised voice. Yep, I'm definitely not going to hold this together, but maybe it's long overdue.

'She's fast asleep. There are two floors between us.' The more I look at him and the more I talk, the angrier I feel towards him. Maybe it's the last couple of weeks, maybe it's relief that she's still alive, maybe it's unspoken hurt that I'm finally giving airtime, but I can feel myself unravelling. 'She won't hear a thing and I need to get this off my chest.' I brace myself, then let go. 'How dare you?' He stares. 'How dare you just waltz back in and assume you can pick things up where we left off?'

'This is about Paul, isn't it?'

I drop against the kitchen worktop, stunned.

'I knew it! When I saw you in the pub. You clearly like one another. Then at the hospital. You were having a heart-to-heart when I arrived. I interrupted you. You have feelings for him, and him for you by the way that he looks at you. I suppose I've come along and ruined it for you. Well, I didn't mean to do anything like that, Lisa, but I do have a right to see my daughter.'

'A *right*?' I shake my head, putting more distance between us, catching sight of the envelope with my hair in it. Maybe it's not all Billy's fault. Although… 'Paul and I are friends. Just as we have been for years.' Billy pulls a face. 'Don't! Don't you dare! You don't have the right to an opinion on that one. My anger with you is founded in your absolute desertion of all responsibilities, then rocking up now like you can just pick things up.'

'Why can't we?'

I laugh. 'Are you kidding me?'

'Alright, maybe not right where we left off but somewhere. I want to be in your life, Lisa. And Poppy's.'

'Why?'

'Because I've realised that I loved you. And that I could love her too.'

'You *could* love her?'

'Yes! If I'm given time to get to know her.'

'And what happens if you realise you can't love her? What if you decide she's not loveable enough? Do you go again? What do I tell her? This is why you didn't want to meet in the village, isn't it? So you could keep some distance if things didn't work out.'

'She's my flesh and blood.'

'Sometimes that's not enough.'

'Two parents are better than one.'

I move around the kitchen, eventually bracing myself against the side, clear on something for the first time in Poppy's life. 'One is plenty, if that's how it needs to be.'

Dad and all he's tried to do, what he's got right, and what he's got wrong, flashes before me. All that I've learned about how I do and don't want to parent has come from him. A single parent. Of course I wish my mother hadn't died, but who can say if my relationship with Dad would have been different if she hadn't? Ultimately, he did his best. As am I. And my best, I know I can do alone.

'Lisa.'

'No! Not yet. You don't get to walk out on us then walk back in and assume it's all going to drop into place. How long are you staying for? Where are you staying?'

He fidgets in his seat, I fold my arms. 'I'm staying at Dougie's.' Dougie is his cousin. 'I've got a bit of time before I need to get back.'

'Get back where?'

'To Edinburgh.'

'Edinburgh?' I frown at him, confused because he never really settled. He told me he didn't like it there. It was too cold, too grey, too… exposing for him, I imagine. 'You went back?' I blink, the news somehow puncturing the part of me that feels like Edinburgh was an opportunity never fully realised. I loved it there, it felt like somewhere I could stay, until he left and Dad brought me home. 'When?'

'A couple of years ago.'

'A couple of years! I thought you'd been travelling, I thought you'd gone off to find yourself. I assumed you must have been away this whole time?'

'I did do that. Then I came back and got a job in a bank.' I double-take. 'I work for Bank of Scotland in their computing department at the moment.'

'You work for a bank?' I look at the beads round his neck and wrists. The tattoos that peek out from beneath his T-shirt sleeve. The casual clothes that look more trekking the Inca trail or sampling psychedelic drugs than systems testing a banking computer system. I imagine the state of my bank account, the one I've tried to fund on my own. Not always just 'managing', Dad bailing me out, even when I really didn't want it. I think about all the times Poppy and I have gone without. I think about the car.

'It pays well. I've managed to buy my own house, it's only small but it's big enough for the three of us and maybe we can make it work this time?'

'You want us to move to Edinburgh with you? I mean, if you're here for Poppy, I want you to be in her life but... moving to Edinburgh?'

'Well... I don't know, the accident made me realise that I can't just rock up and expect you'll want to whisk her away like that. But maybe you could consider it? I mean... maybe we should have both stayed in Scotland and seen this thing through.'

I let out a breath of despair. 'This thing?'

'Lisa. I'm sorry. I've been shit. I wish, I *wish* I could turn back time, make different decisions, be better, but I can't. This is me, Lisa.' He stands in an odd show of alleged vulnerability. 'I'm flawed but I want to make amends. Please... Please don't push me away.'

Chapter Fifty-Seven

Dad arrived back home after just shy of an hour out of the house. I'd just explained to Billy that I wasn't a pushover, that him presenting himself as the kind of father and partner I always wished he could be, did not suddenly mean I was about to up sticks and move to Scotland. It was something of a revelation. That's not to say there aren't things to think about with regards to how Billy and I could make things work for Poppy, regardless of how we feel about one another. But to hear myself stand strong, be assertive, not let him steamroller me like he might have once upon a time… Maybe the changes motherhood brought about aren't a bad thing. I may feel lost on one level, but equally, perhaps I feel found? More so, since Poppy woke up; I have a new focus, some clarity.

Billy left, making me promise to think seriously about his offer. Which I will, of course I will, and as Dad and I drank tea in the kitchen, I felt something like confidence returning.

Until Dad saw the envelope, peering inside to see the hair. He asked me where I got it from and when I tried to take it from him, he just pulled it closer, out of my grasp. I told him it came through the letterbox. That I found it on the mat when Billy arrived. He'd turned my hair over in his hands, the golden plait fitting his palm. A chill came over me and I really wanted him to give it back to me, but he stuffed it back in the envelope asking if I'd seen anyone. He wouldn't look at me. He was off somewhere in his head, unreachable. I'd tried to joke that this wasn't another gift from him, but he didn't respond. Sometimes, when he goes off in his head, he's faked a response when I've tried to gee him up, but this time, there was nothing. His hands shook, his grasp of the envelope so tight that his knuckles turned white.

Then he'd stood, suddenly tall in his kitchen. If I'd wanted to wrestle him to the ground to retrieve it, I think I probably could have, but somehow, I didn't dare move. He had this energy about him, something weird and impenetrable. He left me alone in the kitchen, uncertain what I had done wrong. Which was strange because I'd never really had that kind of feeling before. Yes, there'd been many times when I felt I'd done something wrong, made the wrong decision, been thoughtless or careless. But this time, it was as if I'd done something wrong that was much bigger than skipping school or getting pregnant. Talking to Grandma when he'd asked me not to or smoking with Holly down the bottom of our garden. This time it was major.

When I got up this morning, Dad had already gone out.

I called around for him, his bedroom door ajar, his office door shut. If he'd been in there, he'd have answered and when I looked out of the window, I saw his car had gone. The fire was on in the lounge again, all ready for Poppy to set herself up there for the day. There was a note on the kitchen side from him saying that he was just going over to mine to sort the builders out, then he had a few errands to run. He told me he'd be back soon. I tried opening the kitchen door to let Frank out for a wee, but the door was locked and when I looked for the key in its usual place, it wasn't there. I tried the front door, and again, it was locked, no key in sight.

I started to feel anxious, trapped in Dad's big house. What if there was a fire? I felt hot, too hot. I found myself rummaging through kitchen drawers, trying to find the key, now claustrophobic. I rattled windows which were stuck fast and then I couldn't breathe because what if I need to get out? What if before he came home, Poppy was taken ill, and I couldn't open the door to medical help? I tried calling his mobile but, as usual, it was switched off. I rummaged through the drawers in the lounge, in the drawing room, desperate now for the spare key. I tried each drawer in the kitchen, still no luck.

I jogged upstairs. Poppy was watching episodes of *Peppa Pig*, the theme tune playing out every few minutes marking each new episode. I ran upstairs, stopping outside of his office. I never went in unless invited. It had always been out of bounds. I'm not sure he ever said it was, it just had that vibe. A weird, impenetrable energy. This was his space, the place he worked, organised the home, the place he kept all his important papers. I placed my hand on the handle, guilt settling in my belly. I pushed the door open, the curtains were half closed making the room feel dark and dusty. I went to switch the light on but stopped myself; if he came back, he might see it on, so I dug out my phone to put the torch on instead, carefully reaching for drawers to check for a key.

I didn't dare lift anything, in case I shifted it out of place. The folders of bills, certificates, bank stuff and house stuff. The only key I could find was a small one for the lock on his writing cabinet. I paused, listening intently in case he came back whilst I was here, the only sound being *Peppa Pig* from the lounge. I took the key, carefully slotting it into the lock and juggling it until the lock came free, opening the drawer and peering in. Nothing, no key, just papers. I froze at the sound of a car going past before locking the drawer again and escaping from his room, fearing he'd be able to tell I'd been in there, like maybe somehow, I'd changed as a result.

Out of steam, unsure where to look next, I dropped down the stairs and at the bottom, leant against the bannister, sliding to sit on the bottom step, my belly heavy with dread. I couldn't put my finger on it, but something was really wrong, something shifted last night, the arrival of the hair was significant, but I didn't know why my world was tilting.

When the front doorbell rang, I jumped.

And that's when I found the letter. My name and address on the front but it had been hand delivered.

I jogged through to Poppy, who hadn't noticed my mood. She was snacking on raisins in front of the telly, I'd given them to her especially to help get her fingers working. She was concentrating hard, in between glancing at the TV, picking each one up, carefully, steadily, popping it in her mouth. I plumped up her pillows, planted a kiss on her forehead, loaded the fire up with a few more logs then smiled sweetly. 'Just going to make myself a cup of tea. You okay?'

'Yes,' she croaked, her voice still occasionally breaking.

And now I'm here. My mug of tea steaming in front of me, curling, twisting into the air. Frank sits patiently by the back door, no doubt wondering when I'm going to let him out. The letter rests in my hands and I can't breathe. My world is no longer tilting, it has seismic shifted so far that I can't imagine how I'd ever get it back. It can't be true. It can't be. I'd have known before now, I'd have felt it. Someone would have said. Something would have come out because you can't keep a secret that big for somebody's entire life…

Chapter Fifty-Eight

Dear Lisa,

This is the hardest letter I've ever had to write. I've tried so many times these last few months, and never found the right words. There's no easy place to start, no natural order of things. But the time has come for you to know the truth.

I know that for your whole life, you've believed your mother died. And I know how this version of the story came about. Please, as hard as it may be, don't be angry with those who've led you to believe a version of the truth that could never have been. It's not their fault. Perhaps they did what they thought was best. For you, and for me... I've read the letter over and over since it arrived on the doormat this morning. Landing almost in the exact same space as the envelope containing my hair, the night before.

The truth is, I am alive. I have kept – and been kept – out of your life, but I can't live this lie any more, you have a right to know me, as I do you, if you'll have me.

My throat is constricted, my heart races. My hands shake and everything feels like it spins. I've read the letter so many times, I can almost read it off by heart, though maybe not out loud, because this can't be true, can it?

Digging deep inside myself for focus and determination, I climb the stairs heading straight back to Dad's office. I don't pause or worry when I open the door this time, I know exactly what I'm looking for and where it is. I open the drawer to the files, lifting out the one marked Genevieve. My mother's name. My mother's file. And inside it, I see her death certificate. The same day I've believed for all of my life. Three months after I was born.

A devastating truth they've never kept from me...

I hope that you might find space in your heart to meet with me. I can't imagine how difficult this letter will be to receive, I can't imagine how it will make you feel, but please, forgive me this much until we've had a chance to meet. As hard as it will be, I want to tell you everything.

Chapter Fifty-Nine

Dad's car pulls up onto the drive. I stuff the letter in my pocket, rearranging my face, having already decided that I'm not rushing into this with him. I need time.

I go sit with Poppy, helping her colour in work pages in the book she got sent home by school. Her pen holding is getting better. As Dad comes through to the lounge, I shift a hair from Poppy's face and tell her she's doing a great job, forcing my voice to be light, normal, nothing's changed.

'You two okay?' asks Dad.

Everything's changed.

'Fine, thank you.' I smile as he hovers by the lounge door, watching us. 'I think Frank is desperate to go out though. And I couldn't find a key to unlock the door.'

'Oh really?' Dad pretends to look surprised. I know he's pretending because when he is, he over-eggs it. Always has. He pats about his trousers as if searching for the key before finding it in his inside jacket pocket and rolling his eyes. 'Silly me, I must have picked up the spare without realising.'

'Tea?' I hand some crayons over to Poppy to carry on what she's doing. I stuff my hand in my pocket to make sure the letter doesn't fall out. My hand tingles around it. My heart still pounds.

'Yes. Thank you.' He stands aside for me to pass. He smiles widely, another tell. I try not to be so overtly normal because if I can tell he's hiding something, he'll be able to tell that I am too.

'I've been thinking, Dad,' I say, pouring hot water onto teabags whilst he stands by the back door waiting for Frank to finish his business. 'Would you mind keeping an eye on Poppy for me for an hour or so later? I'd like to pop down to the library and it's only open today until three, then it's closed again until next Tuesday.'

'Oh, is it?'

'Funding I expect.'

'Right, yes.'

'I was wondering if I could get some study books from them.'

'Study books?'

'Well, I know you want me to stay at home with Poppy more and I guess the accident made me realise that time is precious when they're this age. Maybe I should leave my job and stay at home.' The words stick in my mouth because the idea squeezes my heart so tightly. I need that job, I need to be me. But I also need an excuse to leave the house that he'll approve of. 'I think I'd get bored in the house all day on my own, is all, so…'

Frank reappears and Dad wipes his paws without taking his eyes off me. He's still presenting himself as someone without any cares or worries and it still feels weird. I wonder what's shifted for him. Has he had a letter too?

'I thought about volunteering, you know, whilst she's at school, but that's the same as my working, so then I wondered about doing a course at home. You know the distant learning kind? I think they have loads of information about them at the library and I wanted to do a bit of research.'

He takes the tea from me, moving to stand by the kitchen stairs. 'Can't you do that online? Everything's on the internet now, isn't it?'

'Yes, I know, but I'd like to talk to people about it. Get some insight and I think they'd be able to help guide me towards the right course.'

'Can't I help?'

'You've already done so much, Dad. Thank you. This is just something I'd like to do on my own. I'll only be gone a couple of hours.'

'Well, take my car.'

'Oh, Dad. I don't know… I haven't driven since the accident, I'm not sure.'

'Let me take you then, Poppy and I can go and get cake in the cafe next to the library.'

'Dad, please!' He eyes me carefully. 'I'll take the bus. Just let me do this. I won't be long. I promise.' I see the muscle in his jaw flicker. 'I'll be straight there and back. She won't move off the sofa if I go around lunchtime, let her have her sandwiches there and you can carry on doing whatever you need to do. She'll probably have a nap anyway, that's what she's been doing every day, early afternoon.'

He looks uncertain but can tell I won't be turned.

'Very well. What time will you go?'

I look at my watch as if trying to work out what time it would be when actually, I know without doubt.

Please come to meet me, I'll be at the Wetherspoons in Sleaford. 1 p.m.

'I'll leave here about twelve, I reckon.'

If you don't want to know me after we've met, I'd understand. But please give me a chance to explain what happened.

'I'll probably be back by three at the latest.' He frowns. 'Half two, I'll make sure it's half two.'

'Okay...' He studies me for a second and I try my hardest to be cool. Calm. No giveaways. What do they call it in poker? A tell? No tells. 'Just be careful, okay?'

'Course.' I turn around, grabbing a cloth from the sink to wipe down the sides, eventually, I hear him take the stairs, chat quietly with Poppy, then I hear the creak of the main stairs and the opening and closing of his office door.

I take out the letter again, it quivers in my hands.

The gifts were something to try and reconnect. Things to let you know that somebody cared. Things to let you know I've been thinking of you, as I have every day since the day you were born. Things to make you see that despite the lies, you've been in my life this whole time. And now, I'd like to be in yours.

Chapter Sixty

I get off the bus near the library. I walk through town; my legs feel weak. It's market day and the bustle of traders calling out their wares is louder than normal, my ears hypersensitive. Buses and cars trundle along in busy town-centre traffic queues. Some kids from the local school walk down the street, pushing each other and laughing. Their school uniforms uniting them as they move through town; sandwiches and drinks clutched in their hands, lives ahead of them. I wait at a crossing and the beep to say we can walk pierces my ears. Someone brushes passed me, apologising as they continue on their way, and it makes me want to cry. I feel on the edge, not wrapped up but not fully undone, bustled over the road and into the stream of pedestrians that make their way up the narrow paths towards the pub.

I've never been in Wetherspoons here. I've always hated going in places I don't really know. I've hated meeting people I've not met before and I haven't stopped worrying about whether I'll recognise her. Will she look like me? Will it be instant and overwhelming like when they reunite people on TV? Or will it be stilted, guarded, neither of us quite certain what to say? And God, what if she isn't really my mother? What if it's a lie? Despite our challenges, I've never had any reason to doubt Dad. We've talked about Mum, more so when I was little, but even later on, when I fell pregnant with Poppy, we talked about her. The story was always the same, it never faltered. She'd died in a road traffic accident, when I was three months old. I didn't like to bring it up too often, it was clearly painful for him, desperately hard to raise a child alone.

I reach the door to the pub, then hesitate. Perhaps I should go home. This can't be true. Dad wouldn't have lied to me for my entire life. And what about Grandma and Grandad? They can't have lied too, can they?

There were reasons, it's not as straightforward as you might think. Please don't be angry with your family, please don't be angry with me...

But if she sent the gifts. How could she have got the hair, without someone sending it to her? And that photo from Holly's party? Who sent them to her? And she knew my date of birth. The place, the time...

I remember the tiny birthmark on your thigh, it mirrors one on my own...

If it's not her, how can she possibly have known such detail? Was it Dad? Has he kept in contact with her all these years whilst keeping it secret from me? How could he? Why?

The pub is busy, I move through the crowds of pensioners enjoying fish lunches, striped plastic bags at their feet from all they've bought at the market. My eyes dart about, partly wanting to see her straight away, partly terrified of the moment we lock eyes.

And then we do. I stop moving. She swallows. Somebody excuses themselves as they move between us to get to the bar but neither the woman nor I stop looking at one another.

Slowly, she stands as I move toward her. We share the same hair, a dark blonde, Grandma used to describe it as mucky. Mucky blonde. Her lips are thin like mine, her face small. She holds herself close, tight in, her fingers interlaced before her.

'Lisa.' It's not a question. She knows. She scratches at a mark on her hand, her movement quietly frantic. 'I'm Genevieve.' Her voice is glass-like.

I look around as I place my bag and coat down, checking to see if there's anyone I know.

'Erm… can I… do you want a drink?' she says.

'Erm… No. Thank you.'

'Right. Okay.' She goes to sit down, her movement awkward, her body language restrained. She doesn't take her eyes off me despite the scratching of her arm and the energy of someone not entirely at peace. It's like there are micro movements within her stillness, as if she's ready to run at any moment. 'Thank you for coming.'

'It's okay.'

She looks down at her fingers, scrubbing at her arm as if to stop the scratching she's been doing. Her fingers entwine, fidgety. I wonder how she feels. I think about my own heart right now: pounding out of my chest, my belly sick with uncertainty and confusion. Fearful. I don't remember many times when I really felt like a child. I think from a young age I've felt older than my years. When people told me I was mature, I took great pride in the fact and played up further to it, I wore maturity as a badge of honour. Yet now, I feel young, vulnerable, uncertain. I feel like I want a grown-up to come in and fix everything for me, tell me how it's going to be so that I don't have to work it out for myself. Except that I am a grown-up. And so is Genevieve.

'I don't know where to begin,' she says, eventually. I laugh because I can't know either. 'I suppose firstly, I want to say that I'm sorry.'

'For?'

She laughs into herself. 'Everything? The lies. The secrecy. The gifts.'

I think about each one, what they might mean to her, why she sent them. How pertinent some of them were, how significant over these last few weeks.

'I hoped they'd be moments to make you think, bring you some light, and joy, even. Help you with Poppy... but I wonder if perhaps they felt more sinister though. I'm sorry... I guess I've not done this before.' She studies me. 'I've thought about this moment so many times in the last few months. For most of your life, I've wondered if it would ever happen. I've told myself it shouldn't, I've cried because it should. I've wrestled with the need to see you, the want to be your mother, and the knowledge that... you were better off without me.'

'Better off?' I frown. 'How could any child be better off without their mother?'

Chapter Sixty-One

She shifts in her chair, her eyes, flitting. 'It's complicated. I want to explain but… it's difficult.'

'So is receiving a letter from a woman who claims to be the mother you've believed was dead your entire life.'

She looks down, then over to the bar from beneath her fringe. 'Should we get a drink at least? They might think we're being rude to take a table up and not order anything.' Her concern for the rules reminds me of me. Nature vs nurture.

'What will you have?' She reaches inside her bag for her purse.

'Tea. Please. Thank you.'

She takes herself over to the bar, her arms held in close to her body. She's about my height, maybe a little smaller. She's slighter than me too, but only just. She is polite at the bar, I can see her repeating please and thank yous as if she wants them to know just how much she appreciates the drink they're making for us. She can't stand still. Is it nervous energy or is she always like this? She makes her way back through the tables, placing a cup down before me.

I pull it towards me, desperate to cup my hands around the warmth but it's too hot, stinging my palms.

'I heard about Poppy,' she says, her voice barely audible.

'You know about her?'

She sighs, nodding.

'How?'

She studies her cup for a moment. She draws a breath, goes to speak then stops again.

'How!'

Eventually, she looks back at me. 'Elsie. Your grandmother.'

I sit back, stunned.

'Without her, I wouldn't have, but…'

I screw my eyes up, nothing making sense. A couple take up the table beside us, she offers a smile, he buries his head in the menu as if nobody else exists.

'It was a letter to begin with. Then a phone call. She wanted to meet so she could tell me the truth about when she and your dad left with you, but I didn't want to. I couldn't. I'd built a life believing you'd been taken because I wasn't good enough.' I shake my head, confused. 'And I was on my own, I didn't have anybody to talk it through with. It was too painful. I couldn't imagine how we could fix things. It was overwhelming…'

The more she speaks, the more questions I have but I don't know where to begin.

'Then she sent photos like this one…' She reaches into her bag to get out her purse again, flipping it open. The purse shakes in her hands as I stare at a photo of me that I don't think I've ever seen. A yellow knitted cardigan and hat, tied in a wool bow beneath my chin, my face perfectly spherical, my legs chunky and pale.

'I could barely breathe when I saw it.' She pulls it back closer to her, staring at it herself, her eyes fill. 'I didn't want to stop looking at it, I couldn't. Every day, all day, I'd sit with it in my hands, hoping that the more I looked, the more I'd feel, the more real you might become.

I was desperate for things to be different. For me to be different.' She flips the purse closed suddenly, shoving it deep in her bag as if it hurts to look at it now. She wipes a tear just as it falls to her cheek. 'Sorry. I didn't want to cry. It's not fair on you for me to cry.'

She takes a deep breath before looking up at me and I know it's her. I'm in no doubt that she is my mother. We're too alike to question it.

'I feel like I want to tell you everything, but there are some bits that even I don't know.'

I'm in the bathroom, splashing cold water on my face in a desperate bid to regain control of my senses. None of what Genevieve is saying makes sense and yet I know she's my mother, I feel it in my bones. When I look up at my reflection I stare into my own eyes and for a brief moment, can picture how I'll look in sixteen years' time. It's not so far away that it's impossible to imagine.

I pat my face with my scarf and try to force some in-control-of-this-situation composure, heading back out into the dimly lit bar. Genevieve stares out of the window in the same position I left her in, some people have come and gone, the bar is quieter now.

'So, Dad just took me?' I ask after a few moments of sitting back in front of her. She pauses, then gives a shallow nod. 'And you had no idea where we'd gone?'

'That's all I knew. I was young. I was frightened. I was…' Her eyes flick up to me then dart away. 'Things were difficult. There was so much to deal with… I felt so guilty, it was all my fault.'

'It takes two to get pregnant.'

Genevieve looks out of the window again.

'So what did you do?' My voice is flat, one-dimensional. It's partly because I'm not sure how much of the story I believe and partly because I'm terrified of what will happen if I let myself feel anything.

She picks at a handkerchief she's been concertinaing in her hands. 'I was so unwell, for such a long time. I suppose I pretended none of it had happened. I hid. I tried to handle what I was feeling…' Her eyes flick up to mine then away, as they have done since she asked me to promise I wouldn't tell Dad about us meeting. 'I was so alone.'

'In Edinburgh?'

'In Edinburgh.'

I shake my head. 'I lived in Edinburgh when Poppy was born,' I whisper.

'Elsie said. It made me wonder if I'd ever walked past you. Would I have known it was you, if I had?'

'We moved there when I got pregnant. Dad hated it. We argued. He didn't want me to go. My partner left me, and Dad came straight away to fetch me home, wouldn't take no for an answer.' She looks at me, sadly. 'I had no energy to fight…'

We both fall silent. So much to ask, so much to say, too much to wrap our heads around.

'I would have known it was you…' We stare at one another for a second before she studies her drink. 'Your dad had been living in Edinburgh when we met. He got a job up there, working with my dad. They became friends, that's how we met.'

'Dad lived in Scotland?' I wonder why he's never said this.

Genevieve nods. 'He was twenty-six, ten years older than I was. But he never felt that much older than me. I suppose partly because he seemed young, and I always felt quite grown up. We kind of met in the middle, somehow.' She pauses, sipping at her drink. 'I came from a religious family, Dad encouraged him to come to our church to meet new people, make friends.'

'He joined the church?' I think about his lack of religion now, is it connected?

'It was a strange environment. Not like a normal church… they followed scriptures but…'

'But?'

'It wasn't religion as you'd understand it. Not scriptures I could recognise now.'

'And Dad was part of that church?'

'He was. For about a year, I suppose. We were just friends at first. We didn't mean for things to develop.' She drops her eyes. 'My father raged when we told him I was pregnant. Any forgiveness and love that a normal church would show, it wasn't there. We'd let our urges overrule our faith in God. We'd brought shame on the family. My father caused problems, got David fired from his job.' The sound of Dad's name coming from her mouth, the slight Scottish lilt, it sounds unfamiliar. 'I think that's why he moved back home, by the time my father had finished manipulating the story, he had nothing left there. He'd been blacklisted, shamed for a relationship with someone so much younger. We did nothing illegal, and yet my father implied David had taken advantage of me. He had no choice but to leave. Even though he pleaded with my father to let us be together.' Her eyes fill. 'And then…' She looks down at her hands again. 'My parents died. In a road traffic accident.' She picks at the skin on the side of her thumb, it looks raw, sore. 'You were three months old. Your father had been in the car too. As were you.'

'But *you* died in a road traffic accident? That's what I was always told.' She looks up, sharply. 'You said he'd moved away? Why was my father in the same car as me and your parents, if he'd moved away?'

'Because he loved me. And you.'

Chapter Sixty-Two

'Your grandma brought David up to see me. A few months after you were born. She was desperate for my father to let him have access, or connection of some kind. Your grandfather didn't approve of the visit, but she did it anyway.' She pushes at her fingers as if trying to stop the repeated scratching. 'I don't blame any of them,' she says, left turning in the conversation. 'I really think everyone was just trying their best, but my father was God-fearing and felt we had done so much wrong in His eye. My dad was… not a very nice man.'

I think about my own. For all his faults, for all the controlling, for all the judgement, I can't say I ever thought of him as 'not a nice man' and yet, how could anyone tell someone their mother had died?

'There isn't a day gone by that I have not cried for you, Lisa.' Genevieve pushes her hands out towards me, stopping two-thirds of the way across the table, perhaps when she sees I don't respond. She pulls back. 'I understand if you're angry.'

I look down at my own hands. I always thought they were like Dad's, long fingers, 'piano playing hands' Grandma used to say, but now I see they're like Genevieve's. I wonder what she's like, what her personality is. Is she the reason I've always needed to please people, that – apart from where Poppy is involved – I choose not to fight. Is she the reason I will walk away rather than confront, in the knowledge that sometimes people can't be swayed? It's not that I let people walk over me, more that I don't always feel the need to fight. You can't always reason with people who've made a decision about something. I've always rather people be happy, comfortable, heard and seen. Have I passed these things on to Poppy? Is this all inherited from Genevieve?

Except that I could never let anyone take Poppy away. I'd have fought, I'd have moved heaven and hell to get to her. I don't understand how anyone can roll over when their child is taken from them. I can't relate. I look at the woman claiming to be my mother, no real doubt about the biology, but all of the doubt about the truth. It's too much.

'I have to go.' I pull my bag and coat into me.

'Lisa, please. Please don't go. Or let me know when I can see you again, I've waited so long…' Her words trail off.

'I need time. I can't process this. I can't do this. How do I know it's the truth? Why would they lie for all these years?'

She opens her mouth as if to answer, but nothing comes.

'Were you glad to get rid of me? Was it all a mistake?'

It's like I've punched her in the stomach, she reels back. 'Absolutely not!' There's a brief flash of fire in her eyes. 'I loved your father more than anyone before or since. I loved you. That's the reason I stayed away.' I shake my head, it doesn't make sense. 'I'd done enough…'

I think about all the times I've asked him about her, about their feelings for one another. How Dad would tell me that he loved her, he never shied away from that, but it always seemed too painful for him to expand on. Even as a kid, I could see that in him, so I rarely pushed it beyond the days they met. Him noticing her in the choir at church. Their friendship blossoming.

'Your father built a new life for himself, and for you. I just know he will have worked hard to do that and to protect you. He will have put you first, above his own needs, as well he should.' I consider her interpretation of a man I've always found to be stifling, someone who clipped my wings, someone who refused to let me grow and learn and be. Just as Genevieve's parents before him, or so it seems. 'Without my parents, I was alone in a world that I didn't understand because it no longer looked like the one I'd been taught. And it was all my fault.'

This is the first time I lose the ability to control my feelings, the hole in my life that presents now Grandma isn't here. And maybe until now, stood here in this bar with a woman professing to be my dead mother, maybe now is the first time I've truly realised the kind of woman Grandma was, and she is the only person I want to reach out to. The one woman who would have quietly, kindly, gently, told me what to do next. It's the first time I've realised what she meant to me and how carefully she navigated the relationship between herself and Dad, between her and I. She never demanded, she never forced, she was the opposite to Grandad in every way, shape and form. What she did for me is huge, but then… did she know about Genevieve? Surely, she can't have kept a secret as big as this? And now I don't know who or what to believe. I don't know who to blame, or if I even should? How could she take such a lie to her grave? I feel anger and fear and uncertainty. I feel confused, maybe even a little hopeful that things could change, but I don't know how or where to start because I can't just walk into the house and tell Dad what's happened today. How would he respond? How would it make him feel after all of these years?

'I have to go. I'll call you. Just… give me time, okay?'

Genevieve nods. 'My number is in the letter.' I nod. 'I promise I won't keep chasing you. I won't come to your dad's again. But please… let us keep talking. I want to know you, I want to build a relationship. I've lost out on so much and I can't make up for lost time, but we still have time left and I don't want to face the rest of my life without you in it.'

I clench my jaw.

'But if ultimately you decide you can't do this…' She bows her head. 'I will learn to face it. I promise I will. I just want the chance to make things work.'

Chapter Sixty-Three

I don't remember the walk for the bus or buying my ticket. I don't remember taking a seat up at the back or the person that came to sit beside me as all other seats were taken, the further out of town we got. It's only when I notice where I am and I realise I need to get off, grabbing my bag into me and hurriedly asking the lady beside me to move. I hop off by the shop, the place I spent so many childhood summer nights wishing I could be one of the ones who hung around with the rest of my school friends; all the while at home, on Dad's instruction, holed up in my room, all doors locked. Is that why he did it? Is that why my world was so small? For fear that she'd find me? Fear that I'd hear something, a rumour, a whisper that might blow the truth apart? How could he watch me go live in the same city knowing she might still be there and say nothing? Is that why he came to get me back so soon after Poppy was born? When Billy left? Is that why Dad never settled? And how could he never tell me any of this?

I walk the few minutes from bus stop to Dad's, hoping fresh air can fix my face even though I now question everything I thought I knew. I built a version of me, living and excelling, albeit in a wing-clipped life, despite not having a mother, despite being raised by my father. I achieved, in that I did well at school. I was a shining example of getting my education right, even though Dad never seemed to want me to fully realise my potential: when he sabotaged my desire to go away to college, when he stepped in if boys got too interested, when he returned me to the village I grew up in. How must he have felt, knowing I was up there, so close to her? But even before I had Poppy, Dad didn't encourage me to strive. Was that because it might take me too far away? The ambition Billy said I lacked, it was never nurtured by Dad. I am who I am because of what I've lived… so who am I, if not the girl whose mother died?

I pause on the doorstep, my body hunched and tight. I try to stand tall, aligning hips and spine, neck and head. Shoulders back, eyes forward. I push the key into the door and shout out as I head inside. But Poppy isn't in the lounge.

'Poppy?' I call out, jogging up the shallow steps until I reach her bedroom door, I push gently so as not to wake her, but her bed is tightly made, just as I left it when she got up. I call out again, checking my bedroom, then the bathroom. I call out for Dad too, the handle to his office locked. I take the stairs, my heart beating so hard it hurts. 'Dad?' I try, arriving in the kitchen to Frank asleep in front of the range. 'Dad! Poppy!' I try again, trembling. I dig out my phone, trying his number but it goes straight to voicemail. I run back upstairs and out the front door to see if his car is there, not having noticed either way when I got home. But it's gone. And I double over, winded. What if he's taken her? What if he's realised where I went and why and he's angry.

My mind races as I wait for Holly to pick up the phone. 'Hey, you,' she casually answers.

'Poppy's gone! Dad's taken her. Help me, Holly! What can I do?'

'Whoa, whoa, wait a minute, what?'

'I've just been in to town to meet my mother and I think Dad must have realised and taken Poppy to punish me.'

'Your mother, but—'

'I can't explain now. I've got back and Poppy's not here and Holly you have to help me.' I hear her move around. 'Please, come quickly.'

'Okay, okay. I'll be there in a minute. Stay where you are.'

I pace the hallway, glancing up the staircase in case Poppy comes down and I just didn't see her when I looked in her room. I run up, three steps at a time, trying Dad's office again, shaking the door handle to try and free it but it's definitely locked. It feels like hours before the doorbell goes and I race down to let Holly in, but, in fact, my watch says it wasn't much more than five minutes.

'Paul's here too, I was round at his.'

'What am I going to do, Holly? I need Poppy.' The sight of my best friend sends my legs weak and my strength depletes. 'Where is she? Why has he taken her?'

'Hey, hey, come here.' She scoops me up into her arms, Paul just behind her reaches for my fingers and I let him hold my hand. When Holly eventually lets go, I stagger back to the staircase, dropping down onto the third step. 'So, when did you go out?'

'I don't know, a couple of hours ago.'

'Right.'

'She sent me a letter, it was her all along.'

'What was?'

'The gifts, it was Genevieve.' Holly looks confused. 'My mother.'

'But… she died, Lisa.'

'That's what they all told me! That's what I believed but it's her, I can tell it's her. There's no doubt in my mind, well, I mean, I suppose there's a bit, but we look alike, we have the same hands.' I hold mine up to show Holly by way of proof and it's her response that makes me realise how I sound. 'It's true…' I say, my voice trailing off as I begin to wonder myself.

And then Dad's car pulls on the drive, Poppy beaming from the front passenger seat. I push through Holly and Paul and open the door to lift her out, wrapping my arms around her too tight until she complains she can't breathe, her voice still not quite back to normal.

'Have you missed her?' Dad asks with a wry smile. 'Sorry, I wasn't sure how long you'd be. In fact, I thought we might make it home before you, I swung by the library bus stop in case we saw you, but we didn't, did we?'

Poppy shakes her head, still held fast in my arms.

'You look like you've seen a ghost, Lisa, are you okay?' Dad comes up to me, checking me over. He glances around and about, his eyes undermining his jovial tone. He see's something, I'm sure of it.

'I'm… Yes, I'm fine.'

I turn around to hide my face because I don't want to talk to him until I'm ready, catching sight of Holly and Paul who look a combination of confused and concerned.

'How did you get on with your research?' Dad asks, locking his car up then heading into the house. Does he know I didn't go? Has he guessed where I was?

'Oh, yes. Good, it was fine,' I sing-song. Paul and Holly exchange a look. 'I was just… Holly and Paul wanted to hear about it, didn't you?' She nods and he follows her lead. 'I was about to make them a cup of tea actually. Do you want one?' I don't feel as light as I'm desperately trying to sound.

'No, no, thank you. I had one with Poppy. I've a bit of work to do actually so, if you'll all excuse me. Thank you for taking me out, Poppy.'

He shouts it through to the lounge, but she's already tucked up under her duvet with the telly on, looking exhausted from the exertion. Dad pauses, then half smiles at the three of us before heading upstairs. I turn to face them looking sheepish.

Chapter Sixty-Four

'What the hell is going on?' hisses Holly, pulling out the kitchen chair so its legs scrape on the stone floor.

I brace myself against the kitchen worktop, worn out.

Paul takes the kettle and fills it up, moving silently around the kitchen whilst I try and regain composure. He searches out cupboards for the mugs, getting the right one when I point to it. He gets milk from the fridge and tea bags, prepping everything in silence as I work out where to start.

Glancing up the stairs, I begin, quietly, steadily. 'So, I got a letter. From this woman claiming to be...' I pause, listening out before whispering, 'claiming to be my mother.' Holly shakes her head, confused. 'There was an accident. Presumably the one in which I was told she died. But, in fact, it was her parents that died and somehow, for some reason, Dad and Grandma took me from her, bringing me here to raise me as if she was no longer alive.'

'But...' Holly shakes her head as if that might help this all make more sense. 'None of that makes sense. How did she find you?'

'Grandma apparently. They were in touch before she died.'

'Why? Why would she know they'd taken you, then get in touch with her? Surely if you take a child from its mother, you absolutely do not then get back in touch with them? And... if, for some unbelievable reason, that did happen, if your grandma did talk to her, why wouldn't this woman have tried making contact sooner? Think about it. Would you let someone just take Poppy and not then spend the rest of your life trying to find her? You'd never give up, surely? It doesn't make any sense, Lis.'

'I don't know. She was young, maybe she thought it was the best thing for me too? I don't know.'

Holly exchanges a look with Paul who raises his eyebrows to suggest it could happen and she shouldn't be so quick to judge. But she is saying all of the things I've been asking myself since I left Genevieve. Something doesn't add up and I can't put my finger on it.

'And why now? What's so different now that you are worthy of her contact? I just don't buy it. How do you know she's not a total loon? A psychopath. You can't trust anyone these days!'

'Holly…' Paul warns, because he can see she's getting frustrated, angry even.

There's movement up above and we all hold our breath, waiting to see if it's Dad but nothing happens.

I lower my voice. 'I don't know. I don't understand it myself. But it kind of makes sense… maybe?'

'The photo, the hair, perhaps… I mean, it's a bit dark, but maybe it makes sense. But what about the notebook? Or the music? Poppy's dragon book?' Holly asks.

'I think the book was still from Dad…' I run out of steam because I realise I have no idea what I think about any of it any more. Paul stirs the drinks. It would have been easier if they'd all been from him. 'She said the notebook was to help me plan and hope. She said she wondered who'd encourage me now that Grandma was…' My bottom lip wobbles. Paul hands Holly and me a mug of tea. 'But then what about the tickets for the farm park place? How could she have known? And the jumper? I mean, that's just… That's weird?'

Paul coughs to clear his throat, we both turn to him. 'Um…' The colour has drained from his face.

Holly lets out a sound then says, 'Oh God… they *were* from you!'

He pulls a chair out between us both, trying to avoid eye contact though eventually, forcing himself into it. 'I'm so sorry. I can't… I am SO sorry!' I stare at him. 'You were getting these gifts, I just thought you wouldn't notice another one. And I really wanted…' He trails off, burying his head in his hands.

'Oh God, Paul.' Holly rolls her eyes.

'I just really wanted to spend some time with you.' His voice is small, he rubs at his face, before looking back at me, ashen. 'I don't know what to say. I've felt so bad, so guilty about it all. The accident was my fault.' Both Holly and I look up at him. 'It's like you've said before, if it wasn't for those tickets, you wouldn't have been there. It's my fault you had the accident. It's my fault Poppy was so hurt. I have tried, for so long, to hide my feelings for you and it got the better of me, I…' He pushes his tea away from him, standing. 'I don't know how I could ever make this up to you, Lisa, and I'm sorry because you've called us here to help you and now you're telling us the most shocking story and still I've managed to derail things. I should go.'

'Paul!' Holly reaches out to him.

'I'll fetch Charlie from school. I'll meet you back at yours, later. Lisa…' He turns at the door. 'I am so, very sorry. I wish it had been me in that car.' He turns to leave. I hear him exchange a few words with Dad in the hall upstairs and then the front door goes. Holly and I sit in stunned silence.

Chapter Sixty-Five

'Lovely man is Paul,' says Dad, fiddling with the heating in the boiler cupboard.

'You don't know him,' says Holly, trying a joke on for size but the mood not really letting it fly.

'Bit nippy upstairs, thought I'd treat myself to some warmth. It's going to get colder for the weekend, apparently. So the Met Office says.'

'Right.'

'Lisa, I'm just going to nip up to the car dealership. Charles says there's a second-hand Polo just come in, only got eight thousand miles on it, two years old, I think it could be perfect so don't want to miss out.'

'How's Lisa's kitchen coming on?' asks Holly.

'Oh! Erm... well, I think the boiler will be fitted soon.'

'Oh! Poppy and I can go home then?'

'Well... I'm not sure, it depends how long it takes them to put the kitchen back in properly too.' He looks at Holly. 'It's been quite nice having the company these last few days, not sure what I'll do when they've gone. Can't help feeling this old place is a bit big for me on my own. Right.' He pats Frank on the head then goes off up the stairs. 'Lucky we have the space, eh. I'll not be long,' he says, oddly cheery.

When the front door closes, Holly pauses then looks at me. 'Is there a camera somewhere? Is Beadle going to come out in a minute and laugh in our faces?'

'He's dead.'

'So was your mother!' I look up, sharply. 'Sorry. Too soon.' She reaches out for my hand, this time I let it be held. 'So, what do you want to do about it all? How can I help?'

'I don't know. I mean... I don't know. What if you're right and she is just a freak? What if she's lying?'

'But you said you were certain.'

'Well, I think I am... I mean, I thought I was. We look so alike but...'

Holly cocks her head to one side. 'What?'

'Her death certificate is upstairs. I don't understand how we'd have that if it hadn't happened.'

'They're not easy to fake, are they? I never really had your dad down for master criminal.'

'He's not, I mean... difficult sometimes, but maybe that makes two of us. Maybe we're both as difficult as each other. Maybe we're a product of the situation, but no, not a criminal. And yet...'

'I've never pinned you for difficult, Lisa.' She smiles, gently at me. 'You need to get her to take a DNA test.'

'I can't ask her to do that... can I?'

'Of course you can! This is someone claiming to be the woman you thought died thirty-eight years ago. This is a woman who should have been in your life! If she really is who she says she is, this is someone you need to know, Lisa. And if you have any doubt at all, then she needs to prove herself. I don't think it's too much to ask, if you need confidence in the situation, she should give it.'

'I suppose so.'

'You're allowed to ask, Lisa.'

I nod, studying my hands, feeling differently about them, as I do myself. 'I feel like I don't know who I am anymore.'

'Oh, Lis.'

We sit in silence for a while, though I can hear the telly upstairs and the ticking of the kitchen clock. Eventually, I push myself to standing. 'You're right. I'll ask her.' I move to the range, leaning against the warmth of it. Frank stretches out, showing me his belly and I give it a scratch whilst waiting for my phone to connect to Genevieve's number. I fold my arms, holding myself tight, phone up to my ear. Holly watches on.

'Genevieve?' Her voice is distant. 'It's Lisa.' Holly nods at me, encouraging. 'So, I wondered if you'd take a DNA test? Please,' I add. Holly takes our cups, rinsing them out, trying to be quiet as she moves round the kitchen. 'Thank you,' I say to Genevieve. 'I'll find out what we need to do and let you know.'

When I hang up, I let out a huge sigh of relief. 'She says she'll do it.'

'Good, as she should have.'

'Maybe that's proof enough? That she will, I mean.'

'And maybe the test is what you need to make sure you never have any doubt, either way.'

That night, I put Poppy to bed and take myself off to my room. I put BBC Radio 4 on my phone and lay on my bed, eyes fixed on the ceiling, running over the possible scenarios in my head. If she's not proven to be my mother, will I need to involve the police? What if she is proven? I'd need to talk to Dad? She didn't want him to know, but why? Will she change her mind? She can't force me to keep the secret and Dad should have the opportunity to explain what happened. I have a right to know. I need to understand so I can make sense of how I feel about it all, about him. Potentially, he took me away from my mother, how could he have done such a thing? I've barely dared consider my feelings towards him until now. But then, and perhaps I only think this because I'm terrified, if I don't have him, and if I can't find a way to connect with Genevieve, I only have Poppy and whilst she and I will always be okay... do I really want to be on my own without any family support? The shape of it hasn't always fitted, but now, as that shape changes, I've begun to realise how secure I am in the knowledge that he's always been there. Even when I've pushed him away. Even when he's clipped my wings.

My father: the person who, despite whatever has gone on, has always seemed to try his best. He could have left me, had nothing to do with me. Not all men take responsibility for their children, I only have to look at Billy to see that.

Billy.

Just as his name comes to mind so does it spring up on my phone: Billy's calling.

'We need to talk,' he says, before I've even said hello.

Chapter Sixty-Six

What's the saying? It never rains but it pours? The last thing I've wanted to do tonight is come out to the pub to meet Billy. All I want to do is sweep Poppy up into my arms and head to our home, hunker down, hide away from all that is going on whilst I get my head straight and brace for the fall-out of my meeting with Genevieve. Dad was happy to stay with Poppy whilst I came out, though did ask me if it was necessary, and what time I'd be back, and if he could call me a cab there and back. I snapped at him, pointing out it was a ten-minute walk and that I could really do with the fresh air and the exercise. I have to get back to work next week and I feel sludgy and tired. Maybe some of that is the weight of what's going on. I wouldn't have come out at all had it not been for Genevieve, to be honest, just knowing what she and I might have missed out on is the only reason I'm now sat here, in my usual spot in the pub, waiting.

I check my watch. He's late. I shouldn't be surprised, punctuality was never really Billy's thing. I wonder if the bank is alright with such a lackadaisical approach to timekeeping.

A group of Dad's mates sit in the corner, chatting. Normally he'd be with them, but not tonight. I apologised for his absence when I arrived and was quickly informed by Charles that my car would be ready at the end of the week. Dad had already mentioned he'd put the deposit down and I am grateful, I really am, it's just that… I feel like a failure.

'So glad you're here.' Billy puts one hand on the small of my back, planting a kiss on the side of my cheek. 'Can I get you anything?'

'No. Thanks. I'm good.'

'Okay, just a moment.'

He jogs over to the bar, greeting various people along his way. A handshake here, a kiss on the cheek there, a joke that has a group belly laughing before he leans against the bar, ordering his usual. What did he say about the swagger? I remember that I always enjoyed how chatty he was, how outgoing. It was the thing that first attracted me to him when we were kids, there was something in his energy, he was so focused on everyone else, it made me feel special that he also focused on me, and given that I was so quiet, so reserved, his outgoing nature was the yin to my yang. I suppose he can't help who he intrinsically is.

'How's Poppy?'

'She's doing well, thank you. Tires easily, still struggles to get about sometimes, I think things ache and so on, but she's okay. The physio has given us exercises for her to do. I think she'll be better when her voice is fully back and she can get on with life as it was before…'

'Right.' He sips his pint, nodding and winking to someone who's just come in.

He places his pint down, steeples his fingers and leans in. 'Have you had chance to think about my offer?'

I quickly scan the enormity of the last few days, his offer a distant whisper in the back of my psyche.

'Edinburgh. Moving in with me. Starting over.'

'I've… no, it's been…'

'It's just…'

'What?'

'Well, I'm heading off.'

'Now?' I double-take, confused.

'Well, no, not now but… at the weekend.'

'You've only been here two minutes.'

'I'm on annual leave.'

'You're what?'

'On annual leave.'

'I thought you were back for the month? At least. In fact, you said you'd stay, if there was a chance for us.'

He moves about in his seat, looking about the room. Jed the landlord pretends he's not watching us. 'Well… I had a month off. I came here first but, well now I'm due to go to Dubai for a week's holiday with the lads.'

I try and catch his eye, he is not going to get away with being shifty now. 'You're going on a lad's holiday? Now?'

'It's been planned for ages. I sort of hoped it might be one last hurrah before you two come move in with me.'

'When?'

'When I get back. In a week's time. It'll give you time to get sorted and I can meet you both up there. I fly into London then I'm connecting to Edinburgh.'

I stare at him. 'Are you insane?' He looks confused, as if all that he's just suggested is perfectly rational and why wouldn't I just drop everything to move up to Edinburgh. 'I've just had the worst few weeks of my life. My daughter nearly died. I can't possibly just sack everything off to move up to Edinburgh next week!'

'But, we can start again. Be the people, the parents we wanted to be.'

'I already am the parent I want to be. A mum, here in Lincolnshire, to a daughter who goes to the school I work in. In Lincolnshire. I want to be a school secretary and live in my home, Billy. Here in Lincolnshire… which is not remotely Scotland.' I laugh out loud because I can't quite believe him. 'My life is here, Billy. My dad's here!'

'Your dad wouldn't mind, would he?'

My eyebrows shoot up. He has no idea what's going on or how uncertain I am about Dad right now but even still…

'Even if he did mind, this is your life, you have to live it your way.' Billy looks at me imploringly, using the puppy dog look he always gave when trying to get his own way. 'Come on, think about it, Lisa. Edinburgh is lovely. I mean, if you don't want to stay there forever, maybe we can think bigger. I earn well, we can save up, make big plans.'

'I don't think I can plan beyond each day at the moment, never mind beyond a fantasy relocation to Edinburgh.'

'I know, and that's why we're good together, Lisa. I can help you see the bigger picture and we all need to see the bigger picture. That's what would help with this world, if we could understand how insignificant we are. Look at them, over there.' He points to Dad's friends. 'They're insignificant. All pumped up on profile and status, they meet here every week. They're not important.'

'Nice. I mean, I always thought kindness was the thing that would help the world, but apparently it's judgement and assumption,' I say, my eyebrows raised.

'I'm just stating facts. Please, think about it. We could be good together, you and I, Lisa.' He takes hold of my hands. 'We always were, weren't we? I mean, we fitted, like a glove. Weren't we meant to be? Maybe life just got in the way, but here's our chance. Let's not waste any more time.'

I'm about to give him all the reasons this could not possibly work when Paul arrives. He spots us, hands held across the table, Billy looking intently at me, his eyes piercing. I try to pull my hands back, but he spots Paul too and holds them tighter. 'Billy, please.'

Paul acknowledges us but without a smile, before heading over to the bar, his back to us both.

I manage to break free. 'I can't go with you.'

Billy plumps back into his chair.

'I can't, Billy. I have Poppy to think about. She's settled here, she doesn't need any more upset or change.'

'Kids are robust.'

'Maybe. But I don't know if I am.'

'Jesus, Lisa. Just live a little! Take risks, be daring. Why does life have to revolve around the village you grew up in? Look further afield.'

The notebook comes to mind, the encouragement to do more, think more, be more, but the encouragement came from what *my* dreams were, not what someone else assumed they should be.

'I can't, Billy. I can't go with you. Maybe we can keep in touch, talk about you meeting Poppy. You have a right to be in her life, I wouldn't stand in the way of that, maybe you could come back down to see her. When she gets better, maybe we could come to meet you? I mean, you sort of need to meet her properly first though.'

'I can see her tomorrow.'

'Tomorrow?'

'Well… I'm going at the weekend, aren't I? And I've got a few bits to sort before then, so tomorrow really would be the best for me.' His tone has shifted. He's less enthusiastic towards me, more embittered. A three-sixty spin that I wasn't expecting. 'I could see her before I leave. So she at least knows she's got a father.'

'It's not appropriate, Billy.' He shakes his head as if he just doesn't understand me, but it's not hard. 'You can't introduce yourself to my daughter, then disappear for however many months or years.'

'She's our daughter.'

I think for a moment. Paul leans on the bar with his pint. Jed's busy with another customer now, but Paul is definitely pretending not to side eye in our direction. 'She's *my* daughter, Billy. Always has been since the day you walked out and left us.' He goes to speak but I cut him off. 'I'm not saying never. But I am saying not now. She's got enough to deal with, right now. Her full recovery will take time.' Never mind what I've got going on right now. 'You can see her before you go, if you like. But as my friend. When you meet her as a father it's when you've got time to dedicate to her, at least a few days. And we'll need to sort out how it all works, the legal requirements. And…' I bite my tongue a second before deciding, this isn't about my pride. 'And money, you say you're earning well, she needs things. Things I can't always manage on my own.'

'You've got your dad.'

'She isn't his responsibility. She's ours. You need to pay your way.'

He looks at me. 'So basically, I've come back to meet my daughter, and you just want to rinse me for every penny you can get.'

'No. You've come back to pop in and make dramatic gestures you can't back up, when the reality is, you're not even prepared to pay maintenance for your child without making me feel guilty about it.' I down the rest of my drink and stand. 'Have a great holiday with the lads, Billy. I'll be in touch when you get back. Let's sort out how we do this, then, and only then, I'll introduce you to our daughter.'

He drops back into his chair as I head over to Paul and ask him if he has the time to walk me home.

Chapter Sixty-Seven

'Sorry to drag you away from the pub,' I say.

'It's fine. It was distraction really. I've got quite a busy head.'

'Yeah. Me too.'

Paul and I walk on in silence for a bit before he eventually, tentatively asks, 'How's Billy?'

I groan, my breath catching in the cold air. 'He wondered if Poppy and I fancied moving to Edinburgh.'

'Edinburgh?'

'Well, yes, initially, 'til he's saved up enough to whisk us all away for a new life wherever I fancied.'

'Wow. Right... what did you say?' His eyes are dead ahead, his poker face game is strong.

'What do *you* think?' I grab his arm and we come to a standstill a second. Paul shrugs. 'I said no, Paul. I said it's not really what I want for Poppy, right now.'

'Of course. No. Fair enough. Charlie would have been devastated.'

'And Holly.'

'Yes... and Holly.'

We walk on a little further. Lights are on in houses and I can see inside, people sat on their sofas watching telly. Someone is doing their ironing. A young girl jigs around in front of her parents and someone else eats a meal from a plate on their lap. It's normal, regular stuff. Just life happening. I mean, maybe there's drama in their lives but it doesn't feel like it right now as we walk through the streets back to Dad's. It feels normal. It feels like the life I want, have always wanted. The life I've largely had, I suppose, perhaps without fully appreciating it. We walk past one house and a woman sits on a chair with a young girl on her lap, she reads her a book and the girl is laughing. My stomach lurches because I've done these things for Poppy, but I never had a mother to do them for me and I wonder if Genevieve would have been that type of mother. And then I feel sad for little me that never had that, that can never know what a mother's love like that could feel like. And it's not a grief I've felt often in my life. I always knew I'd missed out and when Poppy was born there were moments where I'd look at her and wish I had a mother to guide me, or moments where we'd be doing something, and I'd just wish I'd have been able to do it with my own mother, but honestly? They were fleeting. My normal was not to have a mother in my life. I don't know what it is to be any different. Do I want to know? Is a relationship with Genevieve something that would enhance my life now? Or, like with Billy, has the moment passed?

'You okay?' asks Paul as we turn the corner into Dad's road.

I nod. My head full of what ifs and maybes.

'After today, I mean. With your mum.'

'With Genevieve,' I correct. 'I don't know, I mean, maybe. I just have a lot to think about, I suppose.'

'Do you know what you're going to do?'

'Well first off, she's agreed to do a DNA test, just to be on the safe side.'

'Of course.'

'And then… who knows.'

'You need to do whatever is right for you, Lisa.' We come to a stop at the top of Dad's drive. 'I don't want to talk out of turn but let me just say this.' He stuffs his hands in his pockets. 'You've always been the sort to look after other people. I know you look after you, and Poppy, I know you're not a pushover, but even still, you're so considerate of everybody else. Like today, with the tickets, you couldn't wait to tell me that it was okay. That it wasn't my fault.'

'Because it wasn't.'

'No. Maybe not. But you didn't have to be the one to let me feel okay about it. I have to forgive myself. I mean, of course, it helps to know that you don't hate me.'

I smile at him, a quiet constant in my life that, had he not stuck his head above the friendship parapet, I could be forgiven for not having noticed. 'I could literally never hate you, Paul.'

We look at one another for a second before he says, 'I really am so sorry.'

'I know.'

'I should have said. I should have owned up right away.'

'You should. But it's okay.'

He looks down at the pavement then up to the sky, before focusing back at me. 'Maybe I'm wrong to tell you what I think you need, you're a grown woman after all.'

'You're a mate. Mates have that privilege.'

He half smiles, then nods. 'You need people to put you first, and maybe *you* even need to put you first for a while too. Do whatever you want with your mum... Genevieve. If that's walk away and be without her, that's what you should do.'

His face is lit by the street lamp outside Dad's. A sort of orangey glow. He's familiar, but not in a bad way. It's in a way that, I realise now, stood here, makes me feel like everything's going to be okay. And I've never understood that it was a feeling I've yearned for but never fully had. Or perhaps I have, when he's been around, and I just haven't been aware of it before. I look at him, a man I've known and loved for a long time, a friendship that has evolved without my even noticing. I can feel how his embrace feels, I can imagine what it's like to be held by him, but I realise that what I know is the embrace of a friend, a peck on the cheek at the end of the night, a squeeze to say thanks, see you next time. But I want more. So I stand on my tiptoes, reaching up towards him, kissing him softly enough to suggest how I feel, not so hard that we could run away with ourselves. This isn't a kiss on the cheek from a friend at the end of the night, this is a kiss on the lips that marks the beginning of something I see that I want, something he's seen for so much longer. When I step back, the ghost of his lips still on mine, he's staring at me, as if he daren't move.

'Sorry.' I drag my eyes away, heat rising. 'You said I had to put myself first… I suppose I've wanted to do that for a while.' He allows himself to smile and it makes me giggle, overwhelmed by my uncharacteristic brazenness. 'Moving to Edinburgh isn't what I want for me, either.' I shiver.

He leans in to kiss me this time, before forcing himself to pull away with a 'Go on, get in, it's bloody Baltic out here.'

Heart light, like tissue paper or cotton wool, I turn and go up the steps, rummaging in my pocket for my key. The security light comes on making me squint, him too, I see when I turn around.

'Night, Lisa.'

'Night, Paul.' Key in lock, I turn it, pushing the door open. 'Paul…'

He stops, facing me.

'I never blamed you for what happened, okay?'

He looks at me for a second before nodding gently. 'Night.'

Dad reads the newspaper by the lamplight tucked in behind his chair. The *Telegraph*. He's always read the *Telegraph*. His face is obscured by the pages, just his hands either side of its broadsheet expanse. I hover for a moment, a new sense of purpose has arrived, perhaps it's been kissed into me, I don't know but… I want to ask him everything, even though part of me isn't sure I want to know. I feel as if at any moment my world could unravel, that today's meeting has picked at the tight knot that held it together, yet I also feel anchored. And if it is to unravel, because it hasn't quite yet, I feel I am strong enough to hold on. I don't know if I'm ready, or if I want to face whatever truths may come out, but I also can't ignore everything.

'Dad. I want to ask you about my mum.'

Chapter Sixty-Eight

Slowly, he brings the paper down from his face, watching me over his reading glasses.

'What was Mum like?'

He shifts in his chair, looking back at the paper in the way that tells me he'd rather carry on reading than stop to have this conversation. But it's been years since I've asked him. And before, it was always in bits. Do I look like her? *A bit.* Did Mum like olives too? *No.* How did you meet? *At church.* What was she really like? *Funny, spirited, brave, carefree.* Was it love at first sight? He shuffled his feet at that one, as if the 'L' word was dirty.

There will have been more questions I've asked, over the years. I don't remember the day I asked where she was, or him telling me she was dead. It's as if I always knew. I mean, I guess he must have told me at some point, but I just don't have that memory. He was my only parent, somehow, that's just how it always was. I never lost her because I never had her.

'I want you to tell me all about her.'

Dad closes his paper, straightening the edges out to make sure he can fold it neatly, placing it on the occasional table beside him. He takes off his glasses, avoiding my gaze.

'I want to know, Dad,' I say as gently as my pounding heart allows.

He adjusts himself in the chair, buying time before actually answering. I go to sit down on the sofa opposite. The fire glows amber embers, I pull Poppy's blanket up to my chest, my feet tucked beneath a pile of cushions she's collected from around the house and piled on the sofa.

'I'm tired, Lisa.'

'What did she look like?' I ask. 'What do you remember about her face? Her hair? How she dressed?'

'I don't know that now is a good time for this conversation.'

'Do you really not have any photos of her?'

'It's… very painful, Lisa.'

I pull the blanket up higher. 'It's painful for me too, Dad.' The clock chimes gently to tell us it's nine o'clock. 'And whenever could be the right time for this? Sometimes I've stopped myself asking about her because I'd hate to make you feel bad or bring back difficult memories but…'

'You have questions.'

'I do. I really do. And… I'm sorry if it hurts you to be asked them but… I think I need to know. I'm allowed to ask.'

He clears his throat. He gets up from his chair. 'I don't… I don't know how…' He looks around the room then goes to close the curtains. Diversion tactics I've seen him use so many times before; whenever things get difficult, he's avoided it. And I'm too tired to be angry at the fact now, but it's not fair.

'Dad, please don't…'

He looks at me, shakes his head, goes to try and say something, but the words don't come and after a moment, his shoulders sagging, he simply turns to leave the room. My eyes sting as I hear him take the stairs and see the only time I've been brave enough to tell him what I need slipping away. And I can't say I shouldn't have asked him because

I have a right to know. And I can't say it must be too difficult for him to talk about it because he's not a weak man. And I can't say that I'm okay with him choosing to avoid this because it's time to stop avoiding everything. For both of us. It's all we've ever done, avoid confrontation, avoid feelings, avoid one another when it gets too hard. Should I follow him upstairs? Should I force him to talk? How would I even do that if he's insistent he cannot?

I use my sleeve to catch my tears because I don't want to cry and then I remember that I avoid this sometimes too. And it makes me realise how deeply rooted my need to not feel stuff is. Dad walking away has lit a fire in me that I can feel raging. That he could so easily ignore what I need has sparked an anger that I've always tried to hide. That he could do that on the day I've met the woman who claims to be my mother... I jump up, the blanket falling to the floor. I jump for the door, throwing it open to go up to his room and demand some answers but, as I do, he stands there, a brown envelope in his hands. 'Here.' He passes it to me.

Chapter Sixty-Nine

My hands tremble. I look from the envelope to Dad then back down again. He quietly closes the door behind him, moving to sit back in his chair. He doesn't say anything, just clasps his hands and watches the fire, the most still I've seen him be. I move backwards to the sofa, sitting back where I was, reaching for the blanket now as safety more than warmth. Picking open the envelope, I daren't breathe. It frees easily, the glue now tired and brittle. Has he ever opened it? Since the day he stuck it shut? I'm assuming it was him, but I suppose I don't know that. Peering inside, there are two photos and my breath catches in my throat because if these are of my mother, what if I recognise her straight away? And would it be worse if I didn't?

I pause. I can't rush this, I need to be ready.

Eventually, Dad says, 'I've never trusted myself when you've wanted to talk about her.' I look up from the envelope. 'I've hated you to ask me because I've not been sure what to say or how to say it, how to get it right. Perhaps that's why I've been detached sometimes, I don't know, maybe a lot of the time.'

'Dad.'

'I see you, I see how hard you work to be present, to be loving, to show Poppy how important she is to you, and to the world. You didn't learn that from me.' I look back down at the envelope. 'They also don't give you a book on what to do when the mother is no longer around for the baby. Maybe now you could google it, everyone seems to have answers on the internet, but back then? You just had to plod on and hope for the best, which I know sounds ridiculous. Your mother...' He stops himself. He swallows. He tries to clear his throat. 'Your mother was... beautiful.' My heart skips as he disappears into a memory. I see it happen, the guard he's always had is briefly dissolved, he's in his head and reliving a moment. 'She was so young, Lisa. Too young, or so her father believed.' He comes back with a sniff and tiny shake of whatever it was he almost dared to feel.

'And you met at church, right?'

'Yes. Her father's. I moved to Edinburgh to take a job. I remember Mum and Dad thought I'd gone mad, but I suppose I wanted some element of freedom, I wanted to try something new, somewhere new...' He looks at me as if recognising, for the first time, what my motivation might have been. 'Genevieve's father was a colleague of mine. He was confident, assured, he encouraged me to join so I could meet people. It wasn't like a normal church. It was smaller, quite specific. I was never that interested in religion really, I suppose Dad was so set in his beliefs, perhaps it had turned me away from it, but Genevieve's dad was persuasive. And I was in a new area, I wanted to meet people. I suppose I wanted to fit in too.' He shifts, awkwardly. 'To begin with, it was fun. They were full of energy, they didn't play the kind of choral music my dad always preferred, this church was brighter, somehow. They had fun, they sang and danced. It was more like a night out with mates than a religious experience, to begin with. But the longer you stay, the more... I don't know, the more committed they want you to be. And I'd spotted your mother early on, she sang in this church band they had. We chatted. She was everything I wasn't. That's probably what

I found so intoxicating. I joined a study group because she used to go. We'd huddle together, working through newly written interpretations of lessons in the Bible that her dad wanted us to understand.'

'Written by who?'

'Him. Your mother's father. He was a preacher at the church. He believed there were things in the scriptures that needed teasing out, underlying messages that people weren't appreciating. I suppose some people felt them quite extreme, maybe even I did, but I was in a new city, I wanted to settle in and make new friends. And Genevieve's father was a charming man. Though I don't suppose he would have been, if he knew I was falling for his daughter.'

Dad stares over at the fire. 'Things with your mother progressed from friendship very gently. We'd walk together on weekends, help out locally in the community, we'd laugh, she taught me how to be silly. I wasn't really allowed to be silly, your grandfather thought it a distraction from the important things like school and religion. Genevieve… I suppose you might say she brought out another side to me. A side I hadn't known even existed. She was a mystery to me. She could be giddy and full of life one day, passionate and excitable. She'd take risks, embrace her wilder side, I was mesmerised. Then she'd hit rock bottom the next day. Just out of the blue. Like exhaustion had set in. She'd worn herself out. And nothing I did would pull her round. But when she was up… my goodness, she soared. It was exciting to be around.' He pauses again, fighting. 'We fell in love, well, I did. I can't speak for Genevieve, not really, she was younger than me, though it never seemed it. But I don't know if she really felt the same as me.'

'Love still exists when you're young, Dad. First love, the most powerful even.'

He studies me for a moment then gives a shallow nod. 'Take a look,' he says, pointing towards the envelope.

I take in a breath, reaching inside the envelope, pulling out the photos. There are two. The first is a photo of my mother and I gasp. There's no mistaking it. The hair, the eyes, the only thing missing now is the vulnerability and age; the girl in these photos is definitely the woman I met earlier.

I go to look at the second photo but Dad interrupts as I pull it away from the first. 'Lisa, there is something I need to tell you.' I look down at the photo of a baby in the girl's arms. And though there aren't many photos of me as a baby, I am in no doubt that this is a picture of what must be just weeks-old me, in my mother's arms. My heart splinters and breaks, my hands shake, tears begin to stream.

'She sent that photo to me. Her dad had made it clear I wasn't to see her. Told me he'd cause problems if I did and I was frightened, he intimidated me. The charm had gone, replaced with a menace. But your grandma saw the photo, she told me we had to go back. That I had a right to know you, she said she'd help me fight for you.'

'You left her? Pregnant?'

'I didn't want to. It was the last thing I wanted to do. You have to believe me. But her father saw to it that I lost my job. I had no place to stay. I tried getting something new but every door I knocked on, somehow people seemed to know me. Her dad spread rumours about me, about our relationship. I just didn't know how to deal with it, I was a coward. So, yes, I ran away. I ran away from it all.' He drops his head. 'To my shame.'

I try to focus on the photo again, a photo of me and my mother that I've never known existed. A photo I longed for as a child.

'I haven't known how to tell you what happened.'

I bite down hard on my lip because I don't want to tell him what I know, I don't want to show my hand. I need him to tell me his side.

'There was a car accident,' he continues. I wipe my eyes with my sleeves. Hold it together. Hold it together. 'You knew that much, that your mother died in a car accident when you were three months old.' I wait for the follow-up. I wait for him to tell me that wasn't what happened. 'It wasn't as simple as that.' I brace myself. 'What I never told you, was that… you and I were in the car too.' I focus on him, not daring to take my eyes away. 'It… it was awful. Devastating. She was so young… she had so much to live for…'

'Dad.'

'She could have been…' But his voice cracks and I'm not sure if that's because he can't bring himself to keep lying or because he knows he's about to tell me she's alive.

'She could have been what?' I ask, carefully, hopefully. 'She could have been what, Dad?'

He stares me straight in the eye. 'She could have been such a good mother,' he says. 'Her death was the biggest tragedy of my life.'

I go cold. I grit my teeth. I look down at the photo of the younger version of the woman I met as my dad sits before me with an opportunity to tell me the truth, a path that he's chosen not to take, and it doesn't make sense. If there's nothing to hide, why not just tell the truth.

'Dad. I met her. Today.'

Chapter Seventy

Dad stares at me, so I say it again. 'I met her. Today. In Wetherspoons.' Saying it out loud, like that, it sounds ridiculous. Meeting your dead mother in a local Wetherspoons, it's not exactly the story of romance or great family drama, the truth never so pleasing as fiction. 'She is the one that sent me all those gifts. She told me everything today.'

The look in his eye shifts, but I can't tell what he's feeling.

'Grandma found her. Those gifts weren't from you, they were from my mother.'

'Lisa…'

'I recognise her from these photos, it's her.' He goes to open his mouth, then stops himself. 'Dad, don't lie to me.'

'I wasn't. I'm not. Your mother was—'

'Hiding? Ashamed? Terrified? I don't know, convinced I was going to reject her, probably. That you'd take me away from her all over again.'

'Lisa!'

'She's kept away because she thought that was in my best interests, but you know what, Dad? It wasn't. How could it have been? Why? Why would you tell a child something this awful? How could you let me believe it?'

'Her death certificate is in that pack. I'd never have let you believe anything I didn't think to be true.' He turns away, it's as if he's lost or confused. Like he's been caught out but he doesn't know what else to do but carry on with the façade he's built across my lifetime. 'I would never lie to you, Lisa…'

I stare at him for a few seconds before I know what I have to do. I run out of the room and up the stairs, ignoring his calls for me. In my room, I throw my clothes into a bag waiting for Paul to pick up his phone.

'Lisa?'

'Please can you come and get us from Dad's. I need to go home. Now!'

'I've been drinking, Lisa, I can't drive.'

'But I need to go, I need to leave here, right now. I need to get away from Dad.'

'What's happened, Lisa? Are you okay? Has he hurt you?'

I let out a low, growling laugh. 'You might say that, and I need to leave.'

'I'll be there as soon as I can. Just sit tight, okay. And close the door from him. Are you safe? Is Poppy?'

'Yes. We are safe. Don't worry. Just please, hurry.'

Fifteen minutes later, I'm on the doorstep handing a somehow still-sleeping Poppy to Paul, who buckles her up in the back seat of a taxi. Dad has begged me to stay, he's got angry, he's shouted, and he never shouts. He's told me we need to sit down. That I have to let him talk to me. That he has never lied to me. But he's also never told me the truth, and now I don't know who or what to believe and once again I feel stifled, controlled. I lied to him, this time, told him I was going to Paul's, so he didn't try and follow me and that, plus Paul's calm but looming presence at the foot of our doorstep is presumably why he stopped himself, stepped back, walked away. Just like he always has when things get hard.

Paul jogs up to get our stuff. 'Pass me your bags. Is that everything?'

'It's all I need.'

'Okay, do you want to come back to mine?'

'No, home. I want to go home.'

'But you've no boiler? No kitchen?'

'I don't care. I'll get a heater out of the garage. I'll sort the rest out tomorrow. I just need to go home.'

The taxi pulls away, me in the back, behind the driver, with Poppy, Paul in the front. We're in silence. I stare out of the window. The village I grew up in passes me by. Street lamps lighting the way, nobody out and about. Most curtains are shut now, save for the odd few. I can't see anybody's lives, normal or otherwise. I hold Poppy's hand in mine, more for my comfort than hers. Every now and then, Paul looks back to check if I'm okay.

We pull up on my drive behind a white VW Polo and I frown. Paul pays the driver, whilst I go to the front door to unlock it. When I push the door open, I'm met with the smell of my home, that familiar smell that you don't realise is there when you're always around. A smell that, on this occasion, is tinged with lavender from the plant that Dad or Genevieve or whoever it was that left it for me, still sat on the side where Dad left it when he brought me home that day. And I look around for the scene of devastation from kitchen and boiler, to see nothing. Nothing has changed, nothing has been ripped out or put back in again. Everything is exactly how I left it the morning Poppy and I went to meet Paul and Charlie.

I fly through the downstairs, looking around at my perfect home, the one I've not been allowed to live in. The one I never questioned whether it was really getting all that work done because why wouldn't it be? Why wouldn't Dad have had the boiler and kitchen fixed? Why would he tell me anything different? Which is clearly what Paul thinks when he walks in, Poppy tiny and asleep in his arms. I push past him to the kitchen cupboard to check the boiler, its small orange light illuminated. And I can't believe Dad lied about this too.

Chapter Seventy-One

'I thought…' says Paul, before stopping himself, but still looking around at my not remotely like a building site house.

'So did I.'

'But it's totally fine?'

'How did he think he could get away with it?'

Stunned, I take Poppy from his arms and climb the stairs. Pushing the door open to her bedroom, my legs feel like jelly because it's her room, our home, and we're safe here, we've always been safe here, and I can't believe we've been kept away for so long, at a time we've needed it the most.

'Poppy?' I gently lift her arm to tuck her in, Bear-Bear by her side. 'Poppy?' She opens her eyes, sleepily. 'We're home, look, we're back home.' She dozily looks around, before sleepily smiling. 'Now, go back to sleep, baby. I'll see you for breakfast in the morning, yes?'

She nods, snuggles down into her bed, and within seconds, breathes like she always breathes when she's fast asleep. Like none of this nightmare even happened. Like the world hasn't irrevocably changed.

Back downstairs Paul has brought the bags in, lining them up in the hallway. He's in the kitchen, hand on the kettle, a mug complete with tea bag on the side. 'Are you not having one?' I ask.

'I wasn't sure if you'd want company.'

'I don't think I want to be on my own, to be honest.' He reaches for another mug and tea bag. 'I've got no milk, have I?' I needlessly check the fridge.

'Black tea is still tea.'

'True enough. Shame I haven't got anything stronger.'

'I can run up to the pub, see if I can get a bottle before he closes.' He checks his watch. 'What are we on? Last orders?'

'No, no. Don't worry, it's fine. Tea is probably more sensible really.'

'You want to talk about it?'

I push my head into the back of the sofa, hitting it gently several times. 'I don't know where to begin.'

'Did you tell your dad about Genevieve?'

'Yes. Well, I asked about her. I asked him what she was like. Thought I'd start off slowly.'

'And what did he say?'

'He got out some photos of her.'

Paul waits, perhaps not wanting to ask if I recognised her. He sits on the opposite end of the sofa to me, sitting slightly sideways to see me but keeping himself into himself so we don't touch.

'He has a photo of us.'

'You and—'

'My mother.'

'And you've never seen it?'

'No. Never.'

'But why? Wouldn't it have been nice for you to have seen it? What benefit could come from keeping it from you? It wouldn't have changed the story they told you.'

'I know. Maybe he didn't want to keep seeing it. A reminder of what they did to her. To me.' He shakes his head in disbelief.

The radiator clicks; the sound they make as they cool down. I look over in its direction for a second, shaking my head.

'Did he explain it?'

'Not really. He just repeated the story about the car accident. The only difference was that he and I were in the car, along with her parents. That was new information, I guess. He shoved her death certificate in my face as I tried to pack my stuff up. Proof that Genevieve couldn't possibly be my mother. It was so desperate.'

'But if he has her death certificate... how *could* she be?' he asks the question gently, and it's a reasonable question to ask, one I've kept asking myself, over and over. 'What if the lady today really isn't your mum?'

'But the photo, she looks just like the photo. We are so alike, we have features that are the same. And I feel it, in my belly, I feel it. I mean... I feel it, Paul.'

He sips at his drink before carefully saying, 'What if she had a twin or something?'

'I'd have known, wouldn't I?' But as I say it, I realise I wouldn't have. I realise it could be just another thing that they might have kept from me for reasons known only to the people I should have been able to trust.

'I'm so tired, Paul.'

'You want me to go? I can leave and let you get to bed.'

'I don't think I mean physically, though, yes, maybe that too. And either way, I don't want to be on my own.'

He looks around the room. 'I can stay, on the couch.'

'Would you?'

'Of course, Lisa. Of course I will.'

I search out eye contact, something he's avoided giving me since getting to Dad's. I wonder if he's feeling awkward about my kissing him? Yet it felt like the least awkward thing I've ever done. This time though, he gives in and we sit for a moment, just looking at one another. My heart calms, my breath steadies. 'Let's put on an old film. Something stupid. Something I can lose myself in and stop thinking about this fucking mess. I don't want to think about anything until the morning.'

He reaches to the coffee table for the remote control, passing it to me.

'You choose,' I say, pulling a throw over me and snuggling down.

The credits roll at the end of *Splash*. 'I can't believe I've never seen that film. And I can't believe it's one of your favourite romcoms.'

I look across to Paul, grinning, to see he's fallen asleep. For a bear of a man, he has an eclectic taste in films, and the sweetest expression on his face when he sleeps. I take the throw off myself and lay it across him, shivering with the cold. And then I realise that I don't want to go upstairs to my own bed. So I lay down beside him, stretching the blanket across us both. And when his arm lays across me, pulling me in closer to him, I fight the urge to cry because I realise in this moment that I have never felt so safe, or so understood, before. And with the weight of his arm across me, and the beat of his heart into my back, I close my eyes and drift off to sleep, all questions temporarily paused. Tomorrow, life is going to hurt again, I know it. I can feel myself pushing it away. But for now, this feels like everything I've always needed and never realised I could have.

Chapter Seventy-Two

I wake alone, dozily sitting up, rubbing my eyes, listening out for a sign that Paul's still in the house. The lounge door opens, and Poppy appears, rubbing her own sleepy eyes, Bear-Bear tucked safely under her arm.

'I love my bed, Mummy,' she says, climbing onto my lap and hugging me tight.

'Yeah? You slept okay then?' She nods. 'You want breakfast?' She nods again, yawning. 'Okay, here, you find yourself something to watch, let me get sorted and maybe we can go out for breakfast. I don't think we'll have any food in.'

I pad through to the kitchen as she finds something on telly to watch. There's a note on the side:

Lisa,

I thought it might be easier if Poppy didn't find us on the sofa together this morning. I've bought you a few essentials for breakfast. Sorry I didn't wake you, I thought you might need the sleep. Call me when you're ready. X

I want to call him straight away. Ask him to come round. I want to tell him that I'd like us to not just be friends any more. But I also think I've got too much on and last night was lovely: the film, falling asleep on the sofa, it gave me a pause in what's really going on. This morning though, the reality has hit hard. I open the fridge finding milk, butter and fruit. I open the cupboard to see cereal and bread. I pour a bowl, I put bread in the toaster, I get on with making breakfast for Poppy, but I can't eat a thing. Dad lied to me my whole life.

Iris comes through to her lounge with a pot of tea and a plate with what I can only assume is home-baked cake on it. 'Are you sure you don't want any?'

'I can't eat.' Poppy's next door with Holly whilst I came round. It's lunchtime and I still can't face anything.

'Okay, love.'

'How could Dad and Grandma lie about something like this, Iris?'

'You're asking the wrong person, love, really. What has your dad said?'

'He showed me her death certificate.' She frowns. 'He told me she was dead my whole life. I don't know, I guess he can't find it in him to be truthful, even with it plain to see.'

'But he didn't tell you she couldn't be your mother?'

'Well, no. But he also didn't tell me she definitely was. How could he do this?'

'I don't know,' says Iris, looking off to the middle distance. 'I can only tell you that if your grandma was here, and knew Genevieve had reached out, she would be equal parts relieved, and devastated.'

'How long did you know for?'

She gives me the courtesy of eye contact. 'Your Grandma told me as soon as she found out.'

I shake my head, no energy left for anger, just despairing at the secrets people have willingly kept from me.

'I'm sorry, Lisa. I wouldn't blame you if you upped and left. Or never trusted a thing I said, but I suppose it really wasn't my story to tell you. And you have to know that I really think they tried to do the right thing. It was very painful for your grandma.' She looks back at me. 'The weight of what she knew was so heavy for her. I just don't think any of it is straightforward. It was a different time.'

'It's not that long ago!'

'A lot has changed in that time, life isn't like I knew it. Your grandma hated the secret. When she found out, she pored over your life and the impact: that you grew up not knowing, that your poor mother was left without anybody to care for her. Losing your parents is one thing, but your baby and the love of your life too? How do you survive something like that? I can't imagine.'

'So why didn't Grandma do more? Why didn't my mother fight for me?'

'You need to talk to your father. And your mother, for that matter. I don't have the full picture either and now isn't the time for half stories. You deserve to know the truth, every corner of it. All your grandma asked of me was to let Genevieve know when she passed away. I promised her I would do that. Which I did. After that, I've just tried to encourage her to reach out to you.'

'So, if they all knew the truth, why didn't Dad fight harder?'

She looks down into her cup. 'You're assuming he knew.'

'He must have, mustn't he? He was there.'

'He was in a mess. He had a new baby. He'd been in a devastating car accident. He was back home having tried to work things out with your mother. Your grandad told them both your mother had died. As soon as your grandma learned the truth, after your granddad died, she tried to fix it. I know she did. She tracked her down. She tried to get her to come to Lincolnshire.'

'How did Grandma find out?'

'She found a letter in your grandad's office, shortly after he died.' I scrunch my eyes up because my brain hurts. 'It was your mother – Genevieve – who didn't want her to tell your dad. Or you.'

'I'm her daughter!'

'Things are never black and white, Lisa. I know this is devastating for you, but you all need time to speak, time to listen to what happened. There is almost forty years of hurt and secrets to unpick here. I don't know what really went off, I only know that if your mother is alive, you should have a relationship with her. And like your grandma before me, that's what I've tried to encourage. I…' She puts her cup down. 'Though, I wonder now if I've made a terrible mistake.'

I check my phone, as I keep doing, partly in case Paul messages, and partly in case it's Holly because Dad's turned up at mine. 'You've tried to help.'

'I have. But this is your family business, it's not for me to pry or get involved in. Like I said, your grandma asked me to tell Genevieve when she passed away and I promised her I would. The rest of it, well… All I meant to do was encourage Genevieve to consider if staying away really was in your best interests. Especially now that you've lost your grandma. Look, love, this is a huge shock for you, I can't even begin to imagine. You need to be kind to yourself and try not to be angry with your dad until you know the whole picture. Talk to Genevieve. You'll have so many questions, I'm sure, and you're entitled to know the answers. All the answers. You just need to remember that times were different, not that long ago. And sometimes, what one person feels the need to blame, another has no control over. Yes?'

I frown slightly, pulling back. Then my phone dings with a text. *Your dad's here.*

I jump up to peer out of the window. 'Dad's here.'

'Go. And go steady, okay? Look after yourself. I'm here if you need me. And I'm sorry… if I've made things worse, I'm deeply sorry.'

I bend down to give her a kiss and she pats my hand.

Chapter Seventy-Three

Dad's car is parked over the road, opposite my house, when I come round the side of Iris's. He's sat in the passenger seat and must clock me straight away as his car door opens and he climbs out. We pause, staring at one another. He looks drawn and pale.

'Lisa, please. Can we talk?'

'I'm not ready, Dad. I don't want to talk to you.'

'But, Lisa—'

'You lied! You lied about my mother, you lied about the gifts, you lied about the work on the house! Why? Why would you do that. How did you think you'd explain that one away? What even for?'

He stares at the ground. 'It's… complicated. I panicked.'

'Like Genevieve? Was that complicated?'

'Lisa!' He looks over his shoulder, the idea that anyone should hear us a deep embarrassment to him.

'I will talk to you, but when I'm ready. When I'm ready to question every lie you tell me until you have to tell me the truth!'

He hesitates before saying, 'Anything I've ever done, it has always been to protect you, Lisa. I needed you at my house, in case I had to protect you!'

'I'm a grown woman. I don't need you to protect me anymore, Dad. I needed to come home, Poppy and I both needed to come home.'

He looks up at the house, then over to the car.

'And you can take that back,' I say. 'I don't want the car. I don't want your money. I want you to leave me alone.'

'Lisa, please.'

'No, Dad. Absolutely not!'

'I'm worried about you!' he says, his voice raised before he looks around to check that nobody has heard him. 'Lisa, she might be dangerous. Whatever you think I've done, it has only ever been to protect you.'

'She is my mother!'

He shakes his head. Beryl from over the road turns the corner, pulling her shopping bag behind her. 'Oh, hello, you, are you back?'

I stare at Dad before turning my attention to Beryl. 'Yes, we're back.'

'Oh, I've been so worried about you. And little Poppy. How is she now?'

'She's doing really well, thank you.'

'I'm so pleased. It must have been so frightening for you. We were all talking about how frightening it must have been.'

She gestures to the houses around us, and the tightness of village life creeps into my chest, pressing down on my heart, suffocating.

'You look tired, David,' she says, nodding to Dad. 'Must have been such a worry for you too. I bet you're glad she's able to come back home now, though, eh?' Dad gives a shallow nod. 'You know where I am if you need anything, don't you,' she says, heading up her drive.

'Thanks, Beryl.'

'Not a bother.'

A car goes past. Someone arrives home up the road. A guy I vaguely recognise jogs past with his dog and Dad puts on a polite smile for them all.

'What if she can't be trusted, Lisa?' he whispers.

'And you can?' I motion up to the house. 'I don't trust anyone right now,' I hiss.

He shuffles from one foot to the other. He stuffs his hand in his pocket, bringing out some keys. 'Look, I had to have you home whilst I… looked into things.'

'What? Like, why my mother was wanting to connect with me? So you lied about her being dead, and you lied about the house, because you could see it was all going to unravel?'

'It's not like that. That's why I want to talk to you.'

'I'll talk to you when I'm ready. On my terms.'

'This is the key to the car. Please, at the very least, take it.'

'No, thank you, Dad. I don't want anything from you.'

I turn on my heel, heart racing, and jog up the path to mine, leaning against the door when it's closed behind me. I look down for Frank, expecting him to make his lazy way to greet me before remembering he's still with Dad. Instead, Poppy launches herself at me, arms and legs around me, clinging on tight.

'Me and Aunty Holly have been making puppets, look.'

She climbs down, dragging me into the lounge where Holly sits on the floor, a collection of finger puppets on each hand.

'We're going to do a play for you now, too. Come on, sit down. There you go, Mum.'

Poppy's so happy and confident here, so much more relaxed than when we were at Dad's. The telly is off and she's happy, bounding around the lounge, putting on character voices for each of the little people as she retells a story she and Holly have made up, and I could be forgiven for thinking nothing had changed. Except I hear the car keys land on the mat and know Dad will have posted them for the Polo on the drive, before leaving us to it. And I wish he'd leave me alone.

Chapter Seventy-Four

It's been two weeks since I met Genevieve. I texted her to tell her that I needed some space and time, because it's too much. I want all the answers, I need to know the detail, but I'm so tired. Poppy still needs me, her recovery is happening, but it's slow: some days she's doing really well, others she's tired, clingy, vulnerable even. She is my priority, no matter what, and besides, I feel like I need my world to be small so I can recharge my batteries enough to deal with whatever is coming next. I feel steamrollered, so much has happened in so little time, all since Grandma died. I need to breathe so I can face things.

To Genevieve's credit, she's given me the space I need. Unlike Dad, who has tried calling or knocking on the door every day since I saw him last. Holly thinks I should try listening to what he has to say, but I'm not ready. Paul is trying not to be judgmental about it but each time I see him, I know he is angry on my behalf. He's also holding back, uncertain of what I need… or maybe certain I don't need him asking questions about us, at the same time as I'm asking questions about me. Billy should be back from his boy's trip by now. I've not heard from him.

Poppy has a couple of hours at school this morning, just to see how she gets on. See how tiring it might be for her. She's definitely ready emotionally and she needs to see her friends. I think she needs some normality too, but she's still seeing the physio to keep exercising her muscles, get her strength back on a consistent basis. Thankfully, her voice seems to have fully returned. It's almost like the last month never happened. Except I know it has, because the results for the DNA test sit on my kitchen worktop, next to the notebook I don't seem able to write in at the moment, I daren't open that either. I don't know what I'm afraid of, perhaps that I'm not sure what to do with the truth, or what that means for Dad and I? I'm not sure what it means for me and Genevieve either. I want to know her, but what if I don't like her? What if she doesn't like me? What if it's too hard? What if the relationship I've always imagined I missed out on, is not what she's able to give? Maybe that's why I've wanted to wait, without even realising it. Because I want to see how she reacts too, at the same time as me. What is our organic, natural, instinctive response to the facts going to be?

I wrap myself up in my coat, hiding my chin in my scarf, my hat giving me extra warmth. The bandstand shelters me from the rain that started when I left the house, walking past the car on my drive like I have each day since I moved back home. I have used it a couple of times, but only for Poppy's sake, when we've had an appointment to get to or if she's been too tired to walk to the shops. I don't really want it though, and as soon as the payment comes through for the insurance on my car, I'll be driving it round to Dad's and giving him the keys back. Hopefully when he's out. We still haven't spoken properly.

Water pours off the side of the stand, the wind occasionally pushing it into the opposite side leaving a puddle on the concrete base. Paul is in the coffee shop over the way, waiting like he promised he would. He offered to stay with me until she got here, but I have to do this on my own. I can't see him, but knowing I'm not totally alone helps. I lean on the railings, gazing at the flower beds below. The clipped and precise summer displays have all gone, leaving bare soil that gives off that wet, earthy smell; brown leaves gathering in spots where the wind lets them drop.

'We picked the weather for it, eh?' says a voice behind me and I turn to find Genevieve wrapped up the same as me. Coat, scarf and hat leaving not much of her face visible, just eyes that dart around and her nose, pink with the cold. 'How've you been?' she asks, lifting her chin so I can see her better. There's a twitch to her mouth, like the one I noticed when we first met.

'Okay. I suppose.' She nods, moving towards me, though not quite beside. She leans against the railings then stands, fidgety, uncertain. 'Tired, confused, full of questions.'

'Sorry.' Her voice is small.

'I've got it.' I hold up the envelope that I'd tucked under my arm and she nods. She's here, but not quite, somehow; distracted. She gives furtive looks around and about. At the bar, I remember she mostly sat with her hands tightly together, sleeves pulled down to her thumbs. I remember doing that as a teenager, pulling sleeves over hands and jumpers up to my chin, as I still sometimes do now, little mannerisms that maybe we share. She stares at the envelope.

Part of me doesn't need to open it to know. I can see who she is, I can feel it. But part of me doesn't trust my gut, or maybe her, perhaps that's to be expected, but there's a barrier. Maybe more so today than before, like a force field around her that can't be broken. I wonder how it was for her, doing the test? For me, it was perfunctory, like I didn't think about the implication, simply got on with what was required, taking a swab in my bathroom before packing it off in the envelope. Her, I assume, doing the same at some point so the labs could run the tests.

'Go on,' she says with a shiver.

I take off my glove with my teeth; it hangs from my mouth as I run my finger under the envelope, hands shaking. She watches me reach in and take out the letter, the paper emerges. I'm not sure what I expected, maybe a DNA test card like those you see on hideous morning shows where vulnerable people come on to find out the father of their child. Am I that kind of vulnerable now? Is Genevieve? She certainly looks it, perhaps I do too. A couple run past us, arm in arm through the rain. Do they notice us? Do they wonder what we're doing? Such a significant moment in my life and I'm probably invisible to them. The paper is not a DNA result card, but two A4 pages long full of stuff I don't really understand. I scan down it, trying to work out what all the numbers mean, flicking between the two pages uncertain, before Genevieve peers, then reaches across me and points to the box that says, Possibility of Maternity, 99.9888%.

I stare at the sheet, her bitten fingernails tracing down the page before she stuffs her hand back in her pocket. And even though I knew I knew, seeing it in black and white stuns me. The woman stood to my left, beside me in the pouring rain, sheltered by a bandstand in the middle of a public garden that's now completely empty because it's cold and wet and November, is my mother. Slowly, I look up at her, tears stream down her face as she bites her bottom lip, trying to keep hold of her emotions, her body moves rhythmically to a silent beat.

'I'm so sorry,' she says, her voice wavering. 'I am so sorry that I was never there for you. That I stayed away. That I couldn't be the mother you deserved. I am so sorry I let this happen to you. I am…' But she runs out of words and I can't help but take her in my arms because I don't know what else to do but comfort her.

My hold seems to break the barrier and she sobs into my chest, and it's as if I'm holding her up, as if to let go of her now would see her sink to her knees. Even though everything I thought I knew is nothing like I've grown to believe. I have a mother. I've always had a mother. She didn't die like they said… she's here, in my arms, in this park, and we've been kept apart for my entire life. And she sounds broken.

Chapter Seventy-Five

Paul brings us both a tea over. He moves as if going to sit down elsewhere and leave us to it, but I grab hold of his arm and he sits beside me instead. Just feeling him there, next to me, settles me. Genevieve hasn't stopped crying since we opened the results, though now they're silent tears, streaming down her face. She keeps apologising, then disappearing back into herself, scratching at a mark on her hand, and it seems it's too much for her. As it is for me, here in black and white, on the table in front of us. The innocence of a letter that changes everything. I am not who I thought I was.

'I've thought about this moment so many times,' she says eventually, cupping her tea into her like a tiny protective shield, though still scratching, repeatedly, at her hand. 'And I've rehearsed speeches, the things I really want to say about it all. And I've always been able to say exactly what I wanted in this moment when I've imagined it, yet now, here, I don't know where to begin.'

I watch her, not sure which of the questions I have to ask first because *Why?* feels like it's too big a place to begin.

'I don't blame your dad,' she says, quietly, still unable to hold my gaze for long. 'I mean, maybe I did, once upon a time, but not now. I understand. I get it.'

'Do you?'

She nods, taking a sip of her drink. I hadn't noticed it before, when we first met up, how young she appears. She's not a grown-up, not like the mother you'd expect. She seems brittle somehow. Like she's rarely seen the light of day, never mind the reality of life. 'I imagine he did what he was told. Maybe he was angry with me.'

'What for?'

'How I was? How I treated him? I could be difficult to be around, I know that.'

'But… you were my mother.'

'I wasn't in a good place.'

'You were a kid, how could it have been right?'

She chews on the inside of her mouth, looking at me, then glancing away.

'Genevieve?'

She disappears into herself again but this time I can't watch it happen. She reached out to me, she wanted me to know she was alive. I have a right to ask her questions, I have a right to know the truth and if I can't get that from my father then it has to be her. I look to Paul who gives that look that sort of encourages you, the look where you know you're not on your own and whatever you want to ask can be asked because no matter the outcome, he's beside me and it's all going to be okay. Or a version of okay, at least.

I push my cup away, a kind of steel forming round my heart. 'You talked about a car accident. When we met before. I knew about that, Dad said that's how you died.'

Genevieve flicks up to look at me, there's something in her that I can't quite put my finger on. I don't know that it's fear so much as uncertainty, the brittleness spreading through her, but I push on.

'It was a few months after I was born, wasn't it?'

She blinks and begins scratching at her hand again.

'But he showed me your death certificate. That's what I don't understand.'

She swallows.

'It even says on it, something about injuries caused in road traffic accident.'

The movement she had in the bandstand returns, rhythmic. Steadying?

'Iris said your parents also died? What happened, Genevieve? What are you not telling me? I have a right to know. You can't come back into my life then be coy about why you've not been in it. I need your side of the story, just as much as Dad's.'

The corner of her mouth twitches before she bites on it, repeating the bite as she scratches at her hand, seemingly desperate to stop a host of ticks and niggles that have escalated since we read the letter. Eventually, she says, 'I didn't mean to kill them.'

A chill creeps into my chest. 'What?'

Blood appears on her hand where she's broken through the skin. She's holding my gaze now but the force field surrounding her seems to have returned, perhaps stronger than before. 'The accident, I didn't mean for it to happen. For them to die. I wasn't… it wasn't my fault… not really…'

'Stop!' She snaps to look up as I reach out to her hand, putting mine between hers and her nails. 'You've made yourself bleed.' She studies my hand on hers, then the blood as I move mine away. 'What do you mean, you didn't mean to kill them?'

My eyes flick to Paul, he moves his hand to my knee and I take it, threading my fingers through his.

She snatches her hand out of sight, staring at me. 'They promised they'd never tell you.'

'Who?'

'Everybody! His parents… the doctors… they all promised you wouldn't have to know. I didn't mean to do it, Lisa. You have to believe me.' She reaches across the table, but it feels desperate, needy, almost. 'I didn't mean for any of it to happen.'

She looks around, the surroundings suddenly, apparently, too much for her. She pulls away and it's like I can see her go back inside of herself, glancing at me before she's tucked up again, hands into her body, eyes lowered, jaw tight. She starts shaking her head, gently at first, then faster as she gets up. 'I can't. I shouldn't have. I can't.' She grabs her bag and coat, pulling them tightly into her stomach.

'Genevieve, we need to talk.'

She fixes me with deep, blue, terrified eyes. Wild even. 'I'm not a bad person, you have to believe that… I'm sorry. I can't…' Furtively, she looks around her, aware now that she's being watched by more than just Paul and me. 'I thought I could, I want to, but…' Then she escapes, knocking the table, the last dregs of her tea splash across her, the chair she had sat in, but she doesn't notice.

'Genevieve! Stop! I'm sorry, I'm just… I have questions, things don't make sense, Genevieve!'

She pushes through the other chairs and back out into the rain, still holding her coat into her. I jump up after her, flying through the door, bumping into a couple taking shelter in the cafe entrance. 'Don't go!' I shout, but she runs on. 'You found *me*!'

A man over the other side of the park stares, when I turn back around, people in the cafe are pretending they don't want to know what's just happened and Paul sits, stunned, watching me.

'She's gone,' I say, making my way back to him. 'She's just gone, Paul, why? What did she do? Is that what Dad meant when he said

she was dangerous? Why would she reach out to me like this, then go?
I don't understand what's happening.'

Paul pulls me into him and, safe in his arms, I let myself weep.

That evening, I've put Poppy to bed and Charlie has gone down in
the same room because the kids wanted a sleepover and neither Holly
nor I had the heart to tell them they couldn't. Paul drove me home
from town this afternoon and I sat silently in his car, then blurted out
questions, to which he simply and carefully said, 'I don't know.' I cried
again, then I swore. I asked him to take me straight to Dad's house,
then before we got there, I told him to turn around and take me home
and he did exactly what I asked each time. No questions. Holly picked
Poppy up from school, her first half-day to ease her back in after so
long off, because I couldn't straighten my face enough to pretend I was
okay. And between Holly, Poppy and I, we've just about got through
the rest of the day until the kids have gone to bed, without talking
about what happened, with them both, metaphorically, holding me
up. When I come back downstairs from Poppy's room, Holly sits at
the dining table looking solemn.

'Do you need me to do anything for you? Get you anything?'

'I could do with a stiff drink.'

'Paul's just nipped out to get some.' I look over to the front door
as if I'd catch sight of him. 'He's worried about you. He said it was
difficult today.'

'It was… it was just weird. She just went. Disappeared. It was like
the news was too much for her, even though she knew the truth. I
don't know, I couldn't stop her, she just… left.'

Holly sighs as the front doorbell goes. I jump up to let Paul back in, hoping the bell didn't wake the kids. But when I open the door, it's not Paul standing there, it's Dad.

'Please don't close the door on me, Lisa. Please.' A car goes past, the headlights lighting up the side of his face, but he doesn't flinch. 'I want to tell you everything I know. Please… let me in.'

Chapter Seventy-Six

Dad sits down at the dinner table. Holly gets up from the sofa, then hovers, not quite sure what to do with herself. Dad looks at her as if suggesting she may need to leave.

'Hol, do you want to keep an eye out for Paul?' She peers at me, making sure I mean what I say before heading into the kitchen. I hear the radio come on and the sound of the tap filling the kettle. Knowing her as I do, she'll be doing everything in her power not to stand by the wall with a glass to her ear.

'I spoke to Iris. She said she thought you were meeting with Genevieve today,' he begins and, just as it was odd hearing her mention Dad's name, it's strange to hear him speak hers.

'I did.'

'And?' He takes a deep breath. 'What happened? What did she say?'

I let out a groan, exhausted by the secrecy, games and confusion. 'She didn't tell me anything, actually.' The paperwork rests on the coffee table, tucked into the notebook. I want to give him time to talk, I can show him the paperwork if he begins to lie.

'Right. I see.' He looks to his feet, seeming older than he has before. And different somehow. He's not standing in my house telling me what he thinks I should do about something. He hasn't mentioned the fact that the front door wasn't locked when I opened it, that anyone could walk in and just take the keys to my car on the side, or worse. He hasn't locked it behind him like he always did, and I haven't either because this is my house, my rules.

'What happened?' he asks, tentatively.

'She left me,' I say, purposely starting midway in the story. 'We were talking and she left me. Just… got up and walked away.' He looks up at me. 'Considering…' I pause, censoring myself because I'm still not ready to show my full hand. 'Considering everything, and that she contacted me, I've kept wondering why? I've kept wondering how someone could do what she's done? Tell me she's my mother even when my own father says it isn't so, take a DNA test that proves the fact, without any doubt, then just getting up to leave. Like something else caught her eye, like she couldn't see the conversation through, she was distracted. Is that why she wasn't ever in my life? Because she was too easily distracted? In fact, hey, maybe that's how the accident happened. Maybe she can never focus on anything. Maybe she was incapable and you wanted to protect me from that.' Dad looks away again, staring at the floor. 'Aren't you going to tell me that you told me so? That I should have never met up with her? That I've brought this on myself?'

He starts by shaking his head, then he sniffs. He reaches into his inside pocket for a handkerchief and dabs at his eyes, and I'm so struck by the overt display of emotion that I don't hear the front door open and Paul come back until he's standing in the lounge bearing a bottle.

'Sorry, Paul. Holly's in the kitchen,' I say.

He studies me for a second, checking if I'm okay, I guess. 'Right.' He goes to leave, then stops and looks at Dad, ultimately deciding better of whatever went through his mind and disappears into the kitchen. The door clicks behind him.

I go to sit down, keeping the notebook and therefore the paperwork in reach, just in case. We lock eyes through the mirror before he turns to face me. 'Lisa, I want to tell you the truth, but I'm afraid.'

'Of what?'

'Of everything. Of how you'll feel. Of us unravelling.'

We couldn't unravel any further. I only let him in because Genevieve didn't answer my questions earlier and now, I'm ready for answers.

'I know, I know we've not always got on, I know we've had our ups and downs, our difficulties.' He moves to sit beside me, perched on the edge of the sofa. 'I have tried so hard, Lisa. I've tried so hard and I've made so many mistakes. I did what I thought was best and then it felt wrong so I tried to do things differently, but I couldn't manage on my own.'

'What do you mean? How could you have carried on if it felt wrong? Wasn't that a sign enough? You don't tell someone their mother died if they didn't.'

'But she did.'

Impatient, I reach for the book. 'The test, Dad!' I pull out the paperwork, passing it to him. Now it's his hands that shake, his eyes that fill as he reads. 'Genevieve *is* my mother.' He nods, taking a deep breath. 'Tell me the truth! I have a right to know.'

'So did I, Lisa,' he says, quietly. I frown. 'I didn't lie to you. Not for your whole life, anyway.' My mind races. 'I believed your mother died after the car accident. Look… I need to start at the beginning.' I sit back, waiting.

'When she fell pregnant, I think I said before, her dad made it impossible for me to stay around. I came back here, I didn't want to. You have to believe that, I just couldn't see what else to do. Dad got me a job back with his firm, I left the new world I'd tried to create behind me, but it hurt so much. I felt like I'd let Genevieve down. Your grandma agreed. She thought I should have fought harder, ridden the storm. Your mum and I weren't bad people. We were in love. Yes, she was young. Yes, there was an age gap. I didn't set out to fall in love with someone so young, but she never seemed it. Not to me. And I was young, for my age; like I've said before, we met in the middle. I never took advantage of her, like people thought. I wanted to stand by her and raise you. I asked her to marry me.'

I look up, sharply.

'Genevieve was the love of my life, Lisa. I didn't see you as a mistake, or our relationship as anything dirty or wrong, I know that's how her dad played it, but he was wrong.'

'So she turned you down?'

'Her father turned me down. I was told in no uncertain terms to forget about her. I wasn't welcome in the area. People judged, they talked about me. Her dad had friends all over, I'd walk down the street some days and get shoved or jolted. People called me names. I managed to get a letter to Genevieve, not long after I left. I sent it to a mutual friend we had through church, the only person I could trust to get something to her. I told her where I was, my address. I told her that I'd come get her if she wanted to move to Lincolnshire. That we could raise you down here. She never replied and it broke my heart. But then, out of the blue, she sent me the photo of you both. It finished me off. I couldn't work that day, I remember just sitting in my room, I couldn't stop crying. It all felt so unfair, so unjust. Your grandma found me and decided we had to go to see you.' He gets up, pacing the floor. 'She took money out of the savings account to pay for the train tickets. She and your grandad argued about it, but she was insistent. She stood in my corner, stood up to him, something she rarely did, but she felt that strongly about it. Then, when I got there, Genevieve wasn't the same person.'

'What do you mean?'

'We went when I knew her dad would be at work. Your grandma knocked on her door, spoke to her mother. I walked into the room full of hope, really believing we could fix things, but she looked through me, as if I wasn't really there. She was vacant, somehow. The fire and light had gone, her passion had gone, it was like she existed in a constant fog. I'd seen it before, sometimes she could be like that, up one moment, rock bottom the next, but when I'd seen it before, I could usually help; I could find a way to cheer her up. But then?' He shakes his head. 'She pointed in your direction, you were in a crib beside her. I remember when I first held you, how tiny and beautiful you were. How I fell head over heels in love with you.' He avoids my eyes, looking down at his hands. 'You were a tiny part of us both, living on, and you lay in my hands, just wriggling, so reliant on your mother, on me in that moment, on whoever was going to care for you. I remember you cried, and I looked up to her to see what she wanted me to do, but her eyes had glazed over. It wasn't until her mum said something that she reached out and took you from me, laying you on her lap, staring at you. It was as if she couldn't quite see you either. Her mum tried to get Genevieve to feed you, but everything felt forced, like she just didn't have it in her. And I couldn't understand, it felt like she'd lost a part of herself.'

I remember that feeling after I had Poppy. Not quite sure what shape I was any more. But I'd never have left her.

'I remember pleading with her, trying to get her to see me. To see you. But she'd gone, nothing I said made any difference. The health visitor came round and your mum would perform, sort of present herself as a mother coping with a newborn, but when they left, she disappeared again. We were due to stay for a few days, your grandma extended our rooms at the B&B. She thought it was baby blues at first, that Genevieve needed time and she wanted to let us have that by sticking around. She talked to Genevieve's dad, tried to reason with him. He was desperate by this point too, angry sometimes, at the state she was in. I was surprised he agreed to let me in the house again, but I think he'd have tried anything, and your grandma could be very persuasive.' A small, sad smile touches his lips. 'She didn't do it often, eh, but when she got an idea into her head, she stuck to it, didn't she?' I nod.

'She found a group, local to Genevieve, that she thought would help. A young parents' thing, where they met up and supported one another. That's where we were going, the day of the accident. Genevieve sat in the front with her dad, she hadn't wanted to be in the back with you. I think her dad was fine to have her there too, he had allowed me in the house, but he wasn't thrilled about it. I suspect your grandma had something to do with that too. Maybe you picked up on Genevieve's mood that day, I don't know, but you were particularly niggly. So I was in the back, with her mum and you. Her dad drove.' He comes back to the chair and it creaks as he sits. 'I didn't for a second think she'd try to kill us all.'

Chapter Seventy-Seven

'Dad…' I freeze. Genevieve talked about something not being her fault, but trying to kill us? That feels intended… like she meant to do it?

'The accident… that's what I meant when I said she might be dangerous. It was your mother's fault.'

'Stop. Dad, stop, I can't.' I jump up. 'I don't want to.' I hold my hands up, pacing the lounge.

'Lisa, please. There's more to it.'

'Dad! Just… I need a minute!'

Paul appears in the lounge doorway, concern etched on his face. 'Are you okay?' He takes a step towards me, watching me.

'I'm okay. I'm okay. I just… I need a drink.'

I go into the kitchen, pulling out a glass and pouring it full of the wine on the side. I take a gulp, Holly stares.

'You can ask him to leave, if you need him too?'

'No. No, it's fine. I just… I just needed something to take the edge off.'

Paul comes back into the kitchen. 'Do you want me to ask him to leave?'

'No.'

'What about us? Shall we stay or go? What do you need, Lisa?'

'Erm... I don't know. Maybe it's better if you left. I can call you in the morning when the kids get up, Holly?'

'Or after your dad's gone, I can come back then,' she says. 'Or we both can, whichever.'

'Maybe. I don't know.'

Holly grabs her bag. 'Don't drink it all at once, okay?' she says, pulling me into a hug and holding me tightly before letting go and standing back for Paul.

He hovers. I reach out my hand to him, the tips of our fingers touch. 'I'm here as soon as you call, if you need me, okay?'

I squeeze his fingers but don't let go. Slowly, he lifts my hand to his lips and kisses it, tenderly. Holly looks to the floor as if giving us metaphorical space whilst I step into him, letting his arms envelop me, his touch making my legs feel stronger, my head clearer, perhaps. When I step away, he makes sure our eyes connect, no words needed.

I walk them both to the front door. Holly turns to me, 'Just let us know when you're done, okay?'

'I will.'

Pushing the door closed behind them, I rest my head against it before turning and pausing to look up the stairs. Charlie and Poppy fast asleep. The house now quiet. When I go back into the lounge, Dad is sitting at the little dining table Poppy and I eat our meals at. He has the notebook and paperwork out in front of him. I go to sit opposite him, closing my hands together.

'When I came round from the accident, you were in my room in a hospital crib for newborns. Though you were still small, to me you looked oversized in the crib. Mum told me that Genevieve was too ill, and that we were to look after you for a while, until she was well enough again. I was devastated, I just nodded. I didn't ask for detail, I think maybe I was shell-shocked too. I knew her parents had died. I knew how lucky I was, how lucky we were, to still be alive. And I'd gone from believing I'd never see you, to having you by my bedside. We went home, for a few days initially. She said we'd go back up to Scotland when Genevieve was ready. By then, things started to piece back together in my mind, your mother crying, shouting at voices she said she could hear. I'd been trying to reach forward to calm her, you were crying too. Her father was shouting at her. Your mother just… she just launched herself at the steering wheel.'

I swallow, unsure if I want to hear this, but knowing it's important.

'That's all I remember. And as the days passed, all I knew was that the girl I loved had turned into somebody I didn't recognise. Someone who'd put us all in danger. Someone who had, to all intents and purposes, killed her parents.' He holds his breath a second. 'It sounds so cold, so brutal, but that's what I thought. And on that basis, she could have killed you, Lisa. That fact kept playing in my mind. The girl I loved could have killed my daughter. I couldn't work it out, I was so angry with her, so confused. And then… then Dad told me she had died.' He takes a breath. I wait. 'He said there'd been complications following the accident, that nothing could be done to save her.'

He drops his head, hands hanging between his knees, his whole body crumpled in on himself. 'I was numb,' he whispers. 'The love of my life became someone I didn't recognise, I didn't trust, and then, before I could reconcile any of it, she died.' He looks back up at me. 'Lisa, I have lived my life, your life, believing Genevieve was dead.' He doesn't blink, his eyes tired, sorrowful.

'Until?'

He clears his throat. 'Until your grandma told me otherwise, a few months ago, just before she died. She hadn't known the truth at first either.'

'Iris said she found a letter?'

He nods. 'He said that he felt the only way for us all to move on from that time was to cut Genevieve off. And that he knew your Grandma would reject the idea, so he told her Genevieve had died. He got the false death certificate as proof. Arranged it through a solicitor friend in some men's group he was part of. Lisa, my father lied to us all.'

'Why? How could he do that?'

'We'll never know. I've wrestled with that too. I never thought him to be a bad man, controlling, dictatorial perhaps, but not intrinsically bad... I still don't have the answer to that one.'

'So, what? Grandma found the truth. And told you?'

'Not straight away, no. She didn't know what to do to begin with. Then, eventually, she tried to find Genevieve. She said she hadn't wanted to tell me until she had some facts. She had no idea if Genevieve was still alive, if she could even find her. How Genevieve would react if she did track her down. Eventually, she found her in Scotland, not far from where she used to live.'

'Grandma did?'

He nods. 'I think she hired a private investigator.'

I shake my head, this new side to my grandparents sounding so unreal.

'He found her, gave your grandma all the contact details. Your grandma reached out to her.'

'They met up?'

'No. They spoke on the phone initially. She said that Genevieve was understandably devastated to learn what had really happened. She had always thought you'd been taken away from her because she was unfit. She herself came to believe that, I don't know if others agreed, or if it was just in her head, but your grandma said she was insistent that she was no good for you. She told your grandma that she believed she had the capacity to be dangerous. She lived a life knowing she killed her parents and could have killed you too. Your grandma said she was ashamed, devastated, unable to forgive herself. She refused to risk hurting you all over again.'

'So, she rejected me?'

'She didn't know what else to do, Lisa, I'm sure of it. You'd have to ask her why. Your grandma did all that she could, she sent photos and keepsakes, memories of your childhood… the things you've received in the post, many of them were sent from Grandma to Genevieve, only in the last few years, trying to get her to change her mind.'

I shake my head, stunned and confused by how much there is to absorb.

'In the end, your grandma told me what had happened, but it was just as she was getting ill. I was torn, confused between what to do for you, for her, for Genevieve. I just… I didn't know how to process all this new information. I was terrified, how could I have not known? And how on earth could I tell you? I didn't know if Genevieve was well… and my mother was dying.'

It's my turn to pace now, up to the mirror by the fire. Over to the window. 'So you still didn't say anything? You kept the secret?'

'To begin with, I was consumed by caring for your grandma. I couldn't deal with both things, I mean, maybe that's weak. I probably should have, I just… I needed to focus on keeping your grandma as comfortable as possible. Genevieve had rejected the idea of a reunion, so I knew I'd have a fight on my hands in any case and I didn't want any stress for Mum, so I just pushed it all to the back of my mind. I knew she didn't have long, I thought I could be there for her, then work out what to do for you. When you had your accident… That weekend I went away? I'd gone up to Edinburgh to see if I could find Genevieve. I wanted to try and speak with her, persuade her that we could fix this together if she'd let me. Then you told me about the presents, and I knew they had to be from her. And I was suddenly terrified. That's why I told you they were from me. I couldn't work out what else to say and I risked losing you forever. I'd already been trying to work out how to fix the fracture between us so that, if I could talk to Genevieve, you and I would at least be strong enough for me to tell you the truth. And I suppose I was worried she might be a threat to you, she'd told Mum she couldn't trust herself. And you have to remember, the last time I knew her, she'd caused an accident that could have killed you. I had no idea who she was, or how she'd behave. That's why I lied about the house work, the boiler. I mean, it was stupid, I know… I don't know what I was thinking, what if you'd needed to go home for something? I just felt like I needed you home with me so I could keep the truth from you until I knew what we were dealing with. And then I'd tell you what had happened, I'd explain about why I'd lied. But we were so broken, and I was weak, I couldn't work out how to tell you everything. The days were passing, it was getting worse. All I kept thinking was that I almost lost you before, I couldn't let it happen again. I've got it wrong so often over the years, I've made a mess, made the wrong choices, tried to protect you and made things worse, but I could not lose you.'

I move to the sofa, pulling my knees into my chest, wrapping my arms around myself. 'Is she dangerous?'

He sighs. 'I don't know. I mean… maybe. Maybe not… I have no idea. Lisa. I don't know who she is any more. I've not exactly been bold and trusting when it comes to you, have I? I've spent your entire life worried that you'll get hurt, somehow. I've tried to protect you because I've always been frightened for you. I don't know why…'

'Maybe because she tried to kill us all?'

'But it's not that clear cut.' He shakes his head. 'That's why we need to talk to your mother. I know what I saw, that's the version of your mother I came to believe, but that's only ever going to be half the story. She should be here, she should have a chance to defend herself.'

'From what?'

He glances up at me. 'It's complicated. She was different, your mother. I've said it before, she could be high, full of life, excitable, free, then as quickly, and as surely, she could be rock bottom. Barely able to leave the house. Closed off to the world, to feelings.' He looks at me. 'I could bring her out of it, but, if I was honest, probably only sometimes. Sometimes, there was nothing I could do. She was lost to her demons for hours, days, sometimes. She wasn't well.'

'Clearly.'

'No, I mean it. She wasn't well, Lisa. I was so angry, for so many years, when you were young. It wasn't until years later that I fully understood what had happened to her. Or at least, what had caused the accident.'

Chapter Seventy-Eight

He comes to sit beside me. I shift with the sofa arm against my back, watching him. 'It was your grandma who suggested it at first. Maybe she'd been trying to get her own head around what had happened. I'd never heard of it before.'

'What?'

'Postpartum psychosis.' He swallows and I let the words settle in my mind. 'In the early eighties, mums got the baby blues. They could be a bit down in the dumps,' he says, giving the phrase speech marks. 'They weren't depressed, then. That's not the term that got used. And remember, I knew she wasn't right, I'd seen something, but I didn't understand it. I remember asking your grandma about it again, after Genevieve died... after I thought she had died. I was trying to process all that had happened. Mum felt it couldn't simply have been a case of crying for no reason or Genevieve feeling like she couldn't cope. This had to be bigger, a feeling of needing to die or to protect you so fiercely that you both died. I'd told her what had happened in the car, she'd seen for herself what Genevieve was like. She couldn't shake off the idea that it wasn't straightforward, I think she really felt devastation at the tragedy of Genevieve losing her life, or so she believed at that point. She researched it, she learned of the impact that postpartum psychosis can have, she was adamant Genevieve must have had an almost primal urge, a deep sense, in that moment, that you'd be safer from harm if you were no longer here or at the very least, safe from her, if she wasn't. She said they came from hormone spikes, that things like Genevieve's first period after childbirth could have brought it about.'

Dad's entire body wilts and an ache creeps into my chest.

'To be honest, even with that, to my shame, I couldn't disconnect the diagnosis from the behaviour. No matter what your grandma tried to tell me.' He pauses, looking at me. 'Until you fell pregnant. I'd gone your whole life wilfully believing not just that your mother was dead, but that it was her own fault.' He closes his eyes as if to admit the fact pains him. 'And then there you were, about to have a baby yourself, and I was terrified. What if it was hereditary? What if history could repeat itself? I needed to understand everything I could, then, so I read everything, I watched documentaries. I spoke to a colleague of George's, I wanted to know if it were at all possible—'

'For me to suffer the same.'

'I had to protect you. I had to protect Poppy. I know you've always felt I was overbearing, but I had to make sure I could be there if things went wrong. That's why I brought you home from Edinburgh. It's why I bought you this house. It's why…' He runs out of steam, taking a moment before eventually saying, 'It's why I was so terrified when you bought that car.'

'I would never have done something like that! I would never have hurt her.'

'But that's the point, isn't it? The point I had chosen to ignore for all those years. I don't think for a moment, in her lucid moments, that your mother thought she could have hurt you, and yet…'

He stares at me, not needing to finish the sentence. I think about my own moods, my mental health, the days I've found it tough going, or felt low. I can't imagine feeling so desperate that I'd behave that way, so lost that I couldn't see. So out of control that logic and reason would be so unreachable.

'Genevieve felt life, acutely. I do remember that. Maybe that's what drew me to her, what made her so intoxicating. She wasn't like anyone I'd met before. Sometimes her mood… it was like a switch had been flicked. Maybe she felt it coming on, but I didn't see it. I'd just find she was dark, low, I couldn't lift her. I couldn't make her better. She'd push me away, close off, close down. It wasn't like when you have a bad mood, or you're feeling a bit sad, she was… inconsolable, unreachable, she was inside of herself and nobody could be heard. It made her vulnerable, and, maybe in those moments, I, somewhat egotistically, wanted to be the one to save her, even when she was certain she wanted nobody near. When I went up to see her, after you were born, it was like she wanted to stay away in the dark, just be on her own. I couldn't seem to get through to her at all, though I had no idea why. I thought she was just rejecting me. That she was angry I'd left or didn't love me anymore. But now, I wonder if, when she was having one of those episodes, before having you as well as after, did she even know what was happening to her? I'd have to assume not. I didn't understand it, I just wanted to fix it. But the hormones, whatever was happening in her body when she had you, it made it all worse.' I drop my head. 'I don't mean you made her worse, it was her body, her hormones. There was nothing I could have done.'

I nod, taking everything in. Overwhelmed. 'So… I was here with you? What happened to Genevieve?'

'That is the most heart-breaking part of it all. I have no idea. Like I say, I thought she'd died in the crash. I have no idea where she's been or how she's been living. She told your grandma that she'd been in and out of treatments at various stages of her life. That she's never been quite the same since. Which I guess, you couldn't possibly be.' He stares at the fire again. 'She was trying her best to do right by keeping away, and I was trying my best by keeping you close… too close, I know.' He does one of those half-laughs you do when something isn't really funny, yet you can't help yourself. 'Your grandfather thought that you should have been put up for adoption.' He turns to face me. 'No matter how difficult it was, no matter how much anger I had towards your mother, or grief at her death, no matter how confused and frightened I was, there's no way I could ever have done that.'

'No?'

'He made it so tough.'

'Tough, how?'

'It was the only time I ever heard my parents raise their voices to one another, your grandma told him that she would never forgive him if he forced me to give you away, that she would fight to keep you, if not for me to raise you, then for her to. She loved you, doted on you.' I raise my eyebrows. 'In her way.' He concedes. 'She felt guilt, I think, at how much she'd tried to help, taking me up to see Genevieve, how those few days seemed only to make her worse.'

'That wasn't her fault.'

'I think she knew that in the end, when she realised what had really been happening. To begin with though, she definitely blamed herself. And it's the one and only time I saw her stand up to Dad. I know she had her opinions about things, and I know sometimes she'd say them, but mostly their marriage worked because she kept the peace. She was the home-maker, she lived as he expected. And she'd never threatened him before that… or did after, to be honest. She'd usually say her piece on a subject, then continue making the dinner or polishing the silver.

This time, though, she was different. She said that if you weren't allowed to stay here, to live with us, then she would leave, find somewhere to stay and raise you herself. She said you had already lost a mother and your other grandparents, that she would not stand by and let him take your last remaining family from you too.

Your grandfather stood his ground, so she took you, and she left him. For two, maybe three, days. I had to visit you at Iris's. I was starting an apprenticeship, mechanical engineering; I could see how I could make it a career. How, if I worked hard, I could get a good job, move into management, provide for you. As I have. You were my motivation and I knew I had it in me to succeed. So I worked during the day, then came to see you at Iris's in the evening. When I'd eventually get back home, your grandfather was raging, worse with every day she wasn't there. Furious that his wife would emotionally blackmail him. In the end, I think he wasn't prepared to bring more shame on the family by letting a baby end their marriage. I believe he saw no other option than to give in. His lie about Genevieve had effectively backfired.'

I frown at the choice of words, that something had 'backfired', or that I was something to 'give in' about.

'Eventually, he relented. He arranged a house for me to live in, paid half the rent and I covered the other half with my wages. He let me have his old car when he got a new one. Nothing expensive, but enough to get me to and from work.' The penny of history repeating itself drops. 'My father thought you might be the biggest mistake of my life, but he worked hard, sold shares and bonds he had, to make sure that, along with my own wages, I had what I needed to live and raise you, with your grandmother's support.'

I look around my own house, the bricks and mortar that Dad bought and paid for. The home I've carved for myself and Poppy.

'I have made mistakes, time and time again,' he says. 'But I proved to my father that you were simply not one of them. I worked during the day and Grandma looked after you. Then I took over when I came home. God… I had to learn fast! I am not the best father, Lisa. I am flawed, closed off, unavailable to you so much of the time, I know that. I know me. I've used money to replace affection, and I've used fear in place of reason. But I promise you' – he reaches out to my hands – 'I promise you that I have always done the best I can, even when it wasn't entirely good enough.'

I take my hands back. 'Dad.'

'I know I have got this wrong. I have been so frightened, I've let you down. I've let Genevieve down. But you have to believe me when I say that I love you, Lisa. And I loved your mother. I don't say it because for so long, I don't think I've known how. But I need you to know it now. I didn't lie for all of your life. I just wish I'd been bolder and able to tell you the truth as soon as I learned it, rather than had my hand forced in this way.' He laughs to himself. 'There she goes again, your mother, bolder and stronger than I.'

Chapter Seventy-Nine

It's almost midnight when I pad through to the lounge with a pot of tea for two. Dad takes over, busying himself in the ceremony of pouring: milk first, stirring the pot, sharing the contents until we both have a sufficiently strong cup.

'I miss Frank,' I say, looking over at the spot on the sofa where he should be sat.

'I think he misses you, too. He does a lot of sighing, pottering around, then sighing again.'

'He'd be good for Poppy, something to focus her energy on.'

'I can bring him round tomorrow, if you like.' He checks his watch. 'Perhaps not too early, though, eh?'

'No. Definitely not.'

'So what next?' he asks, with a gentleness I don't recognise. 'What do we do now?'

I think about Genevieve running away. I wonder what she thought I was thinking, or what she assumed I'd believed. I wonder if she realises Dad didn't know she was still alive? I wonder what she's been doing all her life and how she's lived? Dad said she'd been in and out of hospital, over the years. It can't all have been birth hormones, so why? 'We need to call Genevieve. We need to meet her.' He looks up at me. 'Together.'

There's a flicker of something in his eye and I'm not quite sure what it is. 'If she wants to meet with me.'

'I suppose.'

'I worry about her. Leaving you today, it tells me she's still vulnerable. I wonder how we deal with that?'

'I've spent a lifetime trying to look after everyone else, Dad. Trying to make sure that I do or say the right thing, so people don't feel uncomfortable.' He raises his eyebrows. 'Okay, maybe not to you… not lately. But I definitely have, over the years. I watch Poppy doing it now and I hate it. That need to make everyone around you comfortable, so often at the detriment of your own needs. But… maybe now is the time to do that for the right reasons. If there's one thing I've learned about myself these last few weeks, it's that I am stronger than I ever knew. I can handle the worst possibilities and remain standing.'

'I wonder if, despite how it might seem, your mother is like that?'

'I think *you're* probably like that, Dad. You're still here, you're still standing.'

'But what damage have I caused in the process?'

'That's life, isn't it?' He yawns, wiping his eyes. 'Go home, Dad. Get some sleep. I'll call Genevieve in the morning, let's see if we can arrange something that will work for her. There are ghosts to rest here, and none of us can move forward without doing that.'

The next morning, I'm woken by the sound of Charlie and Poppy raiding the kitchen cupboards. When I make it downstairs, bleary-eyed, I find them both with bowls of dry cereal, spillage all over the worktop.

'I didn't want to wake you Mummy but me and Charlie were so incredibly hungry, so we came down and made our own breakfasts and now we're watching telly.'

'I can see that.' I yawn through a smile.

'Can we do something fun today?' she asks.

'Like what?'

'The park or the zoo or swimming or something?'

'Let's see. Morning, Holly,' I say into my phone. 'There are two monkeys wide awake and desperate for fun, how are you fixed?'

'I can do fun. So long as you don't mind Dave tagging along?'

'Of course not.'

'Great. I'll be with you in an hour. Stash them in front of the telly until I get there. Let Charlie know Mummy's friend is coming will you, they've met briefly so he'll be fine, I'm sure.'

'Course.'

'You okay?'

'I think so.'

'Did you sort things with your dad?'

'Mostly.' I head into the kitchen so Poppy can't hear me, lowering my voice. 'He thought she was dead too.'

'What?'

'Until just before Grandma died.'

'Oh God, that's… Wow!'

I scoop cereal mess into my hands, dropping it into the bin before gazing out of the window. 'I know, right. And then, given that the last time he saw her she caused an accident that killed her parents, I think he was terrified about how stable she was. What damage she could do. If she could hurt me. I mean, it's a mess, the whole thing is a mess.'

I've kept thinking what it must be like for Dad. How would I feel if I was told that somebody I loved had died and then, years later, found out they hadn't? A heart so broken he never met anybody else and yet, the one woman he loved had been out there all along.

'My head is mashed, honestly, I don't even know where to begin. Actually, I do. I need to call Genevieve. Try and see if we can finish off where we started yesterday. Then, maybe, we all need to get together.'

'Wow. That's…'

'I know. It feels pretty big when I say it to you this morning. It seemed like a good idea last night but now I'm wondering. What if it's too much for her? What if she freaks out again? What if she can't handle it and I push her too far?'

'Lisa, you can't take responsibility for her. If you need to meet her, to talk with her and your dad together, you've every right to ask the question. Don't talk yourself out of something you need to protect her when she may not need protecting.'

'But she's—'

'Someone who reached out to you. Someone who has lived a life in the shadow of her truth. Someone who got scared yesterday but needs time to face the realities of her life. What did she think your whole life? That the love of her life left her? Didn't care for her anymore? Did she know he thought she was dead?'

'Well, I assume Grandma must have told her when she reached out, but… who knows?'

'There are so many loose ends, Lisa. You've got to try and tie them all up before you can move forward. Maybe all three of you do.'

'When did you get so wise?'

'Fortune cookies. They're much deeper than you'd expect.'

'You're an idiot.'

'I'll be there in an hour.'

Chapter Eighty

I look down the list of names on the door, singling out flat number 6b, the bedsit she's been living in for the last month or so. I press the buzzer, shivering with a fresh blast of wind that whips up my coat. The door clicks and I push it, the draught excluder making a sound on the rough wide doormat into a vast entrance hall. It's an old Georgian building, wide windows and tall ceilings, but it looks unloved, inside and out. It feels unloved too, sort of lost and empty, despite the piles of post and the bikes locked up against a radiator. A door opens somewhere up a sweeping staircase that I imagine, once upon a time, was quite grand.

Genevieve appears at the top of the stairs, wrapped up in her coat. 'Hi,' she says, nervously. 'Come up.'

I take the staircase, each tread shallow and squeaky. I follow her into her room, the door leading me straight to a lounge bedroom. A single bed extends out into the room from the far wall and at the window a small table is set out with two chairs and a bowl of brown bananas. To my right is a door, and to the left of that, there's a sort of box room within a room that I see has a kettle, a worktop cooker and a fridge.

'Take a seat,' she says, motioning to the window. 'Can I get you a drink?'

'Erm, no, thank you. I've just had coffee, actually.'

'Oh, right. Okay.'

I feel bad and wish I could change my mind just to give her something to do and maybe buy me some time. The nerves grew in the coffee shop as I nursed cold coffee whilst staring out of the window for an hour until it was time to come here.

'Thanks for coming.'

'Oh, it's fine. Thanks for agreeing to meet me.'

I try not to look around the room though notice there doesn't seem to be much to give away what she likes or dislikes. There are no paintings, no plants. No soft furnishings or much to suggest this place is anything other than temporary.

'It's a bit…' She plays with her hands as she looks around the room and I feel bad again for not better hiding my inquisitive glances.

'No, no, it's…' I stop myself from saying lovely. We both know I'd be lying.

'I didn't know how long I'd be staying for. It's just temporary until I decide what to do next.'

'Right.'

'I'm sorry I ran away yesterday,' Genevieve says, her voice like china. 'I keep replaying it in my mind, I'd wanted so much to be strong for you. After finally deciding I wanted you to know me, I so wanted to be the grown-up in what must be so… confusing.'

'It's okay. Maybe I didn't handle things right.'

'Is there a right way? I've never done this before.'

'No. Me neither.'

We exchange a smile, which thaws the room a little, though not enough for either of us to take off our coats. She shivers.

'The heating broke. They say it'll be back on by tonight.'

'What happened to you?' I've considered not asking this question, but the truth is, it's all I want to know. Judging by the look on her face

I've caught her by surprise, maybe she thought the heating small talk might last a little longer. But still… 'How did this happen?'

She moves to the chair opposite me, glancing out at the garden below. I follow her gaze to a white fluffy cat that does the prowl wiggle cats do before pouncing on something in the undergrowth.

'I went mad.' She says it so simply, that it takes my breath away. 'I mean, I suppose you shouldn't say that any more, but that's what happened. I went mad. Then, and several times since.'

'How?'

'I don't know. I mean… I know it's hormones. They flood particularly when you get your first period after childbirth.' Dad's research aligns. 'They say that can be really bad… well, obviously. That's an understatement really. But I don't know why me.' She lifts the tablecloth into her hands, fiddling with the lace edging. 'When you were first born, I couldn't have adored you more. I really couldn't. You were a symbol of love for me, you were forbidden, so my dad wanted me to believe, and yet somehow, I'd been able to keep you. You lay in my arms, defenceless, needing my protection. I was overwhelmed but was certain I could raise you. Stupid really. I had no idea what I was doing and…'

'And?'

'Well, clearly my mind had other ideas.'

I think back to when I'd had Poppy. How scary those first few days and weeks were, alone, back home in Lincolnshire, not knowing what had hit me.

'I felt so low after Poppy, I mean, maybe not like you, I don't know, but I was so frightened. I was a grown-up though. Thirty-two. You were so young, I can't imagine how it must have been for you?'

'I don't think I realised, not fully. I knew I was scared. And I knew…' She pauses, adjusting her composure. 'I knew I could hear voices.'

I try not to react, I don't want to give her any cause to stop talking. But voices?

'I'd heard them before, even before I was pregnant. I never told anybody, I was frightened, I suppose. And after I had you, when they reared up again, I didn't want to tell anyone because I didn't want them to take you away. I'd already had to fight to keep you, I couldn't risk anything, so I pretended it was all okay. I thought they'd go away like they had before. At least, I think I thought that's what I was doing. I was sixteen, remember. A young sixteen.'

I remember what I was like at sixteen, barely able to function, never mind be a mother.

'They check you, don't they, when the health visitors come to see the baby.' I nod. 'They watch for your interaction and so on. Somehow, I knew that. I worked so hard when they were there. I'd look at you, really look into your eyes. I'd play with your fingers and toes and I'd talk to you, pick you up if you made even a sound. I was so desperate to prove to them that everything was okay so nobody would take you away and yet, afterwards, when they'd gone, or at night even, when I was totally alone with you…' She takes in a deep breath and gazes back out of the window.

'You don't have to do this now, if it's too hard.'

'You deserve to know what happened.' She rubs the tablecloth between thumb and forefinger, her eyes eventually drifting back to mine. 'It got worse and worse. Maybe to begin with I could ignore my feelings, pretend they weren't there. But after a while, the feelings got stronger, the voices louder. By the time you were three months old, I had endured weeks of voices telling me you were going to be taken away and put in danger if I didn't protect you. Or that I, myself, was an unfit mother.'

'What voices though? Who told you these things?'

'Nobody. I see that now, it was nobody but, in my head, the voices were real. I was unfit. I was exhausted. I'd been trying to fake it for months. And you were getting bigger, you needed more. I remember your dad coming...' A swell of emotion engulfs her, and she can't speak for a second. I wait. 'Your dad came to see us. I so wanted to reach out to him, to let him hold me like all those times before you arrived, when he would. When he'd make me feel better even if he didn't realise it. But I just couldn't let him in. The more he looked at you, and held you, the more I could see that he loved you and I was terrified he would be the one to take you away. Your grandma too, she was bowled over. The more I watched them both, the more of a threat they became. I convinced myself that they'd come to take you away. And that your dad couldn't possibly raise you, that he was a threat to you and to me. Even though I could clearly see that he loved you, somehow, that was frightening. The voices kept telling me you were in danger. And that the only way to protect you was to k—' She clamps her mouth shut.

Chapter Eighty-One

I wait for a second, giving her more time, before eventually, saying, 'You can say it.'

Her voice is a barely audible whisper. 'I really believed the only way to protect you was to kill you.'

My eyes sting, my throat is raw as a tear escapes down her face, she rubs the tablecloth harder. She gives me the courtesy of not looking away this time but her own eyes are teary, her mouth taut.

'I couldn't stop myself, I didn't want to. I just needed to do what was right by you, that was all I could think. We were going somewhere, I forget where now.'

'A young parents' group, apparently. So Dad says.'

'That's right! God... yes.' She pauses.

'He said I was teasy, crying.'

'Right. Yes.'

'If I was anything like Poppy, I'll have done that a lot.'

She forces a sad smile. 'You did. I think that was my fault too. Babies are perceptive.' I nod, gently. 'So he was in the back of the car, with my mum and you. Dad told me to get in the front, but I was going there anyway, I knew what I had to do. Dad took us along a route I knew well. I'd seen the bridge before and thought about what I could do. I'd driven down so many roads with my parents, in the weeks leading up to it. When things were bad, even before I had you, I used to look at walls and bridges as if to assess where might be a good place to drive a car. It's madness, I knew most bridges had crash barriers, you know, on the motorway and things. As we drove that day, I recognised where we were going and I remembered a bridge without a barrier to break the collision. I mean... what a thing to think, and yet... it was perfect. It was like I knew exactly what I needed to do to solve all our problems and I couldn't ignore the noise. It was like I *had* to do it, it was the only way to... I want to say survive but...'

I hold my hands tighter, my body rigid as she tells her story.

'I remember your cry got worse, like you knew what was coming.'

My heart races, thumping in my chest. Part of me doesn't want to hear this and yet, part of me is curious. It feels like she is talking about someone else; it can't be me, it can't be her...

'Mum was shushing you in the back. I was getting anxious; your dad was sat behind me. He reached through to try and calm me, squeezing my shoulder, rubbing at my arm, it made me worse somehow. The voices got louder, I remember shouting. Dad was yelling at Mum to shut you up. He was yelling at me, grabbing hold of my wrists. I managed to pull myself free of him, focusing on the road up ahead...' She pauses, shifting in her seat, no fidgeting this time. 'The roads were greasy, it must have rained that day. As we approached the bridge, I just snatched the wheel, pulling it as hard as I could. I can still remember...' She closes her eyes as if they sting. 'Dad had no chance to rectify it, the damage was done, he lost control, we hit the bridge, then I don't remember anything after that until, I suppose, several days later.'

'Oh God.'

She watches me. I fidget, the truth itching at me.

'I can stop?'

'No... no, I need to hear it all.'

'When I woke up, and they told me what had happened, I lost it. I was screaming, pulling at my hair, howling. They had to sedate me. I think that's when they started to realise there were other issues. Doctors spoke to health workers who talked to the midwives. My files had already been red flagged as vulnerable. Eventually, I was admitted to a psychological mental health unit, intensive care. And that's where I stayed for months afterwards.'

She drops the tablecloth and gets up, startling me. She stands closer to the window, visibly unsettled. Now I really want to tell her to stop because clearly it's too much, but at the same time, I have to know.

'I've been in and out of mental health units, or mental healthcare, for years.'

'But, how? How can you be ill for so long afterwards? Pregnancy hormones go away. I don't understand.'

'I was diagnosed with bipolar disorder. Well, back then it was manic depression. I never knew, I mean, I knew I had mood swings, but I didn't understand why. Pregnancy and childbirth hormones can trigger episodes, make them worse. Periods starting again and things like that, it can all have a catastrophic effect on your levels. My period started that weekend your father came to visit. The first one since I'd had you. They say it sort of turbocharged all the hormones and I had no chance. They say that I couldn't have fought it.'

The look on her face tells me how painful this is. How much she's had to live with. The knowing that through no fault of her own, she could be dangerous.

'I couldn't accept that, not for years. I should have been able to fight it. I should have been stronger, better, more capable. For you. I had you to be that for and I couldn't manage it, that's how it felt, for years. I felt like I deserved to have you taken away. It served me right. It didn't matter that healthcare professionals told me otherwise, I was certain that I was evil and losing you was proof.'

I want to reach out to her, woman to woman, but she's tight into herself, unavailable somehow.

'I have to take medication now, to keep me even. For years, I tried not to take it. I hated how it made me feel, how dull the world seemed when I was on it. Before it, everything was razor sharp, you know? I can only describe it as like on a telly, the brightness or the colour saturation was turned right up and that's how I'd lived for so long, it felt normal. When I was on the tablets, it was like everything was… not quite black and white but not… normal. My normal. Though, I realise now, it's the colour most people live within.'

She sits back across from me. 'For years, I hoped things would get better. Sometimes, when I eventually started taking the medication regularly, I hoped I might be able to find where you'd gone and be the kind of mother you deserved, but then I'd lose faith in myself, I'd punish myself for what happened. Sometimes, things would get better, I'd get better, stop taking the tablets and, in no time at all, I'd have another episode. Gosh, I remember even hoping your dad and I might be able to reconnect at one point.' She shakes her head, wiping her face.

'I suspect Dad would have wanted the same thing.'

'Yeah? I mean, I suppose I always wanted to think so, especially in the early years after it happened. You know, your dad was the one certain in my life. I knew how he felt about me even when everything else felt confused.' Sadness washes over her. 'It was no wonder that he was angry with me. No wonder he hated me, after what I'd done. I couldn't have expected him to stay in touch. I had no idea that it was because…'

'Because he thought you were dead.'

She wipes a tear. 'It made sense when your grandma told me that. I'd spent years thinking he'd taken you and deserted me, that he hated me. That all my fears had come true.'

'But you didn't try to fight for me?'

'Lisa… I didn't know how. I was broken. Inside and out. Looking back, I think I had to believe that you were better off without me. I was dangerous, that's what I thought. And David… your father was protecting you. Maybe if my own mother had survived, things might have been different. Maybe she'd have fought for me, helped me to see things differently, I don't know. As it was, I was alone, I had nobody really on my side. And I had no idea what David had been told.'

'But what about when Grandma found you? What about then? You could have changed things then!' I realise my tone is bordering on anger, and I don't want to frighten her but that's the bit of the puzzle that makes no sense to me.

'I have been telling myself for your whole life, that I had to stay away. I have believed I couldn't be trusted, that I might hurt you. I have believed I am ill, and no good. I killed my parents, Lisa.'

'It wasn't your fault.'

'In theory, when you look at the medical records, that's the case. But it is very hard to accept that's the case when the facts speak for themselves. It happened. How could I be certain it could never happen again? How can I possibly have trusted myself to deal well with turning your world upside down? You were thriving without me. Your grandma tried to persuade me. The pictures she sent me, the letters and cards, the cutting of your hair, they were all designed to get me to agree to meet you, but as much as they were moments that lifted my heart, and I wanted so badly to let you know I was alive… I also believed you were better off without me.'

'So… what changed?'

She pauses for a moment. 'Iris.' A small smile plays on her mouth. 'Elsie gave her my address before she died. She came to meet me. She didn't tell me why, just said she was a friend of the family and she wanted to talk to me. She explained about your grandma. She was so kind, so nurturing, making sure I was okay when she told me. We talked about it. About how you had lost your mother figure, how much Elsie wanted us to reconnect, that your father would be trying his best, but that she wasn't certain he'd know how to deal with this. That she thought it was time I allowed myself to reach out, for all your sakes. I'd had more time to think. I couldn't imagine how devastated you might be at the loss of your grandma.'

'It was hard. Of course it was.'

'We talked about how I might go about it. The gifts were my idea. Little things to help you, or to make you think. Iris wasn't so sure, but it was like a light went on and I knew what I had to do. Little things that might make your dad think, too, in case he questioned anything, and it helped. That necklace?' She motions towards the one Iris gave me that I still wear. 'That was a gift your father gave to me when we found out I was pregnant. My own grandmother had one. I used to sit on her lap and play with it. I told him about it when we saw one, one day, in this little jewellers in an alleyway on one of our walks, before we told everyone I was expecting. He took money from his savings to buy it for me. I wore it every day, for years. I knew that if he saw it, he'd know.'

I take hold of the necklace, the ball in my palm, his reaction when he saw it at the hospital that day, now making sense. 'Iris didn't want to get involved, I really had to beg her to give it to you. It was important, it felt pertinent. Like the music. The hair, because who else might have had something so significant?' She looks down. 'I see now how strange it must have been, perhaps even how foolish the gifts were. I should have done things differently, I just... something like this... you have no idea where to begin. I'm not a bad person, Lisa.'

'I don't think that of you.'

'What about your dad?'

'He's... frightened, I think.'

'He probably hates me.'

'I don't think that's true at all.'

She gazes out of the window, a robin jumps and hops from bush to wall down below. She takes a deep breath. 'Do you think your dad would want to see me?'

'Absolutely,' I say, certain. 'Are you up to it?'

She thinks for a second. 'I am. I think, I finally am.'

Chapter Eighty-Two

Poppy jogs up to Charlie, her face bright and smiling. After much begging on her part, we're trialling a full day since the accident as she's been desperate to stay around for the whole day.

'So lovely to see her happy and well,' says a voice behind me. I turn around to see Felicity Perfect, hair freshly coiffured, gym bunny uniform on point. 'Is she back full-time now?'

'Today is her first full day.'

'How lovely. And are you back to work?'

'Next week now. I was due back, but a few things have come up that need sorting first.'

I see her face change from faux care to hair flick and teeth flash.

'Paul,' I say, turning, knowingly. He stands beside me, just close enough for our shoulders to touch but maybe not so close as Felicity would notice.

'Aren't you just the best uncle doing the school run.'

'It's nice to see Charlie. He's my favourite nephew.'

'Ahhh. Do you have a few?'

'Nope. Just him.'

'Right.' She looks momentarily confused before deciding she's not going to examine what he says any further. 'A few of us are going for a coffee this morning, you're welcome to join us, Paul, as an honorary mum?'

'I'd love to but Lisa and I are heading out for breakfast, I'm afraid.'

'Oh! I see. Right.' She eyes us both as if trying to work out why we're going for breakfast and if it's as friends or something more. 'Must be nice to have the extra time off work and do breakfast. Maybe next time,' she says to Paul before jogging off.

The school bell goes, Poppy comes back to kiss me, then legs it with Charlie and Evie who is apparently over the moon to have her mate back at school and now the three of them can hang out together, have tea at each other's houses, and generally do all the things five-year-old mates do together.

Paul and I walk in unison down the pathway and out to the track down by the river, heading for Loaf, a new little cafe that opened up in the village. We've walked a good five minutes in silence before he asks, 'How you feeling about today?'

I sharp intake my breath because every time I've thought about Dad and Genevieve meeting up, I've not been quite sure what to do with the facts.

'I don't know. I sort of can't believe it's happening. That both my parents will be in the same room at the same time, it doesn't make sense.'

'I'm not surprised. I don't know how you can spend all your life with one piece of knowledge, for it to all be switched upside down so fast. How does your dad feel, do you think?'

'Terrified. I assume. He's been texting me several times, confirming where we're meeting, when, what he should wear, should he bring something for her. He's a weird mix of protective Dad, trying to make sure I'm okay with what's going on, and seventeen-year-old boy about to go on a date.'

'I know how he feels.' I look up at him. 'I mean, I know it's just breakfast but... I feel a bit like a seventeen-year-old boy, too.'

'Do you?'

He looks on up ahead, but a smile plays on his lips. 'You've always made me feel like that. It's kind of nice not to have to hide it anymore.'

His smile makes me smile. Then the feeling of his arm around my shoulders makes my heart flip. We walk on a bit more, my arm around his waist before eventually he says, 'I mean, I feel seventeen, but walking arm in arm like we actually *are* seventeen is uncomfortable, don't you think.'

'Yeah… it is a bit.' Neither of us moves our arms.

'It's like, when you used to walk with your hand in your girlfriend's back pocket.'

'The ultimate 1990s sign of togetherness.'

'The ultimate way to strain your shoulder.' We grin at one another and he moves his arm from my shoulder to my hand, feeding his fingers through mine. 'This is definitely more comfortable.'

'It is.'

'Thanks.'

'For what?'

'Having breakfast with me.'

'Breakfast today, dinner tomorrow… breakfast the day after?' I say, now not able to catch his eye.

He stops walking, turning to face me. We're in the middle of the pathway, tall trees to our left, rushes and the stream to our right. He looks at me then, slowly, leans in, his lips on mine, gentle at first, but there's no doubt in my mind how he feels and my legs go weak. When he pulls back, I'm breathless.

'Dinner then breakfast whenever. There's no rush. You've got important things to sort first.'

And we walk on, his hand in mine, knowing without doubt that time is on our side. He's right, we don't have to rush a thing because, in fact, this was always meant to be. And maybe it was right for it not to happen before now, maybe it took all that we've lived and learned before to show us what we wanted in life, and that – for me at least – Paul was the one who could give me that.

Chapter Eighty-Three

Dad and I wait in my lounge, him sat at the dining table, me pacing the room, glancing out of the window, waiting.

'You'll wear the carpet out.'

'You'll wear the chair legs out.'

'That doesn't even make sense, Lisa.'

'I know.'

Frank stretches, stands, then turns on the spot, his spot on the sofa, tucking himself back into himself, nose stuffed into his leg as he sighs. 'See, he sighs here too.'

'Yeah, but he's definitely happier,' says Dad.

The front doorbell goes and we both jump, banal conversation immediately silenced. Dad had wanted to see her, it didn't seem to occur to him to say no. We were going to do it on neutral territory, but in the end, Genevieve asked to come here. I'm not sure either of us believed she'd turn up though.

Dad swallows and I see a vulnerable side to him too. I wonder if he really does feel like a kid at the prospect of seeing the love of his life again? I wonder if he's nervous, or fearful?

When I open the door, Genevieve offers me flowers. 'I brought these for you,' she says, holding them out for me.

'Oh, thank you, they're lovely.'

'The lavender looks nice,' she says, nodding down to the pot on my doorstep.

'Doesn't it. Thank you.'

She peers inside the door. 'Is he here?'

'He is. Yes.' She stuffs her hands into her pockets, not moving to come in.

'Do you want to…' I motion to invite her, and she looks up and down the road before finally stepping inside.

'Can I take your coat?'

'Erm, yes, thank you. It's warm in here.'

'We have heating.' My lame joke falls on deaf ears.

As she hands me her coat, I notice her arms, marked red and raw in places where she's scratched. The one on her hand from the day before yesterday glistens. I catch her hand and she starts. 'Are you okay?'

She pauses a second, looking at my hand in hers. 'I'm okay,' she says, quietly. 'A bit scared.'

'It's going to be fine.' I give her hand a squeeze to reassure. 'Come through.'

I don't know what I expected from Genevieve and Dad seeing one another again. I mean, I knew it was significant, it's been thirty-eight years and for the majority of those, Dad believed she was no longer alive, but still, I think the reality would have been impossible to foresee. As she followed me into the lounge, Dad stood, staring. I moved aside so she could see him better, so they could get to one another, but in fact they were frozen. Dad looked different; I don't want to say younger because that suggests some shift in psyche that happened as a result of them coming back together after all these years, but I suppose, in some ways, he *did* seem younger. And having only ever seen Genevieve looking vulnerable or uncertain, that she looked this way again didn't come as a surprise, but what did was the way she moved closer towards him, as he did her. They stood in front of one another for a few seconds, neither speaking, before eventually, Dad opened his arms and she wrapped hers around him and he buried his head into her hair and they both cried. And then I cried because I've never seen Dad like this before, and I don't know if he's ever felt it before or maybe he has, with her, when they were young and had life and innocence on their side.

'I see you,' she says to him, when they finally part. 'You're still there, I see you.'

'And you too,' he says, breathless, a kind of pain in his eyes. 'I can't believe you're here, I thought...' She drops her head and he stops himself, perhaps not wishing the moment to suffocate her as before. 'You haven't changed a bit,' he says, which makes her laugh a little. 'Here, come, sit down.'

She takes the chair opposite him and I realise I'm stood in my home, with my parents, both together, looking at me, and this time it's my turn to buckle under the weight of it all.

'Hey, hey, come here. Come on, sit down.' Dad has come to me, his arm around mine, guiding me to the chair. Genevieve watches and I wonder if she realises how unlike him this is. And that's not to say he's doing it for effect, rather that the moment warrants him stepping out of his own constraints and perhaps I should be thankful for that fact.

'So,' I say, wiping my eyes as I regain composure.

'So,' repeats Genevieve.

'Where do we begin?' asks Dad.

Epilogue

It seems strange to say that I'm having dinner with my parents on a Sunday. I've never been able to say it, not for my whole thirty-eight years, and though today isn't the first time, it does seem momentous because it's the first time I've ever taken anyone home to 'meet my parents'. I mean, Dad knows him and obviously he's met Genevieve too, but this is different. We're going together. As a couple. To see my parents.

'You okay?' asks Paul, resting his hand on my knee, the steering wheel in his other hand.

'I think so. You?'

'Definitely.'

I look down at my hand where a new, sparkling diamond sits on my ring finger. When I showed it to Poppy, she was desperate to try it on and paraded around the living room with a sheet over her head, singing the 'Wedding March'. Much to my dismay. The very idea of a big white dress and austere music sent chills down my spine. Thankfully Paul is well up for eloping to Gretna and doing it on the sly... with Poppy, Holly and Charlie, of course. He's been looking at honeymoons in Scotland so we can try a bit of Nessie spotting, Poppy's beyond excited at that.

Mum and Dad don't live together, I'm not sure they're even officially a couple really. They just enjoy one another's company and it is nice to see Dad looking happy. She's got a bungalow that she rents in the village and they see each other most days. She and I have talked more about her life and experiences, about how difficult so much of it has been, how the mental health provision in this country was so poor for so long, how it's better than it was but things still aren't right. For the first time, it's given me something to feel passionate about and today I'll tell them about my plans to retrain as a mental health worker, specialising in postpartum psychosis. It's probably not a great time to enter the NHS or even mental health work in general – I've been shocked by what little funding there is in various counties across the country. Somehow, that's made me all the more determined. I have a mentor in a wonderful psych nurse called Lou. She's been doing it for years and knew exactly what Mum had been through, the hormones, the voices, the need to protect in the worst possible way. She really opened my eyes to how this can still happen. The change being that now mothers are kept with their children as often as possible, just in hospitals that can care for both woman and child.

Dad is on the doorstep when we get there. He definitely looks younger than before. There are crinkles at his eyes where he now smiles. Iris noticed them first, when she bumped into him at the corner shop and rang me straight afterwards to comment on them. She's been thrilled to see how things have unfolded, taking no glory in the fact that, were it not for her, we might never have known Genevieve. She keeps reminding me that it's thanks to Grandma this happened. She maintained a kind of contact, even if she did so in secret for so long. Dad and I have talked about that, about how strange it is to think she did it. That she didn't feel she could say anything to Dad, that she was silenced, seemingly on so many things, by Grandad and his commitment to his faith. A faith I've never really recognised or understood. One that contributed to the silencing of Genevieve.

Genevieve. She steps out from behind Dad, wiping her hands on a pinny he always used to wear when he cooked us a roast. I still can't get on board with calling her Mum. It seems too weird, too much. I think she feels the same, I notice sometimes how things seem to overwhelm her. She continues medication for her bipolar and whilst, for the most part, she is fine and balanced, every now and then she seems to have dips that shift her mood. Perhaps that's normal, nothing to do with her illness. I suppose I'm extra sensitive to it under the circumstances. I'll learn more as I go through my training.

Poppy unclicks her belt and jumps out of the car, running up to Dad. Where once he might have ushered her in, avoiding any contact, now he pulls her into an embrace. I mean, it's clumsy, clunky even, but he makes an effort. More than relieved, I think, that Poppy made a full recovery. The bit that we're all the most relieved about. She runs around, chatters and sings like nothing ever happened. I'm definitely not religious, but some kind of miracle happened the day we had our accident. It saved me for a second time in my life, and for her to be okay too… Life can turn on a sixpence. One day, you're the mother of one, with a father you rarely see and a sense that something in your life is missing but you don't know what. The next, you have two parents, a fiancé, and the knowledge that everything is as it should be, even just for this moment in time.

Holly is preparing for her own wedding. Charlie was just recently told that Dave is more than just Mummy's friend and he was thrilled about it. She and I did talk about a double wedding, very briefly; well, she did. But it didn't last long when she talked about a do in the village hall with a big party afterwards, everyone invited, even the mums at school, apparently. As small as it might be compared to some, it's not for me and Paul.

And Billy? He's back in Edinburgh. He struggled to deal with my rejection to begin with. Took it personally, got angry, closed off pretty much straight away, but something changed after a few weeks of sulking, and he called up to apologise. He's set up a maintenance payment direct from his wages and Poppy knows him as a friend of mine who she talks to on Skype from time to time. He's booked some time off work to come down and be here for two weeks in a couple of months and we're planning during his visit to tell her how he's connected to her. I don't know how she'll take it, particularly as she's really taken to having Paul about. I regularly find them snuggled up on the sofa with him reading to her, her head resting on his arm, but it's important she knows the truth and I know Paul will handle his side of the bargain, brilliantly.

'You got the wine?' asks Paul.

'Yep. Can you get the pudding?'

'Course.'

'Right.' I look up at Dad and Genevieve, both listening intently to whatever story Poppy weaves, stood on Dad's top step.

'Let's do this,' Paul says, taking my hand. He leans in to kiss me, full force on the lips. 'I love you.'

'I love you too.'

'Come on!' shouts Poppy, rolling her eyes at us and we laugh, getting out of the car.

Dad gives me a hug and it's meant, it's felt. And it staggers me that he can show such a display of affection to me as well as Poppy, I would never have imagined it possible. I drape my bag on the bannister, reaching into it for the notebook so I can update them both on the plan for my course, all of which is written down within it. Along with plans prepping for our wedding, and a list Paul and I have written together with things we'd like to do in the future, places to go, ideas for a dream home that Paul wants to design for us, along with ways to raise money to buy a plot of land to build it on. It feels nice to have someone to dream about these things with. The notebook feels like something that roots me, somehow. Writing things down is definitely my way to navigate all that I want, dream, and hope for, something maybe I'd never have known had Genevieve not sent it to me. I see her clock it and we both smile.

Looking back on my life, I now realise just how much I felt a lack of something, something I never really understood. I always thought it was because of Dad, or more recently, the fact I was solo parenting without the guidance of a mother. I don't know exactly, maybe I'll work that out over time, but as I stand in the lounge, Poppy, Paul, Dad and Genevieve chattering amongst themselves, I realise how strong I feel, how strong I am, and, most importantly, how full and content my heart now is. Perhaps that's because Genevieve's in my life, perhaps it's Paul, or perhaps it's the lifting of a secret weight I never even knew I carried.

A Letter from Anna

Dear Reader,

I want to say a huge thank you for choosing to read *What We Leave Behind*. If you did enjoy it and want to keep up to date with all my latest releases, just sign up at the following link. Your email address will never be shared and you can unsubscribe at any time.

www.bookouture.com/anna-mansell

Thank you SO much for taking the time to read my sixth novel. Sixth! I can't quite believe it. I hope you've enjoyed reading about Lisa, her dad, and Genevieve. When thinking about what to write, I knew there was something about the more acute aspects of mental health that I wanted to shine a spotlight on, in particular, how this can affect women with a bipolar diagnosis following childbirth. Devastatingly, Genevieve's story, whilst entirely fictional here, is not unrealistic. Provision and support for postpartum psychosis has improved massively in the last thirty years, but we still have much to learn. That, combined with the dawning realisation of just how many families harbour secrets from the past, is how this book came about. I hope that I've managed to balance telling a compelling story, with some of the truths I learned during my research.

Telling stories for a living really is a privilege and I'm so grateful for all the messages I get from those of you who've enjoyed my writing. If you'd like to chat about this or any of my other books, I can usually be found on Instagram, Twitter or Facebook, so feel free to get in touch. And if you feel you're able, reviews really do make all the difference to authors. It helps others know if we've written something they might like, it gives books and authors more visibility, and it really helps, if we're in the middle of writing a new novel, to see that someone has taken the time to review a previous one… especially if that review is nice. ☺

If you'd like to hear more about my books, please do consider signing up to my Bookouture mailing list. We promise not to spam you!

Thank you again for your time. I am truly, very grateful.

Lots of love
Anna x

 AnnaMansellAuthor

 @annamansell

 MrsAnnaM

www.feelthefearandwriteitanyway.com

Acknowledgements

Okay, so transparency alert, I would rather write a 100k word novel, than a one or two page acknowledgement, mainly because I'm terrified of missing someone out, somebody crucial, without whom I simply could not write. I've recently heard of authors starting Excel spreadsheets to log all those they wish to thank in their novels, I shall be adopting this idea in the future. So for now, it's strictly from my post line edit, midst of a global pandemic addled and exhausted brain. If you think I should have mentioned you, and I haven't, please know that I am beyond sorry, and genuinely appreciative of your time and support; now, more than ever.

So, caveats aside, I would like to thank:

Isobel Akenhead, editor extraordinaire. I have no idea if she knows how brilliant she is for my writing, or how much I enjoy getting her edit notes. They are always intelligent, thoughtful, generous and constructive, making the process of someone picking holes in a story you have sweated over all the more palatable. And look, less swearing in this one!

Bookouture have a habit of employing incredible women, and the wonder crew of Kim Nash, Noelle Holten and Sarah Hardy are no different. They are social media wizards, nurturers, guides, champions and protectors without whom, I suspect, not a single Bookouture author could properly function. They are the reason we gain so much visibility and I am incredibly grateful for their tireless work.

The wider team also make life easier: the copyeditors, the proofreaders, the assistants, the marketing team, all led by (at the time of writing this), outgoing CEO, Oliver Rhodes. Bookouture was still quite small when I arrived, and he has led its growth into one of the leading lights (if not THE leading light) in digital publishing. As he goes on to pastures new, I will be forever grateful for the opportunity his organisation gave me, back when I was a debut author.

Okay, so who else? Bloggers! Now this is where I really could miss someone out and that's something I'd HATE to do because they are an incredible bunch. I have been very fortunate to receive some great reviews and support from some of this group, something they all do for free because they love books, are passionate about reading, and really want to help people find the next great author. Thank you to every single one who has celebrated my publication days, cover reveals, new contracts, and, in particular, the bloggers who have reviewed one or several of my books. THANK YOU, THANK YOU, THANK YOU!

As well as bloggers, there are other authors to shout out. Not least because they are generally the first ones I go to when things aren't quite going the way I want, mainly because they get it! In particular, Barbara Copperthwaite, Josie Silver, Susie Lynes and Miranda Dickinson are positively dreamy to know and chat with. But they are not the only ones, the online author community is beyond generous and I hope that I am able to return the love, whenever it is needed.

This novel explores mental health, but specifically in relation to the impact on pregnancy and early motherhood. Thank you to my good friend, and mental health nurse practitioner, Louise. Our chat, with me furiously making notes, as you shared your experience from over twenty years in this field, was invaluable; any mistakes or errors in interpretation of facts are very definitely mine! On the same point, I spent much time talking with members of the Facebook group, Trauma Fiction, who were incredibly generous in sharing stories of their experience of childhood comas. All of which was then run past my good friend Mel, a paediatric matron... who still found time to help me, despite a global pandemic. I tried not to bother her too much, on that basis, so, as before, any errors or twists for the benefit of the story, are entirely of my doing, but my gratitude remains eternal!

Outside of the writing world, there are my real friends, whom obviously I've not seen in the last three months. When the world shut down, and Zoom piped up, I confess I was not one of those connecting to friends and family via the wonders of technology. I was built for social isolation. Yet, despite this, I hope they know that their messages and, more recently, socially distanced chats as we get our daily exercise, mean everything to me. If you think you are my friend, and matter to me, know that you're right.

I should give a huge thank you to my family. When writing a book, as I've frequently said before, I am grumpy, emotionally unavailable, rarely in the house, and when I am, I refer you to points one and two. On that basis, I imagine I'm pretty challenging to be around... though some may say this has nothing to do with my writing a book! So, for putting up with me, and only asking me for a new computer, a horse, a boat, 43,056 times a week, when I earn my bookish fortune, I thank you. And also, I apologise: we're six books in and I still cannot afford any one of these things. Arguably, I never will... but just imagine how awful I'd be to live with if I weren't able to write... family and friends aside, it is one of the things I love the most.

Which leads me to my final, thank you, from the very bottom of my heart: to every single reader who has purchased my books and read them. Whether you are the reader who shares my books, the reader who reviews them, the reader who messages me, or the reader who simply reads quietly, and moves on to the next, THANK YOU. That I am in a position to write, and have those words published, is not something I take for granted. My privilege is noted and checked. I hope that it continues, I hope that I continue to learn and grow as an author, but most importantly, I hope I write stories that you keep wanting to read.

With love, thanks, gratitude and peace,

Anna x